PRAISE FOR BOOK ONE OF
THE TRIGON DISUNITY

EMPRISE...

Berkley books by Michael P. Kube-McDowell

THE TRIGON DISUNITY

BOOK ONE: EMPRISE
BOOK TWO: ENIGMA

Book Two of the Trigon Disunity

ENIGMA

Michael P. Kube-McDowell

BERKLEY BOOKS, NEW YORK

ENIGMA

A Berkley Book/published by arrangement with
the author

PRINTING HISTORY
Berkley edition/May 1986

ISBN: 0-425-08767-0

For
Marc Satterwhite
Rick Langolf
Art Jolin
former roommates and abiding friends.

And for Janie,
who gives me more than she knows.

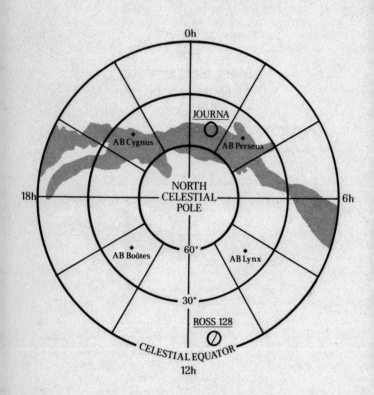

NORTHERN CELESTIAL HEMISPHERE

0h

JOURNA

AB Cygnus

AB Perseus

NORTH
CELESTIAL
POLE

18h

6h

60°

AB Boötes

AB Lynx

30°

ROSS 128

CELESTIAL EQUATOR

12h

SOUTHERN CELESTIAL HEMISPHERE

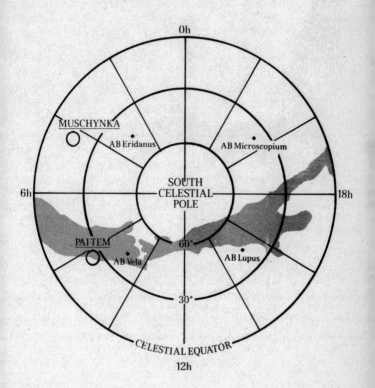

contents

I.

JIADUR'S WAKE

JIADUR'S WAKE

AN ANAMNESIS OF THE NEW HISTORY

Radiation mutates not only organisms but societies. The heat of fire both raised cities and razed them. The electromagnetic waves from Edison's lamps reshaped the cultural shoreline on which they broke. And it was with a halo of radiation that the unmanned Journan museum starship *Jiadur* first made its presence known to Earth.

As is well known now, but was not widely known then, *Jiadur*'s pyrotechnic fall into solar orbit in the year A.R. 35 was not the Journans' first contact with mankind. That honor went to the crude Pangaean starship *Pride of Earth*, which had intercepted *Jiadur* in deep space some eighteen years earlier. And it was *Pride of Earth*'s crew, of course, which first learned the stunning, inexplicable fact that Journans and humans were common genetic stock: twins somehow separated after birth.

It is difficult now to realize what a shock that discovery was. When humankind took its first tentative steps into the interstellar expanses, we were emotionally and philosophically ready for nearly anything, except our own children. But that, of course, was what we found.

Instead of carrying or even relaying that revelation back to its home world, *Pride of Earth* pursued the mystery to its source, ending its days in orbit around Journa. Inevitably, just as Leif Eiriksson's achievements in reaching the New World have been forever subordinated to those of Cristoforo Colombo, it was *Jiadur* which impressed upon the masses the realization

3

that the cold infinity of the Galaxy harbored life. That that life was human turned out, oddly, to be more comforting than discomfiting.

To be sure, many historians and scientists were badly injured by collapsing paradigms. But the average citizen replaced his mental image of a dead, hostile Universe with an equally false image of worlds teeming with humanity—and went blithely about his business. The First Colonization and the Forefathers who carried it out were given an affectionate, semireligious niche in the cultural mythology, and then largely dismissed from thought. Species chauvinism meant that a colony on Journa demanded fewer mental adjustments than a truly alien civilization would have required.

None of this was self-evident in the wake of *Jiadur*'s spectacular arrival. It was a number of years before World Council analysts felt secure enough to advise their employers that the only lasting change *Jiadur* had wrought was the emergence of the Universal Creation Church, a relatively benign successor to Cooke's activist Church of the Second Coming. Convinced that its grasp of (and grip on) the sociodynamics of the single global culture it was creating was complete, the Council breathed a sigh of relief and went about maintaining the prosperity that had purchased a lasting peace.

But *Jiadur* had another lasting impact, one not immediately obvious: It changed the course and objectives of the Unified Space Service.

The USS had been established in the original Articles of Union as an operationally independent but financially dependent arm of the World Council, and for a time had seemed content in that role. But after *Jiadur,* the USS set about parlaying its monopoly on space travel into economic self-sufficiency. By the end of its first century, the USS relied on Earth for only one resource: people. And as the Reunion Day sesquicentennial approached, the Service was fast becoming the tail that wagged Earth's dog.

By then, the Transport branch was operating two dozen packets, a score of mining ships and bulk freighters, a fleet of heavy-lift shuttles, and an assortment of smaller craft. At any given instant, the space tracking centers were keeping an electronic eye on the movements of perhaps a hundred ships scattered between the orbits of Venus and the asteroids.

At the same time, the Resource division's sunsats were

providing a third of the electricity used on the planet. The USS comsats handled virtually all electronic communications traveling more than 100 kilometers. A tenth of the metal used in earthly consumer goods originated in asteroidal ores. Eighty-five families of industrial chemicals were manufactured pollution-free by the robot platforms associated with Unity, the Service's largest space station. The bulk of those chemicals were purchased by the various manufacturing concerns which leased space on USS-Resource's five production centers, each nearly as large as Unity herself.

All this benefited Earth, but none of it was undertaken for that reason alone. Because of the success of Transport and Resource, the Service could independently support a program of deep-space exploration far exceeding what the Council would have been willing to finance. Though the Survey branch operated only a handful of capital ships, each was larger than all save the newest freighters and faster than all save the newest propulsion research prototypes. They were the vessels to which belonged the glamour, the mystery, and, in time, the Galaxy.

Throughout this period, the Council remained strangely blind to the importance of these developments. There was no doubt in their minds that they were that era's history-makers, that universal education and the eradication of poverty were the 2nd Century A.R.'s headlines. But in fact, the cusp point for the human future had already moved from Earth to space. . . .

—Merritt Thackery
unpublished manuscript

USS Security Status: Protected

Clearance for WorldNet: **DENIED**

chapter 1

Jupiter

As Merritt Thackery waited in line to enter the *Amalthea*'s Panorama chamber he felt no special excitement.

In a few minutes, he would be able to look out from the bow of *Amalthea* at the face of the Jovian planet, with nothing between him and it save the thin synglas bubble holding in the liner's atmosphere. Probably more than most of those present, Thackery knew what to expect, and that knowledge took the edge off any anticipation he might feel. He had seen the pictures, and so felt he had seen the planet.

In any event, Thackery regarded Saturn as the system's premiere planet, and the only one which on his own he would have considered visiting (though only if the visit could be achieved in hours rather than weeks). But despite a favorable opposition, *Amalthea* would bring its passengers no closer than a half-billion miles to the tranquil-faced giant and its rings, and the telecamera view offered in the Promenade Theater would be little better than that offered by the lunar and Earth-orbital observatories. Had Saturn been waiting for him in the Panorama, that would have justified some mild excitement.

But it was only Jupiter.

I might as well be in line for the 3-D planetarium at the Smithsonian Science Center, he thought.

Reflexively, Thackery began to study those who waited with him in the steadily moving queue. Even with a total passenger complement approaching five hundred, after two weeks aboard most of the faces were familiar. But then, Thackery had worked harder than most to learn them. He had nearly completed his microsociety study, needing only the time to finish analyzing the third-order sociograms.

"Looking for someone?"

The voice came from behind, from the male half of a couple Thackery had seen parading their fashionably pale, slim, and hirsute bodies in the microgravity mist-pool. Naturalists, both— but then, most of the younger passengers were. By forsaking skin ornamentation, body perfume, and depilatories, the naturalists rejected—and invited rejection from—the economic stratum into which they had been born. Thackery found their conscious avoidance of social affectations an affectation in itself.

"No," Thackery replied. "I thought perhaps Ms. Goodwin might be here, but it seems not."

"Is that the older woman you were playing backgammon with on the promenade yesterday?" asked the female.

The question was impertinent, but then so was the whole conversation. "Yes," Thackery said, helpless to escape until they reached the Panorama.

"I saw her dancing in the ballroom last night, with that tall woman with the rose tattoo on her cheek." She dropped her voice conspiratorially. "From the way they were dancing, I don't think they'll be getting up very early."

"The best way to make sure you find them in the morning is to be with them all night," the male said with a wink.

Thackery smiled politely and used the progress of the line as an excuse to turn away. But when he had taken up the slack, they were right behind him and still eager to talk.

"By the way, I'm Mollis and this is Bellus," the female offered. "You're one of the sweepstakes winners, aren't you?"

"Yes," he said curtly, wondering if she realized the full derivation of her name. Given names taken from new-Latin biological nomenclature were common among naturalists, but *mollis* could mean "weak and changeable" as well as "soft and voluptuous"—not the most flattering self-image. Thackery found the male's name, though unambiguous, equally inappropriate. *Handsome you're not—*

"I thought so," she went on blithely. "Bell thought you might be some sort of security officer for the Titan Line, or a Council observer, the way you watch everyone all the time. But you're a student or something, aren't you?"

"Government Service Academy, Georgetown."

"See?" Bellus said triumphantly. "He's a baby bureaucrat. It's practically the same thing. And I told you he wasn't as old as he looks."

"He's right about that," Mollis said, appraising him with a critical eye. "What are you, third year? You can't be more than twenty-five. But you carry yourself like you're forty. You really need to let yourself relax a little." She reached out and grasped his hand familiarly. "Come on down to the pool after we're done here. I'll introduce you to some people."

Before he needed to give an answer, Thackery reached the threshold with its blinking MICROGRAVITY ENVIRON-MENT BEYOND THIS POINT sign. He allowed one of the *Amalthea*'s green-clad crew to pin the radiation badge to his vest. But he disdained the proffered arm of an usher, and coasted unassisted across the Panorama's uncluttered hemi-spherical volume to an open handhold on the face of the opaque synglas.

He was relieved to see that Mollis and Bellus did not follow him there; they called out to and joined another couple near the periphery of the chamber. A few minutes later, the last places were filled and the hatchways sealed from the outside. Predictably, the Jupiter movement of Holst's "The Planets" sounded from concealed speakers. Then the narration began:

"Jupiter. Son of the Titans. King of both gods and men. Jupiter. Star that nearly was, never to be."

It went on in that vein for nearly two minutes, a mixture of pop astronomy and simplified mythology, as the lights in the chamber slowly dimmed until they were hanging in the dark-ness. The synglas bubble beneath him, above him, before him, remained opaque, and Thackery began to grow impatient. Then the narration ceased, the music grew louder, and the clamshell shields began to roll back.

There was a communal gasp and cries of childlike delight as a band of color appeared across the width of the bubble, but Thackery barely noted the sound. Before him was spread a breath-taking living canvas, an animated palette festooned with whorls and spirals of orange and white and yellow and hues for which he had no name: the face of Jupiter.

And though even the first glimpse communicated the awesome scope of that canvas, moment by moment there was more. The shields moved quickly for their size but in stately pace, as though they were curtains swept back at the herald's call to admit the royal presence.

Outbound, Thackery had wondered why the builders of *Amalthea* had gone to the trouble to include the Panorama when an ordinary observation deck might have done as well. Now he understood. He found himself forgetting the passengers at his elbows. No interior lights or reflections betrayed the presence of the synglas bubble. It was as if the ship itself had vanished.

In one dizzying moment of transformation, he floated suspended between the dazzling stars at zenith and nadir, alone in the void with the Herculean presence of the great gas giant. Vertigo impelled him forward, and he was certain that if he loosed his grip on the railing he would fall the endless fall into its alien depths.

It was as though, having spent his life contentedly viewing the world in two dimensions, a third had suddenly been revealed to him. It was as though he had grasped a high-voltage wire of emotion, and his body sang unfamiliar songs of ecstasy. The swirling storms of Jupiter were part of him, and he of them, a rapturous communion, a participatory consciousness—

And then, without warning, it was suddenly over, the spell broken, the moment lost. The experience itself gave way to simple sense memory of the experience, and he cried a silent, futile protest.

After a time he became aware how much time had passed, and that he was nearly alone in the chamber. Most of the others, Mollis and Bellus included, had drifted away to more diverting or less vertiginous pursuits. For them, it seemed, the family of Jove had been little more than an exotic backdrop to a month of hedonism.

But Thackery, frightened and at the same time angered by the loss of self, ashamed and at the same time possessed by the unprecedented sensuality, remained. He begged silently for the moment to return, anxious to analyze it rather than be ambushed by it. Thus obsessed, he stayed until his radiation badge glowed a warning yellow and began to chime softly.

Only then, and only at the insistence of the Panorama staff, did he excuse himself from the presence of the King.

· · ·

By the time he reached his cabin, Merritt Thackery was angry.

The first object of his anger was chance, a player whose power he previously had held in disdain. Someone had to win, and in that sense it was not a matter of chance at all. But that it had to be him—there was the unwanted touch of the Oddsmaker.

Six months ago, a Titan Line messenger, accompanied by a minicam team, had walked into Dr. Royce's Controlled Market Economies seminar and announced to all present that Thackery would receive a cost-free berth for the *Amalthea*'s first cruise to the realm of the giant planets—one of thirty-seven such gifts, one for each of Jupiter's satellites.

No one was more stunned than Thackery, who had not only not entered the sweepstakes, but had been only vaguely aware that it was underway. Least surprised seemed to be Royce, who segued neatly into an explanation of how such things worked.

Three decades earlier, Royce related, the World Council had cast its critical eye on sweepstakes and lotteries and decided that they pandered to the antirational outlook it was laboring to eradicate. In a move typical of the Council, it did not ban them: It simply set an impossible condition. All citizens of Council states had to automatically be made entrants. It was illegal to require potential winners to take any action whatsoever to qualify themselves.

As a consequence of the new rule, lotteries lost their source of prize money and sweepstakes their promotional value, and both faded away. But the Titan Line, looking to protect its two billion Council-dollar investment in *Amalthea*, won a court ruling allowing it to use the Council's own citizen registration banks for a promotional sweepstakes.

So it was Thackery's twelve-digit Citizen Identification number which had brought him his "good" fortune, and at very long odds; the pool of possible winners numbered nearly nine billion.

Thackery's first impulse was to refuse the award. He had no interest in astronomy, and neither did Georgetown—the subject did not even appear in the Academy curriculum book. Nor did he have time for a sightseeing cruise. His attention was focused on holding his own in the challenging second-tier GS disciplines: Linguistics, Cultural Anthropology, Political

Psychology, Economics of Production. Successful completion of all six tiers at GSA-Georgetown would qualify him for an internship somewhere in the Council's world-wide bureaucracy.

Though only twenty-two, Thackery had worked hard to separate himself from what he saw as youthful affectations, and to take on the habits of thought more appropriate to a mid-level Council facilitator or field agent. He was not surprised that Mollis took him for older than he was—that happened frequently. Nor was he much surprised that she found him stilted, even dull. There was no room for chance or emotional impulse in his plan. He meant his life to be orderly, even tame. That was, after all, the function of the World Council—to see that lives were orderly, even tame. With nine billion lives to consider, orderly and tame was the only acceptable formula.

But Georgetown's administration had intervened, which is why he was angry at them as well. Too many instructors had seen opportunities to use the trip as a practicum in their specialty: sociodynamics, economics, consumer motivation. His advisor had agreed with them, and Thackery was saddled with a half-dozen special projects to be completed before, during, or after the one-month voyage, with never a word to reducing or rescheduling his regular duties. And Director Stowell had approved the plan without troubling to find out what Thackery thought of it.

So he had not come aboard *Amalthea* looking for excitement, or companionship, or even relaxation. He had come because his coming pleased those on whom so much of his future depended. And he was angry at himself for having forgotten it. He had gone into the Panorama not to see Jupiter but to observe his fellow passengers' reaction to it. Instead, he had allowed himself to lose control.

And now he was afraid to go back. Afraid that it would happen again, and afraid that it would not.

For two days Thackery stayed away, while *Amalthea* looped around Jupiter between the orbits of the innermost Galilean moons. In that time, he managed to insult Ms. Goodwin, to start an argument over the current Council that nearly became a fistfight, and, by being conversationally brusque and sexually inconsiderate, to turn a pity fuck offered by Mollis into a disaster.

"What is it with you?" she asked as she dressed afterward.

"Your drug program out of balance?"

"I'm not using," he said, bristling defensively.

"Then maybe you ought to be. What has you so wired? I thought you were all right, just a little naive," she said, not unkindly. "But you knew what you were doing—you just didn't care about my half of it. You can't treat people like this. It isn't right."

I'm fighting myself, he thought. *And losing.* "I'm sorry. It wasn't your fault."

"I don't need you to tell me that."

Chastened, he watched as she finished dressing. "Come to the Panorama with me," he said impulsively.

"I don't think so. Thanks all the same."

"I told you, it wasn't personal."

"That's part of the problem."

When she was gone he sat on the edge of the bed and buried his face in his hands. *It isn't getting better—you're as out of control today as you were in the Panorama.*

You're still angry, he told himself.

No one planned this. It's not anybody's fault.

I'm not angry at anyone in particular, he realized. *I'm angry because I'm afraid and I don't like it. Angry because I let myself be surprised. Angry because*—He balked at completing the thought.

Because—

Because that hour Jupiter had me was the best hour of my life . . . and because it's too late to let that change the course I'm on.

Thackery mulled over that revelation for several minutes, examining it from all sides, looking for flaws. There were none. *All right, then!* he chided himself. *Nothing's changed. Nothing's going to change. So why aren't you at least enjoying it while you can?*

Over the next twelve hours, Thackery entered the Panorama four times, which was as often as the radiation medtech would allow. Each time, he felt anticipation as he neared the threshold. Inside, he was caught up in the complexities of the seething technicolor clouds. The one occasion *Amalthea*'s attitude allowed, he marveled at the fractured surface of Europa, the sulfur-splattered textures of Io. He reveled in the illusion that he was the center of the universe. All those discoveries denoted new additions to his sensibilities. Like a newborn butterfly which had just unfolded its crinkled wings, he felt as though his horizons had been immeasurably broadened.

These are things I could not feel before, he thought happily.

But no more than a hint of his earlier rapture returned, a memory only, an echo. Thackery accepted his lot with equanimity. *How could I ever forget enough to be surprised that way again? How could I ever wipe that impression from my mind? And why would I want to?*

That night, the Panorama staff closed the chamber's clamshell shield for the last time on that voyage, as *Amalthea* said good-bye to Jupiter and began the two-week fall inbound to the Charan Space Operations Center and Earth.

Now things can return to normal, Thackery told himself. To speed that process, he absented himself from the grand ballroom with its continuous music, intoxicants on tap, and seductive star projection. He steered clear of the self-proclaimed beautiful people with their gemstone nosepins and patterned skin sculptures, who hugged too readily and laughed too loudly as though determined to Have Fun during every waking moment. He refused the companionship of the young naturalists, who thought themselves his peers when they were in fact his inferiors.

Thackery stayed within himself, recapturing the discipline and determination of the student, the dignity and distance of the GS professional. By the time the Charan shuttle pierced the atmosphere of Earth, all was as it had been—except for one moment, one memory, the flame of which would not die. And because of that flame, nothing was as it had been.

For the most part, the changes were visible only to Thackery himself. Where he had once prided himself on never pressing the deadline on assignments, now he found himself working late nights to complete work which had gone neglected. Where he had previously preferred to direct group projects he was part of, now he allowed others to take the lead and the responsibilities that went with it.

On more than one occasion, he tapped into the GS databases with the intent of researching one assignment or another only to find his attention turning elsewhere. He read the history of space exploration with a curiosity he had not previously known. He called up hundreds of historic photographs and video clips, including some of the crude bit-mapped images of Jupiter returned by the earliest Pioneer and Voyager probes. And he studied carefully the organization and recruitment practices of the three-headed Unified Space Service.

In all but the most demanding seminars, Thackery's attention wandered. He found the professors pedantic and their observations obvious. In one jarring moment, he realized he had always felt that way, except that he had been too busy trying to garner approval to care. GS Georgetown had always been a greater challenge to his endurance than to his intellect, a gateway to something better.

But in an equally disturbing revelation, Thackery realized that living in the Council's world would mean being surrounded by more of the same boring sameness. And since all Council decisions were collective, the product of committees and studies and consensus, he could not even count on a heady sense of power to enliven his life.

That night he had a vivid dream which found him alone in the Panorama when the synglas itself crawled back. Drawn through the opening, he began to move toward Jupiter, more floating than falling. As it grew nearer he felt its compelling presence and the eager foretaste of union with its substance. He never achieved that union: Whether he awoke first or the insistent alarm woke him, he was snatched back when on the brink of rapture.

For several minutes, he lay drained and shaken on the sweat-dampened sheets. When he finally rose, he was well behind schedule for making his Political Psychology seminar on time. But that did not matter, because he had already decided to skip the session. He went instead to the Evaluation and Counseling Center.

"I want to take the career orientation assessment," he told the clerk, flashing his identity card.

Within fifteen minutes the psychometrician had him wired up in a testing cubicle. "Would you rather dig a ditch or fix a broken toy?" asked the silicon-brained proctor, and the assessment was underway.

As in the past, none of the questions seemed to relate to what people actually did for a living, nor did his own answers seem to have any pattern or to point authoritatively to any particular career. And yet the assessment had high marks for reliability, especially when presented one-on-one by the proctor with the subject wearing a biosensor band on one wrist.

Processing the results took less time than Thackery needed to walk from the testing cubicle to his counselor's anteroom, and Thackery was waved in without waiting.

"What prompted you to ask for a re-exam?" the counselor asked, absentmindedly rolling a touchscreen stylus between his fingertips.

"I find I'm not as interested as I once was. I wanted to find out whether it was fatigue, second-tier syndrome, or something real." It was at least a partially true answer.

The counselor tilted his data display toward himself and glanced at it. "In terms of ideals and skills, you continue to come out as a very strong candidate for GS."

"Oh," Thackery said, both disappointed and relieved.

"But there is one curious finding, which you've already anticipated. Your emotional commitment to those ideals and skills is much weaker than it was on your last assessment."

"What does that mean?"

"Lip service," the counselor said bluntly. "You're just going through the motions." He leaned forward. "What do you really want to be doing, Mr. Thackery?"

"Doesn't that tell you, sir?"

"Of course not. You gave the 'right' answers for George-town, not the right answers for yourself."

"Does it matter where I want to be?" Thackery asked. "I'm twenty-three. It's a little late to be changing my mind. This is the only thing open to me."

The counselor smiled slightly. "You underestimate yourself, Mr. Thackery. You are one of the very best training for a field which, rightly or wrongly, is considered to be the most demanding on this planet. You have options. Whether or not you wish to take them is another question."

Thackery was slow in responding. "Do you mean that other training centers might accept me?"

"I think there are very few that would turn your application down."

"Why are you telling me this?" Thackery asked suspiciously. "Isn't it your job to shepherd us through, to keep us happy here?"

"I *am* trying to keep you happy," the counselor said gently. "If that requires you to take a year off, or even leave here completely, both you and the GS will be better for it. Now— shall we talk about those options?"

• • •

It was remarkable how little there was to pack. The materials he had studied, the music he had played, the art that had decorated the apartment walls—all had been on-line from the GS Depository, and yet they had made the apartment uniquely his. All he really owned was his clothing and a few boxes of what might best be called memorabilia: photos of friends, award certificates from past schools, knickknacks bought on trips with Andra.

Andra. How are you going to take this? he asked his mother in absentia. *How hard are you going to make it?* Thackery did not dwell on the questions, because he knew the answers lay just a few hours away.

He was nearly finished packing when he was interrupted by the paging tone from the apartment's front door. He opened it to find, not entirely unexpectedly, Director Stowell, a somber man whose face and dignity were flawed by a bulbous nose seemingly designed to keep eyeglasses from slipping off. Since Stowell wore contacts, the consensus was that he was afraid of corrective surgery. A minority held that he was a closet naturalist.

"Good morning, Mr. Thackery." Stowell's glance took in the disarray behind Thackery. "I'm glad I turned down a second helping at breakfast. I might not have found you."

"Won't you come in, Director Stowell?"

Stowell threaded his way to the center of the room before answering. "It's not uncommon for second-tier students to withdraw. We expect it. In some cases we welcome it. Occasionally we even request it. But we both know that you are in absolutely no academic difficulty. On the contrary, your work has been uniformly excellent. When you filed your notice of withdrawal with the registrar, you elected not to give your reasons. Would you do me the courtesy of sharing them with me privately?"

Thackery's face wrinkled with discomfort. "I don't think I could properly express why," he said finally.

"Ah." Stowell frowned. "I don't mean to pry, Mr. Thackery. It's only that I would regret to see the Council lose the services of someone with your potential due to some"—he paused to search for the right word—"irrelevancy. I would like to help you, if you'll allow me."

Thackery folded his arms across his chest in a subconscious gesture of resistance. "I've just decided not to continue in GS."

Stowell nodded. "You wouldn't object if I chose to list you as on hiatus rather than withdrawn?"

Guarding his thoughts because he did not trust himself to guard his words, Thackery shook his head. "I don't see any point to it."

"The point is that your reasons for withdrawal may be temporary."

How can I tell you that everything you care about seems shallow to me now? How can I explain about Jupiter? "I plan to enroll in TSI-Tsiolkovsky."

Stowell nodded gravely. "I know."

"I received word yesterday that they would accept me."

"As did I." Stowell settled on the arm of a chair as though he meant to stay a while. "I'm hardly surprised they accepted you. The Technical Service needs people with your qualities even more than we do. But you should be thinking about your needs, not theirs. Speaking frankly, I don't see you being happy in an essentially subservient posture. No matter how skilled a TS graduate is, everything they do is subordinate to decisions from GS—"

Not everything, Thackery thought. *The Council doesn't rule everywhere.*

"—and I've always seen you on the decision-making side of that relationship," Stowell concluded.

"I understand that, sir."

"There is something else to consider. You know that you can be successful here. Your success elsewhere is less certain. Your competition at Tsiolkovsky has been specializing for years, just as you have. You will be a long time catching up—if you ever do. Raw ability is not everything."

"I've considered that, Director," said Thackery, though he had not.

"You've considered that," the director echoed without conviction, chewing at his lower lip. "You should also think of your individual development. The TS institutes offer far greater freedom to set your own pace than we do. Do you understand why? They're only teaching cold science, not providing a total acculturation as we do. There is a dynamism in Government Service that you will not find there, because it is a crucible for human interaction, not chemical reaction."

"I've taken the differences between the branches into account, Director Stowell."

"Then consider one thing further: whether you want to commit yourself to an enterprise which in the scheme of things has no future."

"What do you mean by that?"

"That our investment in space is temporary, ephemeral. Our population is very nearly stabilized, and the infrastructure needed to support it is well on its way to being completed. Once those two conditions are in place, we will have very little need for off-planet resources. The long-term plan calls for stability, not growth. There will be a time, not all that much farther down the road, when we will call the ships home. Oh, we will still be busy in earth orbit, but that's practically an eighth continent. It's the System and Survey ships we'll have no use for. Is that part of your calculation, too?"

"No, sir. I dispute your précis," Thackery said with quiet confidence. "The Council might well call the ships home. But I doubt very much if they would come."

Sighing resignedly, Stowell stood and moved to the door. "A romantic notion. Have it as you wish. I think you're making a mistake. You won't be the first to let Georgetown intimidate you, or the first to bolt. I like you, Merritt, so I hope I'm wrong. But if I'm right, I just hope you're smart enough not to let the door lock behind you."

The use of his first name was an unexpected and jarring familiarity. Thackery drew a deep breath and blew it out his mouth. "All right. I'll concede there's at least some uncertainty. So please put me on hiatus."

Content with that small victory, Stowell opened the door and was gone.

Thackery shook his head wearily and resumed his packing. There was no ready way to prove it to another's satisfaction. But he knew in his own heart that he was running *toward*, not running away.

Nevertheless, turning back Stowell's challenges had exhausted his tolerance for confrontation. He had arranged his schedule so that the turbocopter from Dulles would drop him at Philadelphia's central transport node four hours before his flight to London was scheduled to leave from the outlying PHX airport—enough time to seek out Andra. But when he arrived, he sought out a public netlink instead.

He sat and stared into the nearly blank screen for a long time, composing his side of the conversation in advance. The results were unsatisfying. Then, on impulse, he selected Message mode rather than Call mode. He felt a pang of guilt over ducking a confrontation that way, then washed it away with a wave of comforting rationalizations: *It won't help us to yell at each other. A fight won't change anything—*

Then the prompt bell chimed, and it was time to record:

"Hello, Andra. I'm here in Philadelphia, at the transnode. I'd hoped to come by and see you, but I'm afraid the schedule got squeezed and I'm not going to be able to. I have another flight to catch—I'm on my way to London, to study at Tsiolkovsky. This is a little scary for me, but one of the things that I'm counting on is that you're behind me, and that you're happy I'm getting this chance." He smiled nervously and searched for something else to say. Nothing else seemed relevant. "Take care, Andra. I'll be in touch."

Thackery did not really know what kind of reaction he expected. In his most pessimistic moods, he comforted himself with the knowledge that there was no way she could stop him. "Mother" was a flexible concept without much legal standing, considering all the Alternate Conception variations—fetal adoption, host-mothering, group contract, blind-donor fertilization (Andra's choice). And even the limited powers granted by his Care & Custody papers had expired when he was sixteen. He was an adult in the eyes of the law, an independent agent. The decision was not hers, it was his.

But not being stopped was not enough. He wanted her approval. It had always meant more than the honors and awards he had accumulated with seeming ease, even though it came infrequently and in measured doses. Her blessing would smooth the difficult path ahead. It would give him the reassurance that she thought this, too, was within his reach.

What he got was two days of silence, and then a visitor.

Coming home from his first meeting with the engineering project team to which he had been assigned, he found her waiting for him outside his student flat. They hugged, more out of ritual than warmth of feeling. Her presence made him suddenly anxious, but he was too busy trying to read her mood to realize that he was telegraphing his own emotions.

She cast a jaundiced eye at the inside of the flat, which was bland where it was not cluttered, but said nothing.

"Still settling in," he volunteered.

She nodded absently, examining the netlink. "A 400 series? That's a ten-year-old model."

"It does everything I need it to."

"I suppose," she said, continuing her inspection. "I've been walking around the Institute. It seems more like a warehouse than a school. How many students are here?"

"About twelve hundred."

"Twelve hundred! They can't be very selective."

"It's very competitive."

"Oh, I'm sure, but on what level?" she said, settling in a chair. "Merritt, would you explain why you didn't come talk with me before doing this?"

"It wasn't a hard decision. I didn't have any doubts that this is what I want."

"After I got your message, I went up to Georgetown to talk with Director Stowell. He told me that the door is open for you to return."

Thackery nodded. "I know. I didn't think it was necessary. It was his idea."

"He also told me that you've already damaged your reputation among the faculty just by doing this, that you've raised questions about your ability to take the pressure. He said that if you let as little as three months go by before you return, it'll be next to impossible for you to regain your former academic standing."

Aware of Andra's mastery of the leading question, Thackery wished he could hear Stowell's version of the conversation. "That's sounds about right," he said lamely.

"You're very sanguine about it."

"Andra—you don't seem to understand. I don't expect to go back."

"You don't seem to understand that you have to go back."

"I know this isn't what you were expecting from me—"

"Merritt, I know what the cost of taking time out is. I took time out to give you life. I was thirty-one, right in the middle of my career. My column was getting good placement in all three newsnets. I had good relationships not only with my peers, but with Council insiders. I took two years out, and I never caught up."

"But they held your job open—"

She shook her head. "The rest of the world doesn't hold still. I was on track to become chief policy interpreter for the whole North American zone. I never got there, because of the time I took out for you. I don't regret it—you're the best thing I've ever done. But if you let this opportunity slip away, you're not only making what you've done pointless, you make what I did pointless, too."

Never much for conflict, Thackery's stomach had begun to churn. "I haven't lowered my standards, just changed my goal."

"Do you really think that? Do you really think that your future here compares in any way with the future you can still have in Government Service? Director Stowell agrees with me that you have the potential to go all the way to the Council itself."

"But, Andra—that's your script for my life, not mine. That's not what I want."

"A script? Is that the way you think of it? Then what kind of role did I write for myself? I kept you at home until you were ten. How many mothers waited that long to put their children in full-time childcare? I would have kept you longer if Shelby Preparatory hadn't been residential. Even so, I was always there to help you. I let you use my contacts for your studies. When you were on break, I took you to legislative briefings, agency hearings—not because I wanted to, but because you wanted to know how it all worked. I didn't drag you into the GS track. You wanted it."

Thackery squirmed. It was true enough—for a long time he had taken the lead, had gladly applied himself toward making real what had seemed a sparkling vision. Until very recently he had not even realized that it was she who had planted that vision.

Andra was not finished. "You made a commitment, and I supported you. We both worked very hard for a long time for this. You're a thoroughbred, Merritt. I haven't trained you, others have, but I know the course. You're very close to a big hurdle, and I'm not going to allow you to refuse the jump. I expect you to go back. I will not let you quit."

Torn between incompatible yearnings, Thackery could not mount an effective defense. "All I want is your support," he said pleadingly, his eyes wet. "Why can't you give me that?"

"Because if you stay here, you're going to fail," she said coldly. "Not just fail to live up to your potential. Did any of the track-jumpers who came into Georgetown last? No. You know what happened to them. It didn't matter how bright they were. It didn't matter how much they wanted it. They didn't have the background, and they didn't know how the system worked. They were outsiders, and they stayed outsiders until they gave up. And that's what will happen to you if you don't come back with me."

"I can't," he said helplessly. "I can't."

She stood, and for a long moment searched his face with a hard gaze. "You mean you won't. Which tells me not only what you think of me, but what you think of yourself. And I don't like either part of that message." Stopping at the door, she looked back. "I'm going to arrange a prepaid fare in your name for the transatlantic shuttle, one that'll be good for the next three months. I hope you won't be too proud or wait too long to use it."

For a long time, Thackery had cause to wonder if Andra had been right.

He discovered quickly that the Tsiolkovsky students were no less intellectually able than those at Georgetown. Hobbled by his weak background in physical science, Thackery barely made an impression, much less a splash, in his classes and engineering project team—just as Andra had predicted. Nearly all of his previous training, save for the advanced mathematics, was useless. It took him a month to reach the point where he could follow conversations, and three months until he could contribute to them.

But he did not go back. He viewed the expiration of the shuttle ticket to be a message to Andra, a message that said, *You're wrong, Andra. I can, too, make it here.*

Yet by the end of the first year, Thackery had come to the sobering realization that he would in all likelihood never catch up to his new trackmates. He had started too far behind in a race in which there were no shortcuts. He took solace in knowing that he was stretching himself, was learning how to sustain a higher level of effort than he had ever needed before. And he held on to the hope that though he might never be the best again, he would be good enough.

Toward the end of his second year, he sent Andra a letter that both took cognizance of and ignored the breach between them. He filled it with personal social details and his perceptions of London and environs, while avoiding mention of his studies or plans. A month later, he received a short reply from her in which she similarly avoided any mention of Tsiolkovsky. The fact that she responded at all he took to mean that she had come to at least a grudging understanding that he was not coming back to Georgetown; the way in which she responded suggested that they had established the ground rules for some sort of rapprochement, if not a complete end to hostilities. From that point on, he made an effort to write her every three or four months. Usually she answered.

In all, it took Thackery three years to pass his technical exams. But part of that extra time was a strategic delay. Unlike GS and the various free industries, which snapped up talent whenever and wherever they found it, the USS did not accept applications until and unless they had openings. Instead, it maintained a short "Qualified—Call As Needed" list to fill short-term needs, and posted a Notice of Opportunity when the QCAN list became too short or a new project or ship was approved.

So Thackery waited at Tsiolkovsky, sharpening his skills, avoiding the binding commitments which would have come with graduation. He watched the Placement Services list like a broker with an order to buy until, one morning, he dialed in to find a short-term USS Notice of Opportunity posted. He would not know the reason until later that day: overnight, a fierce chemical fire had broken out in the cargo compartments of the packet *Moliere*. Nineteen of the twenty-five techs being ferried back from Mars' orbital Materials Reprocessing Center were dead.

Thackery went directly to the Tsiolkovsky testing center. Nine hours later, he returned home with his Technical Service Auxiliary (sysawk) rating, a post with USS-Transport, and a seat on the Friday morning shuttle for his first trip to the orbiting city called Unity.

The shuttle *Vulpecula*'s liftoff was smooth and on time. Due to its inverted attitude, the Earth would remain visible through cabin ports throughout the four-hour flight. But Thackery soon tired of looking back, and began to watch for the first glimpse of Unity.

Early in its history, Unity had been home to the offices and ministers of Rashuri's Pangaean Consortium. That highly symbolic "government-in-the-sky" position seemed progressively less important in the years after Rashuri's death, and when the

World Council supplanted the Consortium, it moved to a 1600-hectare free-floating artificial island built for it in the Mediterranean.

Rather than being a blow to Unity's fortunes and status, the departure of the bureaucrats actually opened the door to its explosive growth. Freed of the thousand and one restrictions imposed in the name of security, Unity quickly became the primary hub of orbital activity. Now it was more a city than a space station. It first appeared on the cabin display as a bright star surrounded by five smaller, dimmer satellites. The central star soon resolved itself into the starfish-like radial shape of Unity, the satellites into globular automated production centers.

As *Vulpecula* closed on the city Thackery made out the slender communications masts which extended in both directions from its central hub, giving the structure the appearance of a five-spoked child's jack. New construction was underway, skeletal structures spanning the gaps between the spokes like webbing growing between the fingers of a hand. The dozens of construction waldoids moving among the girders were like so many scurrying orb-weavers, creating their web even as he watched.

Thackery's contemplations were interrupted by a tone from the seat speaker.

"This is Commander Gerhard. The crew and I just picked up something in the intership traffic that we're sure will be of interest to you. The word is that *Orpheus*, the USS-Survey ship working the Vela octant, has discovered a fourth human colony!"

The shuttle's cabin erupted into applause and chest-beating celebration, with Thackery contributing as much as anyone. Gerhard must have been either monitoring or expecting the outburst, for he waited until it moderated to go on.

"We don't have much more information for you at the moment. I can tell you the colony is called Pai-Tem by the inhabitants, which number only about twenty thousand. I can also tell you that *Orpheus* is under the command of SC Alvin Reed, and that the crew and I and all of USS-Transport are damned proud of what our brothers and sisters in the Survey branch are doing."

So are we all, Thackery thought. *It's easy to be proud. But would you trade places with them, Gerhard? Would you give up everything to be where they are?*

"We'll be docking at Unity in just a few minutes, and there may be more information on the basenet by the time we're processed."

There was another spattering of applause as the end-of-message chimes sounded. His seat partner, apparently a member of the Universal Creation Church, joined several others on board in chanting aloud the opening phrases of the hour-long Prayer of Thanksgiving.

Thackery, at once exhilarated by the news and fiercely jealous of Reed and the others aboard *Orpheus,* barely heard them. Fighting to contain both emotions, he turned his eyes toward Unity, his thoughts toward others' past, his hopes toward his own future.

Journa, Muschvnka, and Ross 128—all cold history, discovered long before I was born. And now Pai-Tem. Let there be more, Thackery begged silently as *Vulpecula* eased into the empty dock at the tip of Unity's wing C.

Let there be more! And leave one for Merritt Thackery. One world in a billion. Not so my name is applauded a hundred years later and a hundred trillion miles away. All I want is Jupiter again. To lose myself in the magic of discovery again. Because there can only be one first time.

THE PATHFINDERS

(from Merritt Thackery's
JIADUR'S WAKE)

. . . The radio beacon from Mu Cassiopeia stirred a somnolent Earth into a social and technological metamorphosis, a metamorphosis symbolized by Tilak Charan's *Pride of Earth*. Considering the technological, logistical, and sociological obstacles, the successful construction of *Pride* ranks as the high-water mark of Devaraja Rashuri's reign.

But *Pride* was the product of an infant technology. Its voyage was one of risk and hubris. Its mission meant an encounter with an alien society of unknowable inclination. Because *Pride* never returned nor reported, it was widely assumed that it had failed to survive. But no one could say which of the factors was to blame.

As a result, the USS began to build the only survey ships explicitly authorized by the World Council. What turned out to be a follow-up mission was conceived as a pioneering one, and so the ships were collectively named The Pathfinders. Their individual names remembered the aerial vanguards of Odin and Noah: S2 Hugin, S3 Munin, and S4 Dove.(The honorary designation S1 was assigned "posthumously" to *Pride of Earth* herself.)

Where *Pride of Earth* had been a fragile lifeboat, the Pathfinders were comparative dreadnoughts. Three years after *Jiadur* reached Earth, they set off for the Mu Cass system. There they "discovered" Journa, its inhabitants, and one lone survivor from *Pride of Earth*—a meeting thereafter commemorated on both worlds in the annual Reunion Day festivities.

But that meeting was also the beginning of the Service's colony problem. The Journans claimed to be children of Earth, a claim that proved as irrefutable as it was inexplicable. How could a space-going technological culture have flourished on Earth ten or a hundred thousand years ago and then vanished without a trace? What twisting of history could allow for such a dissonant fact?

There were no answers on Journa.

Absent appropriate instructions, the Pathfinders separated and began a roundabout return to Earth. Their self-set purpose was to define the parameters of the problem by searching for other possible remnants of the First Colonization. If there were none, then perhaps some relatively painless revisionism might suffice—

Then *Hugin,* under the command of Kellen Brighamton, found a neoprimitive human community on a planet orbiting the white dwarf component of 40 Eridani. When Brighamton's report on the Muschynka reached Earth, it became clear that a more ambitious effort to locate and explain the worlds of man was called for. The shipyards went to work, turning out five new survey ships of the Argo series. USS strategists went to work, drawing up a plan to visit each star system within twenty-five light-years of Earth.

Phase I proceeded largely as planned. The inbound Pathfinders and outbound Argonauts recorded visits to more than 130 star systems over a span of a century and a half. And Commander Yabovsky of *Castor* earned permanent fame when his crew discovered an extinct human colony on a cold world orbiting a dim star in the constellation Virgo.

But despite these labors, the colony problem remained impervious to solution. So even as the aging Pathfinders and their Van Winkled crews neared Earth, Survey brass were planning for them not rest but a role in an even more ambitious Phase II. . . .

chapter 2

Ambition

No announcement was made, but everyone on *Dove* nevertheless knew when it was time for the ship to come of out the
craze. Those pulling duty away from the bridge listened in on
the shipnet, while the others drifted by ones and twos into the
contact lab, edrec compartment, or onto the bridge itself.

Among those who came to the bridge was SC Glen Harrod,
commander of the *Dove*. But he made no move to displace
bridge captain Alizana Neale from the pedestal, choosing instead to stand in the back with the talkative, almost childishly
giddy techs and awks.

Dove had come out of craze eighteen times before, and there
was no technical reason why the nineteenth should prove any
more eventful than the others. "Craze" was a fanciful description of what the D-series Avidsen-Lopez drive did to the local
fabric of space. Only a few Service researchers claimed to fully
understand the "why" of the AVLO power plant. It was commonly known that it was a gravity gradient drive (dubbed the
pushmi-pullyu because of the twin bow and stern field projec-
tors). It was also commonly known that to go beyond that
casual description, it was necessary to deal with Driscoll's
abstruse grand unified field theorem.

The drive's effect, however, was easy to describe. The ship
accelerated beyond the speed of light, and the rest of the universe disappeared. No chronometers ran backward, no one's
gray hair turned black again, no theatrical pyrotechnics punc-

tuated the transitions past c, but when you got to your destination the numbers always added up so that you were there
sooner than Einstein said you should have been. A fifteen light-
year craze in a Pathfinder-class ship extracted barely a month
from the crew's biological calendar. When such a ship crazed,
nothing in the Universe could catch it—not even the electromagnetic radiation on which all sensing and communication
depended.

That fact contributed to the secondary meaning of the term
"craze." To some surveyors, referred to unsympathetically as
"the phobes," the blank screens and dead air meant an enforced
isolation in a universe that ended at the ship's hull. Craze fear
had elements of cabin fever, Gansel's syndrome, and prisoner's
psychosis. Unmoderated by drugs, victims of mild cases suf-
fered from anxiety, poor concentration, and irritability; those
more seriously afflicted experienced sexual dysfunction, in-
somnia, and panic.

The one blessing was that few were affected. There were
no acute phobes aboard *Dove,* and only two milder cases. In
that, *Dove* was fortunate—according to one dispatch they had
received, the Argonaut *Heracles* was limping along with nearly
half its crew impaired.

So neither technology nor psychology could account for the
eagerness with which the approaching transition was awaited.
What was special about *Dove*'s nineteenth craze was not how
it was accomplished or how long it lasted but where it would
end. After making visits to eighteen strange suns, *Dove* was
finally going home.

"One minute," the navtech at the gravigation console called
out, and nearly all eyes went to the imaging window at the
front of the semi-darkened triangular compartment. The comtech hunched over his console, checking out instruments that
had sat unused for sixteen days.

"Transition."

In that moment, a crazy-quilt of radiation—light, radio,
microwave, X-ray—began to impinge on the ship's many eyes
as *Dove* regained her senses. Neale looked up expectantly at
the window, and when the dazzle cleared, found herself looking
at a splendid circular starfield, the distortion a product of their
still-tremendous velocity. As *Dove* continued to decelerate, the
view would slowly come to resemble the view from the South
Dakota pasture which had first captured her curiosity.

I started out trying to find Orion in a winter sky for a teacher whose name I can't remember. Look at me now, she thought with a rush of emotion.

"Which one's the Sun, damnit?" demanded a bearded sysawk standing with the onlookers.

Several eagerly, if impatiently, answered him. "There! Right there! Dead on center!"

"That's the wrong color."

"We're still blue-shifted," Harrod reminded the awk gently.

The navtech poked a spotting circle onto the screen, enclosing the small bluish star and settling the disagreement.

"What year is it?" asked someone.

"I make it A.R. 195," said the navtech. "We'll get confirmation once we start picking up our mail."

"A.R.?" asked the medtech, his face showing consternation.

"After Reunion," the comawk standing beside him answered. "They changed the calendar on us while we were gone."

"That's 2205 for those of you still thinking in Gregorian calendar dates, like Bristol there," the navtech added.

That hushed the observers and the bridge crew alike. "A hundred and freezin' fifty-seven years," one said finally. "They better cook up some fine kind of reception for us."

"Speaking of which, we've got just eleven days to get this ship ready to hand over to the yard, and there's a lot to be done," Harrod said. "I'm sure no one wants to be hung up by scutwork when they could be off on leave, so let's get to it."

"Amen to that," said the bearded sysawk. "The Service's already taken a bigger piece of my life than I'd planned on offering."

"Tell 'em, Waite," cheered one onlooker.

Harrod raised a questioning eyebrow. "Just don't forget, there's a whole new generation of ships being built, and they'll be wanting to put some experience on all of them. Be thinking about it. Even you, Waite."

Waite laughed derisively. "I've got other plans."

Neale knocked lightly at Harrod's cabin door. "Glen?"

"Come on in."

She slid the door aside and stepped over the threshold. "Just wanted to tell you she's ready for the hand-over—finally."

"That's good to hear."

"It's been hard to get much work out of them these last three days, with the Earth sitting there in all the screens and getting bigger by the minute."

"Understandable, though, eh? It's been a long sixteen years— or hundred and fifty-seven, depending on how you like to count."

"I'll count sixteen, if you don't mind. Have you gotten word on how they're handling the crew?"

Harrod nodded. "Just came in about an hour ago. We're only the second ship ever to come back—"

"Who beat us in?"

"*Munin*—twelve years ago. Anyway, there'll be a fair amount of fuss. They've been tracking our relatives while we're gone, and there'll be somebody to greet each one of us. Except for Waite." Harrod looked up. "Funny thing, eh?"

"His won't come?" she asked indignantly.

"He hasn't any. I'd have thought that if anybody had left a few genes behind it'd have been that rabbit. But he's got no living relatives, not even a grandniece or nephew. So he's going to be 'adopted'—isn't that considerate of the Flight Office?" His tone carried a burden of sarcasm.

"What comes after? Do they just turn us loose?"

"They've got a place set up in New Zealand where we can 'resynchronize'. Benamira, I think's the name. From the way they talk about it, I'm not sure whether they're more afraid of the world shocking us or us shocking the world," he said wryly. "They'll want to know in sixty days whether we're interested in another flight assignment—though it might be a year or two before they actually need us."

"Any idea what you're going to do?"

"Oh, this is it for me. I've already told them I plan to do a lot of low-tech fishing in a lot of very placid streams. Yourself?"

"I'm going back out, if they treat me right."

Harrod nodded as though he had expected it. "You'll probably get a command."

"That's what I want."

Harrod nodded again, started to say something, stopped himself, and then started again. "What we've seen—where we've been—" He stopped and frowned, searching for the right words. "I guess I don't understand, Ali. What's out there except more of the same? I know we didn't find any colonies ourselves, but—"

"It's not finding them that matters so much. You should know after all this time, Glen," Neale answered, one hand on the door. "I want the answer to the colony problem."

"That burns in you, doesn't it?"

"You know it does. I want to know what makes a mother forget her children. Why did it take the Journans to tell us there had been a First Colonization? There's no more important question for us to answer. I don't know how you can sidestep it."

Harrod smiled a tired smile. "My instinct for self-preservation. Peace of mind." He offered a hand and she clasped it, not as a handshake but as a hug. "You did a good job for me. I wish you the best. Command, without doubt. A colony, at least. Maybe even an answer to your question. You'll have all three, if wanting matters."

"It does," she assured him. "It does."

The broadcast of the welcoming ceremonies reached BT-09 *Babbage* midway between Ceres and home. The asteroid tug, its three-man crew, and its metal-rich, million-tonne catch were falling sunward in a graceful month-long spiral that would end at the Cluster B processing center trailing a half-million klicks behind Earth in solar orbit.

—I think I see them now, Gregory.

—Yes, Nadia, here they come, the two-hundred-year-old space travelers, back home at last after visiting eighteen other star systems.

—That's right, Gregory. It's important that our viewers realize that even though *Dove* did not discover any colonies, her crew is bringing back with them geophysical data on eighty-one different worlds, including samples from the twenty they actually set foot on.

—And of course they were part of the historic Pathfinder mission to the Journa colony, which started everything.

—You're right about that, Gregory. You know, the Unified Space Service tells us that *Dove* has rolled up more than 500 trillion miles since leaving Earth in A.R. 38.

—That's just amazing, Nadia. They're twenty very brave men and women, that's for certain.

"I say they're twenty crazy men and women," systech Brian Hduna said with a yawn, looking up from the small screen set into the console before him. "What do you say, Thack? Lot of fuss over nothing?"

Merritt Thackery was seated before an identical display at the opposite end of Babbage's command console. "Hardly," he said quietly without looking up.

"Hell, what we do on this run counts for more than their whole mission. We're bringing in iron, chromium, nickel—a quarter-million tonnes of it. Think there'll be a band playing when we dock? Hell, no," Hduna grumped.

—Each of the voyagers will be greeted by a member of his own family, Gregory.

—Gone but not forgotten, that's the best way to describe it. We're going to identify them for you as they come out of the shipway. The first out should be Commander Glen Harrod. Here he comes now. SC Glen Harrod, 192-year-old commander of the *Dove,* being greeted by his great-great-greatnephew Tony Harrod.

—And there's SC Alizana Neale, the bridge captain. She'll turn 186 tomorrow, I understand. That's her 85-year-old fourth cousin Randy Stovik waiting there for her.

Hduna made a face. "Can you imagine making it with a 186-year-old woman?"

"Fry out," Thackery said angrily, his eyes burning into Hduna's. "You couldn't have done what they did."

"You make it sound like they're better than we are," Hduna said, squinting at Thackery.

Thackery crossed his arms and looked away, saying nothing.

"If you're not proud of what you are and where you are, maybe you'd just better retire and wait for Survey to call. Wearing the yellow's supposed to mean something," he said, flicking a finger against the yellow ellipse pinned to his collar, the theater insignia for system crews.

Thackery laughed brittlely, "It's none of your damn business, but I transmitted my application this morning."

Hduna cocked an eyebrow, then let out a grunting laugh. "Huh. Well, now I know why you spend all your spare time studying. When'd they post the Notice of Opportunity?"

"Last night. Sixty openings over the next three years."

"Well, well. So you want to wear the black ellipse."

"Everybody who's honest with himself does."

Hduna shook his head. "Not me. Can't see it. Too much to give up."

Thackery laughed. "What's to give up? This billet? Where's the challenge in it? What do we do that couldn't be done just as well by hundreds of others? You used to do your own assays. Now there's a whole team of geologists living in the Belt, tagging asteroids faster than we can haul them in. They're turning the whole Belt into a warehouse, and you into a truck driver. The Council's busy taking the rough edges off of everything, turning this into a finished world. I know. I spent two years being trained to help them."

Hduna snorted. "Hell, I don't know what I'm arguing with you about. You won't even make first call. You ought to know you've got to transfer down a grade to get into Survey."

"That's not in the quals."

"That's the way they do it, all the same. They turn Coms into techs and techs into awks. You're only a awk with, what, six years' experience? What are you going to transfer as?"

"If I don't make it this time, I'll get other shots. They've got a lot of openings to fill, on the new ships and the old ones. I'll make it," Thackery said determinedly.

Hduna laughed nastily. "They're going to have a lot more than sixty openings to get down the list to you."

There was no room at the inn at the Eddington Yards. All five parallel shipways of the voluminous construction base were filled by hourglass-shaped hulls in various stages of completion. *Dove* stood off a kilometre away like a jilted suitor.

Alizana Neale studied the survey ships from the bubble of the jitney. To her right and back a step, Alvarez, the supervisor of ship construction, waited respectfully for her questions.

"How long before they can get on with refitting *Dove?*"

"We'll move the *Tycho Brahe* out within the week so Commander Tamm can get on with preparing it for departure."

"That's the *Tycho* on the far end?"

"Yes—and left to right from there, the *Aristarchus, Kepler, Herschel,* and *Huygens,*" Alvarez said proudly. "We're turning them out at ten-year intervals—the last of the astronomers series. *Copernicus, Hubble,* and *Galileo* are already on station."

"Am I misjudging, or is *Tycho* smaller than *Dove?*"

"Just slightly. But you'll find it actually has more interior volume. No weapons on this class, of course, which helps. And the K-series drive is half the size of that monster in *Dove,* so there's an additional deck for both Operations and Survey.

We've learned some lessons in the last two centuries."

"Haven't we all," Neale said, her voice heavy with irony.

Alvarez crossed his arms over his chest and tucked his hands under his armpits. "I understand only four of you off the *Dove* are going back out?"

She nodded. "Kislak, Tamm, Rogen, and I. Tamm gets *Tycho* and Kislak as his exec, I get *Descartes* and Rogen."

"I guess I'm a little surprised there are even that many—"

"I'll be surprised if there aren't more by the time we leave," she said shortly. "Let's not drag this out, okay? I've got work to do back at Unity. Let me have a quick tour of the section my crew will occupy."

"Of course."

The construction manager brought the jitney in from above and berthed it at a work station inside the bay occupied by *Tycho*'s apparently finished hull. They went aboard via a flex tunnel attached to the aftmost crew portal, near the spherical bulge of one of the four lifepods. There seemed to be little activity aboard, on which Neale remarked.

"We're pretty much down to punch lists and failproofing," Alvarez said as they moved downship on the three-sided climbway ladder. "I've got a test team on the bridge and two mopup crews working in the drive compartment, but you wanted to see your area. Step off here, please."

The climbway ended at the gig bay pressure hatch. On the other side was more of the same: corridors, bulkheads, and doorways. "I'm afraid you'll find you have a little less elbow room here than the ship's main quarters, but it should be adequate. You've got thirteen double cabins and four singles, your own edrec library, and a small exercise area."

"And all this will be pulled once we reach Advance Base Cygnus, I understand."

"Yes. It's modular—three big sections sized to squeak through the bay's space door. The Cygnus folk should be able to break it down and have it out of here and added to their own base in three working days. And because it's intended for reuse, I think you'll find it's not as crude as you were afraid it would be."

"Where's the ship's gig and the rest of the gear that'd usually be in here?"

"It'll go piggyback in a pod amidships on the main hull,

along with the new equipment for *Descartes*. You won't be able to get at it until you reach Cygnus Base, but you won't have need of it, either."

Neale poked her head inside one of the double cabins and gave it a cursory inspection.

"I'll have to admit I was a little dubious when they told me how they were going to ferry my crew out to Advance Base Cygnus, but this should be satisfactory," she said, rejoining Alvarez.

"Hitching twenty-five lights in a gig bay doesn't sound very attractive," he agreed. "Could be worse—they could have put *you* in the pod." He shook his head abruptly. "Slitters. They've got the gain up again. Excuse me a moment, Commander."

Alvarez pressed a finger into the hollow behind his left ear and cocked his head slightly as if listening. "Understood," he said as though to himself, and lowered his hand back to his side. "That was Unity, Commander. Your first call is starting to arrive."

She nodded. "I've seen enough. Let's go back." She knitted her brows and added, "Is everybody wearing those implant relays now?"

"Oh, yes," he effused. "They're awfully damn convenient. Not much to the operation—I'll bet the medtechs could take care of you before *Tycho* heads out."

Neale shuddered. "No, thanks. Being hardwired into the net doesn't come under my definition of duty."

Rocking back in her chair, Neale studied the solemn-faced young awk as he made his way to the empty chair opposite her. "Commander," he acknowledged with a bob of his head as he sat down.

"God, does everyone here do that?" she exclaimed in annoyance. "Don't presume. I'm not your Commander. My name is Neale. Use it."

Thackery nodded, taken aback. "Neale."

She glanced at the flat data-display slate lying on her lap. "So, Thackery, you want to be famous."

"Excuse me?"

"You watched *Dove*'s homecoming and you'd like to go out and become a conquering hero just like its crew."

Thackery's face wound up into a look of puzzlement. "Is that in my file? I never—"

"Oh, come now, it's all right to admit it. I'm one of them, after all. I know what it's like."

"Sir—"

"You're presuming again."

Thackery blinked. "I'd guess I'm more likely to end up forgotten here than famous. More of us will go out than will ever come back."

"Quite true," Neale said, a hard edge to her voice. "Do you know why? Because coming back is a lot harder than leaving. Ask my shipmates from *Dove*, trying to adjust at Benamira. We would never have brought the Pathfinders back if we hadn't promised the crews they'd see Earth again. And we might not have kept that promise if those ships hadn't needed major refits to be useful during Phase II, refits that the advance bases aren't yet equipped to handle. But this is the last time that'll be true. From now on, the advance bases will be the staging points."

"I understand."

"Do you?" she asked skeptically. "Turn your chair to face the far wall and place your hands over the silver band at the end of each armrest. I'm going to show you some pictures and find out what you think of them."

The room lights dimmed, and the first image appeared on the floor-to-ceiling flatscreen: weathered rust-colored spires casting long shadows on the jagged rivercourse.

"Grand Canyon. Northern section, I think," Thackery said.

"This isn't a geography test," she said with annoyance. "The monitors will tell me what I want to know." Glowing numbers on Neale's slate told of Thackery's galvanic skin response and heart rate.

Five seconds later, the Grand Canyon was replaced by a view of the Lagoon Nebula, and both of Thackery's readings jumped. They remained high for the next photo, three bare-breasted women walking along a sun-drenched Mediterranean beach, then nosedived when a nude, well-muscled man appeared in their place.

The images came one after another:

—a snowfield in the Himalayas.

—the hilly streets and Victorian homes of San Francisco.

—two men kissing.

—the Virgo galaxies.

—a young couple holding their toddler on the back of a carousel horse.

—the capital city of the Journa colony.

—Jupiter.

Neale studied Thackery as each new image appeared, while the slate recorded the data from the biosensors. Despite her rebuke, Thackery silently mouthed the identity of many of the images as they appeared, and smiled to himself at the sight of Philadelphia's Fairmont Park. And he jerked reflexively when the portrait which had once accompanied Andra Thackery's newsnet columns appeared.

Then the lights went up, and Thackery shot Neale a questioning look. "What kind of test was that?"

"I find it useful to know something about the strength of a prospective surveyor's attachments," she said idly. "As well as the direction of their sexual proclivities."

"Do I get to know how I did?"

A faint smile appeared on her lips. "No." She touched an icon on her slate and the display changed. "You have an odd background, Thackery. Six years in the GS track, and two at Georgetown—they don't let too many get away. Then three at Tsiolkovsky."

"I've worked hard to develop my tech skills."

"Don't apologize. I like people with odd backgrounds. The candidates I've seen so far could have come out of a cookie cutter. Study linguistics?"

"Eight years. That's a core subject."

"Anything practical in it?"

"I can tell what era you grew up in by the way you refuse to use token honorifics, or to let me call you Commander when I'm not under your command. Most people probably just think you're rude."

She laughed. "You like that kind of reading between the lines, *Mister* Thackery?"

"Yes."

"And you've some skill in sociodynamics, according to this Gordon Stowell."

"He would know."

Neale laid the slate aside. "Thackery, you probably recognize that Survey is making this up as it goes along. We're improvising the rules those that come after will treat as revealed truth. But right now, a Commander enjoys a lot of autonomy in structuring her crew. A ship's a small place when you've been out for three, five, ten years. It gets smaller with every craze. I need to feel good about the people I take aboard."

"I understand."

"I doubt you'd have even made first call for Tamm. You're just not very experienced. On face qualifications only, there's no way to justify making you even a sysawk."

"I realize that," Thackery said, his face showing disappointment. "I appreciate your—"

"I'm not finished. All that notwithstanding, you seem like a right type. How would you feel about becoming a member of *Descartes*'s contact team?"

Thackery gaped.

"Every surveyor needs at least two specialities. I see you serving as linguist on hits and resource geologist on misses," she went on. "I'm guessing that with your background, eventually you might have something to contribute to the overall direction of contact strategy as well. Does that mesh with what you saw yourself doing?"

"Nothing could please me more," Thackery said quietly.

She smiled faintly. "That's what your attachment test suggested. All right. I'll initiate the transfer proceedings right away. Go straight from here to the Survey Medical offices for your pre-assignment screening. It's pretty damn thorough, so don't make any other plans for today."

"Could what they find keep me here?"

"Yes," she said bluntly. "Your general flight physical didn't take into account your genetic endowment. We have to." She paused and marshaled her thoughts. "If you clear, I'll okay a pass downwell and a five-day leave so that you can get your affairs straightened out. Report back on the eighth for orientation. If Tamm can get his people settled, we'll be outbound within sixty days. That's all. You can go." She waited until he had stood and taken a step toward the door, then added, "Oh, one more thing. This Andra—chances are she'll be dead before we come out of our first craze. That all right with you?"

Thackery started, then drew a deep breath. "To be honest, we could hardly be more separated than we are now."

"Dead is a very special kind of separated. So is taking a berth on a Survey ship. You're going to get hit with both, and it'll be worse if you leave with the relationship still screwed up. While you're downwell, get it taken care of. Whatever kind of problem you're having, resolve it."

"I've done about everything I can to make peace," Thackery

said, gesturing helplessly. "We have a kind of a precarious understanding. One of the rules is we don't see each other very often. One of the other rules is that when we do, we don't talk about what I'm doing."

"You're going to have to talk about it. Don't just drift away. Kiss her good-bye or tell her to go to hell. But one way or another, leave it here. Don't bring it along. Clear?"

"Yes—Commander?" he said tentatively.

"Ah, you're learning. Tell them to send the next one in."

By mutual consent, they had not seen each other in four years. The last time had been during the long leave between his reassignment from the transfer freighter *Ripon Falls* to the *Babbage*. They had gone to a sculling race on the upper Schulkyll, then had dinner downtown. Since then, *Babbage* and inertia had kept them apart, save for their infrequent, often impersonal letters.

So he had not been there when she received the Council's Commendation of Merit for Journalism, or when she was retired by the Net the next year at age fifty-eight. He was not there when her hip was broken in a street accident, or when she gave up her colonial row home in New Market for a place in a 28-story glass-faced microcommunity overlooking Fairmont Park.

He sat outside that structure's entrance in his rented car and thought for a long time before he made any move to go inside. Neither the building nor the neighborhood carried any feelings of home. Pity. He would have welcomed a rush of sentiment to thaw the ice inside him.

She let him in wordlessly. The apartment might have been a hostel for all the individuality it displayed.

"Hello, Andra," he said. "How've you been?"

She eyed his jumpsuit coldly, then closed the door behind him. It was the first time he had worn Service garb in her presence, a deliberate breach of the rules. "Do you want a real answer or a polite one?"

"We could at least start out polite."

"Then I'm fine." She settled in a chair in the far corner and rested folded hands on crossed legs. "So what brings you down?"

Thackery sat on one end of the overstuffed russet-colored couch before answering. "I've come here to have a conversation we've both been avoiding for a long time."

"Is wearing that uniform here part of your strategy for making peace?"

"It's not a uniform—"

"Excuse me, 'standard issue shipboard garb, male'—"

"This is part of what I am."

"In case you'd forgotten, I'm not on good terms with that part of you."

"That's not where our problem comes from," he said, shaking his head.

"No? You and I both worked hard to give you an opportunity to be someone special, and you threw it over without as much as a word of warning. You didn't ask my advice, my opinion, or my permission. I suppose you'd like me to forget that."

"It wasn't your place to give permission."

"Don't you think you made that clear? Doing what you did told me exactly what you thought of me and of our relationship."

"What I did had nothing to do with you."

"Exactly. It should have."

"I made the decision I had to to keep peace with myself. I'm doing what I want to do."

She stood and crossed the room to where a drug dispenser sat on the oak dry sink. "I see," she said, fumbling for an ampule. "You prefer hauling rocks to serving on the World Council of Commissioners."

"You're the only one who ever thought that was a real possibility. I never did."

Her head whipped around and she glowered at him with eyes that were fast becoming red and puffy. "You should have. Merritt, I knew those people. I saw them every day, with their public face on and in the back rooms. I knew what it takes, and I made sure that you had it. You were better than most of them, Merritt, and you should be on your way to sitting where they're sitting. With your gifts—." Frustration silenced her.

Thackery looked away. How wrenchingly difficult to be that close to the decision-makers and have no say in the decisions, he realized for the first time. The translator at the summit meeting—the stenographer at a great trial. If you have any ego at all, you would have to want to contribute your thoughts, but you're locked out because of your station.

"I'm sorry, Andra," he said finally. "I'm sorry that it wasn't possible to make us both happy. We've never talked about it, and we should have, a long time ago. But there's something more important for us to deal with."

Her face showed puzzlement. "What?"

"I want to know who my father was."

She turned her back on him, hiding her expression. "I never hid that from you. You've known since you were ten. You were an alternate conception child—I was inseminated at the Human Fertility Institute on Broad Street. Beyond that all I know is that the genes were male, healthy, and compatible."

Thackery rested his chin on his folded hands and shook his head almost imperceptibly. "No, you weren't," he said softly. "You had your prenatal testing done there. But you were already pregnant."

Her back stiffened. "Their records aren't open to you."

"No, they aren't," he agreed. "But they're open to the Service, when the Service is researching a candidate. I'm not an AC. Since I'm male I can't be a partho. And we're too close a match for me to be adopted. I'm part you and part someone else. I have a right to know."

Hugging herself as if chilled, she turned back to him. "The Service can have your genes analyzed. They can learn everything they need to from a skin scraping."

"Which is what they did. But there are some things I need to know that a scraping can't answer."

"No," she said, her eyes wet but her head high and chin firm. "You have no right to that part of my life. Why should it matter? And why should it matter now?"

"It matters now because I know now—because I could have had a father, not just a geneparent. You kept that from me. You kept *him* from me."

"He never belonged to you," she said, turning her head away.

"Did he belong to you?"

She retreated to her chair before answering. "The genes you carry are all he gave either of us," she said softly. "All he could give us."

"Then this isn't how you wanted it?"

She chased the wistful expression from her face and met his gaze squarely. "Don't try to be a mind-reader. You're no good at it," she snapped. "I'll say this much and that'll be the end of it. If what I told you before wasn't literally true, it wasn't a lie, either. There're times that there's no difference between a penis and a syringe."

Inside, Thackery cringed at the crude image. "That may be so, but you wouldn't know. Andra, you can't make me back off just by being disagreeable. I kept growing when I went away."

"I never realized that being 'grown up' meant feeling free to call your mother a liar."

"Only when she is."

After scorching him with a furious look, she bounced out of the chair and headed for the hallway to her bedroom. Thackery moved quickly and blocked her path.

"We're running out of time, Andra," he said gently.

Her angry look gave way to her thoughtful one, and she turned and walked slowly back to her chair. "I see I've missed something here. You said the Service was researching a candidate. Surely they didn't wait all these years to get around to that. But you've only just found out. What aren't you telling me?"

"I'd rather tackle one subject at a time—"

"You tell me now or this conversation is finished. Why are they looking into your records now?"

It was Thackery's turn to wear a desperate look. "I don't want to get the two entangled."

"They already are," she said coldly. "Why are they prying into my privacy?"

Thackery looked away. "I'm transferring to Survey. I'm part of the new crew for *Descartes*, which is waiting for us at Cygnus Base." He raised his head to look at her. "It's what I wanted all along, and I won't apologize for it. But I didn't want to use it as a club to get you to answer my questions."

"Don't worry. It wouldn't have worked," she said curtly. "So—you're leaving us. Well, I can't say as I'll see the difference. I'd throw a going-away party, but I can't think of anyone else who'll miss you, either."

"Ten years ago that might have hurt," he said quietly. "But I know you better now."

She waved her hands in an abrupt gesture of dismissal. "You don't know me at all."

"I've had occasion to wish that were true."

"And now it will be. Well, go, then, and stop pretending what I think or how I feel matters. I'll be fine without you. Is that what you want to hear? Go! You're absolved."

The urge to lash back was almost irresistible. Angry answers filled his head: *You made the choice to be alone, and you will be. Stay here in your room and wallow in your bitterness. Your life is over. I'm going to see places and things no one has ever seen before. Maybe my father would have known how to be proud of me and happy for me. You've forgotten how to love anything you can't control.*

But he squashed those thoughts, saying only in a calm, quiet voice, "My mistake, Andra. When I made my choice, I put myself first. I understand now that I learned how to do that from you." Then he fled the apartment without looking back.

Not until he was safely in the lift did he realize why he had settled for a parting snipe instead of a full counterattack. It was not the fear of hurting her that had checked him, but rather the fear of discovering she could not be hurt.

THE BLACK ELLIPSE

(from Merritt Thackery's
JIADUR'S WAKE)

... In the beginning, it was the rarest gem in the Universe.

It was the rarest because it was a synthetic creation, the product of man's laboratory rather than nature's. It was the rarest because only the Service knew how to make one, and because only the chosen few who held billets aboard the survey ships were permitted to wear one.

The black ellipse was, in fact, the only insignia worn aboard those ships, for a variety of reasons. A survey ship was too small and the missions too long for in-flight promotions, so it behooved the Service to de-emphasize rank. The black ellipse served as a reminder that its wearers were part of a team of equals, not a military hierarchy. The absence of glittery status symbols was thought to remove unnecessary formality and encourage the crew to relate on personal as well as professional levels.

Or so said the director of the Survey Branch.

But despite that ennobling symbolism, life on a Survey ship was usually dominated by an authoritarian command structure and awkward personal chemistry. And what the black ellipse really stood for depended a great deal on whom you asked . . .

chapter 3

Outcrossing

On his return to Unity, Thackery, the other five surveyors, and Contact Leader Rajesh Jaiswal were plunged into a ten-day basic orientation to the Class II survey ship. No more than that was needed, since it was only in the direst emergency that surveyors would pull operations duty. Thackery was not sure how much help they would be even then. Few surveyors had even minimum quals in any of the operations technicals: AVLO drive, gravigation, communications, ship's ecology, and library and electronic systems.

The team then moved from Unity to *Tycho* for a six-week hands-on familiarization with the extensive array of surveyor's equipment. During this time Jaiswal, an Asian biologist, proved himself likable despite his high expectations and swift, sharp-tongued rebukes. Thackery also got on well with Gregg Eagan, a slender African a year or two Thackery's junior. They spent a good deal of time together, since Eagan was Thackery's "inverse"—the prime resource geologist, and the backup linguist.

Thackery saw less of the other four surveyors, but still enough to have largely good feelings about them. Two were Europeans: Derrel Guerrieri, the astrophysicist, and Jael Collins, the interpolator. Michael Tyszka, the technoanalyst and gig pilot, hailed from the West Coast of North America. Donna Muir, the exobiologist, called South America home.

The one glaring weakness in the Contact Team was the

absolute lack of experience. Not one of them was a Phase I vet. Collins and Jaiswal were even Service outsiders, with no prior Orbital or System experience.

That weakness became painfully apparent during the mock field exercise in Queen Maud Land, Antarctica. From the moment *Tycho* moved into the appropriate polar orbit, the exercise was marked by indecision and error. Thanks to the snow and ice, Eagan misread the spectroscopic data and underestimated the resource base. Muir missed the rock lichens which were the test zone's primary life form. Tyszka found but initially misinterpreted the artifacts placed there by the Service. Jaiswal allowed the team to return without seeing to proper decontamination precautions.

Though they were surely not all his fault, the misadventures cost Jaiswal his position. When *Tycho* returned them to Unity, Thackery and the other surveyors moved into the station's D wing to begin preflight gnotobiotic conditioning. Jaiswal did not. The stiff-necked answer to their queries was that he had been reassigned. Whether it was voluntary or involuntary was not open for discussion.

No immediate replacement was forthcoming. There was talk that the Service was desperately courting the vets in search of an experienced Contactor for the *Descartes*. In the meantime, the team members concerned themselves with reclaiming their personal possessions from the decon crew and determining if the objects had survived the irradiation and other processing.

Bayn Graeff, the dark-complected, husky-voiced *Dove* vet who had signed on as *Descartes'* bridge captain, then took charge of the team. She shepherded them through meetings with the investors who would handle their compensation accounts, the fitness experts who laid out their diet and exercise programs, the psychologists who retested them for craze fear, and the gnotobiologists who rearranged—for the worse—their inner environment.

As far as Thackery was concerned, gnotobiology was a synonym for misery. The necessity was inarguable: Since the colonists were full human stock, any successful contact brought with it the risk of crossinfection. It was not merely a matter of seeing that they were free of active or latent pathogens. Even the 1200-odd grams of ubiquitous human microflora—primarily intestinal bacteria, but including significant colonies on the skin, and in the mouth, lungs, eyes, vagina, and nose—had to be eliminated. The ship and the crew had to be made, insofar as was possible, germ-free.

That meant not only numerous injections of broad-spectrum antibiotics, but a complete blood replacement for anyone carrying active viral particles, be they from past infections or from past immunizations. At the same time, the doctors flushed each crewmember's intestinal tract with a diet of antibiotic-laced food, then provided each with microflora capsules to reestablish the benign, symbiotic anaerobes. The resulting five days of diarrhea left a permanent stain on Thackery's romantic conception of being an interstellar traveler.

What made matters worse was that all the misery only eliminated half the risk: the chance of the Contactors infecting the colonists. The chance of the colonists infecting the Contactors was still very real, and though there were steps that could be taken should the occasion arise, Thackery knew the Contactors would remain vulnerable. But that was a risk the Service found acceptable, and as he prepared to leave Unity for *Tycho*, Thackery knew he would have to find a way to view it in the same light.

His arms full, Thackery pressed the door release with his elbow and shouldered his way into his cabin. At a glance, he saw that the compartment was more roomy than the one he had occupied on *Babbage*. Though cramped and lacking some amenities—most notably privacy—it would certainly do for a month. Coming downship from the aft portal, Thackery had caught a glimpse of one of the relatively luxurious cabins in the Survey section, and expected that the same awaited them in *Descartes*.

Three metres away and seemingly oblivious to Thackery's presence, a red-haired awk stood facing the far wall, beyond which lay the consumables storage section of *Tycho*'s gig bay. The man's fingers were tracing the almost invisible zipweld between two plates of structural composite.

"Hey," Thackery called, tossing his haversack on the nearest bunk.

The awk looked back over his shoulder. "Hi. Do you know anything about materials science?"

Good to meet you, too, roomie. "No."

"Oh." He tucked his hands in the belly pockets of his jacket and turned to face Thackery. "I was just wondering how strong this is."

"Couldn't tell you." Thackery settled on the bed and opened the neck of his bag. "I've seen you during training but I don't know your name."

"McShane. Daniel McShane. You're Thackery. I asked." He smiled a nervous smile. "I guess you've never been out, either."

"I've been to the Belt."

"I meant gone through a craze."

"No. That I haven't done." He laughed. "You can't get near those vees in a tug."

"I guess not." McShane rubbed his neck. "There's storage under the bed for your gear, and that's about all. No drop-downs or hideaways back here."

"Tourist class."

"Temporary." He laughed nervously again. "That's something, isn't it, going into deep-space in a temporary structure?"

"We're still inside *Tycho*."

"In the bowels of the beast. Sure. Sure. Look, if you haven't been out, maybe you should know. Anybody who comes down with craze fear will be put off at Cygnus."

"I hadn't heard that."

"Oh, yeah. They'll be watching us real closely on this leg."

"Good to know. Are you worried about it?"

"No, no. Except that it means we're not in yet. There's one more hurdle to get over."

By the time *Tycho Brahe* was ready to leave, Alizana Neale's list of grievances against the Service in general and Lin Tamm in particular had grown too long for recitation.

It was bad enough that Tamm, junior to her on *Dove* in rank if not in experience, had been gifted with the brand-new *Tycho*, while she had been assigned to *Descartes*. Though operationally identical to *Tycho*, *Descartes'* oversized and inelegant cargo blister marked it for the one-time freighter and transport it had been.

Like all its sister ships in the Pioneers series, *Descartes'* first job had been to ferry the components of an Advance Base to a spot decreed by Service planners: In this case, twenty-five light-years in the general direction of the distant supergiant

Deneb. With the construction crew transformed into the A-Cyg staff, *Descartes* waited there like a white elephant for a survey crew to take her further. Neale's crew.

But the *Tycho* had been designed for just one purpose. It was a better *Dove*, not an unwieldy hybrid. Its L-series drive made it 5 percent faster than the *Descartes;* in Neale's eyes, its newness made it 100 percent more desirable. *It should have been mine,* she thought almost daily. *But they gave me the hand-me-down.*

When she expressed that complaint privately to a sympathetic rating in the Flight Office, she learned of a second affront to add to her list. Her appointment had come by the narrowest of margins, 3–2; her opponents would have given the position to Keene Rogen, her exec.

"They're both recidivist sexists," her source confided. "Everybody knows they didn't want to give it to a woman, but they were careful to build up Rogen instead of tearing you down. Otherwise they'd have been reprimanded for sure. So they gave you *Descartes* as a compromise."

The idea that "everyone knew" but no one did anything kept Neale simmering for several days. No better received was hearing the way Tamm described her and her crew during his appearance on an interview show broadcast net-wide.

"I understand *Tycho*'s first task, though, will be to serve as kind of a space taxi," the interviewer had ventured.

"That's right," Tamm had responded. "We'll have thirty passengers to ferry out to Advance Base Cygnus, at the fringe of explored space. We'll drop them off, then continue on to begin our prime function of surveying planetary systems."

We'll be right on your heels in Descartes, *damnit,* she thought furiously. *Don't make it sound like you're going to scout the whole freezin' octant by yourself.*

"But isn't the prime function finding more First Colonization civilizations?" the interviewer demanded.

"Not really. There are so many systems, and we have so little basis for saying this one or that one might have a colony, that we really have to think of surveying as the number one task," Tamm began his answer, and the subject of the second crew never came up again.

Even while the show's closing credits were still appearing, Neale was on the phone to Alvarez, the supervisor of ship construction.

"I want a mock bridge for my crew," she demanded. "Something we can use for training simulations en route, and slaved to *Tycho*'s bridge for current status displays. We'll give up the exercise space."

Alvarez had started to shake his head almost immediately. "That's not enough room for one, and there's not enough time now if it was."

"I don't want to hear why it can't be done."

"Not hearing them won't change the facts, Commander Neale," Alvarez said, bristling. "You'll have full shipnet access down there, but there's just not enough time to rig something as complex as a training mockup."

"Then I want access to the real bridge."

"There I can't help you. That'll be up to Commander Tamm."

It wasn't until the next day that she tracked down Tamm, only to find she needn't have bothered.

"Look, Ali, I can't see the sense to disrupting my crew's routine as well as yours," Tamm told her. "After all, it's not crucial that you be ready to jump in *Descartes* and roar off the instant we reach A-Cyg. You can stay there a week, two weeks, a month for orientation if you want to. There's really no rush."

You're enjoying this, she thought, studying his face. *You like having the upper hand.* The discovery puzzled her, since she could think of no residual friction traceable to their time on *Dove*.

"The fact that there are no deadlines doesn't justify wasted time," she retorted.

"Oh, of course not. But I'm sure you can find some way to see that your people's first craze isn't wasted," he said superciliously. "It's only fifty-three days to Cygnus."

When at last *Tycho* was ready to leave, Neale and Rogen were the only members of the *Descartes*' crew invited forward to view the departure from the *Tycho* bridge. Neale suspected that, were it not for the fact that bridge video was being made available to Worldnet by the Service, even that small courtesy would have gone by the board. Any sense of commonality among *Dove* alumni had apparently faded quickly.

Tycho was given an escort comprised of five ships, including a World Council yacht bearing John Langston. Langston was the best known of the several retired Councilors still living, having held a seat in that body for an unprecedented and generally distinguished nineteen years. From him came the traditional "Cleared for departure" signal.

Angling up out of the ecliptic and leaving the escort behind, *Tycho* also received a spectacular salute by means of a kilometre-wide ring of starshell mines. When detonated, the charges formed a perfectly symmetrical yellow halo through which the departing ship passed. It was the first time Neale had seen fireworks in space, and though the *Tycho*'s own monitors failed to capture the effect, the view relayed from Unity reminded her of the opening of a space-warp from early video fiction. She wondered if the parallel were intentional.

"Are we combining our outcrossing ceremony with *Tycho*'s?" Rogen asked.

"We're not welcome to," Neale answered curtly. "Don't you know? The Net wants their ceremony to cap the coverage of *Tycho*'s departure." She sighed. "That's all right. I wouldn't want it that formal anyway, with the Council anthem and the Service fanfare and all the rest."

Rogen took a moment to digest that news. "We'll be leaving the heliosphere pretty quick. We should probably go get ready for our own, then," he suggested as the comtech poked a view of fast-diminishing Earth onto the bridge window. Unity was already invisibly small.

"In a minute," Neale said wistfully and gestured toward the screen. "I kept trying to find a way to prepare the new crew for that sight, and never did. As little good as came out of coming back, I still think it's harder to face the second time than it was the first. Because this time we know we'll never see it again."

When Neale finally left *Tycho*'s bridge she went directly to her cabin, delegating the outcrossing preparations to Rogen. Half an hour later, shortly after the announcement came over the shipnet that *Tycho* had passed beyond the heliosphere, Rogen came by for her. He carried a book-sized leatherette case under one arm.

"The lesser colors are assembling in the library for the pinning. So whenever you're ready—," Rogen said deferentially.

Neale lay aside the slate on which she had been reading a translation of Ptolemy's *Almagest*. "Let me see."

Holding the case in front of him, Rogen tipped it and opened the lid so that Neale could see its contents: twenty-five Service deep-space theater insignia, twenty-five gleaming black elliptical jewels.

"Never saw so many of them in one place before," she said, taking the case. "Damnit, I hate this. Giving them out like candy to kids. They've done nothing to earn them, but you put one on them and they'll think they're as good as you or Sebright or Waite or any of the vets. It cheapens the insignia."

"It's just not going to be such an exclusive club anymore," Rogen commiserated.

"You know, I'll bet I could still tell you the original complement of all three Pathfinders," she went on. "We knew everyone who wore the black ellipse. Now I need to use the library just to remember the commanders of all the ships. I've never even met most of them."

"There're a lot of new faces everywhere," Rogen agreed. "They tell me Homal had twenty-seven lessers when he took out *Galileo*."

Neale shook her head in disgust. "Come on. Let's get it over with."

There was much happy talk and some braggadocio among the twenty-five crew waiting in the crowded library. Thackery did not take part in either, content to listen and defend the corner of the workstation he had staked out as a seat. He had too many conflicting feelings to freely enjoy the anticipation of his pinning.

For one thing, he had heard that the outcrossing was to be televised. But it was obvious now that that was not true—which meant that he was already gone as far as Andra and any Georgetown alumni who might remember him were concerned. Not that Andra would have been likely to watch, but, still, the ceremony's importance had been diminished.

At the same time, he remained proud of what he had accomplished. He had set a goal for himself, what seemed an outrageous goal at the time, and—more easily than he had thought possible—he had achieved it. True, that pleasure in his accomplishment remained internal, somewhat tainted for lack of anyone who could revel in the feeling and reflect it back to him. His crewmates were unsuited to that role, having matched his success on the strength of, in most cases, even more experience and expertise.

It's like going from the top rung of one ladder to the bottom rung of the next. The people you left behind are impressed only to the extent that they want to be where you are—and the people that you've joined aren't impressed at all.

He came to his feet with the others when Neale and Rogen appeared. All talking ceased, and all turned to face the officers. That was all Neale and Rogen expected; the Service's heritage lay with the merit-oriented Pangaean Consortium, not the militaristic International Police.

"Since the days of Charan Rashuri, commander of *Pride of Earth,* it has been the ship commander's obligation to recognize a moment of transition for those among his crew new to the Survey branch," Neale began.

"I have no doubt that some among you have invested the outcrossing with far more meaning than it deserves. It is an occasion for the exchange of theater insignia. You give up the blue Orbital or yellow System ellipse you now wear. You receive the black Intersystem ellipse. But the difference in color is meaningless in itself."

Then why do you vets call us lessers? Thackery wondered, fingering his own System insignia absently.

"Contrary to what many of you believe, this is not a promotion. The Service does not honor you by doing this. All we do here today is to mark the beginning of an opportunity for honor—honor you will have to bring to yourself in the months and years ahead. You wear the black ellipse, but you have not yet earned it."

A tech to Thackery's right nudged him and whispered, "Trying to scare us with the tough bitch routine, huh?" Thackery ignored the comment.

"In the last two months, I have even heard some of you use the term 'cadet'. You mislead yourself if you think of your role here in those terms. There are no 'cadets' in the Survey Branch, and even if there were, there would be none in the crew of *Descartes.* A cadet is expected to make mistakes and learn from them. You are expected not to make mistakes. Remember that, always."

She handed the case to Rogen, opened it, and took out the first insignia.

"Technician Jessica Baldwin," she called out.

When Thackery's turn came, he came forward suffused with pride despite Neale's deflating remarks. She made the exchange smoothly and wordlessly, deftly removing the yellow, handing it to Rogen in exchange for a black, and pinning the new jewelry in place. Then the moment was over. But as he turned away he was conscious of the new weight on his collar all the same.

I didn't see it happening this way, he thought as he walked back. *Not full of down-talk, not as part of a human assembly-line, not in a crowded temporary compartment in the hold of someone else's ship. But damnit, I'm here. We're on our way. And this is what I wanted, no matter how it comes packaged.*

As Neale was pinning the next-to-last tech a shipnet comtech broke in to announce: "First warning. Craze in thirty minutes."

Neale waved the last auxiliary forward and called out instructions as she pinned him. "First command watch, forward to the *Tycho* bridge. Second watch, monitor from here. In both cases, I want the navtechs and comtechs to prepare an annotated log and critique of *Tycho*'s watch procedures. Everyone else out of here, they need room to breathe. Questions?"

There were none, and the gathering broke up quickly as the officers left and the various crew scattered to their posts. Thackery fought his way through the congested corridor and caught up to Neale and Rogen at the former's cabin door.

"Commander, a request?"

Neale looked back over her shoulder, then turned to face him. "Thackery," she acknowledged.

"Permission to observe the craze from the bridge, Commander?"

"I've sent them as many observers as they will accept. I'm the commander of *Descartes*, not of *Tycho*."

"Then permission to observe from the library."

She shook her head. "There'll be time enough for that later."

"What's your interest, Thackery?" Rogen interjected.

Thackery glanced sideways at the bridge captain and hesitated before answering. "I understand that any phobes will be rousted out at Cygnus."

"That's correct. They'll be transferred to the permanent staff there."

"Well—I'd like to find out right away."

A bemused smile slowly spread across Rogen's face, and he walked away chuckling to himself.

"The craze phobia is psychological, not perceptual," Neale said coldly in answer to Thackery's baffled look. "If that were not the case, we would be able to screen for it more effectively."

Flushing rapidly, he said, "I always heard it compared with claustrophobia—"

"An analogy only. Its effect becomes evident only over a period of time. So we won't know right away whether you are fit to continue on this ship," she said pointedly. "You have as much to prove here as anyone, Thackery, if not more—and not just in your flight adaptation. So I would suggest you spend less time letting the vets mislead you and more time working to improve your skills."

She turned her back and entered the cabin, leaving him alone in the corridor.

The moment Neale's door closed, Thackery smacked his thigh sharply with a fist. *Idiot! How could you—*

"Second warning. Fifteen minutes to craze," the shipnet intoned. "Prepare to terminate local telemetry handshaking. Receiving final inmail. Last call for personal outmail."

Unable to readily shed the foolish feeling or forget the sound of Rogen's laughter, Thackery made his way back to his quarters. Mercifully, McShane was with the second watch in the library. Mercifully for him, considering his contribution to Thackery's blunder.

Thackery flung himself lengthwise on his bunk and blew a weighty sigh between his lips. *Well, let's add up the day. You had to come aboard without being able to reach Andra, found out your new commander thinks most of her crew isn't worth a straw, and then you proceeded to prove her right. A great start, Thack. A great start.*

Unpinning the Intersystem insignia from his collar, Thackery held it up at eye-level and stared into it, the first time he had had a chance to examine one closely. True to its reputation, the black crystal's invisible internal facets created a marvelous illusion of a dimensionless void. Though barely three centimetres across the long axis, it was almost possible to believe that it contained a universe as infinite as the one in which it existed.

My compliments to the crystallurgists.

Thackery recalled having heard on Unity that a vet from the Hugin was arrested for trying to sell his black ellipse to a Filipino businessman. Though nothing had appeared in any official media to confirm any part of the story, the asking price was said to be €75,000.

How many are there, six hundred scattered through 65,000 cubic light-years?—And I have one of them. How could he sell it? Why would he even consider it?

Meaningless in itself, Neale had said. *You're wrong, Commander,* Thackery thought as he returned the insignia to his collar. *It means enough to make up for what we gave up to get it, what we put up with because we wear it, what it will cost us to keep it. And on days like today, it means everything.*

"Thack?"

He reached across and tabbed the shipnet. "Here."

It was Baldwin. "Just passing the word. You got mail."

"What?"

"In the last dispatch before we crazed. It was a big batch. We were receiving almost right up to the last minute."

"Oh. When can I access it?"

"It's already queued up under your file number."

"Oh. Thanks."

Thackery retrieved his slate from one of the drawers beneath his bunk and switched it on, wondering what he had left unfinished or who he had failed to settle with. To his surprise, there was not one but three messages in the queue.

Touching an icon, he brought the first of them to the slate's display. He recognized the header immediately: It was the formal letterhead of the Government Service Academy at Georgetown.

The face of Director Stowell appeared . He smiled briefly. "Good morning, Merritt. Or at least it's morning where I am. I don't suppose that term applies where you're heading.

"One of the things I've learned in twenty-two years as an educator is that the talented students will find their own way, no matter how bone-headedly determined the institution is to hinder them.

"I believe I told you once that I couldn't see you as a follower. I didn't realize then that you had it in your head to be a pioneer. I never had the desire to be where you are today, but the task you have chosen is an important one, and I wish only that your part in it brings you great satisfaction." He smiled again, in fatherly fashion, and the picture was replaced by a fax of Thackery's student record. In the space where it had once said ON HIATUS, the legend now read WITHDRAWN WITHOUT PREJUDICE.

The second message was text only, and Thackery found it puzzling at first. There was no header, only a twenty-four-year-old clip from POLINET.

> FOR RELEASE: 3:00 p.m. GMT May 12, A.R. 172
>)CAPITOL ISLAND—World Council insiders are pointing to Associate Director John Merritt Langston as the most likely candidate for the seat of 75-year-old retiring Councilor Den-Buodi Kuoinmoni.
>)A 52-year-old native of Newfoundland, Langston would be the youngest ever selected to the 17-man executive body, and the first North American so honored since the turn of the century . . .

The rest of the article comprised an unusually positive biography of Langston, in which he came off as being bright without being snobbish, fast-rising without being ambitious, and one who practiced traditional values without being a shill for them. It was sharp, well written, and incisive. And it made not a whit of sense until Thackery reached the end and the creditline:

> A NEWS ANALYSIS BY ANDRA THACKERY,
> POLINET CORRESPONDENT.

Even then, he only understood who had sent it, with just the barest hint of why. It took Andra's trailing note to fill that gap.

> Merritt—son—
> Within an hour of your leaving that day, I came to admit (I always realized) you did indeed deserve to know. Since then I also realized other difficult truths: Most importantly, that when I could not have him, I tried to make you into him, and that I think is a far greater offense.
> Even so, I can only make myself tell you now because you are beyond reach, and you cannot disturb him, or me, with your hunger for an alternate past. Don't wonder at his silence, for he never knew—another choice I made for all of us.

It is impossible to control and too late to change what you feel toward me. But please believe that I am as proud of you as I can be. I have asked a friend to drive with me into the country and help me find Cygnus, so that I can look into the night sky and think of you often.

Andra

Numbly, Thackery asked the netlink for a picture of John Langston. He looked a long time into the eyes of the gaunt face which appeared on the display, then asked for a younger picture. The eyes became stronger, the chin firmer, the folds and wrinkles fewer. He asked for a younger picture yet, and a chill went through him when it appeared. It was as though he were looking into an unfaithful mirror, or at the face of a brother, or—

There was one message remaining in the queue, and for one brief moment of wish-fulfilling weakness Thackery allowed himself to hope it might be from Langston—from his father. Even now, as little as it would be, it would mean so much—

But there were to be no tidy endings. The final message was a routine congratulatory from the current dean of Tsiolkovsky Institute, a man whose name meant nothing to Thackery and whose words were formal and meaningless.

Thackery retreated to his bed as a wounded animal goes to his lair. There was almost deliberate cruelty in the way Andra had told him, for it was already too late for him to use the knowledge. There was no way to reach out to Langston, no way to heal the trauma. *Descartes* had crazed, and the wall had gone up. When it came down again, Langston would be dead.

And so would Andra.

He saw with renewed clarity how selfish she was, even at the last. She had given him what he had demanded, but only after waiting long enough to render it valueless. For all her apologies, her message did more to free her conscience than it did to restore what had been stolen from him.

Damn you, Andra! Better you hadn't told me at all than to tell me now, in this way. You've made leaving harder, not easier. And instead of redeeming yourself, you've given me another reason to hate you—

Except that she was dead, and he was beginning a new life.

In his mind's eye, he would still her voice and freeze her form, and he would bury her. With a will, perhaps he could forget her.

That way, he would not have to find a way to forgive her. Because he did not see how that would be possible.

THE VETERANS

(from Merritt Thackery's
JIADUR'S WAKE)

. . . For some reason, the Flight Office was eager to see that there was Survey experience aboard every outbound ship. Older surveyors saw it as a sign of creeping conservatism, since the all-novice crews of the Pathfinder and Argo ships had managed to cope with what they encountered.

Nevertheless, the Flight Office worked hard to see that, at minimum, the commander, exec, and contact leader on each new ship were veterans. That was a deceptively ambitious goal. To place three vets on each new Pioneer-class ship and keep even that number for each refitted Pathfinder-class ship, nearly half of each returning crew had to be coaxed into going out again.

But asking a vet to sign a second contract, even a limited-term, three-year mission contract, meant asking them to give up the country-club atmosphere of the resynchronization center at Benamira, New Zealand. It meant asking them to pass up figuring out how to spend the enormous fortune which resulted from sixteen years' salary invested (even at the Council-imposed ceiling of 3 percent) for more than a century.

There were only two kinds of veterans to whom returning to space was the more attractive alternative: those happy few who had found their identities there, and those unhappy few who had lost their souls . . .

chapter 4

Hysteresis

Contact Leader Mark Sebright sat on the edge of the lab workstation, crossed his arms over his chest, and surveyed the expectant faces of his surveyors. The team was studying him just as intently, for they had seen little of him since he came aboard.

The last name added to the *Descartes* roster, Sebright was the long-awaited and often despaired-of replacement for Jaiswal (who, according to rumor, had left the Service entirely and gone back to teaching at Hzui-Tyu). And he promised to be a more than adequate stand-in: Sebright was not only a Pathfinder, but a veteran of *Hugin*, the ship which had discovered the Muschynka colony in Eridanus.

Sebright's assignment was finalized a bare five days before departure, the minimum required to pass him through the gnotobiotic tortures, and two days after the team had transferred to *Tycho*. Thackery had caught only a glimpse of Sebright since then, as the vet had spent most of his time huddled with Neale, Rogen, and Dunn. What little Thackery had seen encouraged him. The rangy, tangle-haired Sebright comported himself confidently and casually. Where Neale seemed to be constantly on edge, Sebright had the worldly-wise eyes and demeanor of someone for whom life holds no more surprises.

"Morning," Sebright said, his inspection complete. "This won't take long."

There were several skeptical smiles, for that was a promise

Graeff had made often and never kept.

"I've been over your records," he continued. "You're a damn sight more educated than we were. Half of you have quals in specialties that didn't exist until we found out the Service needed them.

"Unfortunately for you, the Com doesn't agree with me. She says we don't know enough. She wants to solve it by sending everybody up for another qual test when we reach A-Cyg. That'll be worth a few more Coullars in the pay account, so I suppose there's some of you who won't kick too hard," he said with a shrug. "But the way I see it, it's not that we don't know what to do—"

Eagan, sitting at Thackery's elbow, whispered, "He should have seen us in Queen Maud Land."

"—It's that what we know how to do doesn't need doing yet," Sebright continued. "I suspect she's a lot more worried about idle time on the leg out than she is about your quals. If it were up to me, I'd say enjoy it while it lasts. It'll probably be the last vacation you have until you die or transfer out.

"You wouldn't know it from your simulations, but once we hit our first system, we'll be working harder than anyone on board. And when we leave the first system, we'll be running three shifts during the craze just to analyze the data we collected. Unfortunately, we'll reach the second system before we're done with the first—and the backlog will build from there."

He paused and scratched his chin. "So I can't tell you what freezin' good passing another technical will do you. But Neale expects it. I'll leave it up to you to see that you're ready. Pick a new area or try to move up to the next level in your current ratings, I don't care which. And you can sync yourself to whatever shift you choose."

"Do you want to approve our study plans?" asked Tyszka.

Sebright shook his head. "I don't even want to know that you have one. Hell, you're not students or trainees. You're professionals. That little trinket you're all wearing proves it, right? So start living up to it these next few weeks." He stood up and tucked his hands into the thigh pockets of his old-fashioned jumpsuit. "That's all."

As the meeting broke up, Muir planted her gamine body in front of Thackery.

"What do you think?" demanded the exobiologist.

"I think I like him, Donna," Thackery said, watching Sebright out the door.

"Did you hear? He intended all along to bump someone from either *Tycho* or *Descartes*."

"So?"

"He didn't tell them until the last minute because he wanted to avoid the 'nuisance' of preflight training."

"Where'd you hear that?"

"From someone in the Flight Office." A cross look took over her face. "They should have let Raji stay on. It wasn't his fault we screwed up down south."

"Sure it was. He was Contact Leader," Thackery said, standing. "Look, Sebright is the only one aboard, command crew included, who's actually been involved in a successful Contact. We're going to learn a lot from him."

"I don't think so," Muir said, shaking her head.

"You come to conclusions too fast," Thackery retorted as he edged past her. "You'll have to watch that. It's a bad habit for a surveyor."

The rush of good feeling stayed with Thackery, and at midrats he pursued the topic with Collins. "We've done really well, you know?"

"What do you mean?" she asked.

"To have five vets in our crew."

"I thought there were four."

"The Com, the exec, Graeff, Dunn, Sebright."

"Oh—I forgot about Dunn. He's that quiet one, isn't he, who's always in a little crowd of awks."

"He *is* senior tech. Anyway, we are lucky, aren't we? There's only three on *Tycho*."

"I suppose," she said, nibbling the edge of a pastry. "I wonder sometimes what they're doing here."

"The *Dove* reups are easy to understand," Thackery said defensively. "They have something to prove."

"Because they didn't find a colony? Maybe there aren't any more." She sighed. "No, I shouldn't say that, it'll jinx us. But they've seen—well, look at it this way. When they step out on their patio at night and look up, there are eighteen flickery points of light that to them are real places. They can point and say, 'I've been there. That's a place that I know.'" She shook her head. "That must be the most wonderful feeling in the world. I don't know what else they could want."

Thackery smiled. "Maybe the best feeling isn't remembering, but being there."

"Then why don't they all go back? Oh, I don't know. Did you hear about Sebright?"

"Stalling the Flight Office? Yeah, that's made the rounds."

"No, this is something I heard from Jessie. I guess Sebright doesn't have full Contact Leader quals."

"No?"

"No, you know they're supposed to be qualified in all six survey specialties, like the Com is on operations specialties. But he's only passed resource geology and technoanalysis. Kind of makes you wonder how far down they had to dig to get him."

Thackery shook his head. "There're face quals and real quals. Raji had face quals, and we saw how that worked out. Sebright's going to be good for us. Besides, I figure the reason he doesn't want to be bothered with our study plans is because he's going to be busy with his own."

"Maybe. He just better not try to tell me how to do my job until he knows at least as much as I do." She looked at her watch, then wiped her lips on her napkin. "Speaking of which, I've got some work to do with Donna," she said, pushing back from the table.

She took two steps, then stopped and came back to where Thackery sat. "Look, you're not one of those ones who's going to think that because we had a conversation, I want to change cabins, are you?"

"No," Thackery said uncertainly.

"Fine. Because Donna and I are perfectly happy rooming, all right? You can pass that word around if the subject comes up."

"Sure."

Her seat had barely begun to cool when Tyszka came up behind Thackery and slipped into it.

"You getting anywhere with her?" he asked earnestly, resting his folded hands on the table before him.

"Not trying to. I haven't even been thinking in those terms," Thackery answered honestly.

"You'd better start," Tyszka said, clucking. "The numbers aren't good to start with, and some of us are going to be left out." He stood and surveyed the nearly empty wardroom, then clucked again. "Maybe Donna's up in the library. I'll see you when the war's over, okay?"

Thackery chuckled. "Right."

Thackery spent the afternoon with Eagan upship in the survey laboratory, being glowered at as interlopers by members of *Tycho*'s contact team and trying to make the best use of the time on the linguacomp that had been granted them.

"This is your specialty, not mine," Eagan said dubiously as he regarded the machine's 318-character keyboard. "Why doesn't it have voice input?"

"It does," Thackery said, unfolding the operator's seat from its storage space against the wainscoat and settling in front of the terminal. "It can monitor any shipnet channel, and do character scans off any medium. This keyboard's not for input. It's for processing."

"I thought all we had to do is tell it the text we want and let it go to work."

Thackery laughed mockingly. "Don't we wish. The L-comp is smart. It's not clairvoyant. Say we feed it a sample of a language it's never seen before. What can it do with it?"

Eagan scratched his cheek. "I'll let that be rhetorical."

"If the sample is too small, it can't do anything. A lesson from cryptography—sufficiently small sequences are undecodable. But even if your sample is unlimited, there's a limit to the L-comp's abilities. Here," he said, pointing to the screen. "Here's the first cut on a Journan text sample."

The complex display was arranged in groups of three lines: The first showed phonetic Journan, the second a standard English translation, and the third a series of two-digit numbers.

"Try reading the English lines and you'll see this is no universal translator. If it was, they wouldn't be still trying to figure out how to talk to whales," Thackery observed.

"The numbers under each word are the confidence probabilities?"

"Yes. Now, I can highlight the object-words, the action-words"—he touched a key, and the display now resembled a tree proof—"or forget the words entirely and look at the proposed syntax."

"Most of the percentages are between thirty and seventy," Eagan noted, then wrinkled his nose. "But the L-comp knows Journan."

"I hid that part of the knowledge base from the inference processor so I could show you what we might be facing. We're here to operate the L-comp, but we're also here to make the decisions the L-comp can't."

"Or there's no Contact."

"Or there's no Contact," Thackery agreed. "What are you fluent in, again?"

"English, Russian, and Latin."

"That's right. The science languages. All right, here's the program. We'll rehearse by trying to Contact each other. I'll take a language you don't know, compose a 1000-word practice message in it, and then set up the sign-on so that language and any first cousins are hidden from the processor when you're working. When you've got it translated, compose a standard Contact message in that language. I'll let you know how you did."

"And I'll do the same for you."

"Right—all the way into A-Cyg, as much as they'll let us use this thing. Now, watch. I'm going to show you how to set a knowledge base restriction."

Later, resting in his room, Thackery reflected on the task he had taken on. The machine's limits were even more severe than he had acknowledged to Eagan. If the language did not parallel a significant number of Earth dialects—for instance, the Romance family—the confidence level for individual words rarely went above 60 percent.

A purely oral language posed its own daunting difficulties. How did you break the flow of sound into words? Were variations in pronunciation mere dialects, or meaning units in themselves? Even with a linguacomp to create the graphemes and search for repetitions and correlations, there was much guesswork and gruntwork involved.

Eagan would learn of those problems, too, when he could face them without concluding that the task was impossible.

For there was no room to think of the task as impossible. Should *Descartes* prove a lucky ship and carry its crew to a First Colonization world, it would be up to Thackery and Eagan to lay the groundwork for the Contact. Unless they and the linguacomp could come up with a satisfactory decoding of the natives' language, there would be no Contact landing. The team would be limited to whatever could be learned from orbit and from landings outside the inhabited areas—something that had never happened before.

Three months ago, he had accepted the responsibility without truly understanding its dimensions. Now he silently vowed to himself to do everything necessary to see that he was equal to the challenge. He wanted Sebright to have confidence in him. He wanted Neale to have confidence in him.

But before others could, he would have to have confidence in himself.

There were two disadvantages to sharing a cabin with McShane. One was that his bunk and desk seemed to autonomously generate clutter. The other was that he seemed constitutionally incapable of falling asleep without holding a protracted conversation first.

So far the topics had ranged from the contents of the *Tycho*'s entertainment banks (McShane holding forth on the merits of both the inclusions and exclusions) to the mysteries of the AVLO drive (McShane finding it very significant that no one could make him understand how it worked). His favorite time to begin seemed to be just as Thackery was about to fall asleep.

The fifth night out, the question that came out of the dark was: "Did you ever wonder why they named our ship after Descartes?"

Thackery let a portion of his groan become audible, then a portion of his impatience taint his tone as he answered. "No. He was a key figure in the scientific revolution, and an outstanding mathematician."

"But he was also the one who said that the world around you only existed because you believed in it, and that if you stopped believing in it, it would disappear."

Thackery laid his head back on the pillow and squeezed his eyes closed. "I'm not sure that's a fair summation of his ideas about reality."

"That's what one of my instructors said," McShane said defensively.

There followed a long silence that encouraged Thackery to think he had successfully shut McShane off. It was not to be.

"I wonder whose dream this is. I've tried to make it disappear but it doesn't."

Thackery could not be sure McShane was joking but chose to take it that way. "Neale's, I think."

"Maybe." Another long pause. "I haven't seen her much. Do you know her well?"

"No." Thackery hesitated. *If he's determined not to let me sleep, then at least we can talk about what I want to talk about.* "Do you see Sebright? I mean ever?"

"The Contact Leader? No."

"I was asking Michael today whether Sebright had said anything to him about a briefing on the Muschynka contact. He said he hadn't seen Sebright for three days."

"He's probably sync'd to the C or D watch schedule."

Thackery missed the impatience in McShane's voice. "No, because I left a message for Derrel—he's on that cycle—and he said he hasn't seen Sebright either."

"So, Sebright's a recluse. So what?"

"He's supposed to be here to give us the benefit of his experience," Thackery insisted. "We're five days out and I can't even find anyone who's met with him. He doesn't respond to pages, he doesn't answer messages, and he's never in his cabin."

"Look, I've got problems of my own," McShane said irritably. "If you've got a real grievance, go see Neale. If you just want to complain, find some of your own people to listen."

"McShane, you're a selfish son-of-a-bitch," Thackery said tiredly.

McShane jumped up from his bunk. "Damnit, I'm the one with responsibilities on this craze. You don't have to stand watches. You don't have Rogen and Graeff breathing down your neck looking for an excuse to replace you. You're on a freezin' vacation."

"Whoa, easy," Thackery said, snapping on the light. McShane shivered oddly, hung his head, and stood a moment with arms akimbo.

"Sorry," he said at last. "If your problems aren't my fault, I guess mine aren't yours, either." He sighed expressively and settled back on the bed. "He's got a single, doesn't he? Break his damn door down and wait for him. He's got to show up there sometime."

Thackery laughed tiredly. "Unless he's moved in with some little awk from *Tycho*." He turned out the light and turned on his side. "Who knows," he said to his pillow, "maybe that's what I ought to be concentrating on, too."

For two days, Thackery shifted Sebright to the back of his mind. In that time, he made a token (and profitless) attempt at courting Jessica Baldwin, got off to an encouraging start on his studies for the exobiology qual, and solved the first test message Eagan had composed for him.

But on one of his many trips from the passenger hive upship to the *Tycho* library, he cast a glance as always from the climbway down the corridor onto which Sebright's door opened— and saw a woman he did not know push that door open and disappear inside.

For a moment Thackery was torn by ambivalent impulses. Then impatience won out over propriety, and he stepped off the climbway and stalked down the short corridor.

But there was no answer to the page button, no answer to his insistent knock. "Concom Sebright," he called out, listening for sounds beyond the closure. "This is Merritt Thackery. Can I talk to you?"

There was no answer, no sound at all. Frustrated, Thackery smacked the door release with a balled fist and began to turn away. But the door, which had been locked every time he had been there before, slid open.

Sebright was lying prone in the narrow single cabin, his ankles strapped in a microgravity exercise cradle and one hand gripping the crossbar. Beads of perspiration stood out on his cheeks and forehead, and the longish hair was matted. But his eyes were closed, as though he were sleeping. An instant later, Thackery saw why: The fingertips of Sebright's right hand were in the grasp of a small black box lying on the bed next to him.

Thackery took in all that in the moment before the woman rose up from the chair beside Sebright and rushed toward Thackery, protectively blocking the view with her body.

"Out," she demanded.

"He's on a tranq machine," Thackery said, disbelieving.

"I'm only going to ask one more time. Then I'll remove you myself," she said fiercely.

"He's on a tranq machine!" Thackery repeated, this time indignant.

"That's none of your damn business."

"He's my supervisor and an officer of this ship," Thackery said, his voice rising. "I've got as much right here as anyone, and more right than you."

Glowering at him with piercing black eyes, she reached behind him and closed the door. "Thackery—look," she said in a more modulated tone. "He told me he was going to do this and he asked me to look after him. I give him nutrient shots and sponge baths and make sure the exerciser doesn't hurt him. I read his messages and answer the ones that need answering. If he's needed somewhere, I come in and wake him up."

Thackery cast about for a plausible explanation to the inexplicable sight on the bed. "Is he a phobe?" he asked, almost hopefully.

"No. He just—prefers to absent out sometimes. He—doesn't tolerate boredom well. It's not my place to talk about it."

His eyes narrowed by suspicion, Thackery asked, "Why are you doing this?"

She smiled tolerantly. "It's not what you're thinking. I'm his four-gen grandniece. I met him when *Munin* came in twelve years ago—I was his greeter. Look, I've told you more than I needed to. Now will you go, so I can take care of him?"

"I want to talk to him," Thackery said stubbornly.

"Why? To see if I'm telling the truth?"

"No. About the team. About Survey business."

"It can wait."

"Damnit, no!" Thackery exploded. "He's got responsibilities. This isn't just for me. There are six green surveyors that he ought to be working with. Wake him up."

"No."

"Why? Will it hurt him?"

"No. But he doesn't want to be disturbed."

"You're not in his chain of authority. He'll have to tell me himself."

She crossed her arms and shook her head stubbornly. "He'll do his job when it's time to do it."

"Part of his job started a week ago." Thackery paused and looked down at Sebright, then continued in a voice that was quietly threatening. "If he's getting messages, then there are people who don't know about this. Like Neale, maybe?"

"People know."

"Some would have to. But not Neale, right? If you don't wake him up, she's going to."

Her eyes spat angry sparks, but she moved to Sebright's side all the same. A touch on the tranq box controls, and the metal bands opened to release the vet's fingers. A few moments later, stirred by an influx of amphetamine molecules in his blood, Sebright opened his eyes.

"Morning, Yolanda. What's happening?"

Scowling, she jerked a thumb in Thackery's direction.

"Concom," Thackery said, taking a step forward.

The older man pulled himself up to a sitting position. "Thackery, isn't it? The linguist."

"That's right."

"What's up, Thackery?"

"I'd like to talk to you about Muschynka."

Sebright looked from Thackery to his grandniece, then back again. "Read about it in the Op Recs," he said gruffly. "I've answered those questions too many times already."

"But—"

"Sure, you only asked once. But a thousand other people have asked once, too." Resting his folded arms on the crossbar and his chin on his arms, he looked up at Thackery. "You know how when you try to tell someone about a dream, you're really trying to tell them about an experience, but you end up telling a story?"

Thackery nodded uncertainly.

"Every time I tell about Muschynka, I lose a little bit more of the experience. Pretty soon all I'll have left is the story. The story becomes the experience."

"I don't understand—"

Sebright nodded. "I didn't really expect you to. Listen, Thackery. Don't do this again. You'll see enough of me once we're aboard *Descartes*. But until we *have* a ship, we're not a crew, and my only responsibility is to myself."

"So you won't hold a briefing for the team?"

"They can read the Op Recs, too," he said. "Any more questions, since I'm up?" A hint of a sardonic smile touched his lips.

"Just one. Why did you bother to sign on again?"

Sebright was immune to the venom. "No. Try Dunn. He's only been back two months. He may still want to talk about it." He laid back and poked Yolanda playfully with a finger.

"Anything to eat around here?" he asked her, and Thackery took that moment to move toward the door.

"Sneaking out, Thackery?" Sebright called after him. "For future reference—you'd be smart not to push in where you haven't been invited. You can't afford to alienate people on a little ship."

His picture of Sebright savaged beyond repair, a benumbed Thackery made the climb to C deck and the library. Having absorbed most of his values from Government Service, he felt personally betrayed. Information was a free good, freely available, freely exchanged—the Ninth Article. To have a Contact treated as a personal possession was unthinkable, as unthinkable as a Contact Leader who refused to lead, who chose to spend eight weeks in a drug-induced black-out—

The Op Recs. Maybe the answers are *there—if there are any answers for a man like that—*

The story of the Muschynka was not new to Thackery. Hundreds of anthropologists had fallen over themselves in their eagerness to sift through the contact records and publish their findings. There was even a standing request before the Flight Office for a follow-up mission, since the Muschynka represented a form of human society no longer available for study on Earth: a polytheistic, communal-living patriarchy employing slash-and-burn agriculture.

But if there was any explanation in the voluminous contact report for Sebright's attitudes, it was beyond Thackery to see it. There was plenty of data on the Muschynka's dependence on lightning for fire, on their movable longhouses, on their death beliefs and funereal customs. But there were no answers in the records for the questions he would have asked Sebright: How did it go? What was it like to be there? How did you know what to do?

Any wisdom that had been gained in the course of the Contact had been stripped of its anecdotal elements and made part of the general Contact protocol. Any narrative power in the account had been erased by the third-person-impersonal voice. The feeling of the moment had been reduced to dry history and cold science.

Is that what they tried to do to you, Sebright? he wondered. *Did you come back because you wanted to dream again?*

That thought replaced most of Thackery's accumulated resentment with a troubling premonitory vision. *Is that what I'm doing? Chasing a piece of the past?*

Thackery pushed the thought away. There had to be better reasons. Sebright's was the quest of the addict for a remembered high, he decided—one so exquisite that it made normal life unbearable. But *Dove*'s crew had sustained themselves through an abstinence enforced by unfriendly Chance. There had to be better reasons, and the *Dove* vets had to know them—or those now aboard *Tycho* would not have chosen to accept their new assignments.

Late to be wondering why you're here.

You know why you're here, he answered himself. *You just don't know what will sustain you now that you are.*

A day later, Thackery found Thomas Dunn in *Tycho*'s ward-room, conducting a training session on the AVLO drive for Baldwin, Behnke, and four of the awks. The silver-haired senior tech was soft-spoken, but he clearly knew both his subject and how to communicate it. Thackery listened with interest from the doorway as Dunn held forth for twenty more minutes, then moved toward him when the class filed out. "Mr. Dunn? Sebright said you might be able to help me."

Dunn cocked his head and squinted. "Aren't you Thackery? The inquisitive one?"

Thackery's face wrinkled up. "You heard—"

"Didn't you think we veterans talked to each other?"

"I didn't think anything worth talking about happened," Thackery said stiffly.

"Privacy has an exaggerated importance on a survey ship. You'll understand after a while."

"Is that a warning not to ask you any personal questions?"

"No." Dunn settled cross-legged on the table. "I try to be a little more sympathetic to novices than Mark is."

Thackery settled in one of the recently vacated seats. "I was wondering why you came back."

"To the Service? I'm not *that* sympathetic. Next question."

"Well, what about Sebright? What makes somebody like that come back after five years out?"

Dunn craned his head and looked at the ceiling. "I don't think that I can speak for someone else, Thackery. If I'm guessing, I might be wrong. If I know, I have no right to violate their confidence."

Thackery's face showed his growing exasperation. "So don't talk about him specifically. You spent time at Benamira. How do the vets feel about what they did, about where they are?"

Dunn swung his crossed legs back and forth. "Until you feel it yourself, it'll just be words."

"Tell me anyway."

Nodding, Dunn said: "Some of us come back knowing what the parameters are. Some only need a few weeks at Benamira to learn it. Some resist and spend a few years trying to fight it."

"Like Sebright?"

His eyes clouding, Dunn only smiled faintly in answer. "You see, the Service has to be your family, provide your loves and mates, even take care of you when you age. Because Earth will forget you, and if you ever return there you'll find it strange, almost incomprehensibly so—even with the Council doing its best to put the brakes on change. My advice would be not to return. You've done more than change jobs, Thackery. You've changed lives. Your old one is now forever out of reach."

Dunn's words struck Thackery as unnecessarily melodramatic. "That's no secret. Any fool would know it. And the Flight Office warns us."

"You won't begin to understand until much later," Dunn said with that same faint smile. "It's almost as though there's a grace period—which is just as well. It's not a reversible decision. You're already out of time."

"I thought that's what Benamira was for—to put you back."

Dunn chuckled knowingly. "When I was growing up, the world government was led by statesmen. Now it's in the hand of bureaucrats. Back then, everyone knew who Devaraja Rashuri was. My father *worked* for Benjamin Driscoll. But say those names to someone from this era and you'll get a blank stare two times out of three." He threw up his hands. "I don't like the music of today. I find the styles of clothing garish. I consider body adornments self-mutilation. What can the Service do to help me? Yes, they wanted Benamira to be a halfway house. But it never cures anyone. More accurate to call it a hermitage—and some vets aren't made to be hermits."

"What about Neale? Is that what moves her, too?"

Dunn's eyes twinkled. "So you're mystified by the Space Lily?"

Thackery grinned uncomfortably. "Where'd she pick up that tag?"

"That's one of her several nicknames, none of which you should ever let her hear you using. A horticulturist at Unity hung that on her. When you were home, did you ever grow any lily-of-the-valley?"

"I think I've seen it."

"It's small, unobtrusive, and looks delicate—and the next thing you know it's taken over the garden. You follow?"

"No."

"She'll make it clear to you at some time or other, I'm sure," Dunn said, in a way that made clear the subject was closed. "Well—have I satisfied your curiosity, Thackery?"

"Less than you might have."

"You incline toward the painfully blunt, have you ever been told?" He brought a hand to his mouth. "Let me be equally forthright. Have you paired yet? Are you happy with McShane as a cabinmate?"

The question cast Dunn's willingness to talk in a new and unwelcome light.

"I'm fine," Thackery said, too quickly.

But Dunn took no offense. "We'll be out a long time. I hope you'll keep me in mind when you're ready for a change."

A glimpse of the rainstorm building on the horizon pulled Thackery off the climbway and onto the *Tycho* edrec deck. The landscape was playing on all twelve of the screens ringing the huge circular room.

Iowa, Thackery thought. *Or maybe eastern Nebraska.*

One chair had been turned to face the darkest part of the clouds, and above the fabric of the shoulder rest projected a shock of reddish hair.

"Dan?"

He was answered with a grunt.

"You pick this?" Thackery asked, settling in a chair nearer the center of the deck, where the illusion was better.

"Yup."

"Something up, or are you just trying to depress the hell out of everybody?"

"I got chewed out by Graeff today, in front of everybody."

"Deserve it?"

"No. She's got it in for me. I work twice as hard as any bridge awk, and everybody knows it. She's just busting me."

"Don't argue. Vets know everything," Thackery said cynically. From behind he heard the faint ringing sound the climbway made when someone was near. A moment later Tyszka bounded off the ladder and joined them.

"Is this the meeting of the *Descartes* Masturbators' Society and Sewing Circle?" he asked loudly, striding across the deck and plopping into the chair to Thackery's right. He craned his head and took in the landscape that was playing. "God, how depressing. If I tell you how it comes out, will you put on something else?"

"Put on what you want," McShane replied disinterestedly.

But Tyszka made no move toward the control pedestal, instead sliding sideways in his chair and hooking one knee over the arm. "You two look like you've already heard the news."

It was Thackery who offered the obligatory response. "What news?"

"It's done. They're all gone," Tyszka said, clucking and shaking his head. "And unless my intelligence is faulty, none of us have one. I warned you, Thack."

"*Now* I know what you're babbling about."

"Will someone tell me?" called McShane.

"Women, my son, women. They're all spoken for. I know. I just helped the last one move in with my roommate."

"No doubt a painful experience."

"Considering it was Nakabayashi, I would say significantly painful." He made a loud clicking noise. "We don't need them, though, right?"

"Celibacy forever," McShane rallied.

"That's right," Tyszka said, pounding the padded armrest for emphasis. "We resisted, despite their crude attempts to seduce us."

"We were too smart for them," Thackery said, trying to get in the spirit of the foolishness.

"We refused to let them sap our vital life fluids," declared McShane.

"No matter how much they begged."

"Right. They didn't meet our standards."

"Not a one of them."

The patter became rapid-fire, self-reinforcing improvisation. Thackery sat back and listened, the laughter building in him but showing only as a wry smile.

"Muir."

"Too butch."

"Abrams."

"The ice queen. Uibel is still defrosting."

"Shaffer."

"Whitewear."

"Too fragile."

"DeLaCroix."

"Too experienced."

"Too crowded in her bed."

"Baldwin."

"Big sister."

"She'll tuck you in but she won't fuck."

That brought the first involuntary, half-embarrassed laugh spilling out of Thackery, and his laughter triggered theirs.

"Graeff," McShane managed to say, trying to keep it going.

"Untouchable," Tyszka fired back.

"Neale."

"Unthinkable," Thackery blurted, and as the landscape dissolved into rain around them, they dissolved into the silly, out-of-control laughter of the tired and the stressed. Thackery laughed until his chest hurt, until his throat rebelled with rough coughs and his eyes brimmed with moisture.

"Well," Tyszka said as decorum slowly returned, "if the Concom was right, maybe we'll be too busy to notice."

The mention of Sebright wiped the remaining smile from Thackery's face. "I don't know how much stock to put in him these days," he said soberly, then kicked Tyszka's chair. "Change the freezin' tape, will you? This *is* depressing."

Ten days from A-Cyg, Neale posted a schedule of crew interviews—four a day in two-hour blocks. No purpose for the interviews was given. Some of the interviewees came back in fifteen minutes, while a few stayed the two hours, and Nakabayashi was gone for three. None would discuss the interviews or even divulge their topic. The consensus in the hive was that the interviews were fitness reviews, and the anxiety level of those well down on the alphabetical list climbed precipitously.

To minimize his distraction, Thackery refocused his attention on increasingly difficult Contact simulations. Almost before he realized it, his appointment was imminent. He convinced himself he was at ease by eating a normal lunch just before he was due in officer's country. En route from the mess to Neale's cabin, Thackery detoured to his cabin to retrieve his slate.

He was startled to find McShane there, sitting cross-legged on his bed and hunched over a portable netlink, a unit similar to the slate but with input capabilities.

"What's up?"

McShane did not look up, and Thackery moved to peek over his shoulder. The screen was filled with two columns of names, none of them familiar.

"Aren't you supposed to be on the bridge watch?" Thackery asked, glancing at his watch.

"I've got to get this finished first."

"What the hell is it?"

McShane touched the scroller several times and the list jumped downward. "There," he said. "There you are."

Thackery's name was in fact on the screen, along with the names of several other crewmembers.

"Some sort of personnel list?"

McShane craned his head to look up at Thackery. "Do you remember the name of the woman who passed us through the Unity screening center?"

"No."

"Come on, the blonde with the long hair. The young one."

"I barely remember her. What are you doing, anyway?"

He turned back to his machine. "I'm trying to make a list of everybody who ever knew me. I mark them with a caret if they were friends, and an asterisk if I had sex with them. Everybody else is just an acquaintance. See, your name has a caret."

"Why are you doing this?"

"So nobody forgets. Are you sure you don't remember her name?"

"I don't think I ever knew it."

"Damn. Oh, all right. I suppose I can leave her off."

"Don't you think this could wait until your watch is over?"

"No," McShane said placidly, then abruptly changed the subject. "Thack, do you know what happens if you die out here? They can't give you space burial—there's no place to send you to. I wonder what happens to the soul, whether it has a way of escaping the craze."

"Dan, maybe you should go see Pemberton," Thackery said tentatively, naming the medtech.

McShane snapped his fingers. "That's a great idea. I'll bet he had to work with her on the screening. He ought to remember her name."

With an anxious glance at his watch, Thackery picked up his slate and moved toward the door. "Dan, I wish I could stay, but Neale is expecting me. Go upship and stand the rest of your bridge watch. I'll go see Pemberton with you later."

His back to Thackery, McShane shook his head. "I've got to finish my list first." He sighed. "I wish you could have seen Karen at Lake Ponchetrain."

With an effort of will, Thackery made himself open the door and leave the compartment. *How do you help them?* he asked, sagging against the corridor wall. *How do you bring them back?*

But there were no ready answers, and Neale was waiting. *First things first,* he told himself, and hurried off.

When Thackery arrived, Neale's cabin was full of stars in motion—a time-compressed, asymmetric scale projection of the Expanded Local Group, 10,000 stars in a 100–light-year radius sphere centered on Earth. Four of the stars were a brilliant green: the colonies. Thackery stepped through the doorway and into the swirl of stars.

"Chair to your left," said Neale's disembodied voice. Thackery moved that way and felt his way into the seat.

The motion of the stars suddenly stopped with three of the four green spots within Thackery's reach.

"Do you know them?" she asked.

Thackery studied the projection. "Pai-Tem," he said, pointing at one. "82 Eridani, that's Muschynka. Journa. And Ross 128, over there in Virgo."

"Very good." The lights came up, masking the projection. Only then could Thackery see Neale, who was almost swallowed up by a padded recliner modeled after an orbital acceleration couch. Neale's fingers beat an irregular rhythm against the arm as she stared the thousand-mile stare.

Her gaze drifted sideways and found Thackery's face. "I'm sorry to say that only about half the operations crew can cor-

rectly identify all four without prompting," she said. "I'm re-
assured to find that my surveyors are more knowledgeable."

She crossed her arms across her smallish breasts. "Have
you thought much about the First Colonists, Thackery?"

"No."

"I'm surprised. I marked you for more intellectual curiosity
than that answer suggests."

"I've thought about what it would feel like to take part in
a Contact, about my responsibility if *Descartes* should happen
to find a colony. But about the First Colonists themselves, no.
It's hard to see how there's any profit in the effort."

"Do you think that all of the colonies have been found?"

"Life, I hope not."

"Then wouldn't there be profit in making our search more
effective?"

"If there were some chance in knowing what the First Colonists were like and what motivated them. But it's all guesswork. Unless there's been some recent discovery I don't know
about, we don't have a single FC-era artifact."

She wagged a finger at him. "How wrong you are. We have
four very significant artifacts. You named them earlier."

"But the colonies don't remember their founders any better
than we do the civilization that produced them. Even the First
Cities of Journa turned out to postdate the colonization by
thousands of years."

"There are conscious memories and unconscious memories,
Thackery. Don't mistake one for the other. If we don't remember the Firsts, then we need to look more deeply into ourselves.
They left their mark on us, I have no doubt. But set that aside
for now. How would *you* choose the destinations for a fleet of
colony ships?"

When Thackery made no answer, treating the question as
rhetorical, she went on.

"So many of your generation think it's so easy—just pick
a dozen or two stars similar to ours in temperature and spectrum, long-lived and stable. Journa's sun is the perfect example,
a pretty little G-type star. So is 82 Eridani."

"Yet they passed up Tau Ceti and Alpha Centauri A."

"Exactly!" She sat up in the lounger. "Some of the other
colonies are around some of the most improbable suns. Pai-
Tem has a K binary, for life's sake! And it's no wonder the
Ross colony failed, orbiting a M-star so cold it takes a green-

house effect to make the planet livable. But they chose it deliberately. What did they know that we don't? What fact would unscramble the puzzle? There's the fascination, Thackery. That's the magic of the colony problem."

She sat back and waited for his reply. When he said nothing, she gestured. "I asked you here to tap you. I want my crew's best thoughts, honest thoughts. Otherwise we'll never solve this thing."

"I think it's a mistake to worship the Firsts and act as though there was some magical wisdom in their choices," Thackery said tentatively. "Maybe they ended up where they did because they had no way of continuing on—we've never found one of their ships to know their capabilities. For that matter, there might not be any ships to find, maybe there are other instrumentalities. Or maybe all that was special about them was that they were first."

The lights dimmed as Neale touched a control on the arm of her lounger. "You disappoint me, Thackery," she said as the spherical halo of stars once again took over the room. "You lack imagination."

"Commander, I'll be happy to devote some attention to this now that I know of your interest—"

"Don't bother," she said brusquely. "You haven't the vision for it, and I don't need another flufflicker." She continued mechanically, "I invoke your pledge of confidentiality. You are not to discuss this interview or any of its subject matter until I free you from the pledge. There will be a general announcement to that effect when the remaining interviews are completed. Good day."

Descending toward the hive, Thackery heard the commotion coming up the climbway before he saw the gathering. There were five or six awks and techs crowded around the open door to his cabin, peering inside as best they could.

"What happened?" he demanded, shouldering his way between two of the spectators.

Guerrieri, standing closest to the doorway on the right, looked back and saw who had asked. "It's McShane. The craze got him."

"He was screaming something about the hull splitting open," another offered.

Thackery bulled his way to the doorway and surveyed the

room. McShane was stretched out motionless on Thackery's bed, with Pemberton crouching beside him monitoring vitals and Dunn looking on. McShane's own mattress was leaning crookedly against the far wall, as though the vertical zipweld had started to open and McShane had used the mattress to try to seal off the leak.

"Oh, Dan," he said feelingly.

Dunn looked up. "Ah, Thackery. Did he give you any warning on this?"

Thackery took a step into the cabin. "No. I didn't know he was having trouble." The half-lie came easily, too easily.

Dunn nodded acceptingly. "Sometimes it's like that," he said softly. "Sometimes they're clever enough to save all the madness for their private moments, even though they're not clever enough to see where that leads. Do you want him moved upstairs, Pembe?"

The medtech stood. "Yes. He's stable now, but we'll want to watch him. He'll be on antianx and antidep right in to A-Cyg."

"Where he'll stay," Thackery said involuntarily.

"Afraid so," Dunn said, grunting as he gathered up McShane in a fireman's carry.

Thackery stepped aside to let Dunn pass with his burden. "It's not fair. He was working so freezin' hard."

"It happens," Dunn said from the doorway. "Wanting to do well's not enough. Some don't have what it takes."

"First warning," the Tycho gravigator announced sonorously. *"Thirty minutes to transition. Com officers, prepare for reacquisition of signals. Repeating, first warning, end of craze."*

"That's a freezin' shame. He didn't miss by much," one of the onlookers said, shaking her head as she turned away.

"Coming?" asked Guerrieri from the corridor.

With a sudden violent motion, Thackery reached out and slammed the cabin door shut, sealing out the curious who had not already scattered. When he turned back to face the disarray, the sight of it resonated with his own internal disharmony. He drew a series of long, trembly breaths, then gave in and sat down where he'd been standing, letting the tears of frustration and disillusionment run quietly down his cheeks.

This is not how it was supposed to be—not at all—

A FRIENDLY FACE IN A DISTANT PLACE

(from Merritt Thackery's
JIADUR'S WAKE)

. . . Search the stars for planets. Search the planets for life. So simple in concept, so incredible in execution.

Even today, there are few in or out of the Service who can grasp the dimensions of the project. The AVLO drive has salved our battered imaginations, just as trans-Pacific shuttles make the voyage of the Kon-Tiki inconceivable.

But consider: the Local Group, those stars clustered within twenty-five light-years of the sun, consists of some two hundred glowing motes. Extend your view to the hundred light-year radius of the Expanded Local Group and your gaze now takes in more than fourteen thousand stars scattered through a volume of four million cubic light-years.

Mercifully, many of the stars are found in groups of two or three or even more. Some are barren, and, if they are close enough to a first-class observatory, that absence of planets can be detected and that system bypassed.

But even with the AVLO drive, even excluding the close binaries and trinaries, excluding the unstable giants and the fiery short-lived O-spectrum dwarfs, excluding all but the M-K-G spectral classes thought most favorable for habitable planets, a survey of the Expanded Local Group still called for a thousand-year plan.

The broad outline of the strategy was shaped by the geometers of the Strategic Planning Office. With a stroke of their lightpens, they partitioned the sphere of space centered on

Earth's Sun into eight equal sectors, four north of the celestial equator and four south of it. Onto that playing field came the survey ships, built by the Procurement Office, equipped by the Research Office, staffed by the Flight Office, first one ship for each octant, then three, with plans for five and finally eight if the millenium-long plan stood up.

It was not enough, however, to simply loose a fleet of survey ships into the Galaxy. For the most part, these great vessels were self-sufficient—had to be, or the entire emprise was unworkable. But ships and crews alike had useful lifetimes. The former could be refitted; the latter required rejuvenation and, eventually, replacement.

The planners anticipated other needs as well: for communications relay points, for nearby support centers for the colonies, perhaps even for hub points for commerce among the not-yet-Unified Worlds. It was implicit in the name given to the long-ago founding of Journa and its sisters that the Service saw itself the agent of the Second Colonization.

For all those reasons and more, the Advance Bases were conceived and constructed, one in each octant, frontier outposts which were to become tomorrow's metropoli. In a Ptolemaic perversion of astrography, each was named, not for the star near which it was located, but for the constellation in which it appeared from Earth: Perseus. Lynx. Bootes. Cygnus. Eridanus. Vela. Lupus. Microscopium.

But that cleptic confusion was the least of the problems faced by these nascent communities. For, while they were close to those they were expected to serve, they were also very far from Earth and the authority of Unity—far enough that some came to have their own ideas about what they were there for . . .

chapter 5

Cygnus

Tycho picked up the A-Cyg navigation beacon immediately on coming out of the craze. The beacon consisted of an eight-bar musical theme, the tracking pulse, a timemark, and a voice message:

"Welcome to Advance Base Cygnus, located just west of Infinity on the Far Edge of Nowhere. Your hosts are the men and women of the 'we'll go anywhere we're told' Unified Space Service, Survey Branch. Your innkeeper is Wayne 'don't bother me with details' Coulson. Request you transmit crew directory to speed check-in. We monitor standard frequencies A and D."

There was laughter on the bridge, but Neale did not join in it. *Damned unprofessional,* Neale complained to herself. *I wonder if the base commander knows what's being broadcast.*

Tamm seemed amused, however. "Sounds like they've been a bit lonesome out here," he said. "Let's let them know they'll have company for dinner."

"The ship's transponder is already putting out our identification signal," the communications officer noted.

"Let's be a little more personal," Tamm said. "Give them a hi-how-are-you and repeat it until we hear from them live. Navcom, how far out are we?"

"Ninety-two light-minutes."

Tamm nodded. "We should hear from them right about change-of-watch."

Still hurtling at high velocity despite the steady gravitational braking of the AVLO field aft, *Tycho* closed on the commonplace M7 star which was host to Cygnus Base. Well before nolag communications were established, the telecameras picked up the silhouette of the complex. The station was orbiting just sunward of the fourth of the five small planets comprising the system. At first, only the two huge energy sails were visible. But as the image grew larger and more refined it quickly became apparent that not all was as expected.

"What the hell have they been up to?" Tamm demanded indignantly. "Let me see the station fax."

The comtech turned to his console, and a moment later, an architectural diagram shared the window with the telecamera view.

"You've got the wrong damn document," Tamm said with annoyance.

"No, that's Cygnus—file number AB21N," insisted the librarian.

"Scale them the same."

"They already are."

"What? They must be ahead of schedule. Show me the station development plan."

The librarian complied, and Neale walked forward to study the display. "Here," she said, pointing to one of the more symmetrical shapes. "This section wasn't supposed to be added for another five years." She swung her arm to point to an irregular mass which seemed to have grown tumorlike from the central cylinder. "And whatever this is, it isn't in the development plan at all."

She looked back at Tamm, and the commanders exchanged puzzled glances.

"They were sent out here with a hundred-year plan for expansion of the base," Tamm said, nonplussed. "What the hell are they doing ignoring it after just five years?"

"Seems like the discipline problems go all the way to the top," Neale said critically.

They stared together at the bright image of A-Cyg. The neat symmetry of the original design was badly marred by the new additions. "Not our problem, I guess," Tamm said, standing and stretching. "We're not staying."

"Where's *Descartes?*" Neale asked suddenly.

The ship was nowhere in sight. The station's single dockport was empty.

"Give us a wider field," Tamm ordered, and the image of Cygnus Base shrank. Almost immediately, Neale loosed a noisy sigh of relief. Powered down and empty, *Descartes* trailed several kilometres behind Cygnus in the same orbit.

"Looks like you won't be staying, either," Tamm said with a wink. "What'd you think they'd done with it?"

"Considering what we've seen already, I was afraid to guess."

On docking, Tamm and Neale were whisked through an ebullient throng to the administrative level and the opulent office of Wayne Coulson. The corpulent base director bounded out of his chair to greet them, shaking hands vigorously and ushering them into the room.

"I've just been told before you got here—you're keeping your crews on board?" Coulson asked, the disappointment keen in his voice.

"At least until we've worked out the arrangements with you," Neale said.

"Oh, heavens, there's no need for special arrangements. We're all set up for you. Please, call over there and give them liberty," he urged earnestly. "We've been planning for this for most of the last year. My people are very eager to meet with your crew. You're three weeks overdue, did you realize?"

Tycho's a brand-new ship. We stayed around to have some little problems fixed—can't expect it to come out of the yard perfect," Tamm said, smiling. "Never stopped to think that we'd be missed at this end," he gestured. "Use this netlink?"

"Of course—it was probably wrong of us to pin so much on the schedule. It's been five years for us but thirty-two back on Earth. The program could have been delayed, even canceled. We had to wonder."

"Everything's still go. There'll be more following us," Tamm assured him, then turned to the netlink. "Kislak, I'm authorizing liberty for the second, third, and fourth watches. We'll continue to stand one-in-four until further notice. Make sure everyone understands that."

"Yes, sir. Does this order include the hive?"

Tamm looked to Neale, who shook her head emphatically and turned away. Tamm shrugged. "No. Not the passengers. Just our crew."

"Is there some problem, Commander Neale?" Coulson asked, his eyes narrowed by concern.

"Commander Neale doesn't approve of the discipline here," Tamm said, then moved toward the bar to avoid Neale's baleful glance.

"Is he right, Commander?" Coulson said, a puzzled expression wrinkling his round face.

"I do have some questions about your priorities," she said stiffly, settling herself in the least plush of the several chairs. "We spent sixteen years on *Dove* without this sort of breakdown, and you've been here barely five."

"What breakdown is that?"

She waved a hand in the air. "Your hailing message—your abandonment of the development plan—"

Coulson likewise took a seat. "We haven't abandoned the development plan—not yet, anyway. We've adapted it. If you'd had time to analyze what we've done, you'd see that our modifications won't prevent us from building what was prescribed. That's not to say we may not yet get tired of waiting for structural components from Earth and do it our own way."

"You have no authority to make that decision."

Coulson spread his hands expressively. "This is home, Commander. We have the right to make it livable. We have the right to make it ours. I would guess that your sixteen years on *Dove* were busy ones. But once we had the cylinder sealed and the energy panels erected, there hasn't been a whole lot of urgency to what we have to do."

"Unless you feel like you're doing for yourself, rather than for some distant authority," Tamm said between sips of his liqueur.

"Exactly," pounced Coulson. "And that requires a certain latitude on less important matters. Commander Neale, I assure you we came to this out of necessity. The first three years we went by the book. At the end of that time, most of us were ten kilos overweight and averaging one fight a week. Every work team was anywhere from a month to half a year behind schedule, and I was turning into an autocratic son-of-a-bitch because of it. We even had two suicides and a half-baked mutiny—that's why we moved *Descartes* off-station. Frankly, for a while I had doubts about our community surviving until you got here."

"So what happened?" Tamm asked, enjoying Neale's discomfiture.

Coulson smiled. "We had a town meeting and took a good

hard look at ourselves. The end result was that we reclaimed control over our own lives. We'll do things because they need doing or because we want to, but never just because the Service said so. We apply that same principle locally. You can call me Director if you prefer, but the truth is that I'm more like an elected city manager. I represent these peoples' interests. I don't tell them what their interests are supposed to be."

"That's insubordination," Neale said sharply.

"Yes, I suppose it is," was Coulson's casual reply. "But we're too far away to allow ourselves to be dependent on Earth. I believe the hundred-year growth plan was nothing less than an attempt to lock us into a structural technology which would keep us looking to Unity at least that long. We choose not to be so bound. That planet down there has accessible hydrocarbons, which we're tapping to process our own construction material."

"Is that what you used for that addition?"

"Yes. You should make a point of seeing it. We're very pleased with how it turned out—"

"What is it?" Neale demanded.

"A playroom."

"A playroom!"

"For the children—and the adults. Everything from soccer to gymnastics to hide-and-go-seek—"

Tamm interjected, "You're having children already?"

"Yes—another modification of the plan. It's the best way I know to make a place feel like home," Coulson said simply. "There've been six born already, and that many more are on the way. We've got fifty-four people here now. But we've already built the base up to where it could handle over a hundred."

"Plenty of guest rooms," Tamm said, chuckling.

"You may laugh, but that image has been useful to us," Coulson said soberly. "We try to be happy with ourselves, but the simple truth is that this community is too small and our memories of Earth are too strong. We need to believe that others are coming—not just visitors, but emigrés. I look forward to when they start calling me the landlord instead of the innkeeper."

There was a long silence when Coulson finished, a silence broken at last by Tamm.

"Listen, Wayne," he began tentatively, "I don't know how

this fits in with what you've told us, but those cargo blisters on *Tycho* are full, half of it yours and half of it ours. And I was expecting your people to yank the temporary compartments out of our hold and generally help get the *Tycho* in mission configuration."

Coulson nodded. "We'll do that for you, just as we got *Descartes* ready before we moved her out. As to making use of those modules in the hold, as you've seen we're hardly hurting for *lebensraum*. But we are eager to see the rest of what you've brought us. How soon do you think we could arrange to duplicate your technical and edrec libraries? We've got some catching up to do."

"I'll have my librarian get together with your people immediately and work out the transfer." Tamm finished his drink and set it aside. "Very nice synthesis, this," he said, gesturing at the empty glass. "How long do you think it'll take your people to strip the hold?"

Coulson pursed his lips and considered. "I'd say a good week's work at least."

Tamm frowned. "I was hoping you could get us out faster than that. If it would help, I have some people with construction experience—waldoid and teleoperator—that I'll make available—"

"Commander Tamm," Coulson began, smiling benignly. "We understand how eager you are to begin your mission. And we won't make your stay here any longer than it has to be, even though we might be tempted. There's not much out here to do except work, eat, and have fun, and we're good at all of them. Give us a week and let us show you what we can do."

Tamm laughed easily. "All right, Wayne. I think we understand each other."

"What about my crew?" Neale demanded. "We need to get aboard *Descartes*."

Coulson shrugged apologetically. "I can't do anything for you until we're finished with *Tycho*. We only have the one dock, after all."

"Then take us out to *Descartes*, if you can't bring her in here."

"You're not at Unity, Commander. We don't have sixteen-seat peoplemovers and interorbit ferries. I don't even have a long-range backpack available to put your senior tech aboard. We disabled them all after the mutiny."

"You could have thought to make a second dock part of your building spree," Neale complained.

"We don't have many traffic jams here, Commander," Coulson said lightly. "Besides—here you are, asking favors from us, and you've done nothing to let us enjoy the benefits of your crew's presence."

Neale stared at him for a long moment, then walked to the netlink.

"Channel A," Coulson said helpfully.

"Rogen," she said with a note of annoyance. "Pass the word to the crew that anyone—make that anyone who passed their upgrade or requal exam—is free to come over to the base if they choose."

"Thank you, Commander," Coulson said smoothly. "And we'll be happy to put you up here while our work crews are disassembling your former quarters. There's not much in the way of amenities, but we certainly have the room. And we'll do our best to see you're entertained."

The first thing Thackery saw on disembarking was the last thing he had expected to see: children. There were three, one very tiny one sleeping in its mother's arms, one perched on his mother's shoulders, and one standing on wobbly legs and clinging to her father's leg.

But the welcoming committee of which the children were part was no surprise. The exuberant reception which had greeted Tamm, Neale, and the first watches to leave *Tycho* had been audible all up and down the ship's central climbway. By the time *Descartes'* crew was released an hour later, the gathering had thinned to thirty or less. But the welcome was just as warm, all clapping and spontaneous hugs and beaming faces.

A small podium with a microphone was set up in the shipway. As each *Descartes* crew member emerged from the tunnel they were guided to the dais to give their name and birthplace and accept the applause of the group. Each was then met by a Cygnan escort and led from the chamber.

While he waited his turn Thackery's attention was captured by a bright-eyed, raven-haired female technician standing near the front of the gathering. The bright embroidery covering her USS jumpsuit made her stand out as much as the body it so flatteringly concealed. When he introduced himself and she moved lithely forward in response, he silently exulted in his good fortune.

"I'm Diana Marks," she said, taking his hand familiarly and leading him away. "I'll be looking after you while you're here."

"I'm glad you waited for us."

She smiled. "We knew you'd be out before too long. Coulson promised us that. Is Merritt what people call you? It seems too formal for everyday—don't you have a nickname?"

"Not one I like."

"Then I'll call you Merry, and try to see that you are," she said, then grimaced at her own pun. "What would you like to do first? The grand tour? Lunch? What?"

"Is there a place from which you can see your planet—" He paused, searching his memory. "Does it have a name?"

"After a fashion. Astrography calls it Survey General Catalog 182 Cygnus-4."

"That seems too formal for everyday," he parroted. "Doesn't it have a nickname?"

She laughed easily. "Planets should be named by the people who live on them, don't you think? And no one lives there." She paused, then added, "Though some of us think we could."

"Are you that lonely for natural gravity?"

Her face became serious. "No—for open spaces. For a place to stand facing a world instead of a wall. When I joined, I was thinking about roaming an infinite universe. I never really stopped to realize that I'd be seeing it from inside a series of very finite, fragile bubbles."

"Sometimes you can forget the bubble's there," Thackery said, remembering.

"I never have," she said with regret. "Come on. We'll go down to the playroom. You can get a good view from there."

Seen through the binocular telescope mounted at one of the playroom's viewports, the unnamed world wore a crust of sludgy brown and orange. Forgetting Diana standing beside him, Thackery scanned its undulating surface. He noted the thin arc of atmosphere visible at the sunward limb, studied briefly one of the turgid hydrocarbon fountains, watched the advancing shadow of night race across a lifeless world. But despite his eager yearning to do so, Thackery could not engage his emotions in the viewing.

"Nothing," he said in a soft sad voice.

"Why do you say that?"

He had not meant to speak aloud, and her question invaded a private space left momentarily unguarded.

"Nothing like home," he said, straightening and turning away from the telescope.

She seemed to accept the elaboration at face value. "Does Earth still feel like home to you?"

"Doesn't it to you?"

"I can't let it," she said simply. "Not if I want to be happy here."

Her honesty demanded an equally self-disclosing answer. "Force of habit," he said with a weak smile. "At the moment nowhere really feels like home."

"Until you get on *Descartes?*"

Thackery nodded absently, looking around the playroom. The semi-circular white-walled room was part gymnasium, part resort courtyard. A multiplicity of colored lines on the floor of a sunken central arena attested to the room's versatility.

"Would you like to see the rest?" Diana asked suddenly.

"The rest?"

"Come on," she said.

From a compartment adjacent to the playroom, Thackery was led up a ladder into a tunnel bored out of a solid mass of spongy, rough-textured porifoam. Before they had gone a dozen steps the tunnel began to close in on them, driving them to hands and knees in order to continue. Moments later, the station's gravity fell off dramatically, and their awkward leaden scrabbling became the graceful touch-and-push of the micrograv veteran.

Wondering but unquestioning, Thackery followed Diana through a maze of tees and branch tunnels. They passed tiny alcoves, dove confidently through a many-entranced spherical chamber, and caught glimpses of—but never caught up to—other visitors.

"What is this place?" he called ahead to Diana.

"It's a good place to get lost—so stay close," she answered, a playful note in her voice.

At last she stopped, curling through the opening to one of the alcoves. He followed and found her floating in the synglas half of a small surface blister. Behind her was star-glitter and the disc of the bronze planet.

"Close the privacy panel," she said, her pupils large.

He turned and complied. When he turned back, she had anchored herself with widely-set toeholds. Locking eyes with him she reached up to her throat, and the top of her jumpsuit fell open to bare soft skin. A moment later, she undid in one smooth motion the long zipper which ran from instep to groin to instep. Underneath was all Diana.

"I hope you like this view better," she said.

After fifty-nine days of celibacy, he didn't question his luck. She was supple, hot-skinned, lubricious, and he came to her eagerly. They tasted each other, explored each other's contours, then joined in a coupling prolonged and intensified by the restraint forced on them by the absence of gravity. Thackery took from her a pleasure uncomplicated and untarnished, and she took the same from him in a mutual selfishness which left both satisfied and neither cheated.

"Tell me about the last time you saw home," she whispered afterward, clinging to his shoulder.

He chewed at his lip as he thought back. "When *Tycho* left Unity—"

"No—not from orbit," she said quickly. "The last time you were there."

Thackery thought back farther. "I'd gone downwell to tell my mother that I was joining Survey, and to be with her. She took it badly, so I had some extra time. I went down to Cape May. I walked along the breakwater in front of the old gingerbread houses, and on the beach at the point."

She dug her fingers into his arm. "Make me see it."

Thackery closed his eyes to help sharpen the memory. "There was a strong breeze off the bay, and the smell of the salt marshes. Green-head flies were biting. There was a charter fishing boat coming in, with a flock of gulls following off the stern, begging for an easy meal. The sand was hot, even through my shoes, so I took them off and walked along the tideline with the sandpipers. I found a horseshoe crab shell, with the tail and three of the legs still attached." He opened his eyes and smiled wistfully. "I wanted to bring it along, but it didn't survive the sterilization procedures."

"That's a good last time."

"I guess it is. I wasn't planning it as one. It's just a place I liked to go."

"I know." She pulled away from him and began to restore her clothing to its previous tidy state. "We have to go clear out your cabin on *Tycho*."

"Why?" he asked, reluctantly following her lead and dressing himself.

"They'll be starting to strip the hold soon."

"Where will I stay?"

She slid the privacy panel into its hideaway, then looked back at him with head cocked to one side. "Didn't I tell you? You stay with me tonight."

When they reached her room, they fell into each others' arms again. This time she urged him to a harsh vigor with whispered entreaties, opened herself for him and invited his entry, clutched at him and made little moaning cries as they drove their loins together. Under her spell, Thackery disengaged his mind and lived through his senses, his nostrils full of her scent, his eyes fixed on her rapturous face.

And again, when they were spent she clung to him and wanted to talk.

"I picked you out, you know," she said with uncharacteristic shyness.

"How's that?"

"When your crew data came in, they called in the volunteers and let us pick whom we wanted to escort. I picked you."

"I can't imagine why—but I'm glad you did," he said, bending over and planting a kiss on her forehead.

Snuggling in closer, she coaxed him to talk about himself. He told her about Georgetown and Tsiolkovsky, about *Babbage* and *Descartes*, even about McShane and Andra, though that was difficult. He even tried to explain about Jupiter, though so awkwardly that she seemed not to understand.

At last, arm benumbed and eyelids drooping, he yawned convincingly enough that she turned off the light. But his thinking was clouded by a lingering testosterone high and the happy fatigue in his limbs, and he slipped away without realizing he had learned nothing of her at all.

Seated on *Tycho*'s nearly deserted bridge, Neale watched as a trio of waldoids unshipped the *Tycho*'s gig from the port cargo pod and nudged it free. The whole process seemed painfully slow, like everything the Cygnans did. It had taken the work crew four days to clear the hold, and only now were they beginning to transfer to it the equipment which had been stored away in the temporary hull blisters amidships. Yet Tamm, who had been so impatient to begin the mission, seemed not to mind at all that the original seven-day schedule was already being projected out to ten days—

"Ali?"

Neale turned away from the monitor and saw that it was Rogen who had interrupted her. "Yes?"

"Coulson has been trying to locate you."

"I know."

"He wants to talk about the personnel transfer—to go over some candidates for our opening."

"I know." She saw his look of consternation and added, "I've been avoiding him. I can't stomach the man."

"Tom Dunn keeps prodding me to get it settled, so he can start breaking in the new awk."

She sighed. "I know. I suppose I have no choice. Any problems with the rest of the crew? Anything else I need to talk to Coulson about?"

"No problems."

"No problems with the locals?"

Rogen's smile was almost a smirk. "Hardly, sir."

"Accommodations satisfactory?"

"More than. I've never seen the crew this happy, the men especially. They're going to hate to leave. But they'll be glad for the rest, if you know what I mean."

Her eyebrow shot up. "I don't. Explain yourself."

A trapped look appeared on Rogen's face. "Well, I'm sure it's no surprise to you, eh? Didn't you work out the arrangements with Coulson?"

"What arrangements are those?"

"The Cygnan escorts—Commander, you had to know. Commander Tamm knows about it."

"Knows what?"

Rogen spread his hands, embarrassed. "That they've been more than friendly. My girl, Kiena—well, hell, you'd expect some of it just because of the new faces. Coolidge effect, eh? But they act like they've been going without."

"Son-of-a-bitch suit slitter!" she exclaimed, coming to her

feet. "Curse me for a goddamn fool. Where's Coulson?"

"He paged me from his office, I think."

"Call him! Tell him to park his freezin' ass until I get there. Those words exactly, hear me?"

Wayne Coulson wore the sanguine expression of an over-confident matador as he awaited Neale's charge. Arrayed comfortably in a reclining chair with his feet up and a drink at his hand, he waved Neale into his office with the air of a gracious monarch.

"Am I suitably parked?" Coulson asked sardonically.

"Your people are screwing my people," Neale said bluntly.

Coulson reached for his drink. "You sound surprised. Didn't they believe in sex on *Dove?*"

"Your women are fertile," she accused.

"We hope so. Most of the menstrual cycles are in sync, and your arrival timed out perfectly."

"Damn it, I should have known when you talked about having brats. But I assumed you'd at least be planning the births, not just throwing the whole thing wide open."

"We did plan it. We went over your personnel files and let each woman choose among the hets in both your crews."

"That's damned mechanical, don't you think?"

"Let's not be puritanical, Commander. They'd have been bouncing the beds anyway just for novelty. What matter if there's a practical side, too?"

"What practical side?"

"Why, doubling our gene pool right at the outset, of course. Commander, an Advance Base is not a ship. We're going to try our damnedest to be a normal community."

"A community of liars. Or do our men know what's going on?"

"No. Why should they?"

"My people deserved the right to say no."

"I can assure you no one was dragged into this against his will."

"How about her will? What kind of woman would let herself be used this way?"

Coulson shook his head back and forth slowly. "Commander, I guess you've never discovered it, but being pregnant isn't all nuisance and misery. Having a baby is a beautiful experience. I didn't twist any arms."

"But you weren't honest. You've turned my people into freezin' sperm donors."

"We think this is the best way. We accept the responsibility of raising any children that result from this . . . exercise. If you tell your crew, what will it gain you? You'll sour what for most of them has been a very pleasant experience, and fill their minds with thoughts of the son or daughter that maybe they're leaving behind."

She turned her back on him for a moment. "I hate agreeing with you on anything, but you're right about that. I won't tell them," she said finally. "But I want *Descartes* brought to the dock within twenty-four hours."

"Or what?"

"Hmm?"

"If you were my superior, that would be an order. But you're not, so it must be the first half of a threat."

Neale cast about for a suitably large stick. "I'll report this to Unity—"

"You're so proper you're going to do that anyway," Coulson interrupted casually. "Besides, by the time they receive the report and can do anything about it I'll be dead of old age. Face it, Alizana. You can't move me and you can't remove me. So why don't you relax, and stop being so damned jealous."

"Jealous!"

"Of course. Whether you're jealous of the men or the women is the only question I can't answer. Want to give me a clue?"

"You're a shit, Coulson."

"When it's to my advantage, Commander. Now—shall we talk about finding you a replacement Auxiliary?"

It was Diana's hands fondling his hardness that woke Thackery, drew him slowly and pleasurably up out of a dream that briefly blended with reality. He reached for her but she brushed aside his touch and moved to straddle him.

"Let me," she whispered, and lowered herself on him. She rode him with a gentle rocking motion that, all too soon, ended in wet shuddering spasms.

"That wasn't fair," he complained good-naturedly as they held hands. "You rushed me."

"We didn't have much time, and I wanted to look at you," she said tenderly. "You're being called back to *Tycho*."

"What? What for?"

"I don't know. You're due on board in a half hour."

"Did Neale or Sebright make the call?"

"I don't know. They want everyone, with gear."

Thackery sighed unhappily. "I'd guess I'd better be there, then. Shower with me?"

She smiled coyly. "We'd just get started again, and we don't have the time. I'll wash up later."

When he returned from the bath, she had donned a soft robe and gathered his extra clothing into his bag. At the door she kissed him sweetly, a kiss that lingered on his lips after contact was broken. "Thank you, Merry—for being nice to me."

"I'll be back."

Her smile was small and poignant. "I don't think so."

Dunn and Sebright were waiting at the gangway to check in the arrivals.

"Almost left without you, Thackery," Sebright said with world-weary bemusement. "Down to G deck and join the queue."

"Left? What's going on?"

"Where've you had your head?—as if I didn't know," Dunn said salaciously. "It's moving day. Next ferry should leave in about twenty minutes."

"Leave for where?"

"*Descartes*, of course. You didn't think we were going to stay here for ever, did you?"

"But it was supposed to take a week—"

"It didn't," Sebright said succinctly. "The Com found us some transportation—*Tycho*'s gig. What's wrong, you having second thoughts?"

"Diana—"

"You didn't fall for that, did you?" Dunn asked cattily. "She only wanted to improve her chances of getting picked for *Descartes*. But the joke's on her, isn't it—she was sleeping with the wrong man."

"Lay off, Tom," Sebright said sharply. His tone became sympathetic. "This is one of those things you wanted me to tell you, Thackery, except you wouldn't have understood. When it comes to relations outside the ship, you've got to have your emotions in neutral. If you don't, you're just asking to be kicked."

"But I *care* about her—"

"You can't afford to," Sebright said. "Because you can't stay, she can't leave, and she won't be here if you ever get back. Like it or not, that's the way it is."

Thackery answered him with a hostile scowl and moved off toward the climbway. Dunn's unkind laughter followed him, but he did his best not to hear it.

Despite the bustle of activity on board, the atmosphere of *Descartes* had the chill and fuggy odor of an unused basement. At the center of the bustle was Tyla Shaeffer, processing the new arrivals.

"Thackery," she pronounced when he reached her. "E deck, cabin 5."

"Where's Neale?"

"Commander's on bridge deck. Don't you want to know who your roommate is?"

"No," he said. "Is that all?"

"It's Voss, the new awk." When he showed no reaction, she went on, disappointed. "Pick up your personal gear in the hold and put your cabin in order. Then Sebright wants a power-up checkout of the equipment in the survey lab."

Nodding acknowledgment, he brushed past her.

The cabin lock responded to his touch, and he tossed his bag onto one of the bunks. Sliding into the only chair, he switched on the netlink.

"A-Cyg net," he requested.

"Restricted. No personal communications." It was the system's voice, not the comtech.

"Authority."

"By order of Commander Neale."

"Page op, please."

"*Tycho*—excuse me, *Descartes* com," said a new voice.

"Is that you, Jessie?"

"I think so," Baldwin said, chuckling.

"Why the com restrictions?"

"I think they're uploading data from *Tycho*."

"That wouldn't affect the whole net, would it?"

"Hey, I'm new here myself. Excuse me, the bridge is paging."

"Can you get Neale for me?"

"She's on her way down the core to see Abrams about the drive."

"Thanks."

It was just a few steps down a short corridor to the climbway. Stepping off the deck, he started to ascend hand over hand toward the bridge deck. He felt the vibrations of other traffic, and, looking up, spotted Neale.

"Portside up, starboard down, mister," she snapped at him when her feet were within a few rungs of his hands.

Chastened, he crabbed around to the other side of the ladder. "Commander Neale, will you lift the com restrictions when the data upload is finished?"

"No," she said, moving past without pausing.

"Will we be docking at the base before we leave?" he called with a note of desperation.

The reply was the same.

Thackery scrabbled downship to stay with her. "There's someone on base I need to talk to—"

Neale stopped and gazed unsympathetically at Thackery. "No."

"Commander, I have a right to my private life—"

"Forget her," Neale said bluntly. "It wasn't what you thought it was, whatever you thought it was."

"It meant something—"

"Grow up, Thackery," Neale growled irritably, "before I start wishing I was leaving you here with your old roomie."

She went on downship, leaving him feeling helpless and hating it. *This is going to stop happening*, he thought determinedly. *Go back to what you know. You learned the game at Georgetown, that you make your place not by worrying about your needs but by meeting theirs. Accommodation, compromise, living within the rules, that's the game here, just like it was there. You wore that suit once and it's time to bring it out and dust it off again.*

IMPERFECT
KNOWLEDGE

(from Merritt Thackery's
JIADUR'S WAKE)

. . . The linguacomp's inference processor represented the highest successful application to date of expert systems technology—thinking machines. But despite the heuristic marvels of
the Interlisp-P programming language, the inference processor
could do nothing without an extensive knowledge base. Aboard
the survey ships, that knowledge base consisted of a syntax
and vocabulary file for every known language and dialect, from
dead languages such as Latin and Gaelic, to invented ones such
as Esperanto and Cobol, to the native languages of Journa,
Muschynka, and Pai-Tem.

But the linguacomp was only one application of a basic
technology for which a bigger job was waiting: the colony
problem itself. The inference processor was ready whenever
the knowledge base was large enough. The Service was hungry
for information, a hunger barely slaked by the hundreds of
entry and exit dispatches streaming back from the survey ships
to Unity, filling more and more volumes of subatomic memory
with the portraits of a profusion of suns and worlds. Every
colony discovery was a feast, a thousand more pieces for the
billion-piece puzzle.

At some point, the knowledge base would reach a threshold
of completion, and the machine would at last unravel the five
fundamental mysteries of the First Colonization—to where
from where, when, how, why, and, most tantalizing, what
happened afterward. That was the hope, nay, the expectation,

of the Committee on the ReCreation of First Colonization Planning. They had nothing else on which to pin their hopes, convinced as they were by their own failures that the intricacies of the problem were beyond the scope of an individual human mind.

But until that threshold was reached, until the machine proved itself the equal of those expectations, it was the insights and energies and inspirations of those individual humans on which so much depended. . . .

chapter 6

Redemption

At first, the star and planets comprising 118 Lyra were mere dimples, tiny space-time pocks on the gravigator's mass detector. Then *Descartes* dropped out of the craze, and, with an urgent curiosity that seemed to belong more to the ship than the parasites within, reached out with her many senses and made them worlds.

The ship was already within the heliosphere, that living, pulsating halo of charged particles which bathed some planets in death and battered relentlessly at the magnetic armor of the rest. On the bridge, the immediate priority was to sample the plasma pouring outward from the cool orange star and gauge its threat to the crew.

If, as the remote survey had suggested, the host star was a normal Main Sequence inhabitant in stable mid-life, then the Survey Protocols would come into play. But if 118 Lyra were an undiagnosed flare star or other miscreant, *Descartes* would leave hastily and with no regrets, for no star hostile to *Descartes* could be a friend to dirt-bound life.

Downship in the survey lab, a cheer went up when Guerrieri confirmed that it was a planetary system, and not a primordial nebula, which was responsible for the excess infrared measured by the A-Cyg observatory.

"We've got rocks!" he exulted. "Two, no, three big ones—looks like eight altogether." But Sebright did not join in the celebration, and his reserve put a damper on their exuberance.

The gravigator's data was already being processed into a map of the system and a timetable for visiting its components. But most of the instruments lay inert, and would remain so until *Descartes* fell into orbit around its first new world. Only the telecameras, probing the still-distant face of the nearest planet, and the com scanner, searching hopefully for new voices in the ether, were in use.

Presently, lights flickered throughout the ship as the entry dispatch, a high-intensity burst of radio waves carrying the report of their arrival, was transmitted toward Earth. The lights flickered again, less severely, as the same message was directed at A-Cyg. It was one of the ironies of the Service that had either message been one of real urgency, it would have been necessary for *Descartes* herself to return, since the dispatch was bound by a celestial speed limit which the ship's drive was empowered to ignore.

At last the ship's ecologist gave her blessing to an extended stay in the system, and the real work of *Descartes* began. By that time Muir had determined that only the second planet fell within the star's biosphere, as defined by human-biased criteria. But her pleas to begin there fell on deaf ears.

"There's three planets more or less between us and Two that need surveying first," was Sebright's reply.

"But Commander Neale—"

"Doesn't know enough about stellar ecology to start telling us how to set our priorities," Sebright finished for her. "I know, the Com's real eager to find a colony. But possible isn't the same thing as probable, and probable's nothing close to certain. We're going to do this efficiently, without a lot of jumping around and doubling back. Be patient. Anything that's there on Two now will be there ten days from now."

So the first world to be studied was Seven, a cold gray-green globe tracing a slow, lonely path near the rim of the system. In the course of twenty-four hours, more than 95 percent of the planet's gaseous face was scanned simultaneously by more than a dozen instruments: photopolarimeters, imaging radars, ultraviolet spectroscopes, magnetometers, and more. Data poured in far faster than it could be reviewed, much less analyzed, forcing each team of specialists to focus on just one or two key items.

Eagan and Thackery mapped the thick atmosphere in three dimensions and determined its composition, while Guerrieri and Tyszka gauged mass and rotation and listened in on the squealing and booming of the magnetosphere doing battle with the stellar wind. At their elbows Muir and Collins worked out Seven's energy budget and modeled its unpromising ecosphere. Sebright contented himself with the narrow-angle telecamera and its subjective portrait of the planet's face.

They expected few surprises, and found none. In truth, the Service had only modest interest in planets per se. A few facts sufficed to place most new worlds firmly in the Rogermann planetary classification system: the major constituent of the planetary mass (ices, oxides and silicates, or gases), the primary source of internal heat, and the primary constituent of the atmosphere.

Virtually all possible combinations of those three characteristics had been seen during Phase I, and most of them more than once. Uranus had a hundred known cousins, and Mercury a thousand. As a consequence, unless there was some compelling anomaly, no uninhabitable planet warranted more than a day's intensive study. Not even Seven's third satellite, an ice world puddled by nitrogen lakes fed by nitrogen rain from a dense nitrogen sky, was deemed worthy of a lingering look.

The lesson of Rogermann's system was that it is in the fine structure that worlds achieve uniqueness. The Valles Marineris of Mars and the Great Red Spot of Jupiter, the lobate scarps of Kapteyn's Star Three and the equatorial plateau of Muschynka—from such things proceeded all individuality, all identity. A corollary lesson was that such considerations matter only on a world which harbors life or temporarily enjoys its company.

It was the search for such life, then, and not reflexive scientific hoarding or the need for exacting classification which prompted the wholesale collection of data. The story of the Pai-Tem contact provided a sharp reminder of the wisdom of that practice. That small, pretechnological colony was discovered not during the initial survey, but during the analysis of data on the craze to the next star.

The alternating six-hour watches, which began the day before a planetary encounter and ended a day after it was concluded, were eye-fatiguing and bottom-numbing. The surveyors took short breaks when they could, most often at their consoles or no more than a few steps away. Housekeeping went by the board, and meals were eaten on the fly if at all.

"Sebright wasn't exaggerating, was he?" a yawning Tyszka asked at one point during the encounter with One, a parched cinder orbiting just outside the star's Roche limit.

"About what?" Thackery said, eyes trained on the columns of numbers rolling up the screen of the geoscience console.

"About how hard we'd be working. Even if I had a sex life, which I don't, I wouldn't have one now."

At the other end of the lab, Muir rolled her eyes and turned away.

"It isn't so bad," Thackery said.

"No? I get maybe four hours sleep in a six-hour block. And I'm developing lower back pain from spending too much time sitting in this damn ergonomic chair."

Thackery shrugged. "I'm getting along all right."

"Come to think of it, I haven't heard you complain—not even when Sebright's away." Tyszka peered narrowly at Thackery. "What's your secret?"

"No secret."

"Give, or I'll tell the joke about the Councilman and the pavement princess again," Tyszka said threateningly.

"For life's sake, tell him," Muir pleaded. "I've heard it four times already, and it wasn't funny when it was new."

Thackery grinned. "No secret. I keep thinking that a single system, even a single star or planet, would be a lifetime's work to properly study, and that there's no telling when anyone will come here again. Makes me want to make the most of the time we have."

"Stars, a serious answer. How dull," Tyszka said disappointedly. "Didn't think you cared that much for this part of it. What happened, did Gregg infect you with rock fever?"

Thackery shook his head. "I want to do my part. I realize I may never get a chance to prove myself as a contact linguist. So if I'm going to contribute, it has to be this way."

"Nice speech," Muir said cynically. "Should have saved it for when Sebright was around."

Tyszka clucked. "Now, Donna, you wouldn't be impugning Thack's motives here, would you?"

"Ask *him*."

"Woof," said Tyszka to himself as he turned back to his work. "And I thought *I* wasn't getting enough sleep."

During the first watch at Four, Thackery amassed enough data to demonstrate that the planet was a volcanic nightmare, the heat from its rich lode of radioactives driving a restless geothermal engine which continually bathed the surface in a patchplaster of liquid rock.

"Let's send down a couple of spike seismographs," Eagan said after reviewing the report.

"I thought you might want to. I've got some candidate sites picked out. . . ."

Passing up the chance to return to his cabin and sleep, Thackery stayed and helped prepare the two-metre-long torpedo-like instruments for deployment. Then he hovered behind Eagan at the teleoperator station as he flew the first of them down to a stable landing and a successful implant.

"How about letting me handle number two?" Thackery asked as Sebright entered the survey lab and joined them.

Sebright raised an eyebrow, but Eagan genially said, "Why not?" and gave up the chair.

Conscious of the appraising eyes behind him, Thackery shrugged off his fatigue and marshaled his concentration. Un-expected upper-air winds in the turbulent atmosphere threatened to carry the seismograph downrange, but he was able to kill off the extra velocity with a series of controlled stalls and guide the glider to a gentle three-legged landing within metres of its intended target, half a globe away from the first.

"I thought languages were supposed to be your long suit," Sebright said afterward.

"They are," said Thackery, unaware that his answer came across as bragging. *This part isn't so different from what I was doing aboard* Babbage, he was thinking. *Wouldn't that give Hduna a few laughs at my expense—*

Sebright grunted. "Well, it's good to know we don't lose too much when Gregg's catching his six."

You don't lose anything, Thackery thought but did not say. *And before I'm done you'll know it.*

At last *Descartes* moved on to Two, a clear-skied rust-faced world with the thin air of the Himalayas and a temperate-zone climate like a sunny November day. At the end of five orbits Sebright called the team together. Their subdued expressions spoke volumes about their findings.

"What's the prospect?" asked Sebright.

Muir responded as though the question had been addressed to her alone. "Gregg says there's no methane signature in the atmosphere. None of my instruments are showing any ground cover. The oxygen's all in the crust and the water vapor's all in the air, and the geochemical cycles that might move them are sluggish or nonexistent."

"Conclusion?"

"Livable, but not without a fairly high level of environmental technology," Tyszka offered. "A level we would have detected by now."

"So nobody's home."

"In a word, no."

"Did you seriously expect otherwise? On our first semi-terrestrial planet in our first system?"

He was answered with sheepish smiles.

"All right." He squinted at them. "Anyone living upstairs? You are, aren't you, Mike?"

Tyszka nodded.

"Get yourself moved down here, pronto. You'll be bunking with—"

"Me," said Thackery. "You'll have to move out Voss."

"With Thack. Find his roommate and tell him he's being chased."

A grin broke out on Tyszka's face as he realized what the order meant. "Right away," he said, and left the room with long, bounding strides.

"We're going down?" Eagan asked, surprised.

Sebright nodded.

"But there're no indications to justify it. This has every earmark of an ordinary B2N world. Oxysilicate crust, primary nitrogen atmosphere, three-strength magnetosphere—God knows I wish it were a more interesting place, but it's not."

Sebright waited patiently until Eagan was through. "I intend for us to make a survey landing on every surface where a minimum E-suit is enough protection," Sebright said. "Or at least one in every system."

"But what about the Survey Protocols—"

"I haven't read them," was Sebright's offhand reply.

"Survey Protocols are advisory," Thackery offered from his station at the far end of the lab. "The Concom has discretion in all matters related to landings."

"The protocols say that, do they?" Sebright mused idly.

"Yes."

"Well, good. Then let's go down and have a look." He reached across the board to the shipnet. "Ali, this is Mark. We're going into isolation mode in thirty minutes."

Neale's tone communicated her displeasure. "There's no colony on Four, is there?"

"No indications of one to this point."

"Then I assume you have some other good reason. This will hold us here for at least another day, and there're four more planets to look over before we can move on."

The corner of his mouth curling upward, Sebright glanced at Thackery. "It's just a three-hour survey landing, Ali. Per the Protocols."

Neale sighed audibly. "All right. Flag your landing site on the map and I'll see we're moved into an appropriate orbit."

Switching off, Sebright grinned. "Let's make a house call. Donna, Gregg, Derrel, get going."

As the trio rose and hastened out, disappointment flashed momentarily across Thackery's face. Then the mask fell back in place—but not so quickly that Sebright missed the transition.

"What's the matter, Thack?" Sebright said, standing. "Think you should be going?"

Thackery's response was quick and evenly modulated. "No. Backups take part in planetary landings only when the primary specialist is unavailable."

Sebright snorted bemusedly and shook his head. "I almost believe you mean that. All the same, I don't think I'll play any poker with you. Don't worry—you'll get your chance."

"I'm not worried," he said, jumping up. "Any objection to me going down and helping them with their E-suits?"

Sebright regarded the younger man thoughtfully, and for a moment Thackery thought he had gone too far.

"Never mind," Sebright said, sighing. "Go ahead and give them a hand."

By universal agreement, the difficult part of an E-suit was the gloves. The suit itself, a close-fitting single-piece garment, resembled a Service allover and was put on the same way. To that basic foundation were added boots, gloves, and a soft helmet, all made of the same thin polymerized sandwich of synthetics and all attached by rigid and uncooperative binding rings. A wearer could usually get both boots secured in place, frequently the helmet, rarely the first glove, and almost never the second glove.

When Thackery reached the dress-out room at the foot of the climbway, Guerrieri was already dressed and aboard, beginning his checkout of the gig. Muir had donned all but her helmet and was trying to help Eagan with his gloves. The E-suit fit her more closely than her usual garb of choice, leading Thackery to a quiet and favorable reevalution.

"Oh, good, Thack," Muir said on seeing him. "You can do this. My gloves are so freezin' slippery I can't get a grip on his." Tossing the glove she had tucked under one arm to Thackery, she stepped to the hatch and dropped through.

"That's so the microbes can't get a grip on them, either," Thackery called after her. He waited a moment for a laugh that didn't come, then turned to Eagan.

"I don't know if I should let you do those," Eagan said sparingly as he held out his hands.

"Why?"

"I think you want my job."

"Banish the thought," Thackery said as a loud *clack* announced that the first glove was properly seated.

"I don't know. You've been busting cee all week—no, since we left A-Cyg, really. Even Sebright's noticed, asked about you."

"When was that?" Thackery said, and then bit down on his lower lip as he applied leverage to the remaining glove.

"I don't know, one of my watches. After Four. What was all that bowing and scraping about up there, anyway?"

Clack.

"I don't know what you mean," Thackery said, stepping back. "You're all set."

"Sure you don't. All the same, better watch it, it's hard on the knees," Eagan jibed. "You going to stay here and help Mike?"

"Yes. Go on, check out your gear."

It took another forty minutes to get all three of the surveyors on board and the gig checked out to Sebright's satisfaction. Watching on the bay monitor in the dress-out room, Thackery did not hear the go to proceed. But there was no mistaking the hissing and the basso thrum of pumps as the air in the bay was drawn into a storage reservoir. Now it was the pressure hatch at the foot of the climbway, and not the bay's wide clamshell space door, which *Descartes'* internal pressure held firmly closed. A few moments later the gig was released from its anchors, and slid sideways out the space door and away.

The picture shuddered as the wind grasped at the camera pylon, extended two metres above the fuselage of the gig. The picture was of a rock-littered desert stretching out to meet a pale violet sky.

"Wish we were watching upstairs on the edrec deck," Tyszka said wistfully.

"It's being recorded. Later," Thackery chided. *It looks like a recording now,* he added silently, disappointed. *Mars, or maybe Procyon Six—I've seen so much video this seems like just one more. Connect, Merritt—your friends are down there.*

"Here they come," Collins said suddenly.

At the bottom of the screen appeared heads, distorted by the foreshortening of the wide-angle lens. In that moment, as the landing team walked out onto the landscape, kicking up the dust of a new world, Two lost its patina of familiarity for Thackery.

"This is fantastic!" crackled the voice of Eagan. On the monitor, the shortest of the three figures raised his arms to each side and made a slow pirouette. "I haven't even seen them yet and I can tell you the pictures don't do justice."

Another of the blue-suited figures turned and waved vigorously toward the camera. "For something that clogs up the whole damn bay, the gig sure looks tiny down here," Guerrieri radioed. "Man, I was starting to forget what a wide-open space really looks like. This is going to spoil the edrec room for me for a while."

"I can practically feel the wind right through the suit," Eagan crowed. "Look at this! I feel naked."

Sebright chuckled. "Best advice is not to follow through on that impulse."

In the background, Muir had been edging away from the others. Now she broke into a trot, heading toward the horizon. She stumbled and almost fell, and they heard her laughter as she caught herself and kept going, dancing nimbly among the rock obstacles.

"Don't go out of sight," Eagan called after her.

Without breaking stride, Muir reached up and switched off her radio.

"Stay with her, please," Sebright counseled, and the two men started after Muir at a brisk walk. Two hundred metres out, she disappeared over a rise. A few moments later Eagan and Tyszka followed her footprints into invisibility.

"Hey, Donna."

They heard a long sigh of pleasure. "No walls. No people. Oh, what a wonderful place."

"She's got something there," Guerrieri said fervently. "If I turn my back on these guys, I'm all alone here. It's like I always have been alone here, you know? Because the gig's out of sight, and that's the only reminder that I was ever anywhere else. It's a very strange feeling."

"Understood, Gregg," Sebright said. "Now if you folks would wander back, we'll take a look at item one on the survey landing checklist."

An answer came not from down on the surface, but from upship and the command deck and in the terse, angry voice of Neale. "Mark, are you there?"

"Yes, Ali."

"I want to see you, the minute you break isolation."

That minute was a long time in coming. After the gig was safely nestled back in its moorings inside the bay, it took three hours to process the landing team through primary decontamination. Beyond that stretched a 48-hour incubation period during which the contact decks continued to be sealed off physically and environmentally from the rest of the ship. By the time the team was pronounced healthy and the isolation mode terminated, *Descartes* had moved on to Five.

But Neale had no trouble summoning up her simmering anger when Sebright at last appeared before her, especially since by that time it was also clear that the scientific results of the landing were, to be charitable, trivial.

The encounter was in the privacy of her cabin anteroom, and she did not waste words on protocol. "What was the purpose of that display down on Four?" she demanded. "Is that a sample of the kind of leadership you've brought to this ship? Whatever his other failings, your predecessor wouldn't have asked for a landing on a world like Four. He wouldn't have allowed that landing to become an undisciplined frolic. He wouldn't have wasted the time and resources of this ship on a private self-indulgence. Explain why you did it."

But her emotion seemed to wash over Sebright without affecting his sanguine expression. "Walking out onto a new world is a high," he said simply. "I want them to learn how to handle it when it doesn't matter if they screw up or their attention wanders."

"That's not good enough."

"It is for me."

Neale scowled. "You could at least make an effort to persuade me that this was a valuable rehearsal, or something to that effect."

"Why?" Sebright said, stretching out his legs and resting one ankle on the other. "Look, Ali, I could argue that we really needed a full test of the gig so we knew we could count on it. I could wax poetic on how much we learned from a dry run of the isolation procedure. I could try to make you think we needed some physical samples to keep Gregg and Thack busy during the next craze. Most of that is even true."

"Then do it, dammit, and let's get this behind us."

"Ali, if we get lucky, you want the contact to go smoothly. You want the contact team paying attention to the colonists and not the surroundings. Right?"

"They don't need practice to do that. They need discipline."

Sebright scratched his chin and studied her. "Maybe we should take you down with us. I'd be willing to bet that in all your time on *Dove,* you never made a landing."

"It wasn't my place to," she bristled.

Sebright nodded. "I know that. But you wouldn't say that kind of thing if you had that experience. Look, when this business was first starting and the astronauts would come back from a flight, everyone asked them what it was like to see the Earth from space. It was a very exclusive experience, and it seemed like only members of the club could make each other understand—and they didn't need to. Maybe you even felt that way when you made your first orbital. I know I did."

"So?"

"So now things are reversed. We're used to the sight of a planet from orbit. It's going down to walk on one that pushes those buttons for us. Don't take my word for it. Go down with Jael and the others on the next one."

"No," she said sharply. "First, ship commanders belong on

the command deck, not in a landing team taking unnecessary risks—certain tapes in the edrec library not withstanding. And second, there aren't going to be any more of these excursions."

"Survey landings are at the Concom's discretion," Sebright said quietly.

"Subject to *my* review. You don't run this whole ship, Mark. You don't even seem to be running your part of it with any particular distinction." She looked away and exhaled sharply. "I'll accept your other reasons for this landing, so there'll be no more trouble over it. But you've used those reasons up, and until you have some new ones there'll be no more survey landings."

"I gave you another reason."

"If you mean that nonsense of yours about needing to 'adjust' to making landings, I reject it. Every planet's different anyway, so 'adjusting' to one won't do a damn bit of good on the next. What they need is to be taught to put their responsibilities first. That's how to make these things go smoothly, whether it's a survey landing or a contact landing."

Sebright stood, his face offering an unflattering opinion of what he had heard. "There'll be some trouble, bad feelings, if the others don't get to go. You have to let me have one more rehearsal landing."

"No, I don't. Your bad judgment created the trouble," she said curtly. "You deal with it."

After nineteen days in the system, *Descartes* crazed again, carrying them on to the next star. Thackery left feeling as though the task he had set for himself was already half accomplished. He knew he had done a good job, and he knew that Sebright recognized it. That pleased him in two ways: because Sebright was his superior, and because since A-Cyg Thackery had seen a different Sebright, one that in time he might grow to respect.

Unfortunately, the obvious but unacknowledged falling-out between Sebright and Neale meant that Thackery could not count on that favorable impression filtering upward. To move up in Neale's eyes, Thackery knew he would have to do well in something close to Neale's heart.

And there was only one solution to that equation. The colony problem was more than Neale's primary interest—it was a preoccupation verging on an obsession. Already it was a standing joke that anytime Abrams, the senior electronics tech, could not be found, she was probably in Neale's quarters working on the star projector.

Yet there were risks in such a tactic—the risk of succeeding too well. If he were to somehow generate a real advance in First Colonization theory, he could count on arousing not her approval but her professional jealousy. Certainly he could not expect to retain credit for any minor insights shared with her. She had already shown with her crew interviews, particularly the lengthy exploration of Nakabayashi's slow-ship/fast-ship argument, that she had no compunction about appropriating others' ideas for her personal dispatches to the FC Committee.

No, for Neale a slightly different strategy was required. The road to her approval was not to be a high achiever, a rival expert, but to be seen as taking the colony problem seriously. Then his interest would be reinforcing, not threatening. *They always want confirmation from others that what they think important really is,* he thought. *Well, that I can give her.*

Despite that modest goal, Thackery knew he had to be properly prepared. Enthusiasm would not be enough; he had already felt the quick scorn Neale reserved for the self-serving and opportunistic. Nothing destroys the illusion of sincere interest faster than an ignorant question, he reminded himself, and nothing establishes credibility faster than an insightful one.

Time for that preparation had to be found in a schedule nearly as hectic as that they had kept insystem. But by arranging to be assigned responsibility for analyzing the data from the four worlds least likely to support life of any kind, Thackery was able to steal hours from his regular duties without risking an embarrassing oversight. He spent those hours studying the direction FC theory had taken since *Jiadur* and Journa.

Thankfully, he was still a quick study, especially on matters sociological and theoretical, and two days before the craze ended he judged himself ready. But there was still the problem of arranging a private consultation, especially since Neale rarely met with ratings except at her own request. After weighing the alternatives, he chose to intercept her as she was leaving the wardroom after what he hoped was a satisfying meal.

"Commander Neale?"

"What is it, Thackery?" She did not stop, and so he followed her out into the corridor.

"I've been doing some thinking about the colony problem—"

"As I recall, you badly needed to do some."

"Yes, sir. Commander, I've reached a bit of a branch point, and nobody seems to be able to tell me whether I'm going the right direction. If you could find a little time to spare me, I'd very much appreciate the benefit of your experience in keeping me on track."

"What's this 'branch point'?"

"Commander, what I'm really hoping for is some guidance in evaluating the alternatives to the standard First Colonization paradigm."

"You think there are any alternatives?"

"Well, I thought so, at least one interesting one—but that's why I really need the advice of someone who's been involved in this from the beginning."

There was a long pause. "All right. I can give you ten minutes. Not here. My quarters, two o'clock."

She kept him waiting several minutes, but acted as though the reverse had been true. "You don't have much time, so let's hear it," she said as she settled in her lounger.

Thackery took a seat facing but not too close to her. "As I understand it, the reigning First Colonization theory is that there was a great civilization in Northern Europe during the last glacial interstade, some 25,000 years ago."

"Yes, the Mannheim hypothesis," she said. "But you oversimplify. There are some theorists who place the civilization in the U.S.S.R. during the Valdai glaciation, and a number that would push the date of the Forefather culture back much farther, to the Ipswich interglacial. There are probably a hundred variations on that basic idea. We're obliged to look back at least as far as the Weichsel—we have too good a picture of history since then."

"And if I understand Mannheim's argument, the civilization was wiped out by a subsequent fast glaciation, and any remaining traces were destroyed during the reoccupation of the continent, accounting for the lack of any historical records or physical artifacts of their culture."

"Not exactly. Most members of the Mannheim school believe that the rather remarkable and historically sudden development of Middle Eastern civilization from the Sumerians to the Greeks was built on refugees who brought at least some of their knowledge, if not their technology, down from the north."

"I see," Thackery said, though he had already known that detail. "Of course, the higher the technology with which we credit the FC culture, the harder it is to explain why they didn't anticipate or find some way to cope with the glaciation. And even a fast glaciation is slow in human terms."

Thackery's comments consciously echoed those in a paper Neale had written after the end of the *Dove* mission, and she studied his face a long moment before responding. "I believe the First Colonization *was* their response to the glaciation. It's possible the Firsts had an incomplete knowledge of planetary climatology, and thought that when the ice started to return it meant, in essence, the end of the world. They couldn't have known or even had reason to hope that the ice would only advance as far south as Kiev and the Spanish-French border."

"They must have had an excellent understanding of the basic nature of the Galaxy, though."

"Oh, obviously, of course. They must have had their Anaxagoras, their Copernicus, their LaPlace. They must have known that the planets were other worlds, and must have believed that the stars were other suns."

"Has any linguistic analysis been done comparing the early Mideastern languages with the colonial languages?"

"Yes, not very fruitfully. Have you been considering that avenue of research?"

"If I had access to the proper materials, I'd certainly want to go over what has been done and see what's left to be done." Thackery made that commitment knowing full well that the ship's library did not contain facsimiles of the ancient documents he would need.

"I doubt anything conclusive could come out of it, or it would have been pursued elsewhere."

"Most likely," Thackery agreed quickly. "Now, the way I understand it, one of the hard questions has been why the colonists weren't able to maintain the level of technology that brought them there."

"That's right. On Earth we can blame a combination of the ice, the cultural stress imposed by the colonization effort, and a society-wide fatalism that came out of their misunderstanding of the situation. Out of the four colonies, only Journa was even close to being capable of space travel, and it was only the spur of contact with the Founders—us—that brought that out of them."

"And even that was accomplished in primitive fashion, with a nuclear-pulse slowship and no computer technology."

She nodded. "But their hydromechanical switching and logic systems still represent the highest level of technology found on the colonies."

Thackery shook his head as though bemoaning a regrettable twist of fate. "And no records or remnants of the FC starships have been found."

"Well, of course, for a while, we thought *Jiadur* was one, left in orbit and then pressed back into service for the Reunion. But the Journans apparently built it themselves."

"Is there any chance they were following an FC design?"

She crossed her arms across her chest, which to Thackery was a telling bit of body language; he had noted that there was no information in the Journan contact record about Jiadur's designers. "That's a question that probably hadn't been looked into as carefully as it might have been," she said carefully. "But we know a lot about how they built it, and it's pretty obvious that it was something fully within the reach of the contemporaneous Journan culture."

"Let me be sure I understand. Even though the Mannheim hypothesis holds together analytically, there's no hard evidence to support it."

"No, there isn't. Which is why the door is still open, at least a crack, for alternatives. Which is what you said we were going to talk about."

"How seriously is the possibility of a second-species intervention taken?"

"It's called the Daniken hypothesis, which if you understand the reference is one of the problems." She sighed. "It would be taken very seriously, I suppose, if anyone could nominate a second species that might be responsible. You know what the Service has found. The Galaxy is not exactly fecund. There's a lot of worlds that could support at least some life, but very few of them actually do, and little above the complexity level of a sea sponge. Even the colony worlds tend to have a fairly simple native ecology."

"But the theory doesn't require fecundity. It would only take one other species reaching the level we have, but ten or fifty thousand years sooner. And second-species intervention eliminates a lot of the difficulties," Thackery said with manufactured earnestness. "It would explain why the colonists 'lost' their high technology, because it would mean they probably never had it. I would explain Earth 'forgetting' an earlier technological age, because it would never have had one. It would eliminate the problem of accounting for the choice of colony stars and worlds in human terms."

"And this magic is worked through an even more farfetched series of postulates than the Mannheim hypothesis requires," she said sharply. "Every serious student of colony theory considers this 'alternative' at some time or another—because it's easy. What questions it doesn't answer it makes unanswerable, because it transfers both the problems of means and motive to an unknown and unknowable alien intelligence. The Daniken hypothesis is wishful thinking. I would not waste any more time on it."

The answer was no less than Thackery expected—in fact, he privately agreed with it. "I appreciate your frankness, Commander," he said smoothly, rising. "And I'll follow your advice and concentrate on the question of proof for the Mannheim hypothesis."

She nodded approvingly. "That's the only profitable course. Not that you've shown me any reason to think you're capable of making a contribution. There was nothing new in anything you had to say. But at least you've moved beyond the ignorant mental meanderings you displayed the last time." She glanced at her watch. "Your time is up, Thackery. You're excused."

Despite her words, it was an effort to keep the grin of self-satisfaction off his face as he left. It was an effort to keep from dancing a celebratory jig down the corridor. For he knew without any question that he had achieved his purpose. He was a long way from a complete redemption, and even farther from achieving the status he hoped eventually to reach, but he was on the way.

He knew that not because of his confidence that Neale's next personal dispatch would include a speculative commentary on the origin of the design of *Jiadur*. He knew it not because she had implicitly included him in her comment about "every serious student of contact theory."

Rather, he knew it because his ten-minute consultation had taken the better part of an hour to complete, and it was not until the end of it that Neale had noticed or cared. For the moment, that was all the confirmation he required. The rest would come in time, as it always had.

PROTOCOLS

(from Merritt Thackery's
JIADUR'S WAKE)

. . . Easily overlooked in evaluating the wisdom of the Service administrators is the qualitative difference between the Phase I and Phase II searches.

The crews of the Pathfinders, and in particular their commanders, were expected to show initiative and exercise judgment. They carried a burden of trust which freed them to focus on results rather than procedures. They responded to that challenge with courage, integrity, and responsibility far exceeding any narrow definition of duty.

By contrast, the crews of the Pioneers were expected merely to follow the Protocols. There were Flight Protocols limiting the discretion of the commanders, Operations Protocols governing the work of the crew, and Survey Protocols dictating the priorities of the surveyors. If the need ever presented itself, there were voluminous Contact Protocols as well.

The Protocols were meant to be the accumulated wisdom of the Service, stronger than recommendations, less rigid than regulations. It was always understood in the Planning Office that the Protocols could not be inflexibly applied, that they represented the past and would not always pertain to the present. The acknowledged risk was that a crew might remember to follow the Protocols and forget to think, might substitute the judgment of the dead and the distant for their own.

But the veterans of the black ellipse perceived something else entirely. The Protocols represented a loss of faith, a presumption of incompetence, a failure-oriented psychology. There were few of Command rank who did not realize that the standards against which they would be judged had been changed, and that "I followed the Protocols" would be a stronger defense than "I did what I thought best at the time."

So it turned out, with bitter irony, that the rules which were intended to prevent mistakes instead guaranteed them. . . .

chapter 7

Gnivi

Though Thackery could cope with catching his sleep four or five hours at a time, that did not make him any more accepting of being awoken in the middle of such a session. But there was no ignoring a shipnet priority page—if the piercing tone did not rouse him, the annoyed occupants of the adjacent cabins would.

"Here," he said, standing on unsteady legs in the darkness.

"This is Jael. Better come on up," she said. "I think this might be the one."

"I'll need a shower if I'm going to keep my eyes open," he said. "I'll be there in a little bit."

Thackery knew immediately what Collins' call meant: that the planet they were now orbiting might be the kind of docile B-type world to which Sebright had sent half the contact team some two months and three crazes ago. Since then his promise of more such landings had languished unfulfilled as they looked down on a seemingly unending series of hostile worlds.

Even based on the inbound scans Thackery saw before the change-of-watch, 605 Cepheus-5 was clearly bland-faced and lifeless. But it was also benign, with a climate not far removed from that of the ice-free valleys of Antarctica. When Thackery had turned over the geoscience console to Eagan and left the contact lab, the orbital studies had just begun. Collins' call told him all he needed to know about how they were progressing.

The pitch of excitement in the contact lab and the eagerness with which Thackery was greeted provided confirmation.

"This is the one, Thack," Collins said with proselytizing fervor. "It's our turn."

"It looks good. It looks real good," Tyszka said. "Tell him, Gregg."

"You'd better brush up on your piloting, then," Thackery jibed, moving to look over Eagan's shoulder. "I don't want any landings on the bounce. What about it, Gregg?"

"Everything I've seen says that minimum E-suits would do," Eagan offered, leaning back in his chair. "There's a few nasty spots along the equatorial fracture zone, but nobody says you have to go there."

"I wish Sebright would get down here," Collins fussed.

"When's he due?"

"Twenty minutes ago."

"How long till we need to make a go/stay decision?"

"An hour. We're only programmed for three orbits."

"Well—he'll probably be down," Thackery said, turning out his hands in a gesture of helplessness.

"Look, he's got to be awake by now," Collins insisted. "I think I should call him and get the okay to start preparations."

"Maybe it'd be better to go on up there in person," Eagan suggested.

"No," Thackery said firmly. "That's not a good idea."

"You're putting too fine a point on it, the way I remember," Tyszka said dryly.

"He'll be down," Thackery said with more hope than confidence. "He saw how this planet was shaping up before he went off-shift."

But too soon, the third orbit was completed, and the expected call came down from the flight deck:

"Contact lab, are you clear?"

Thackery glanced around the room. "Who's today's watch supervisor?"

"I am," said Eagan. "Look, I can't help you. I can give the clear, but I can't authorize a landing. And the fact is, all the studies *are* finished. But if I tell them that, Neale'll take us out of orbit."

Collins and Thackery exchanged glances. "If I go get Sebright, will you wait?" Collins asked Eagan.

"If you don't take too long." He tapped into the shipnet.

"Hold a little while, will you, Navcom? We're going over the checklist."

"Be quick about it. The Boss is itching to move on."

"Understood. We'll have an answer for you post haste."

Shortly, Sebright appeared at the lab doorway, trailed by Collins.

"—like you did for Donna and the others," she was saying to him.

"Just hold on," Sebright said, going to the central netlink and placing a finger on the actuator. "Current. Survey. Summary." The words brought data to the screen, which Sebright scanned quickly.

Then he reached for the net switch. "Bridge, this is Sebright. We're clear." He turned a hard face to Eagan. "Why couldn't you decide this?"

"Just a minute—what about our landing?" Collins demanded.

"A landing's not indicated," Sebright said curtly.

"But you said—"

"Read your Protocols. A landing requires anomalous geology, indigenous organisms, or some other Priority 1 phenomenon. Do you have anything like that? Jael?"

"No, but—"

"Mike?"

The technoanalyst shook his head.

"Thack?"

"No."

"Then what the hell did you need me for?" Sebright demanded and stalked out, leaving the room in stunned silence.

"Well, no field trip, class," Tyszka ventured finally. "I wonder if Neale didn't call him down for the last one."

"Then why didn't he tell us so?" Collins demanded.

Eagan shrugged. "Command loyalty, maybe. What d'you think, Thack?"

"Probably," Thackery said slowly. "Vets sticking together." The disappointment was already fading, the hope having been so recently kindled. "He might have told us sooner. He could have warned us not to expect anything."

Eagan tried to offer a hopeful outlook. "We'll just have to find you a Priority 1 anomaly, eh? They aren't that rare."

But Collins tossed her head angrily. "That's all right for you. You've got lots of possibilities. But, Thack, I'm surprised at you. The only thing now that will get any of us to the surface is a colony," she said bitterly. "Want to give me odds of less than six figures on that?"

No one did.

Descartes spent the succeeding months wandering within the tenuous remnant of a nebula which had given birth to a small cluster of young T Tauri stars. Since they were barely a half-million years old, the nebula's children were considered poor prospects for life of their own. But spectrographic studies of the nebular remnant showed it was rich in second-generation elements—oxygen, silicon, iron, and other atoms cooked in the hearts of long-dead stars—which made the stars good candidates to form terrestrial planets.

So young were the systems that the first *Descartes* visited, 312 Lacerta, was caught still in the process of planet formation. The stellar nebula had condensed into a flattened disk revolving around the protostar, but the inner edge of the disk was only beginning to be driven outward by the T Tauri wind, the blast of energy pouring out of the newly ignited fusion furnace. It was only the second time that a USS survey ship had come upon a system in that state (though several had been studied telescopically by the Service's High-Inclination Observatory orbiting the Sun in the cis-Cytherean space).

"Looks like they set out to build Saturn, but the engineers dropped a decimal point," was Thackery's observation. But that image came only from imagination and, later, computer modeling, since in close quarters 312 Lacerta appeared as little more than a vast cloud, lit from within by sporadic electrical discharges and masking their view of half the Galaxy.

As there were no planets to be evaluated, Thackery spent much of his time at Guerrieri's elbow, trying to sharpen his understanding of the gestation of planets. His own discipline of resource geology was only interested in geohistory to the extent that it made assays of the crust more accurate. Unfortunately, the seminar was a brief one. *Descartes* made a single, 22-hour mapping run across the north face of the disk, then continued on.

At their next stop they found but a single planet and a thin glittery remnant of a nebular disk. But the planet was a hundred times the mass of Jupiter, a third the size of its parent star and very nearly a star in its own right. Seen in visible light, the planet's coral and ochre atmosphere seethed and surged from the heat generated at the core by gravitational collapse. Seen in infrared, the planet literally shone.

Two crazes later, they reached a system which none of the crew would ever forget. The three inner planets of 298 Lacerta were undergoing a breathtaking bombardment as they swept the remaining nebular debris out of the ecliptic. Even from a safe fifteen million kilometres above the activity, the telecameras showed at least one spectacular strike blossom into a shortlived crimson flower every two or three seconds.

"Some show," Muir said, who along with Thackery and several off-shift operations awks was watching the spectacle on the edrec screens.

"Isn't it just glorious?" Thackery said.

"Typical male comment—it looks like a war. Like a goddamn nuclear war."

"No, you're not looking at it right," Thackery said earnestly. "It's a birth—a little bloody, a little stressful, but when it's all over and they get cleaned up we'll be looking at brand-new triplets."

"Save it," Muir said tiredly.

"Don't you understand? We only ever get to see worlds in middle age, just snapshots that make you think they've always been that way. Seeing this, it's easier to remember that they change, that they have beginnings and ends—that there're cycles longer than we can see."

She looked at him with surprise in her eyes. "I actually think you mean that. When did this happen?"

He looked back at her and laughed a little self-deprecating laugh. "I don't really know."

"Maybe you pretended you were interested so often that the idea took."

"Maybe," he said, and paused. "Was it that obvious?"

"Yes."

Thackery frowned. "I think maybe it's that I've brought my expectations in line with reality. This isn't a bad life. It isn't what I was expecting. But it isn't all bad, not nearly so."

She looked back at the screen just as an enormous double strike mushroomed near the pole of the second planet. "Not nearly so," she echoed. "Keep this up, Thackery, and I might actually start to find you tolerable. Not attractive, mind you. But tolerable."

There was a great deal of interest in 214 Cygnus-2 right from the start. It was the first world on which there was enough free water for the familiar dynamic of the water cycle to influence the topology. It was the first world on which the clouds held rain, not burning acids or strangling smog.

Even so, the three discontinuous seas were modest by comparison with those of Earth. The largest, dubbed Mare Australis both for its size and location, averaged barely a thousand metres deep across its four million square kilometre expanse. The smallest, a circular body comparable in size to the Caspian Sea, appeared to be a Hudson Bay–type astrobleme. From the regularity of the shoreline and the surrounding plain of jagged ejecta, Eagan estimated the asteroidal impact had occurred less than a quarter million years ago.

From the beginning of the first orbit, it was on those seas that the contact team's attention focused. Free water was a Priority 1 anomaly, and there was no question but that there would be at least one survey landing for samples and soundings. However, Sebright had not announced whom he would send— the primary survey team of Muir, Guerrieri, and Eagan, or their impatient backups. Collins, at least, thought that the question was still an open one.

"He's got to even things up," she said confidently to Thackery during the first orbit. "As long as things don't get too interesting down there, he can justify sending us. Unless there's something really special down there, he can't justify *not* sending us."

The discovery that the water of Two's seas was brackish and poisonously mineral-laden made Thackery wonder if Collins might not be right. But it was Thackery himself who made the observation that quashed that hope.

"Donna?"

"What?"

"Anything on the shoreline?"

"Not a hint. Too many salts and heavy metals. Anything that could grow there would have to have cell walls made of ceramic."

"Agreed. That's what you get when a pluvial lake shrinks over time, during a warming period. But Mare Australis does have active feeder streams. What about conditions upriver?"

"Show me the feeders."

She watched over his shoulder as Thackery tracked the sinuous path of the largest of the three shallow rivers. For several hundred kilometres there was no change in the signatures returned by the infrared mapper: weathered rock, salt flats, and mineral deposits. At irregular intervals, the river even disappeared underground, only to reemerge a kilometre or more further along.

"There," Thackery said suddenly. "What's that?"

"Looks like a grassland," she said, hurrying back to her own console. "Oh, blessed, look at how big it is. Five thousand kilometres on a side."

"How'd we miss it?"

"We didn't. I'm looking at the data from the first pass. Damn, there's even some variation in the flora—four or five different signatures, all mixed together."

"Like farmland?"

"Oh, no. It's got to be a natural distribution. But it's still the best we've found so far."

Thackery turned the console over to Eagan a few hours later, along with a request from Tyszka and Muir to construct a model of the grassland's aquifer and drainage patterns.

"Michael? What kind of resolution do you and Donna want on this map?" Eagan called to the other end of the lab as he settled in.

"What do you usually do?"

"Three-metre contour lines."

"That won't do. Can you give us one-metre?"

"I can give you half-metre—it just takes longer to process."

"We'll take it. The distribution of plant species here is a little hard to figure. Donna hopes the answer is microclimates."

"I'll try to have something for you before end-of-watch."

The task, though time-consuming, called for no new observations. The Nebraska Prairie—as Muir had dubbed it—had already been scanned, and all data was always collected at the maximum resolution of the various instruments. The information Eagan needed was safely stored in the radiation-shielded memory modules which filled *Descartes*' hull just downship from the bridge.

Ordinarily, the data would have remained there until needed for analysis during the outbound craze, or until the post-Contact

exit dispatch to Unity. After the dispatch, only an abstract of
the data would be retained on board for future reference. The
rest had to be purged to make room for new observations on
the next system. It was left to Unity to study the data to ex-
haustion, and at every order of resolution.

But one of the reasons for having a crew on board at all
was to maintain flexibility. For *Descartes'* purposes, and particularly the ecologists', the finest resolution was not the most
useful. Too much detail blurred the picture, obscuring the patterns and relationships which gave order to their science. But
if the ecologists needed that detail, Eagan was prepared to
extract it.

The bulk of the work, the plotting of the ground contours
and the extrapolation of the Nebraska watershed, was done
automatically by the geoscience computer. Nevertheless, at
such a fine resolution the processing revealed dozens of to-
pological features which cried out for Eagan's attention.

In the course of monitoring the mapping routine, Eagan
took a closer look at one of the regions where the river became
subterranean. To his surprise, he found the contour lines on
either bank to be severe in the vertical dimension and angular
in the horizontal, forming a hill-and-rill pattern reminiscent of
spreading ripples on a pond. A central longitudinal rift split
the circles into complementary arcs.

Curious, Eagan called up the telecamera survey in place of
the mapping radar. When the image of the sector he had been
studying materialized on his display, Eagan's breath caught in
his throat. The hills were rows of buildings, the rills concentric
streets.

"There's a *city* down there," he breathed.

So congested was he with emotion that no one else in the
lab heard him—not Muir, who was by the door laughing with
Sebright about something, not Sebright, not Guerrieri, who
was yawning and rubbing his eyes tiredly. When there was no
response, he whirled a half-turn in his seat and shouted as
though insulted, "Didn't you hear me?" That they heard clearly,
but not having caught his first utterance, it only made them
look at him wonderingly. He spun back to face his console and
mashed the shipnet contact under his fist.

"Page. Eagan for Commander Neale," he demanded.

The answer came from the net's silicon caretaker. "Page

mode not available. Commander Neale is—"

"Jessie!" Eagan pleaded.

"Here, Gregg," Baldwin broke in. "What's—"

"Stop talking and listen! Get Neale up. Get her down here. There's a city below us, on the Nebraska. A city, d'you hear? We've found a colony! We found a freezin' colony!"

When the news reached her, Neale was alone in her room in the embrace of an exercise cradle, performing the twenty-eighth of a planned fifty leg lifts, the last element of her thrice-weekly program. By the time she had disengaged herself from the machine and hastily wiped the perspiration from her face, an update hard on the heels of the first alert added the welcome detail that the city was occupied, its streets filled with life. That fillip drove out of her mind any thought of a quick shower and change of clothing.

There for you, Glen Harrod, she thought in triumph as she danced down the climbway. *There for you, Lin Tamm*. Her short-cut hair was damp and tangled, and bands of perspiration streaked her singlet between her breasts and in the middle of her back. But her eyes were bright and eager, glowing with the triumph of her moment. *There for you, Wayne Coulson. You all tried to get in my way, but you couldn't stop me.*

This time, the familiar descent down the climbway was endless, its hundred rungs seemingly a thousand: down through the enclosed tunnel of the systems section, through the open spaces of the middecks, past a noisy celebration on the edrec level, through the longer tunnel piercing the drive, then at last to the aftdecks and the lab level. The contact lab door was closed, and Sebright was waiting for her outside it.

"This is wonderful, Mark, just wonderful," she exulted, throwing her arms around him in an uncharacteristic display. "Are your people all together in there? I want to meet with all of you, hear everything."

He shook his head stiffly. "Not yet."

"We have to lay out our timetable—"

"No, Ali," Sebright said composedly. "Not 'we.'"

She stepped back and squinted at him. "What?"

"You've already heard everything. Gregg spotted a city on the Nebraska, straddling the river. The population might be as much as fifty thousand. There's some evidence in the ecological data which suggests cultivation in the surrounding prairie. We're searching right now for other cities. That's all we have, to the minute."

"Which is why we need to review our strategy—"

"No, Commander," Sebright said, more sharply than before. "There's pressure enough on them right now. I won't have you adding to it."

His words, his very attitude, brought a flash of rage to her gut and a cold rigidity to her features. "What exactly does that mean?"

"We'll make this Contact as expeditiously as possible. But that may mean six weeks sitting up here learning what we can about them. It may mean six months."

"I understand that."

"I doubt very much if you do. Everyone on this ship knows how much you've invested in the colony problem."

She stored her anger in a tightened spine, keeping the tension from her face. "What exactly are you accusing me of?"

"It's not an accusation, just an observation. You have one objective, getting information. I have a whole series of them— a good survey, a safe landing, a successful Contact, and then, only then, data on the colony problem. I don't want you suggesting to those people that the first three are any less important than the last, or infecting them with your impatience. If we're going to do this right, we're going to have to take it step by step."

"Are you telling me I don't know how to handle my own crew?"

Sebright crossed his arms over his chest. "No. I'm reminding you that they aren't your crew. Not now. When we're crazed, *Descartes* is all yours," he said calmly. "But when we're surveying, the Concom sets the agenda. Maybe I haven't asserted that as much as I should have up to now. But we're on Sebright time now. Before you go in there you're going to have to acknowledge that."

"I do, do I? Will you tell me what to say when I get in there, too?"

"After a fashion. You can go in there to congratulate them, and you can go in there to talk them up for what's coming. You can tell them you have confidence in them and you can tell them you'll be looking forward to the results of their work.

And that's all. I won't have you down here looking over their shoulders and getting in the way."

"You make it sound like they're children. Do they know how little confidence you have in them?"

"When it comes to this, they are children. And I don't want you getting them excited about the carnival across the street before they've learned how to look both ways."

Tight-lipped, she asked, "And later? Do you have a script for me then, too?"

"We'll hold an update briefing at every change of watch to go over new material. You're welcome to monitor those sessions, or even to come and sit in as a spectator."

"How very gracious of you. And how exactly do you intend to enforce your edicts?"

"I don't need to," Sebright said. "Because you know I'm right, and because you know I'm within my rights. You know this is the way the Flight Office meant for the chain of command to go, why they wanted a vet and why they weren't happy with my predecessor."

"You're awfully confident of my good will."

"No. Of your professionalism and your sense of duty. Ali, you did your job. You got us here. But you're not the expert now. We are. Let us do *our* job."

Be damned if I'll let you have anything, least of all my colony, she thought fiercely. *This is a grab for glory, nothing more. And it won't work. It won't work.* But for the moment, she could do nothing. Maddeningly, infuriatingly, Sebright was right.

"I'm not entirely convinced that anyone's an expert," she began curtly, "considering that this is only the fourth colony Contact the Service has attempted. And I hope this discussion isn't a sample of your ability as a diplomat. Luckily for you, I'm able to separate what you had to say from the downright abrasive way you said it. And to overlook being accused of something I wasn't about to do. We'll proceed according to the Protocols—as I always intended."

But as she moved past him into the lab and congratulated each member of the team individually, her mind was occupied with far less conciliatory thoughts. *I've outlasted and outmaneuvered far better than you, Sebright,* went the silent refrain. *And I'll deal with you, too, soon enough.*

• • •

"Padwa gnir par batu."
"Sar tan we—"
"Belotoy gnivi."

Gnivi, with a hard G. Thackery and the linguacomp agreed that it was the colonists' name for the city, but it had quickly been adopted as the name of the planet and the people as well. It seemed only fair, since Gnivi appeared to be the only city on its surface. There was a rural population numbering perhaps a hundred thousand scattered throughout the Nebraska, but their most complex social organization appeared to be the family, and their ties to the city seemed to be stronger than to each other.

The sound of Gnivian voices had been a constant in the contact lab for weeks. The night after the city had been discovered, Tyszka had taken the gig down to scatter a hundred pebble-sized relays across the city in a nighttime, lights-out pass five hundred metres above the rooftops. Sixty-four of the peepers had survived, and fully a dozen had fallen where they regularly picked up conversations and relayed them back to *Descartes*.

Of that group, the most useful was Number 41, which had come to rest on the sloping roof outside the second floor greatroom window of a Gnivian merchant family. Since the Gnivi did not seem to have invented glass, the team was treated to a fairly intimate aural glimpse of Gnivian family life.

Next most useful was Number 5, which lay in the courtyard of an open-air eatery, from which it relayed the discussions of a much wider strata of Gnivian society. Though even with the directional selectivity of the instrument, the cacophony at the peak of business was often more a source of humor than insight.

Nevertheless, the constant influx of information allowed Thackery and the linguacomp to make steady progress on what seemed to be a very basic, functional language with simple constructions, little use of modifiers, and few if any inflections. A handful of the peepers were located where Thackery could use the telecameras to get at least an overhead view of who was talking and, thereby, a clue of what the topic of discussion might be. With that boost, the confirmed vocabulary list of what Sebright called the "language hard to lie smilingly in" grew daily.

It was Sebright, not Thackery, who had decided the feed

from a choice peeper should be audible in the lab during at least half of each watch. Thackery actually joined Muir and Collins in protesting that their concentration would be adversely affected by the alien chatter.

"Even if you don't understand it now, you'll have the sound of it in your ear," Sebright said in rebuffing them. "When it's time to start learning Gnivan, it'll come to you that much faster."

The work of the rest of the surveyors was proceeding nearly as smoothly. What surprised them most was how little surprised them. Each new revelation fit neatly into the patterns and ranges established by ten thousand human societies through ten thousand years of Terran history. For the biologists, it was more evidence that biology was the primary shaper of human behavior. For everyone else, it added up to an irresistible urge to identify with the Gnivi.

"They're so like us," Collins blurted out during one early change-of-shift briefing.

"They're *too* like us," was Sebright's gruff response. "I trust you're all making an effort to remember that they *aren't* us."

But it was through thinking in terms of the known that most progress was made. It was impossible not to use terms drawn from the anthropological bank of their own experiences, and once those terms were firmly attached to some aspect of Gnivi, it was impossible to be uninfluenced by their previous associations.

One example was Eagan's map of the city, which was full of familiar names. Gnivi's only two entrances, East Gate and West Gate, lay at either end of Broadway, the great central corridor which bisected the city. At each of the entrances, a half-dozen major thoroughfares fanned out from a great plaza like fingers of a hand, leading into other parts of the city. The thoroughfares were officially identified by letter codes, but it was Eagan's more informal names—Camino Del Real, Via Appia, Champs-Elysées—which gained currency.

To the bare bones of Gnivi's physical layout the team quickly added details of the patterns of traffic, commerce, and habitation. Within the first few days, they identified an industrial sector along the presumed path of the river, a civic complex at the heart of the city, and scattered residential and business districts. No one quarreled with the anthropocentric flavor of the labels.

There were more cautionary parallels, as well. Overall, Gnivi had the look of a walled fortress city. Each half of the outer ring of buildings was in fact one contiguous structure, an unbroken barrier which clearly marked the boundary between the city and the prairie beyond. Not even the river breached the fortress wall, for the Gnivians had bridged over its waters and built part of their city atop it. Inside the city, even though many smaller, secondary streets branched off of the main byways, all were dead ends, channeling traffic—or invaders—along those main roads rather than between them.

But there were no fortifications, no ramparts along the "wall," no patrolling guards or armaments. Nor was there any evidence that the rural peoples could muster any serious threat to the city. In fact, the rurals were seen daily entering the city with two- and four-wheeled carts drawn by unidentifiable draft animals. Coming in, the carts were loaded with foodstuffs; going out, they carried cold-rolled iron implements from the Gnivian forges, cloth from Gnivian looms.

It was clear even to those who were not interpolators that any period of conflict had ended long ago, leaving as its only legacy the layout of the city. And if any doubt existed, it was banished when the archaeological base yielded up a long list of Earth cities, including Beijing, Delhi, and dozens more, whose fortress design had lived on into more peaceful eras.

Gnivi's industrial economy was based on the power of the river that flowed beneath it. From the differing elevations of the river on either side of the city and measurements of the kinetic energy lost in between, Tyszka postulated that the underground waterway included a series of small dams driving dozens of overshot water wheels. He was eager to see the complicated ligature of shafts and pulleys which would be needed to distribute that energy to the various workplaces.

"Imagine!" he said during one briefing. "They may've built themselves a completely mechanical power distribution net, completely analogous to an electrical grid, with transformers, substations, feeder lines, and branch circuits. That was done in single factories at the start of the Industrial Revolution, but never that I know of was a whole factory district tied together."

All this screamed to Collins of a planned city, one that had been laid out in every detail before the first brick was laid, rather than evolving haphazardly as economics and individual initiative dictated.

"I think there's a good chance we're looking at a First Colonization city plan that's remained almost unchanged since the beginning," she declared during another briefing "Gnivi may be the clearest clue yet to how large the FC ships were and how they chose to adopt their technologies to the world they colonized. They weren't afraid to take big steps backward. They may even have had a strong cultural preference for simpler ways and a nonexpansionist lifestyle. That's why none of the colonies have had spaceflight, or radio, or even the steam engine."

"Except Journa," Tyszka pointed out.

"The exception that proves the rule. They had the search for the Founders as a driver. Since they found them—us—they've been very conservative about introducing any new technologies to their general society. They've even let some *Jiadur*-era technologies go."

To back up her argument, Collins could point to the otherwise unexplained observation that despite its apparent vitality, no construction was underway in the city except for what could be described as maintenance. The buildings were thousands of years old, but kept fresh and livable by what seemed to be an army of plasterers, mudworkers, and masons.

"When we get down there, I think there's a chance that we could pin down the time of the First Colonization with a precision nobody's even dared hope for," she concluded triumphantly. "We just might crack this thing."

For all the optimism around him, Sebright showed little inclination to hasten the day of the contact landing. In fact, during the update briefings Sebright never spoke of a landing at all. His interest was in what was known, in what remained unknown, in cross-fertilization between the disciplines, as though there were no objective beyond building an accurate portrait of Gnivi and its inhabitants. To Thackery, it seemed to be a clear message from one who had been there to those who had not that the team was not ready.

But as the days slipped by, a week, then two, and the questions fell one by one, Sebright's recalcitrance became both more obvious and more puzzling. He acknowledged their progress without ever acknowledging what they were progressing toward, always providing a new task to replace one completed.

The contact landing team was diplomatic enough not to bring it up in the presence of either Sebright or those who would not be landing, but when they were alone together in the lab they began to wonder out loud.

"Aren't we ever going down?" fumed Collins, the most impatient of the three.

"When we're ready, I guess," Tyszka said with a shrug.

"But we are ready," she insisted. "I'm beginning to pile up my interpolations three deep. We've exhausted what we can do from here. I need some fresh data. I need to get down there."

Thackery found himself in the unfamiliar position of defending Sebright. "When we do go down, Sebright's got the heaviest burden. Maybe it's not a question of whether we're ready, but whether he is. He has the responsibility to speak for us, to negotiate for us, to explain for us. By comparison, we're just going along as tourists."

"Well, damn it all, how long is it going to take him?"

"He's working harder than any of us," offered Tyszka.

"I know he is. He understands the language as well as Thack does, he can recite back my own findings to me, and ' > even seems to understand what Guerrieri is talking about. That's why this is so frustrating. What's he waiting for? What else does he need?"

"You could go ask him," Tyszka said with a grin.

"Oh, no," she said, playfully filliping a crumb of her breakfast in his direction. "I learned that lesson the last time. I'll do my bitching to you two, thank you very much."

"The Concom's gain, our loss," Thackery said, for which she hurled a headset his way.

But others had noticed Sebright's behavior as well, Thackery discovered one night when the piercing tone of the shipnet awoke him two hours before his alarm would have.

"Page. Commander Neale for Thackery," the machine announced.

Groggy, Thackery swung his legs over the side of the bed and groped his way to the desk before the tone could sound again. "Thackery here."

"I trust I haven't disturbed you, Merritt?"

"Oh—no."

"Good. I'd like you to do something for me."

"Certainly, Commander. What is it?"

"Before I tell you, let me find out how you personally feel about the progress of the team."

It took no great insight to know where the conversation was leading. Thackery knew that Neale had been monitoring the briefings; Sebright had made a point of warning the team so they could avoid saying anything that might have repercussions. Thackery had welcomed the news, since it meant that Neale would have a chance to see him at his best.

"I can't judge for everyone, Commander," he said. "I know that *I'm* feeling very comfortable. Four days ago I was sitting in the lab working and listening to the feed from Gnivi that was on the speaker, when I suddenly realized that I was thinking in Gnivan—that I had stopped translating back and forth from Gnivan to English in my head."

"So you *would* be ready for a landing."

Thackery did not want the responsibility she was implicitly offering. "That's for you and the Concom to decide. All I can say is that our language data surpasses the criteria specified in the Protocols."

"Very good," she said. "What I want from you is this: Sometime during the next update briefing, ask for a summary evaluation of the team's readiness for a Contact."

Thackery's nose wrinkled. "I don't quite understand, Commander. I thought that's what the whole briefing amounted to."

"You've been spending a lot of time on things that are peripheral to the main objective, guessing about things that we can go down and ask them about," she said briskly. "I want to see people put on the spot. I want everybody to have to say 'I'm ready' or 'I'm not ready until X.'"

"I don't know if it's really my place to ask for that—," Thackery began apprehensively.

"I'm sure you'll find a way."

Thackery did not have to work for an opportunity: Sebright himself created one, at the end of every briefing.

"All right," Sebright said. "Let's go round the table once. Gregg, anything else? Jael? Donna? Thack?"

Thackery took a deep breath. "I've got a question."

"Go ahead."

"I think it'd be useful if we knew where we stood by departments. I know that I'm ready, but I don't know enough about the requirements for the rest of you to know how close you are."

Sebright cast a piercing glance in his direction, as though he knew exactly what was behind the request. "Fine," was all he said. "Thack thinks he's ready. How about you, Jael?"

Her "yes" was firm and hopeful.

"Mike?"

"Just give the word."

"How about the rest of you?"

There were some nervous glances exchanged. "I don't have any problem with my own material," Guerrieri said tentatively. "But I've been going over Thack's transcripts and Gregg's map. I can't see any evidence they've got the necessary astronomical knowledge to understand what we have to tell them."

Collins had a quick answer to the astrophysicist's objection. "They don't need to be able to think in terms of our own perspective. In fact, you can be sure that they won't. They're not obliged to understand our worldview. But it's incumbent on us to understand theirs."

"From what I've found so far, I don't think they have one," Guerrieri said. "I don't know if they've ever looked up."

"I would project a very primitive astronomy," Collins persisted. "There's no compelling nighttime body, such as a major satellite. The planet has a minimal axial inclination, so the seasons are very modest. They don't travel, so there's no navigational impetus. And all the farming is done by the rurals, who apparently don't do much more than organized foraging and probably don't have any need for a planting cycle."

"So," Sebright said, cutting off any further discussion. "You all vote go. Let me point out a few things to you. Thack, you may know basic contact Gnivan inside out. Do you know how to insult them? Do you know how to *keep* from insulting them?"

He did not wait for an answer but turned to the rest of them. "If the importance of that is too abstract for you, try this one. The Gnivians have potential farmland right outside their front door as good as any anywhere in the Nebraska. Why don't they use it? Why depend on the berry-and-campfire types? For that matter, why don't the rurals use it, instead of dragging their goods in from all over the map? When we get some of those questions answered, then we can start thinking about a landing."

"We can answer the questions we have left better down there," Thackery said.

Cocking his head to one side, Sebright gazed penetratingly into Thackery's eyes. "See if you can understand this, rookie. Every pre-Contact profile has been wrong in at least one important way. Not just a little wrong. Not just wrong in the details. Every crew has missed something big enough to endanger the Contact, only they got by. We're missing something, too. You just can't learn about a society by flying overhead."

Thackery's ears burned, but his example had emboldened Collins. "So what are we going to gain by waiting?" she demanded.

"Time," Sebright said curtly. "Enough time for you folks to come down off your high and start thinking again. When that happens, then we'll visit Gnivi. Now, before we break up, I have some additional studies to assign. . . ."

That night, Neale called Thackery to her cabin.

"Which is it, Thackery? Are you ready or aren't you?"

Thackery squirmed uncomfortably, anticipating the choice he was about to be forced to make. "I'm really not the one to ask. I can only speak for myself."

"Um." She walked toward him and sat on the edge of the credenza. "You know, you and your teammates have done first-class work. In little more than four weeks, you've given us as complete a picture of the Gnivi as I could have hoped for. You've brought us to the point where we're ready to close this out. We have a lot of questions for the Gnivi. I think it's time we started asking them. In my judgment, Mark is being too cautious. What do you think?"

When he hesitated, she reached out to touch his knee, adding, "It's time to choose your friends."

Thackery slowly drew a breath. "There's a certain irreducible risk in a contact landing. I think that the Concom could be overly occupied with that aspect of the decision."

She was not finished. "In your judgment, will the work you're now doing materially affect the chances of a successful Contact?"

"No. I don't think it will."

"Do you know any specific reason why Mark should delay the Contact?"

"No."

"What about the land around the city not being farmed?"

"Jael projects that the rurals are emigrés from the city. Depending on the circumstances under which they left, they may have been forbidden to come within a certain distance of the city. The ban probably evolved into custom and taboo."

"Then there's no reason not to begin the contact landing on the next cycle."

Thackery rubbed his forehead. "I don't see any," he said finally.

"Then say so at the next briefing. And be ready with answers for his objections."

"But—"

"I'll be sitting in. Leave the rest to me."

It's amazing, Thackery thought as he watched Neale and Sebright face each other down across the table, *how much can be communicated without words.* Since the briefing had begun, Neale had said nothing, though she had made a point of talking to each of the team members before a late-arriving Sebright had appeared. Since his arrival, Sebright had been hardly more communicative, saying only as much as was necessary to arbitrate the meandering discussions of Gnivian diet, time-keeping, and ethics.

Yet there was a tension between the two officers, a negative energy flowing back and forth across the table. A shift in position, a raised eyebrow, a loud exhalation—these were the elements of the code.

They've had this out before, Thackery realized belatedly. *He knows what she wants, and she knows what she has to do to get it—put him on the spot in front of us. Through me. And anything I gain with her by doing it I'll lose with him.*

He had not recognized the choice so clearly before. He knew Sebright better, knew him and had to work with him day in and day out. Thackery's early harsh judgments had been tempered by the experiences of the last few months. But Sebright had no ambitions. He was where he would be until he resigned. On the other hand, Neale was not yet finished. She was still climbing, and might take others who had been useful along with her.

Thackery was not entirely comfortable with the criteria on which the decision was turning. But neither was he comfortable with the thought of facing Neale after failing her. The time to say no had already been lost.

Only the hope that he was right consoled him when the moment came.

"Concom Sebright, concerning our discussion at the last briefing? I would like to formally recommend that we proceed with the contact landing," Thackery said in a voice less sonorous than he had hoped to muster. "As far as I can determine, the data we've collected exceeds in every category the minimums established in the Protocols. We should be able to function effectively among the Gnivi."

For a moment, Sebright did not respond.

"Do you want seconds on that?" Eagan asked.

"No," Sebright said. "A landing would be premature at this time."

His tone invited Thackery to pursue it no further, but Neale's presence was a more powerful motivator. "Sir, I think the team would appreciate it if you could identify your specific areas of concern."

Sebright shook his head. "I have no specific areas of concern."

"Then why are we waiting?" Collins demanded. "Because you don't trust us?"

Resting his chin on his folded hands, Sebright met her level gaze. "It's not a question of trust."

"What, then?" Tyszka asked. "Why the delay? We have a right to know."

"I had hoped that some of you would see it yourselves. Or are you all completely insensible to the effect we're going to have on the Gnivi?" Sebright asked. His eyes swept around the table, accusing each in turn. "The moment we go down there, we've changed them forever. Whatever uniqueness of thought, whatever social harmony they've evolved over the centuries will begin disappearing the moment they're confronted by our existence. Is what we're after so important that we can't take the time to at least record what they were like?"

"Salvage ethnology," Collins said, surprised.

"Exactly. Preserving what we know we're about to destroy. The data we're collecting now is all there'll ever be. We have an obligation to do what we can to help them remember what they were. As far as I'm concerned, it's worth whatever additional time it takes."

"Except that doing so is not part of our charge," Neale said quietly. "There's no provision in the Protocols for this kind of undertaking."

Sebright scowled at her. "So everything not required is forbidden?"

"It'll take six months or more to do a proper salvage study," Collins complained.

"We lose years by the fistful every time we craze. It can't matter much to Unity if our Gnivi data comes in a few months later."

"If Unity were the only consideration, I would have to agree," Neale said. "But is such a project proper use of this ship and this crew's time? We're equipped and staffed to initiate Contact. Anything beyond that will have to wait for the follow-up mission."

Sebright crossed his long arms over his chest. "That'll be too late. We'll already have contaminated their culture, just like we did the Muschynka and the Pai-Tem."

Belatedly, Thackery understood Sebright's objection. *So this is why you didn't like talking about Muschynka. But why shoulder the guilt when the decision was made by someone else? Neale's right. The Planning Office isn't willing to commit a survey ship to each colony just to find a way to mitigate the shock of Contact—*

"Cultural contamination is the whole reason this ship exists," Neale was saying unsympathetically. "I think Thackery's original question is still on the table. Is the team ready, or not?"

Thackery marveled at how neatly she had manuevered Sebright into a position where he could not say no. With the salvage issue out in the open, any refusal to proceed with the landing would be suspect. He could not fight, because he had no allies: Neale, the Protocols, and the threat of dissonance on the team all stood against him.

But Sebright was a long time in answering, as though he were not convinced that the issue was lost. He sent Thackery a sideways glance which was an indictment, and locked gazes with Neale in a silent, furious battle of equipollent wills.

"The team will consist of myself, Thack, Jael, and Mike," he said finally. "Derrel will fly the gig and drop us off on the East Gate road during local night. We'll enter Gnivi the next morning. That gives us about thirteen hours before we want to be on the surface. I suggest you spend the first eight hours of it sleeping."

Afterward, they came to congratulate Thackery, to clap him on the shoulder and praise him for saying what they had been eager but afraid to. All except Sebright, who quietly left, and Neale, who caught Thackery's eye and nodded approvingly before following. To Thackery, the celebration seemed hollow. *I'll do the rest,* she had said. And so she had, but never in a way that committed her, never in a way that risked anything. She had gotten him to take the risk for her.

You'd better remember, he thought. *You'd better take care of me. Because if you don't, then I've been used.*

The road was crushed rock cemented by rain and centuries of booted feet and iron-rimmed cart wheels. They walked toward the city until they could see its walls outlined against the night, then squatted down to wait for the dawn.

Collins and Tyszka quietly practiced their Gnivan together, while Thackery fussed with his nostril filters in a vain attempt to get them to draw freely. Sebright sat apart from the rest, craning his head, listening to the night sounds of Gnivi and staring into the darkness as though there were more than a deserted grassland to be seen.

When morning came, they waited until the first traffic emerged from the East Gate, then rose, dusted themselves off and started in. As they drew near they saw that the city was adorned with all the detail and glitter of an illuminated manuscript. Instead of the bare off-yellow stucco the orbital views had led them to expect, the outer wall was a continuous work of art which was coherent without being patterned.

"Not representational," Collins said. "Pure decoration."

"They must teach graffiti in school," Tyszka said drily.

"It's beautiful," Thackery said.

They passed two groups of outbound rurals, each with a half-full cart, without incident.

"Early risers," Tyszka said, taking note of the empty road between them and the city.

"Did you see those animals?" Collins said excitedly. "That's a canine breed of some sort, just like on the other colonies."

"From the size of them, I hope they breed them to be tooth-less," Tyszka wisecracked.

"Everybody have their transceivers in and on?" Sebright asked. When they gave assent, he nodded and said, "Page. Contact-1 to *Descartes*. Jessie, do you have a good signal on everybody?" The message was relayed by his own transceiver, nestled in his right ear canal like a hearing aid.

"We've got you all," came back Baldwin's voice, as clear in Thackery's ear as the voices of those with him.

"Thanks, Jess. Contact-1 EOT."

As they neared the gate Sebright reminded them, "Remember, hands visible at all times, and answer their stares with smiles." He said it in Gnivan, which was in itself another reminder.

They had made no effort to disguise themselves as either rurals or Gnivians, and so expected to draw some attention. Thackery, Tyszka, and Collins wore the royal blue allovers, Sebright the same in red. Walking four abreast, they entered the city.

Just inside the gate, the plaza which served as the intersection of the nine great boulevards was full of foot traffic. Yet they crossed it without difficulty, the stream of traffic parting effortlessly to permit their passage.

"They know we're here," Thackery said. *"Ni pag todya,"* he added, ducking his head in greeting to a woman frozen staring by the sight of them.

"Good," Sebright answered. "We're not here to surprise them. I *want* the civil authorities to know we're coming well before we get there."

Thackery scanned the perimeter of the plaza. Each boulevard seemed to have its own color scheme, its own characteristic whorls and filigree. "Broadway straight ahead," he said.

Swapping ends, Collins came up on Thackery's right. "There's too damn many of them talking," she whispered. "I can't understand a word."

"I'm having a little trouble myself," Thackery admitted.

"I think there's your first writing, Thack," Tyszka said, pointing at two vertical plaques cut into the corners of the entrance to Broadway and filled with bas-relief characters.

"Street signs."

"'This way to our leaders.'" Tyszka laughed. "God, I feel great."

Broadway was a canyon through the heart of the city, its walls rising a story higher than those of any of the other thoroughfares. The plaza traffic and its noise fell behind them, and the sound of their own footsteps echoed loudly off the hard walls. They were as alone as they had been walking into the city, with only a few of the natives visible in the distance.

Suddenly fighting panic, Thackery pivoted his head quickly to either side and stared at the decorated walls. There were dozens of fist- and head-sized openings incorporated into the design, from waist-height to high overhead. He looked again and saw not decorations but disguised machicolations, positioned to provide a crossfire from which there would be no hiding.

"Mark!" he cried, stopping and grabbing the veterans' arm. The others carried on a step or two further, then stopped and half-turned to look back.

Collins' eyes widened dramatically, and she pointed past them back toward the plaza. "What are they doing?"

Thackery twisted to look over his shoulder and saw a solid wall of Gnivians, standing across the entrance to Broadway. They were watching, waiting, as though they knew something—

Pfwtt. Pfwtt-pfwtt. Pfwtt.

The sound was of birds' wings beating. But there were no birds on Gnivi. Yet things flew all the same, swooping down from the battlements of Broadway, things with backbones of hardwood and beaks of barbed iron. Thackery turned back and took one step toward Collins. As he did she fell toward him to her knees, the lost look on her face as devastating as the angry red flower blossoming on her chest. On the periphery of both sight and consciousness he knew that Michael, too, was down and screaming.

Pfwtt. Pfwtt.

Thackery dove forward to the pavement, already running with Collins' blood. He lay there beside her as she plucked helplessly at the shaft of a second deathbird projecting from between the swell of her breasts. He heard the wet rasp of her breathing and saw her frantic writhing weaken from instant to instant. He did not know why they did not fire again and let him share her pain.

Then someone was shouting at him in Gnivan, and a pair of strong hands was hauling him to his feet. He stood frozen for a moment, staring at the wall from which the attack had come. Then the insistent hands jerked him along, and he suddenly understood the shouted words, that he would die lying there beside her if he did not run.

And, understanding that if nothing else, he ran before the birds could fly again.

REGRETS

(from Merritt Thackery's
JIADUR'S WAKE)

...There is no greater pain than the pain of avoidable failure...

chapter 8

A Coin For Charon

It was barely fifty metres to the end of Broadway, but to Thackery it was an infinite expanse of pavement which he had neither the right nor the hope of crossing safely. Fear crawled in the middle of his back and guilt churned in his bowels as he ran, barely aware of Sebright following close on his heels.

The crowd of spectators meant sanctuary to Thackery, a place where the deathbirds could not find him. But even as he neared them and began to think *yes YES I'm going to make it*, Thackery could find little compassion on the faces of those who watched. A few even called out to him, jeering, taunting:

"Ne corti lormo e huji lormo. The blood of your wives runs in our streets and you run from the fight."

At the same time, there was a roaring in Thackery's left ear, noise that was without meaning until Thackery forced himself to concentrate on it. Then the roaring became Guerrieri's insistent, anxious call, "Contact-1, report, report."

From the ranks of the spectators a tall man stepped forward, his face grim. He wore the vest and leggings common to the rurals, plus a red scarf knotted around his right bicep. If the clothing had not marked his class, his sun-browned skin and laborer's physique would have.

"You have broken ten *muri* of *gtorman* by your foolishness. Why did you not heed the warning?" he demanded as he stepped into their path.

Thackery looked helplessly to Sebright. "We heard no warning," the veteran said.

"Is it beyond you to raise your eyes and read?" their accoster demanded, gesturing at the terra cotta plaques. Then he craned his head to look to either side and called, "Marnet!"

"Here, Par," said a whippet-like woman, moving into view a few steps away. Thackery stared. It was the woman to whom he had called a greeting.

"Why did you not stop them?"

"Look at them," she pleaded. "They are not from the Green Lands. Therefore they are Gnivi. How could I know they did not have safe conduct?"

"Clearly they are not Gnivi," Par said with hard scorn, turning back to Sebright. "You did not have safe conduct, and you did not heed the warning of the gate. Where are you from that you want death so badly?"

Sebright parried the question with one of his own. "Our people," he said, sweeping a hand toward the crumpled, now-still forms of Collins and Tyszka. "Can anything be done?"

"Are the bodies of value to you?" Par asked with surprise.

"Yes."

Par studied Sebright with a hard look. "You speak with the clumsy tongue of a Gnivi, yet you are not Gnivi. You are not Green, yet you claim to share our death-customs. I look forward to explanations." Gesturing to Marnet to follow, Par turned away toward the plaza.

Guerrieri had fallen silent during the conversation, but in the momentary lull took up his page. "Contact-1, Contact-1, come on, Mark, give us a word. Contact-1, are you still receiving?"

"Shut the hell up," Sebright snapped, reverting to English.

"Contact-1, *Descartes* observers report two of your team down. On my way for a pick-up. I'll put the gig down in the East Gate plaza. Estimate four minutes max."

"Absolutely not," Sebright barked. "Stay the hell away."

"This is straight from Neale, Concom, no options."

"Goddamnit, you keep that thing away from here," Sebright barked. "I'm on the scene and you'll take your orders from me. If we need a pick-up we'll call for one. You bring that thing in here now and you'll put us that much farther behind."

Catching Sebright by the elbow, Thackery protested, "We've

got to do something for Jael and Mike."

"Something's already being done," he said, pointing.

In the middle of the plaza, Par and Marnet had commandeered a two-wheeled dray. As Thackery watched, they tipped it on its side, spilling its load of foodstuffs across the ground. Each taking one side of the T-shaped drawbar, they dragged the dray toward Broadway at a trot, calling *"Dar mator!* Let us pass!"

Thackery retreated out of the way as the dray rumbled by. As he did, he realized that the crowd had thinned dramatically, and all those around them now wore the stamp of the rurals—make that the Green Lands. The Gnivi who had jeered and taunted them had slunk away in the wake of Par's arrival.

"Pan tura! Pan tura! For the dead," cried Par as the dray advanced. He held his free arm upraised, his hand open, and Marnet did the same.

There was a grinding sound, and beyond the bodies a block of pavement as wide as the street rose up as though on hinges, forming a waist-high barricade from wall to wall. Several armed men rose up behind it and pointed their crossbowlike weapons directly at Par and Marnet.

"This whole damn city is a fortress," Thackery exclaimed under his breath.

"I know," Sebright said, tight-lipped. "Tell me why and you'll have done me a favor."

"Contact-1, Contact-4," Guerrieri paged. His voice had lost its impatient edge, lost all expression whatsoever. "Just thought you might like to know. *Descartes* says negative, negative, negative on both Mike and Jael's vitals." The next sound might have been a sigh or an instant of interference. "I'll hold at angels 20 until you need me."

"Acknowledged, Flight-1," Thackery said when Sebright was silent. "It shouldn't be long."

Par and Marnet took no note of the guards and the barricade except to direct their pleas of *"Pan tura!"* in that direction, and advanced until the dray was within a few steps of where the bodies lay. Then, while Marnet held the dray level, Par bent down and picked up Tyszka, cradling him a gentleness that betokened respect. When Par had placed the corpse on the dray bed, he retraced his steps and gathered up Collins with equal reverence.

As they turned the dray to begin their retreat one of the

Gnivian guards raised his weapon to eye level and loosed a deathbird. It flew between Par and Marnet to impale itself in the dashboard of the dray with a *thunk* and the sound of splintering wood. The Gnivian laughed, and Par and Marnet quickened their pace. But the attack ended there. As the dray reached the plaza the guards descended into their warren, the barrier was retracted, and normal traffic resumed, the dust of their passage muddying the blood of the dead.

Thackery rushed to the dray and leaned over Jael, taking her clammy-cool hand in his. The sharp stink of feces, her blank open eyes, the jagged bloody rent in her clothing and chest, set Thackery to retching, and he turned away.

"Thank you," Sebright was saying to Par. "You are a man of conscience."

"I cannot say the same of you. What was your purpose there, for which you sacrificed half your party?"

"To speak to those in the Atad. Are no outsiders permitted?"

"But rarely. I have been there, and a few others. That you must ask the question tells me much about you."

"Then make us equal by telling me something of you."

Par stiffened as though insulted. "I am Par, of the Urmyk. That has always been enough to know." He nodded sharply toward the dray. "There is no mystery in you. You are Gnivi, and you are mad, though I repeat myself too obviously. Take your dead away," he said, and moved off to make a settlement with the dray's owner.

Sebright circled the dray and joined Thackery where he crouched. "I don't know how far I can carry one of them," Thackery said pleadingly, the stench of vomit still on his breath. "We need to bring the gig down."

"This Par has influence. He knows things. I don't intend to let him get away."

"What are you thinking?" Thackery demanded shrilly. "We botched the Contact, and Jael and Mike are dead."

"Hold the postmortems until we're back on *Descartes*. We can't help the kids now. But maybe we can still save the Contact. Is there a Gnivan word for priest? Do you remember hearing anything about their funereary rites?"

"No and no. What? Do you think he's going to get us into the Atad?"

"He may not have to," Sebright said, and left without further explanation. Several long strides caught him up to Par, who had finished his negotiation and was moving off. Sebright planted himself in Par's path. "If you are a man of conscience, help us."

Par scowled. "You require more help than I have patience for."

"A simple matter for Par. We must go to the Atad, for we must speak with the wisest of all men, the exemplar of conscience, he whose domain reaches from one end of the Green Land to the other."

Par spat at Sebright's feet. "You will not find such a man in the Atad."

"Where, then? We have questions for him, and news of places beyond the Green Land."

"You would pursue this while your dead wait for their release?" Par asked, pointing back toward the dray.

Sebright's face took on a thoughtful expression. "I cannot give them release."

"You have no *tomen* to say the words over them?"

"None."

"Do you wish the words said?"

"I wish all to be done as prescribed."

Par crossed his arms over his chest and studied Sebright. "I will take you to Marja."

The change in plans meant renegotiation of the settlement over use of the dray. While Par attended to that detail Sebright returned to where Thackery waited.

"Switch your transceiver to local send and receive," he said to Thackery, walking past without stopping.

Thackery slowly complied, raising his hand to his right ear and pressing the short stub projecting from his ear canal.

"We're going to have an audience from here on out, so I'm not going to be able to hold long discussions with you or stop to explain everything I do," Sebright said in his ear, taking up position on one end of the crossbar. "Keep your eyes open and your mouth shut. Don't contradict me, don't question me. I need as much status as I can get with these people, and I'm starting out pretty damn low. If you spot something you think I need to know about, go off by yourself and say it. I'll hear you fine and we won't give them a reason to be suspicious. Understand?"

The request was reasonable, even prudent, but somehow still felt like *this time, stay out of my way.* Thackery accepted the reproof as his due but could not stay silent. "Why are you tying yourself to these people? That can't help us. Sometime we're going to have to come back here and try to make Contact with the people behind the walls, or at least their bosses."

Then Par joined them, denying the opportunity for an answer. He circled around the back of the dray, stopping when he reached the deathbird projecting from the dashboard. With a yank and a twist, he pulled it free, then tossed it into the dray with a clatter.

"That way," he said, taking the free end of the crossbar and nodding toward the gate.

Thackery fell in behind the dray as they passed through the gate and onto the east road. From there, Collins and Tyszka were always in his field of view, the shafts of the deathbirds still projecting obscenely from their bodies. He forced himself to stay there, to look at them, as a kind of self-flagellation.

If I hadn't been so eager to cozy up to Neale—if I hadn't helped her pressure Sebright—you would still be laughing, Mike, instead of lying on your face in a bouncing dogcart. Jael'd still be making everyone crazy—and I'd still be the bright kid with a future. If, if, if. What a useless emotion regret is. As if the words "I'm sorry" can banish guilt, or excuse stupidity. I'm sorry all the same—

There were few interruptions to dislodge Thackery from his recriminations, for Par showed no inclination to talk. Sebright took his cue from the Urmyk and did not press him. Then, about an hour out from Gnivi, their guide suddenly became voluble.

"You were never in Gnivi before today," Par said.

"Yes."

Par nodded approvingly. "I would have been told. We would have heard of your death."

"How often do such things happen?"

"From time to time. Rarely in the Atad Corridor, because everyone knows it is forbidden. Even the common Gnivi are barred."

"Then you can be shot down on other streets as well?"

"There is no public place where you are not watched, where they could not strike at you if they so chose. There are a hundred tunnels and ten thousand watchplaces." Par paused. "How can you know the Atad and not know things that are taught to children?"

"We have not yet had the chance to learn."

"You are not Gnivi."

"Yes."

"You are not Urmyk."

"Yes."

Par banged the palm of one hand hard against the crossbar and shook his head.

"You're presenting him with a paradox," Thackery offered. "Using their verb formation, one and only one of those statements can be true. You just told him they both were."

"Then you do not even understand why you are alive to make this trip," Par said.

"Is there a reason other than luck?"

"The guardians prefer not to kill all of any party. That way there is someone to carry back the word that Gnivi is strong."

"I understand."

"They want to see fear. If you had not shown it, they would have killed you as well."

"But they did not try to stop you and Marnet."

"Because we gave the sign of submission," Par said exasperatedly. "This is how things are done." Releasing his grip on the shaft, he threw his hands up in the air and took several long, angry strides that put him well out in front of the procession.

"We've got him thinking about us," Thackery said hopefully.

"They're not all good thoughts. We put him in a position where he had to humiliate himself to help us," Sebright said, shifting his grip. "Get on up here and help with this, huh?"

The Urmyk home to which Par took them was less than a village and more than a camp. In a copse of smooth-rinded, waxy-leaved trees was an elevated platform for the storage of food, under which were stowed an array of hand tools, two drays, and a larger four-wheeled farm wagon.

Slung between the surrounding trees in groups of two or three, often one above the other like a multistory house, were some two dozen sleeping hammocks. Some of the hammocks were rolled and tied, as though to keep them from collecting rain and detritus. Other hanging places were empty, as though some of the community were away for an extended time.

Leaving the *Descartes* men to stand by the dray and accept the questioning stares of the Urmyk, Par went into a huddle with a wrinkle-faced gnome of a man whose silver hair was combed straight back into what appeared to be a permanent tangle.

"This is more organized than we had given them credit for," Sebright said. "They aren't just gatherers. They've got to be doing some farming."

"They also have to have some ground-living pests. Everything is up."

The conference over, Par led the older man toward them.

"Marja," Par said, and walked away, his disgust evident.

The old man reached out to finger the material of Thackery's allover, then stepped back and squinted at them. "You are not of the Urmyk. Why do you ask our death-customs be followed? Have you none of your own?"

"Our friends died in your lands and at the hands of your enemies," Sebright said.

"They died in the city of despair and at the hands of cowards," Marja said, more a correction of fact than a reproof. "What are the names of the dead?"

"The woman is Jael. The other is Michael."

Marja turned to the others looking on. "Prepare *canuta*," he ordered.

Because of the difficulty the Urmyk women had with the zippers and stays, Thackery was drafted to help undress and bathe the corpses. It was an exceedingly unpleasant task, the more so since he had from time to time imagined undressing Jael in a far different context and circumstance. Those pleasant fantasies were irrevocably trashed by the sight of her brutally violated death-white skin, and he found it difficult to touch her.

The three Urmyk women, particularly a round-bodied middle-aged woman named Taj, showed no such compunctions. It was Taj who wrestled the barbed heads of the deathbirds from the two corpses and then neatly tucked back in the ragged edges of the wounds. Taj also took the time to take note of every subtle evidence that the Descartans were not-Gnivi, not-Urmyk:

their teeth, their smoothly trimmed nails, their thinly calloused feet, the transceivers plugging the left ears, the small strawberry tattoo on Jael's hip, the appendectomy scar on Michael's abdomen.

She said nothing about her observations, either to Thackery or to her two assistants, but she absented herself before the preparations were through, disappearing in the direction Marja had gone with Sebright. Meanwhile, the other women produced several lengths of coarse fiber rope, and proceeded to tightly bind each corpse at the ankles, knees, wrists, and elbows.

"Contact-4, got a moment here. Somebody just corralled Marja for a conference. He's been showing me the fields," Sebright said in Thackery's ear. "The Urmyk idea of farming seems to be to keep a natural mix of crops, not in rotation but at the same time. So they don't really have fields, more like cultivated foraging areas. They prune out the weaker plants and lay them out for the pests. By the way, I got a glimpse of one, and if it wasn't a mouse, it was something you wouldn't mind calling one. If you're free to talk, let me know how things are progressing. Any idea yet whether we're looking at burial or cremation?"

"Not really," Thackery said. "Is that person talking to Marja a stocky woman, forty-ish, wearing a vest a couple sizes too small for her?"

"That's her."

"Then the conference is about us. She gave Mike and Jael a real close going-over, and she's probably giving him an earful about just how strange we are."

"Good," Sebright said, inexplicably. "Looks like we're going to head back. See you presently."

As dusk came on, the bodies were taken to the west edge of the copse, where they were laid side by side near the base of a tall waxleaf tree. The Urmyk formed a one-deep circle around the bodies, and Marja moved into the center. He stood over the bodies and spoke to them.

"Spirit of Jael. Spirit of Michael. Witness the service we now do you, that you may depart to the place and condition where you now belong."

The Urmyk then began to chant, voices hushed as though a group whisper:

Spirit free
Fly to heaven
Leave friends in peace
Accept your ending

Par came forward as Marja retreated, knelt and grasped Jael's corpse in a headlock. In his other hand flashed a small tool Thackery could not recognize. The Urmyk's body blocked Thackery's view of what was happening.

"What are they doing?" he demanded of Sebright, who stood at the opposite end of the circle, chanting with the others as he looked on.

"Trephination."

"What?"

"Drilling holes in the skull."

"That's barbar—"

SPIRIT FREE, FLY TO HEAVEN

The chant suddenly grew louder as Par leaped to his feet and held the plug of scalp and hair high above his head for the group to see. Then he knelt by Tyszka and began again.

"Think what you like, but keep it off your face," Sebright said. "If you show disapproval, you may ruin what I'm trying to do."

"Which is what?"

"Win us an audience with the man we came to Gnivi to see."

The chant grew even louder as Par stood again with another trophy. Then he brought the plug from Michael's body to Thackery, and from Jael's to Sebright.

"My words, now," Sebright called out suddenly, and stepped forward. The chant died away to a murmur, and both Par and Marja showed displeasure at the interruption.

But Sebright took no notice. Kneeling between the bodies, he bowed his head and began to pray, "Creator of the numberless worlds, Architect of the design of life, Guardian of our immortal souls, accept these Your servants into the everlasting peace of death, preserving them in Your living memory for the infinite time to come."

The prayer was a double-barreled surprise for Thackery. The first was that Sebright chose to say it loudly and clearly in English, though it was perfectly translatable. The second was the prayer itself: It was part of the Rite of Death of the Universal Creation Church.

But the prayer seemed to please the Urmyk, who cheered Sebright as he left the circle and came to stand with Thackery.

"Was that just for show, or are you a Creationist?"

"Most human cultures have an abiding respect for mysticism, even someone else's mysticism."

"That doesn't answer my question."

"I know."

In the meantime, the Urmyk had taken up their rhythmic, poetic chant again. Sebright joined in loudly, elbowing Thackery to do the same. They looked on as two young Urmyk men came forward and hoisted the bodies pick-a-back, their bound arms giving Collins and Tyszka an unflagging grip on their respective bearers' necks.

"Pallbearers," Sebright said in an aside to Thackery.

Then, in a startling display of strength even for an 0.8 gravity field, the Urmyk began to climb the tree, hauling themselves upward from limb to limb with an agility that defied the dead weights with which they were burdened. Within a short span of time, during which the chant took on a more belligerent tenor, Collins and Tyszka were left hanging naked from a high branch of the tree, dangling from ropes looped under their armpits.

The sight of it brought all of Thackery's accumulated outrage welling up. "We can't leave them there," he said angrily. "They were our friends—shipmates. To see them like this—what kind of deal are you making with these people? What can they do for you that will be worth this kind of disgrace?"

Sebright took Thackery by the arm and steered him firmly toward the yellow fires which marked the heart of the copse, falling in step with the Urmyk who were scattering, laughing and jabbering, to their chores and games.

"Disgrace? Can't you see the beauty in the ceremony?"

"Boring holes in people's heads!"

"Cro-Magnon people did it while the patient was alive, to exorcise demons," Sebright said. "With the Urmyk it's different. They seem to fear recrudescence, as if the dead person has a choice between reanimating the body and passing on. That explains everything we saw—binding the body, the trephination, hanging them in a high place. They want the dead to stay dead, so they load the choice, encourage the spirit to leave—think about the chant. All of which means they have the profound self-awareness to know that something leaves the body at death, and the humanity to wish well for it. You judge them too harshly."

"You may say so—"

"Stop introducing your cultural biases. Accept them on their own terms. You may see things you can't now," Sebright said sharply. "Look, Marja has provided a hammock for each of us. I'm going to make good use of mine. I suggest you do the same."

But before he could settle in, Sebright was intercepted by a young Urmyk girl. "Marja wants you, at the tree of the dead," she said, then skipped away.

A crooked grin lit up Sebright's face. "I think this is it," he said, and started back the way they had come.

"What do you want me to do?" Thackery called after him.

"Eavesdrop," Sebright threw back over his shoulder.

Thackery lay in his hammock and listened, feeling useless and extraneous.

—We have all watched you, and none can say when they have seen such before. Par believes you are spies from the Gnivi, that the Atad plots again to make its dominion grow. Taj believes you are golem.

—We are neither of those things. We are brothers. We breathe as one, our hearts beat to the same rhythm. We are part of you, and you are part of us.

—So my eyes tell me. But where have you come from? And why have you come here?

—The last I have told Par already. We come to talk with the wisest of all men, the exemplar of conscience, he whose domain reaches from one end of the Green Land to the other.

—Then talk, for I am he.

Braggart, Thackery thought.

—First there are things I must understand. Why is the city armed against you?

—They fear us because we are strong. They hate us because they must depend on us.

—For food?

—Yes.

—And you depend on them for your metal tools, for the wheels of your drays—

—We depend on them for nothing. We need none of that for ourselves, only for what we do for them. If you traveled farther from the city, you would see none of these things.

—Why do you feed the Gnivi?

—It is the price of peace. So long as they need us, the Atad dare not anger us too much.

—Why do they not come out of the city and gather their own food?

—Because I will not permit it.

—You could defeat them?

—In our lands, as they could defeat us in theirs.

—How long has this been the order?

—Thirty generations.

—And you are content with it?

—They see us come into the city, and know that we are free, and that they are not. In time, the Gnivi will grow tired of their imprisonment, and place new leaders in the Atad.

—What about before?

—Before, we built the city.

Thackery sat bolt upright in his hammock, nearly falling out in the process. "These are the real Gnivi," he exclaimed aloud.

—Who was the first Urmyk?

—No one knows.

—I know. He was one of us.

—And what is that? Where are you from? From the Lake of Salts? From the Brown Lands?

—If you climb to the top of the highest tree, can you see all men everywhere? Can you see to the end of a road when you stand on it? Or are there men and places beyond seeing, even the sight of the wisest of the Urmyk?

—There are.

—We are from such a place, of such a distance that no Urmyk alive has ever traveled there.

—We have been the length of the river and the breadth of the Green Land.

—You have not traveled into the sky.

Silence.

—Is Taj right, after all? You come from the place of the dead?

—The sky is larger than you have imagined, and there is room enough for both the dead and the living. Every light that you see above us is a land larger than that the Urmyk know.

—A place too far to see—

—Yes.

—Each star—

—Every one.

—In times recent, there was a new star—There. See it there.

The canopy overhead was too thick for Thackery to see through, but he doubted *Descartes* was even a second magnitude star. The fact that the Urmyk had noticed it said much.

—That is our home. When the sun rises, I will call down a dray from it. My companion and I are needed elsewhere. But if you will accept them, we will leave others, to stay with you, to learn from you about you, to teach you of us. Will you accept them? Will you make them part of the Urmyk?

There was barely an instant's hesitation.

—We will.

In the morning, they waited for the gig in the field to the east of Marja's camp. *Your finest hour,* Thackery thought as he looked at Sebright. *You plucked triumph out of the disaster I created.*

Sebright caught the look. "Regrets?"

"Jael and Mike."

"They bought us our introduction. You still regret leaving them?"

"No," he said truthfully. "They died here. Where else should they be?"

"Something else, then."

Thackery shrugged. "You didn't even need me."

"Because you did your job right when we were still on board. I didn't want to need you here. Or anyone."

Then Marja joined them to watch the gig spiral down. As it grew nearer and its size became clear, several of the Urmyk fled to the safety of the edge of the copse, and when the noise of its engines reached the ground most of the rest joined them there. Marja flinched but stayed at their elbow, and was the first to move forward when the gig had come to rest.

Thackery hung back as Eagan and Muir disembarked and Sebright made introductions. There were muted words of congratulations and bittersweet hugs. Then Eagan pressed past and came to where Thackery stood.

"You screwed up," he said, his face hard and unfriendly.

"I know," Thackery said.

But his admission of guilt did not end the chill. It lingered as they worked together to unload the two trunk-sized cases containing the deep-space transmitter and the two satchels of personal gear, and passed the equipment and their owners into the custody of Marja's family. Muir did not speak to him at all.

All too quickly, there was nothing left to do but board the gig and leave, nothing more to postpone the accounting. Thackery had his hand on the ramp railing when one of the girls who had helped prepare the bodies—Thackery did not even know her name—ran from Taj's side across the field to him.

"You still grieve," she said, breathless from running.

"Yes."

She pressed something into his hand. "So that you might replace those who are lost," she said earnestly.

He opened his hand to find a black wood statuette, two-faced, Janus-like. One side was female, a woman with a distended belly and pendulous breasts, the other male, improbably gifted and triumphantly erect. The craftmanship was superb, the symbolism obvious. It was a fertility icon.

The gift was a gesture as poignant as it was pointless. His eyes moistening, Thackery closed his hand over the icon and looked up at the girl's hopeful face.

"Thank you," he said, and turned away to climb the ramp.

But his grief was not over Jael and Michael, for their trials were ended. It was for himself, and for the realization that in leaving Gnivi he was closing out his career, that he would never walk on a world other than Earth again. His ambition had cost the lives of two of his friends, and he could not imagine that either he or the Service would be willing to forget that.

PARADOX

(from Merritt Thackery's
JIADUR'S WAKE)

... The Service's carefully laid out scheme of expansion very nearly came apart even as it was coalescing. Problems of logistics, erratic morale at the Advance Bases, and a shortage of ships to back up the advancing survey vessels were all factors. But at the heart of the problem was communication.

For, despite the fleetness of the AVLO-drive ships, communication between them, the Advance Bases, and Unity was limited by the electromagnetic medium and its 300,000 kilometres per second speed limit. Through the first half of Phase II, every advance in Service communications technology had to do with compressing data, extending the useful range of transmitters, or increasing the operating efficiency. Nothing could be done about speeding the message on its way.

That created a curious situation wherein the fastest way to deliver critical news was to send a messenger. There was no Einsteinian paradox involved, no more than if you should mail an invitation to a neighbor, then walk next door to cancel it before it was delivered.

But there were problems all the same. Every base, every ship, was on its own time zone, and the time zones were not hours but decades apart. A dialog between installations was impossible when your nearest "neighbor" lived far away in the past or in the future. Contemporaneity was fast becoming a lost concept except to Service historians, to whom it was a continuing nightmare. In short, the vast expanses which the Service had conquered threatened to divide and conquer the Service itself. . . .

chapter 9

Not On My Watch

When the gig docked, Guerrieri did his best to make up with enthusiasm for what the reception lacked in numbers. Later, there were many calls of congratulations from upship: Tefft Voss, Jessie, Bayn Graeff, even Dunn. But the congratulations left Thackery cold, unaffected.

I have no claim to the success of Gnivi, only to the disaster, he told himself, and there was no one to argue.

As Thackery had anticipated, Neale was already preparing *Descartes* for a quick return to A-Cyg with the Gnivi data. He had expected that they would at least wait out the thirty-six hour post-Contact isolation period, giving the liaison team a chance to settle in and report any problems. But within an hour of the gig's return, the order was given which sent *Descartes* climbing out of orbit to begin its return trip. Baldwin caught one encouraging dispatch from the liaison team before crazing, but that was all.

With two lost and two left behind and the isolation hatch still sealed, contact country was suddenly a large and lonely place. Thackery rattled around aimlessly, unable to concentrate on the work that needed doing, withdrawn into himself. Even the sound of Guerrieri's hammer dulcimer, which Thackery had always regarded as bright and joyful, seemed funereal and mocking instead.

But when he stopped by the astrophysicist's cabin to ask him to stop or close his door, Thackery found himself hungry for companionship, and instead walked in and sat down.

"Hey, an audience," Guerrieri said, the mallets light in his fingers, flashing precisely against the taut steel strings. "Thack— I was wondering—do you want to double up?"

"No," Thackery said, shaking his head.

"Like the elbow room, eh?"

"I just don't think it's a good idea."

"Post-Contact blues?"

"How many ships do you know have lost crew in landings?"

Guerrieri stopped playing and considered. "I know *Hugin* lost one, because that's how McAullife's Planet got its name. *Nestor's* gig crashed, so they lost half their team. Those were both survey landings, though, not contact landings. Is this the first time anyone's lost people during a Contact?"

"Unless someone has since we went out."

"Well—I wouldn't dwell on it. We did find a colony. The Flight Office is going to care a lot more about that than about Mike and Jael."

"That's nonsense. They can't just shrug it off."

"I suppose not. Still—it wasn't your fault, eh?"

"Wasn't it?"

"No, of course not. If you want to be fair about it, it was the Gnivi."

"But it wouldn't have happened if we'd waited until we knew more about them."

"Sebright made the decision, didn't he? And Neale was right there."

"But I made the recommendation," Thackery said sullenly.

"They didn't have to take it." Guerrieri shrugged. "You don't need to worry unless Sebright decides to pin it on you."

"He's never said so much as one word of reproof. I wish he would. Waiting for it is worse."

"Sounds like you're going to be okay, then."

Thackery shook his head. "You don't understand. I *am* responsible. I don't intend to duck it or fight it. I accept it."

Guerrieri reached for the mallets. "You're too rough on yourself. Nothing's going to happen. Don't you think they expected to lose some of us? Probably more of us than they have. Back in the office this won't be seen as a screw-up. Back there this is just kismet." He resumed playing, the haunting sound engaging ambivalent emotions as it chased Thackery back to his cabin.

• • •

The inquiry hearing was held behind closed doors in the library.

"They're here," Shaffer reported to the waiting board, which consisted of Neale, Rogen, and Dunn. "Would you like them one at a time or together?"

"Thackery first," Neale told the awk, raising an eyebrow in the direction of the others. "Unless there are objections?"

The others demurred, and Neale nodded to Shaffer. "Show him in."

There had been a change in Thackery, Neale saw immediately. As he walked in and took his seat there was nothing of the eager-to-please lesser who had walked into her Unity office for his first interview, nothing of the calculating new black he had been for most of the mission to date. There was something new in his bearing, something which suggested he would be less tractable. *No great loss,* she thought. *I'm almost done with him.*

"You understand that the purpose of this inquiry is to determine the circumstances which led to the loss of Technoanalyst Michael Tyszka and Interpolator Jael Collins during the Gnivi Contact," Rogen was saying.

"Yes," said Thackery.

"This is not a fitness review nor a personal evaluation. This is an inquiry into the performance of the entire team. It is not the role of this board to recommend to the Flight Office any action on behalf of or against any member of the team. This is purely an informational exercise."

"I understand."

"Very well. Commander?" Rogen said, deferring to Neale.

"Merry, would you describe the events leading up to the attack by the Gnivi guardsmen?"

It was the first time he had been called that by anyone except Diana, and he decided immediately he did not like it. He could not tell from Neale's expression whether she used it knowingly, to goad him, or innocently, to relax him. Either way, he hoped she would not make a habit of it. "There's not much I can add to what's in the telecamera and transceiver recordings."

"Go ahead anyway," Neale said pleasantly.

The telling took several minutes, starting with the entry at the East Gate and ending with the appearance of Par.

"Thank you, that's enough," Neale said, cutting him off.

"In your estimation, would an immediate pickup have afforded the injured members of the team the medical attention necessary to save one or both of them?"

"I—don't know. From what I saw of the wounds later, I doubt it."

"The Gnivi weapons weren't explosive, were they? You had no indication that a poison was used?"

"No."

"Then they bled to death."

"I have basic Service EMT training, that's all. I can't really say," Thackery said. "I didn't see much of Michael. Jael was closest to me."

"But they lived for several minutes."

"Those aren't the easiest circumstances to keep track of time. I suppose they did. Didn't the biotelemetry tell you what happened?"

Neale ignored the question. "In your estimation, wouldn't a more prudent course have been to make a preliminary Contact with the pedestrians in the East Gate plaza?"

"It sure looks that way now," Thackery said. "But in my opinion, the mistake was made earlier."

"Oh? When?"

"We landed prematurely. We should have taken more time to evaluate the Gnivian society. As linguist, I should have insisted on planting peepers among the rurals as well, as a cross-check on dialect and as a source of an alternate perspective. If I had done that, Mike and Jael would still be alive. And we knew that Gnivan was a written language, but I didn't think it was crucial to the Contact. I was wrong. If we had been able to read the warnings at the entrance to Broadway, Mike and Jael would still be alive."

"So you blame yourself," Rogen said.

"I do."

"Do you have command responsibility, Mr. Thackery?" Neale asked lazily.

"No. But the Contact Leader is obliged to rely on what we tell him. If we tell him things that aren't true, or are only partly true, he can't be held accountable for the decisions that flow from them."

"Thank you for your thoughts," Neale said. "Do the rest of you have any other questions? Very well, Merry, you can go."

In the few moments between Thackery's departure and Sebright's arrival, Dunn turned to Neale. "Very forward about taking responsibility."

"That's Thackery's style," Neale said idly. "Very conscientious. We have to remember, though, that he's also loyal to the Concom. Who wouldn't be, in that situation? They were the only two to survive, and it was Sebright who got Thackery out of danger. You have to expect him to feel an obligation."

The door opened then to admit Sebright. When he had settled himself before them, Neale rocked back in her chair. "All right, Mark. What went wrong down there?"

"I think it's pretty obvious. We walked into the middle of a jacquerie."

"How is it possible that we sent a team down there not knowing that?"

"The Gnivi have had two hundred years of armed standoff to prettify their fortifications so their populace isn't constantly confronted with reminders of war and potential war. That concealment made it possible for us to misread the balance of economic and political power between the city-dwellers and the rurals."

"And whose fault was that?"

"No one's."

Dunn leaned forward and rested his forearms on the table. "How can you say that?"

"We were forced to proceed on the basis of incomplete information."

Neale's eyebrow shot up. "Again, whose fault was that?"

"You're *always* going to have incomplete information from an aerial survey. Cultures don't assay as neatly as rock formations, Commander. We made the best guess possible under the circumstances. We were wrong."

"And who was responsible for making that guess?"

"There's no hard line in a contact team separating one person's responsibility from another's. It's a group effort."

"Please," Dunn said tiredly, "let's not try to protect anyone, Concom Sebright. Who was responsible for the miss?"

"Since you insist," Sebright said, meeting Neale's gaze, "it was really Mike and Jael's call. It was Mike's job to assess the technological level of the culture. He underestimated the level of the rurals, which reinforced our natural bias toward the city as the seat of power. And it was Jael's job to read between the lines and see the inconsistencies in the model."

"Now isn't that convenient, if the dead were responsible for their own deaths."

"You're the one who wanted names. I don't look on it that way. Everything that happened, good and bad, belongs to all of us equally."

"A very egalitarian outlook," Neale said. "That will be all."

"Not quite, Commander. I'd like a word with you outside."

After a moment's hesitation, she pushed back her chair and followed him out.

"I know what you were trying to do in there," he said, leaning close. "You wanted me to name Thack. That stinks, Ali. You know the position you put the kid in. How can you climb on him now for doing what you asked?"

"You don't need to worry about Thackery," she said reassuringly.

He squinted at her suspiciously. "I have your word on that?"

"You do."

When they came out of the craze a fortnight later, it was impossible to see the base they had left and the jewellike city revealed on the monitors as the same structure. Cygnus had done more than grow—it had undergone a metamorphosis as dramatic as that experienced by any hymnopeteran.

For all Thackery could tell by looking, the original base had been either discarded or completely disassembled. Instead of a slender spire, Cygnus now had a cubic structure easily a hundred times the previous volume. Atop the base, extended from the "roof" like antennae, were two tall docking masts. Slung beneath the bulk of the station, also two in number, were the familiar upside-down U shapes of shipways. One of the 'ways was occupied by some sort of capital ship, though Thackery could not see enough of it to know even which series.

But Thackery could not spend too much time sight-seeing. *Descartes* had regained its senses a mere five hours out, truncating the final leg of the journey. Just an hour later, the word came down from the bridge:

"After discussions with base authorities, Commander Neale advises that all personnel will leave the ship at Cygnus. That's the good news, folks—a change of scenery. The bad news is that you have to clean up after yourselves before you go."

Thackery had already anticipated leaving the ship, so his own quarters were in order. But with that news, there were

Michael's things to look after, and Jael's, and an empty cabin to police, and samples to be readied for transfer, and a contact lab to put in order. By the time Thackery and Guerrieri were ready, most of the awks and techs had already departed.

Thackery's last stop was his own cabin, to pick up his gear. On the way out, he paused at the door, the duffle bag slung over one shoulder, and looked back at the now-empty compartment. He thought about Danny McShane, his first cabinmate, and about Michael, his last, and he felt the sadness welling up from his chest. *It didn't go well for any of us, did it?*

A few metres down the corridor, Guerrieri emerged from his cabin and joined him.

"Not getting sentimental, are you now? You'll be back," he said, clapping Thackery on the shoulder.

"No," Thackery said soberly as he pulled the door shut. "Not to this cabin, or this ship. That much I know."

A-Cyg's port facilities had improved to the point that there was no need for *Descartes* to attempt to maneuver its bulk in close to the fragile structure of the base. Instead, *Descartes* stood off a thousand metres while a six-place people-mover shuttled back and forth between the D-deck hatch and one of the docking masts. Except for the dour-countenanced pilot, Thackery and Guerrieri were the only passengers for the ten-minute run.

On reaching the docking mast, they squeezed into a tiny lift for the descent to the top level of the base. Then it was down a long, brightly lit, gently downward-sloping corridor which ended at a transfer lounge reminiscent of those at Unity: plush seating and carpeting, comfort stations, skylights through which the docking masts and the silhouette of *Descartes* could be seen. The expansive lounge was capable of handling fifty or more people at a time, but the only other person there was a green-clad awk sprawled in a chair and watching the basenet.

"Check-in to your right," the awk called to them without looking up.

To the right, three contiguous Synglas-enclosed offices under a TRANSFER PROCESSING sign made a barrier to the concourse beyond, with broad red lines in the carpet showing where queues should form. Beyond the offices, Thackery could see a row of speedlift doors and what appeared to be a gift shop.

A young woman—hardly more than a girl—sat behind the sickle-shaped desk in one of the offices, watching the newcomers expectantly. They took the cue and headed for her.

"One at a time," said the aide sharply as they tried to enter together.

Guerrieri and Thackery looked at each other. "You go ahead," Guerrieri said with a shrug, and retreated outside.

The door slid shut with a hiss. "Have a seat," she said, gesturing. He could not help but briefly stare at her legs, naked to the thigh except for the Greek-style crisscross lacings which climbed upward from her sandals. When he looked up, their eyes met, and he realized guiltily that she had noticed—and probably misread—his interest.

"You've done remarkable things here since we left," Thackery said as he settled in the chair, trying to redirect both their thoughts. "What's the population now?"

She considered a moment before answering. "We just hit eleven thousand permanent residents, plus a few hundred temporaries. Including you. What's your name?"

"Merritt Andrew Thackery."

"Assignment?"

"Contact Linguist, *Descartes*."

"And your Service number?"

The question surprised Thackery. "I don't know. We don't use them on board."

She tsked and shook her head. "Better learn it. You'll need it for everything around here. How long are you staying?"

"I don't know."

"Well, I just came on, so I don't know—." She glanced at a note posted to her right. "Oh, here we are. *Descartes*'s in for Kleine refit?"

"I don't know what that is. We're just back from the Gnivi colony."

"I know. But you're still going to get a refit. The schedule says thirty-one weeks."

"I don't expect to be on her when she goes back out."

Her instructions apparently left no room for variables. "At the moment you're officially attached to her, right? Then you're looking at thirty-one weeks. Which means I can get you a double-wide instead of the standard apartment, and it'll only cost you another three hundred a week."

Thackery gaped. "I'm supposed to pay for this?"

"Well, of course. What did you think?"

"I thought we were all Service—"

She straightened up in her chair. "We are, but that doesn't mean we can afford to give out free room and board. How do you expect us to earn our trade credits, if not by servicing the ships and looking after the crews?"

"But I don't have anything to pay with—"

"Silly. Here's the balance in your Service account," she said, rotating her display toward him.

The figure was a little over € 600,000, which stunned Thackery to silence.

"With that kind of money, I wouldn't think you'd worry about the extra for a double-wide," she continued.

"My account was being managed at Unity," he said, confused. "When did they transfer it here?"

"Transfer it? No, you don't understand, your account is updated every day. We're linked to all the Unity records. Oh, wait a minute. That's right—*Descartes* doesn't have its Kleine yet, so you wouldn't know about all this. See, we're in constant contact with Unity. I can call them about as easily as I can call someone down on Seacrest Level."

"How is that possible?"

"Oh, God, I don't know, I'm just an Operations aide. We've had it for sixty years, though. You'll be one of the last ships to get it."

The proposition implicit in her words was so jarring to Thackery's sense of the way the Universe worked that rather than deal with it, he set it aside. "This can't be anything like a full-time assignment for you. How much traffic are you folks getting in here these days?"

She seemed not to mind the digression. "No, not full time. But we get a packet every three months from Unity, plus the odd survey ship every now and then."

"Every three months?" Thackery thought a moment. "That means there'd have to be forty or so packets en route at any given moment. Eighty, if you count the ones on their way back."

"Why, sure, I guess so."

"I didn't think the Procurement Office would ever get us ships in those kind of numbers."

"It hasn't. The packets are operated by USS-Transport."

"Do the crews wear the black?"

"Well, sure," she said. She brushed her longish hair back and showed him her own black ellipse, worn like jewelry on the collar of her blouse. "Everybody out here does. What's the matter?"

"I don't think you'd understand," Thackery said, subdued.

She did not notice his change of mood. "Anyway, there's a packet due in about six weeks, so you'll get to see one then."

"How many survey ships are working this sector now?"

"Three, when they're all out: *Tycho*, *Munin*, and your ship. But you and *Munin* are both here now. *Tycho*'s about eleven lights out. We don't hear much from them."

That answered the question of which ship he had seen in the yard. Thackery pursed his lips. "Look, try not to take this the way it sounds, but is everyone taking the Contact with Gnivi pretty casually?"

She laughed, a musical titter. "Oh, no, you're wrong. We were beginning to think we'd be the last octant to find a colony—even to worry a little that there might not be any out this way at all. We're really happy about you people. This puts Cygnus on the map, and'll mean that much more traffic for us. Honestly, we've just been scraping by with the Unity shuttle traffic. But now we'll start getting noticed by the Intercolony Support Office, and that's where the profit is."

Not everything she said was meaningful to Thackery, least of all the last part. He had never heard of the ISO, and the motive she cited seeming jarringly out of place. "There wasn't much of a reception," he said, jerking his thumb in the direction of the awk, now dozing in front of the screen. "It seems like there'd be a little more fuss over the fifth colony."

"Fifth? Try eighth. Gnivi is the third colony in two months. Don't worry, though. I'm sure there's going to be a dinner honoring you, and probably some commendations handed out, too."

"Oh." Again, Thackery was brought up short by a reminder that time had not stood still while *Descartes* had been on station. "What about my room, then?"

"Your apartment is on Scirocco Place, number 76," she said, handing him a magcard that appeared at a slot near her elbow. Glancing at it, he saw that it bore his face, name, rating, and Service number. "There's a help menu on the basenet that will tell you all about restaurants and recreation," she went on, "just about anything you want. And you can always page the base library or our offices if you can't find what you need."

He slipped the card into a pocket and stood. "Thank you."

"You were the linguist," she said, cocking her head to study him. "You went on the landing."

"Yes."

"Look, I have to take care of your friend out there. But if you want to wait, I'll be happy to help you find your apartment, show you around..." Her voice trailed off, making the offer open-ended.

Memories of Diana came rushing back, unpleasant, painful. "How old are you?"

"Nineteen," she said brightly.

"I'm a hundred and sixty-six," Thackery said coldly. "I don't think we'd have much in common." As he passed out of the office into the concourse, he shut his eyes to the wounded look that appeared on her face.

Thackery found his apartment without difficulty, and having done so found himself with nothing to do but wait, wait for the bureaucratic wheels to grind round, wait for the word to come down that would end this misadventure and give him a chance to start again.

While he waited he made use of the basenet to try to fill in the blanks remaining from his conversation with the Ops aide. The biggest blank was the Kleine transmitter, so he started there.

According to the Worldnet announcement made some fifty-five years ago, the Kleine was exactly what Thackery had surmised: a transrelative deep-space communications system. It was not instantaneous, but the lag between Cygnus and Unity, lying some twenty-five light-years away, was a mere three minutes. "Transmitter," however, was a bit of misnomer, since no one had been able to measure or even detect anything physical being transmitted.

The system was named for Arthur Kleine, the Technology Office drive engineer credited with the admittedly serendipitous discovery, but the homonymous suggestion of the crazy geometry of a Klein bottle was equally appropriate. Kleine had designed new development instrumentation for a pair of identical prototypes of the O-series drive. During the first field test of OX-1 in deep space beyond the Oort Cloud, the data meant for the screens of the test team appeared almost instantly on the monitors before the techs preparing OX-2—half a light-day away in the labs of the Technology Office research center. The system seemed to have only two limitations: It only worked in conjunction with an AVLO drive, and it, too, did not work during the craze.

"That's too damn easy," Thackery protested aloud. "God knows the Service needs it, but really—"

Indignation sent Thackery in search of the technical reports on the Kleine system. To the extent that he could understand them, he found no hard data, no cogent explanations, only speculation disguised as theory. *Just like drive theory.* The most frequently cited paper, by Walters and Highsmith, proposed that an operating AVLO drive created "energy corridors" with every other AVLO drive, through which the Kleine units propagated their transmissions.

But there was vanishingly little evidence, experimental or mathematical, on which to evaluate the Walters/Highsmith theory. In fact, considering its metaphysical flavor and the impossibility of direct observation, the theory had all the marks of being both unprovable and irrefutable.

Which is no doubt why it's so popular. Where's Karl Popper when we really need him? Thackery thought wryly as he cleared the screen to take up a new subject.

Thackery found the "free enterprise" turn that Advance Base operations had taken to be, after examination, equally incomprehensible. He freely admitted that biases carried over from Georgetown and his first career track were at the root of the problem.

Except for the capital-formation mechanisms and a few independent corporations left alone for efficiency's sake, the World Council had diligently rooted out the profit motive from the Earth's economic life. The financial infrastructure that remained, transfer payments and community service fees, salaries and prices, merely provided a familiar handle on what was, in effect, a planet-wide barter market.

With a less complex system and a better educated population, the Survey service had foregone even that crutch. Since boarding *Tycho* ever so long ago, Thackery had not once needed to think of money. His salary was nothing more or less than a recruitment bribe, paid according to mission elapsed time (but earning interest according to Unity elapsed time) and collectible on his return to Earth and its monetized economy. He had never expected to see a penny of it until then.

But suddenly he was in a pay-as-you-go world, drawing against that account for every minor service and amenity. There was an immigration fee, a lodging fee, an environmental services fee, a net access fee, a maintenance and housekeeping fee—Thackery had only begun to learn the variations, and already the list seemed endless. Though the rates quoted by the Ops aide would hardly make him a pauper, not even through the remainder of a full normal lifetime, Thackery bitterly resented every debit and considered the entire practice piracy and worse.

It was obvious from the Ops aide that the residents did not share his outrage. The four-place packets, their run sliced to eleven years actual, sixteen days perceptual by the I-series drives, brought in trade goods, emigrants, USS inspectors, even a few tourists. Cygnus Base could have anything Unity had to offer—when they could pay for it.

Their community-wide goal was full shipbuilding capability, the stated intent building, staffing, and supporting a survey ship to be named *Cygnus*. But there were also studies underway on the feasibility of opening "corner-to-corner" trade routes with the Advance Bases in adjoining octants, or, barring that, selling packets to USS-Transport itself.

If this is what the Service is coming to, then it's past time I got out, he told himself lugubriously.

Dispirited, Thackery asked for a summary directory of the colonies. The directory confirmed that Gnivi was, in fact, eighth on the list. The new colonies were Daehne, thirty-three lights out in the constellation Serpens, discovered by Weber in *Magellan;* Dzuba, twenty-nine lights out in Canis Major, credited to Hiscox and *Amundsen;* and an extinct colony on 22 Hercules-5, uncovered by Higuchi and the crew of *Hillary.*

And in none of the Contacts had any surveyors died.

Turning off the display, Thackery settled back on his bed to mull over what he had learned. And when he was done, he walked three blocks to a rec outlet and brought back a jeroboam of the local sweet red wine.

When the wine was half drunk and Thackery thoroughly so, he returned to the basenet and tried to access one last bit of data to fill in one last blank. When he could not, he corked the bottle, left the apartment, made an unsteady trip to Castle Place to see the base librarian.

"This may seem like a strange request," he said, his words less slurred than they seemed to him, "but I wonder if you could get me some information on one of the base's original crew."

"Of course," the Com aide said brightly. "May I have your card, please?"

Thackery felt several pockets before finding the one to which he had consigned the hated object. Extracting the card with some difficulty, he slid it across the counter.

"That's actually a fairly common request for people of your era," she said, clued by his low Service number. She was unconscious of the insult in her words, but at that point so was Thackery. "What's the name?"

"Diana Marks."

"It'll be just a moment, those records aren't kept online. When were you last here?"

Thackery had to make an effort to remember. "'13."

"Oh, my, you have missed a lot. Here we are. Marks, Diana Elizabeth, chemical technologist. Shipped to Cygnus in *Descartes* as part of the pioneer team, as you said. Productivity award in '19—not much else. Had a daughter in '14, name of Andrea—make that Andra. Mother and daughter both shipped out back to Earth in '21 aboard the packet *Audubon*."

The alcohol coursing through Thackery's body diminished the impact of that news, but it could not fully abate it. Leaning heavily on the counter, he closed his eyes and rested his forehead on his folded hands. "Is there anything in there about the father of the girl?"

"She gave it as an M. Thackery, no further information. Apparently Vital Statistics wasn't able to confirm that, because it's listed as anecdotal rather than genetic." The aide's eyes suddenly widened. "M. Thackery—is that you? Was that your child?"

Thackery did not answer. He was already tottering toward the door with all the speed his rubbery legs could muster, his stomach churning threateningly. He made it to the corridor before the cramps won and dropped him to his knees in a puddle of second-hand wine and tears.

"I did it, too," he sobbed, his pain making him oblivious to the stares of the library aide and the pedestrians in the corridor. "Freezin' Christ, just like my father. I did it, too."

•   •   •

It was a chastened and subdued Thackery that was released from the A-Cyg detox center at eleven the next morning. He went directly home, curled up on the bed fully dressed, and took a three-hour nap. When he arose from it, the lingering effects of both the alcohol and the concoctions the center had used to banish it were finally gone. The memory of what had triggered his display, unfortunately, had not.

Declaring war on self-destructive thinking, Thackery turned to the entertainment channels, switched off his mind, and filled his eyes and ears with, in succession, a flatscreen historical, "Gone With The Wind," a concert by a long-dead folksinger, and a nude trio grappling on a grassy hillside, all watched with equal detachment. The sex show had just ended, with everyone except Thackery satisfied, when the door page sounded.

It was Dunn, smiling familiarly and dressed casually in a V-neck shirt and softskin slacks. "Heard you had a bit too much excitement last night," he said, stepping past Thackery into the apartment. "I thought I'd see how you're doing."

"I'm just waiting for the word."

"What word is that?"

"My discharge from Contact."

Dunn settled on the edge of the bed. "Why are you expecting that?"

"I earned it with my performance at Gnivi, don't you think? Hell, you were on the inquiry board."

To Thackery's consternation, Dunn laughed. "Don't you understand? Neale can't discipline you without bringing her own actions into question. It's Mark who'll take the blame."

"Mark—"

"He's the one she wants. You just made it easier for her. So perk up. When *Descartes* goes back out, I promise you you'll be on her."

"I don't want to be. If they don't release me, I'll resign."

"If you feel that way, why haven't you resigned already? Wait—you'd have to forfeit the compound interest on your salary, wouldn't you?"

"I don't care about that."

"No. Then what is it?"

Thackery sighed weightily. "I just want to face up to it."

"Resigning before they had a chance to can you would offend your sense of honor."

"I guess that's what I mean."

"You want to stand up straight when they shoot you. Won't even ask for a blindfold."

"What—"

"Be honest with yourself, that's what it amounts to. You feel responsible for the people we lost. You made that clear enough at the inquiry. Do you think if they run you out for it you'll feel any better about it?"

"That's not what I want."

"Sure it is. And it won't come that way."

"Don't you understand?" Thackery shouted. "I'm responsible! *I* screwed up. They didn't do anything to deserve what happened to them! They died, and I didn't. I'm sure as hell not going to let someone else take the blame."

"It's out of your hands," Dunn said. "Don't you understand? Neale knew what you'd say. She set it up so Mark'd look bad—and he did. That wasn't an inquiry. It was a hanging. Mark's gone, or as good as."

"That's not right."

"But you'll learn to live with it, and the guilt. Merritt, try to think straight for once. Farther out in this octant are the Veil Nebula, the Cygnus Star Cloud, the Great Rift—we've barely begun. How could you want to be anywhere else?"

Thackery shook his head grimly. "I'll wait until that next packet is ready to leave for Earth. If they haven't removed me by then, I'll do it myself."

Thackery vegetated five days away before he had another visitor. This time it was Guerrieri.

"Hear you're talking about leaving us."

"It's not just talk."

"Heard that, too. What's going on?"

"There's nothing complicated about it. I've got no reason to stay in, not one. But now I've got a reason to leave."

"Which is?"

Thackery hesitated, then told him about Diana.

"You're not the only one," Guerrieri said with a wry smile. "Rogen left one—he's been having lunch with his granddaughter. So did a couple of the awks. Even Mike, which is kind of nice." He flashed his eyebrows. "Guess I was shooting blanks."

"Diana took her back to Earth."

"And that's your reason for going?"

Thackery nodded.

"Better think that through. Unless one or the both of them kept moving, all you're going to find is a grave."

"I still have to see."

"They can talk to Unity now."

"I already tried."

"And?"

Thackery sighed. "Unity says that Diana was released from the Service in '50. And her Earth records since are protected by the Right to Privacy provision of the Articles. They have nothing about her—our—daughter at all."

Guerrieri frowned, then lifted his shoulders in a little shrug. "Guess you have to make up your own mind. What do you think about this Kleine transmitter business? You realize, if we'd had one we'd wouldn't of had to come back. Have you been down to the yard? They've got the ship all torn up amidships."

"It's crazy."

"It works."

"It's still crazy," Thackery said emphatically. "Do you realize that the two inventions on which this whole business rests are a complete mystery to everybody?"

"Not to *every*body."

"Everybody. Did you ever study drive theory? What makes an AVLO ship go? The drive doesn't provide the energy needed to create the gravity hole—it taps it. How? From where?"

"The multiplier effect—"

"Is an invention of the physicists to preserve conservation of mass-energy. It's a fancy fudge-factor."

"Come on, you're no drive tech."

"McShane was. He told me that no one really knew where the ship was when it crazed—that it couldn't be in normal space, but that the drive couldn't function in any of the postulated hyperspaces. And now we've got a com system that uses shortcuts nobody can find and follows rules nobody can figure out." He shook his head in disgust. "This is just insane, the whole thing."

"The engineers are just a few steps ahead of the theoreticians, that's all."

"No, it's crazy, all of it."

Guerrieri said nothing for a time, then a sympathetic cast came into his eyes. "What's up with you, Thack? Are you all right?"

A bitter laugh answered him. "All right? My whole life is screwed up and I don't even know why. I can't even figure out how I got here. I mean, I can remember the events, but it doesn't feel like I was in control." He tried a smile, but it was unconvincing. "I just can't do this anymore. Do you understand?"

"I think so," Guerrieri said, edging toward the door. "Look, I'm expected—"

Thackery waved a hand in the air. "It's all right."

"I'll stop by and see you again. Or you could come out and see us."

"Bring a bottle. I'll be better company."

But Guerrieri did not return, and Thackery languished, counting down the days until the arrival of the packet *Raphael* and waiting for the word that seemed would never come. But one morning, with the countdown at seventeen, the page light on his apartment's netlink lit up at last. The conversation was brief, but it was enough:

"Merritt Thackery?"

"Here."

"Report to Carl Heiser in the Flight Office at 10 A.M."

Lifted out of his gloom, Thackery bounced around the apartment expending his restless energy in cleaning and straightening. An hour before his appointment, he showered away three days' worth of olfaction and shaved off a six-day growth of beard. Dressing in a clean allover—available thanks to a laundry services fee rather than his own foresight—he looked deep into the black ellipse for a long moment, then pinned it above his left breastpocket for the last time.

Leaving the apartment earlier than he needed to, Thackery found himself waiting outside Heiser's office with Fowler, one of the awks from *Descartes*. Then when the office door opened, it was Jessica Baldwin who emerged. Heiser appeared behind her only long enough to call "Fowler," then disappeared inside again.

"Thackery," she said, with what seemed to be a genuine smile. "I'm glad to see you here."

"Hello, Jessie."

"Look, all of the techs are getting together at Tom's apartment on Simonton Place to talk this over. Why don't you come on up when Heiser's done with you?"

The invitation puzzled Thackery, so the head bob that acknowledged it was reflexive and perfunctory.

"All right, then," she said brightly. "I'll see you later."

Fowler was inside some ten minutes, and then it was Thackery's turn.

"You mind if I take a moment to get myself some coffee?" Heiser asked as Thackery entered, waving him to a chair. "This has been a crazy morning—appointments since 7 A.M. and still half a dozen to go."

"No—"

Heiser stirred something briskly into his cup and returned to his desk. "Well, Thackery, how are you feeling? Ready to go back to the wars?"

"Excuse me?"

He pushed a piece of fax across the desk toward Thackery:

Unified Space Service—Survey Branch
Flight Office
Cygnus Annex

--------------------Notice of Personnel Transfer--------------------

Thackery, Merritt Andrew   S.N 0001091
  Current Billet: Contact Team Linguist, *Descartes* (USS-63)
      Pay Grade: C-4
    New Billet: Contact Specialist, *Munin* (USS-3)
      Pay Grade: C-5
     Effective: As Dated
  Term of Tour: Open. As required by Mission.

"This is a promotion," Thackery said, unbelieving.

"Of sorts."

"I don't understand. I don't even know what a contact specialist is."

"To be honest, we're not quite sure either," Heiser said, rocking back in his padded chair. "*Munin* won't carry an ordinary crew—but that's only right, since her mission's not an ordinary one either. *Munin* is going to the colony Sennifi. If that name sounds unfamiliar to you, don't worry. It was to everyone until a week before your arrival, and we've been very closed-mouthed about it from the beginning—for good reason. This is a follow-up mission. We're sending you out to try to pick up the pieces of a botched contact."

Heiser paused to sip at his coffee. "As far as your new assignment is concerned, my understanding is that you won't be part of a contact team as you've come to understand the term, but will serve as an aide to Mission Commander Neale. Since she's directly responsible for the negotiations, that should put you right in the middle of things."

"Why was I picked?"

"On Commander Neale's recommendation. You certainly would have been selected for the mission in any event—your language facility and your Gnivi experience put you well up on the list."

This is Neale's payoff to me, Thackery realized suddenly. *Dunn was right. Oh, damn him, Dunn was right.* "What about Mark Sebright?" he demanded.

"What do you mean?"

"Is he on the crew manifest for *Munin?*"

"No—"

"Then that's my answer, too. No," Thackery said, coming to his feet. "I'm not available for this assignment. I'm resigning from the Service."

"I had no notice—," Heiser began.

"Here's notice for you," Thackery said, tearing the black ellipse from his allover and throwing it down on the desk. "I want out."

"I don't understand—"

"All you have to understand is the word 'No'. I'm not going," Thackery shouted, and stormed out of the office past the questioning eyes of Guerrieri and Taylor-White.

By the time Thackery reached his apartment, there was already a Priority message waiting on the netlink, insisting that he report to Neale immediately. Unable to purge it from the system or silence the ringer, he ignored it. Twenty minutes later, the door page began to sound. Thackery ignored it as well, until the combined and continuing demands exhausted his minimal patience.

"Go away!" he hissed, flinging the door open. "I'm done with you!"

But it was not Neale. The strong hand that caught the door before Thackery could slam it shut, the shoulder that pushed it open again, belonged to Sebright.

"My turn to butt in," Sebright said, stepping forward without waiting for an answer.

"What are you here for?"

"You know."

"To break the news that they've found some way to keep me from resigning."

Sebright shook his head. "No. They know they can't make you stay."

"Then they must have sent you to talk me into it."

"No one sent me," Sebright said, crossing his arms over his chest. "You insult me. Do you think I'd do anything for them now?"

Thackery dropped his gaze to the floor, and his shoulders slumped. "I'm sorry. I wasn't thinking."

"You've had that problem a lot lately."

"Then what are you here for?"

Sebright paused a moment before answering. "Derrel came by a week or so ago and told me a lot of things you probably rather he hadn't. Tom filled in the rest, or enough of it. When I heard what happened this morning, I decided it was time to stop listening and start talking."

"Talking about what?"

"I think you should go to Sennifi. Not because they want you to, certainly not for Neale. Because I think it's the right thing for you—and because I can't."

"They're trying to give me a damn promotion. Neale's paying me off for helping her get rid of you."

"I know. But she's not the only one who recommended you."

Thackery stared.

"This is an important one—the most advanced society since Journa," Sebright said. "The Sennifi have a unified planet-wide culture with a high level of intellectual achievement. Their language is sophisticated, very subtle. And they've told us to mind our own business."

"What about you?"

"What about me?"

"If it's so important, why don't they want someone with your kind of experience?"

"Neale won't have me," he said easily. "She's probably right, too, though for the wrong reason. I'm a good Contactor, Thack—"

"I know. I've seen you work."

"But I'm a lousy Contact Leader. I don't delegate responsibility well, I can never be bothered to explain myself, and I'm not interested in 'managing' people—only in getting the job done."

"So what are they going to do to you?"

"They haven't decided yet. I'm not even sure what I want them to do. I'll never tire of the work. Strange as it may sound, I loved every minute on Gnivi. But I'm very tired of the bullshit that goes with it."

"Come back to Earth with me in *Raphael.*"

Sebright shook his head. "That's the wrong choice for you, Thack."

"Why are you so sure?"

He sighed. "You once tried to get me to tell you what it was like to be where we are now. You're here now, and you still don't seem to see it. I don't know what waits for you at Sennifi and beyond. But I do know what waits for you on Earth. You've had a taste of it here on Cygnus, if only you'd realize it. Try to understand what it would mean to see this kind of change when you have an emotional investment. You think you're going back because of Diana, but what you're really trying to do is go home. But home isn't there anymore."

"I have to see for myself—"

"No. I've been watching you ever since you came on board *Tycho.* You've spent all of your life letting those around you define what you are and what you should do and how you should feel. Isn't it time to take charge and do that for yourself? If you go back, it's only because you're desperate to go back to an environment that will treat you more gently than the Service has, flatter you and make you feel good about yourself again. But that environment isn't Earth. It's childhood, and there's no getting back there. Your eyes are open now. You can't forget what you've seen. Life is short, brutish, and unfair—but it's the only game in town. If you ever try to run from it, it wins, and you lose. Don't go to Earth, Thack. Go to Sennifi."

Slowly Thackery raised his head until his eyes met Sebright's. "You're the only one I would have accepted this from."

"I know."

Thackery nodded, his eyes growing wet. "All right. Sennifi, then."

Sebright nodded approvingly. "Then you'll need one of these," he said, holding out his hand and opening his fist. Lying on his palm was a black ellipse.

"How did you get that back from them?"

"I didn't," Sebright said. "It's mine." He stepped toward Thackery and pinned the insignia on his chest, above the tear in the fabric. Thackery looked down at it, then up at Sebright, and tried to speak, but his voice failed him. In the next moment, naturally and unselfconsciously, the two men fell into a long, emotional, and reassuring hug.

Thackery could not say for certain, but he thought it was the kind of hug a father would give a son.

II.

MUNIN

chapter 10

Sennifi

The first time Thackery got a look at the Sennifi records, he understood perfectly why Neale had insisted on leading the followup mission:

FC 09—Summary and Index (Internal Release Only)

$<\neq>$ Primary sun: 2 Aquilae
$<\neq>$ Planet: Type B4N (Fe-silicate-oxide crust/active core/ N atm)
$<\neq>$ Highest lifeforms: (Dreyer hierarchy) Homo sapiens aquilae
$<\neq>$ Civilization: planet-wide, city-based, geoforming
$<\neq>$ Technological Scale Rating (preliminary): 7.48
$<\neq>$ Social-Ethical Scale Rating (preliminary): 8.10
$<\neq>$ First contact: *Tycho Brahe* (USS-81), Cmdr. L. Tamm
$\wedge$
-TOUCH FOR MORE --

The key was in the last line: Neale could not pass up a chance for a final victory over an old rival.

As it turned out, *Tycho* had stayed at A-Cyg a full six months after *Descartes'* departure. The first third of the delay was apparently due to the distractions of the base, the remainder

by the installation of its Kleine system. *Tycho*'s Kleine was
the first in the octant, trans-shipped aboard the first of the new
packets and intended for the base itself, but placed on *Tycho*
when the opportunity presented itself.

But after that bit of fortuitous timing, *Tycho*'s luck turned
sour, and its log became a record of unparalleled futility. Every
system they visited was painfully ordinary. Every planet they
studied was completely lifeless, either an inhospitable gas giant
or a radiation-seared rock nugget without so much as a pro-
tobacterium to call its own.

That track record made the unexpected sound of Sennifi's
planetary radio-band communications a compelling siren song.
Skipping over the four inner planets of the 2 Aquilae system,
Tycho had rushed to settle in orbit around Sennifi. Her linguists
eavesdropped on the radio traffic, while her technoanalysts and
anthropologists spied on the cities—sixty-eight in all, scattered
through the lightly vegetated temperate zone. The physical
scientists, forced for the first time to stand in line for instrument
and processing time, grumbled but were ignored.

Then things started to go wrong. Without warning, the Sennifi transmitters fell silent, after the general form of the language had been identified but before much vocabulary or
grammar could be deciphered. The population surveys gave
erratic, ultimately contradictory results. And when a four-man
contact landing team was set down outside one of Sennifi's
cities, they entered it to find it completely empty.

There were no signs of the disorder of an evacuation, and
every sign of a city in use—except that there were no Sennifi.
Yet the telecamera records from the last light of the evening
before showed normal street traffic. The only conclusion possible was that the Sennifi had somehow known the team was
coming, and had gone to great lengths to avoid meeting them.

In the grasp of both impatience and frustration, Tamm then
made what proved to be a tactical blunder. By asking the Sennifi
for permission to land the contact team at a site of their choosing, he gave them a chance to say "No."

They said no. Firmly and unequivocally.

Nonplussed, Tamm appealed to A-Cyg for guidance. Guidance came back in cold tone and insulting detail. Finish geological and geopolitical mapping. Transmit all data back to
A-Cyg. Continue on to the next system. After a cooling-off
period, a special team will follow up on Sennifi.

It was a double blow to *Tycho:* having their sole discovery wrested from them, and locking in the ignominy of their failure to complete the contact. Together, they would likely seal forever her reputation as an unlucky ship.

Poor Lin Tamm—

It was not really his fault. Six times, USS ships had appeared in the skies above an FC colony to say, in effect, "Hello— we're here—you're not alone." After a varying period of shock, the answer had always been, "By our gods, it's good to see you!"

But the Sennifi had told *Tycho,* "We know. Go away."

It was up to *Munin* to find out why.

"How long?" Thackery called anxiously across the bridge of *Munin.*

The gravigator—the only other person present in the semi-darkened compartment—looked up blank-faced.

"How long?" Thackery repeated. "Till we come out of this craze?"

The gravigator checked his instruments unhurriedly. "Thirty minutes."

"Not enough," Thackery said under his breath, turning back toward his display screen. Scrutinizing the rows of green Sennifi symbols—each a logogram, much like in early Earth Chinese—he continued processing them though the lingua-comp's error-proofing program. The contact message had to be ready, and it had to be right. Unfortunately, Thackery was behind his self-imposed schedule, and the combined probability of error was holding at 19 percent—due, no doubt, to the limited Sennifi vocabulary bank with which he had been provided.

"Mass-touch on 2 Aquilae," announced the gravigator over the shipnet. Thackery sighed and deleted a sentence from the message. The probability of error dropped encouragingly to 12 percent. Close, Thackery thought. *Better get it down to five.*

As he tinkered, the command crew began to appear on the bridge, manning stations that had sat unused throughout the 32-day craze. Captain Russell Cormican appeared presently and checked with each tech in turn, lingering at Navcon and Communication. For Thackery, he had only a single question: "Is the contact message ready?"

Thackery touched a key and a small "4.7%" disappeared

from his display. "Yes," he said with a hint of a triumph.

The captain nodded absently and moved on down the line.

A winded Dr. Amelia Koi appeared at the top of the climb-way and looked uncertainly around the compartment. Thackery beckoned the interpolator over.

"Where's Commander Neale?" he asked as she neared him.

"The Commander is in her cabin," Koi replied, settling her pert frame at the open station to Thackery's right. "She asked to be called when we make Kleine contact with A-Cyg or radio contact with the Sennifi, whichever comes first. Speaking of which, did you get the contact message buttoned up?"

"After a fashion. But to get the level of confidence Neale wanted, I ended up making it very simple. Not much more than, 'Hey—you—over there!'"

Koi's answering smile was friendly. "How much longer?"

Thackery glanced at the clock. "Minute or two."

"Good," she said fervently.

Thackery caught the tone and realized she was avoiding looking at the two-metre wide bridge display centered above the tech stations. "You all right?"

"I'm one of the 'phobes," she confessed. "I don't like the craze. I know better, but I can't stop thinking that the rest of the Universe is gone and not coming back."

"Are you tranqed?" he asked sympathetically.

She pulled up her right sleeve so he could see the medipump. "Not enough."

"There—Navcom just shut us down," he said, nudging Koi and pointing past her to a display at the next station. "Here we go."

"If the Universe doesn't come back, I'm holding you personally responsible," she said with a nervous smile.

Thackery looked expectantly at the imaging display, and when the dazzle cleared, found himself looking at a splendid golden planet mottled with lacy white cloud patterns. "Gorgeous," he said. *As beautiful as any since Jupiter,* he added silently.

"It doesn't look inhabited," Koi said at his elbow.

"They never do," said Thackery, surprised at her naiveté. But a joking reproof went unsaid as he saw on her face the same anticipation and excitement he was happy to be feeling. *Thank you, Mark. This could be fun after all—*

• • •

With his long gray caftan sweeping the ground and with his long smooth strides, J'ten Ron Tize seemed to flow, rather than walk across the chamber floor. His caftan bore on its hip the three golden slashes that marked his rank among the scholars: Tize, or "he of clear vision." Waiting for him at the table beneath the highest point of the arched ceiling was the highest ranking scholar of Sennifi, wearing the four-slash green caftan that no other was permitted to wear.

"*Sekkh quil e'nom,*" said J'ten as he reached the table. His use of Paston's Language marked the seriousness of the meeting. "They have returned, as I predicted."

"There is no glory in the successful prediction of evil," Z'lin Ton Drull chided gently. "Sit, J'ten."

J'ten settled in the empty chair. "We were wrong to send their first envoys away. They do not follow the courtesies of Kemar. Now we have gained nothing—except perhaps their enmity."

"Either your *ize* or your memory fails you, J'ten. They chose to leave. We could not have forced them to go. We have neither the means nor, I am afraid, the will. Not that it matters. You begin to forget what we were once like. They are like that now. They would come, and come, and come—." The Drull seemed tired; his head seemed to teeter on his slender neck.

"They again ask to meet with us, to share knowledge."

"And nothing has changed. We must refuse again. We cannot let them see what we are, know what we know."

"Or become what we have become," J'ten said softly.

"Yes," Z'lin Ton Drull said slowly. "The knowledge would mark them, as it has us. And yet, what can we do?"

"May I presume—"

Z'lin gestured his approval.

"In these years, I have studied them, considered what might be done should they return. You are correct to say we cannot refuse them. *But there is another way,*" he said with surprising vehemence. "We are not yet reduced to cowering in their presence. We must test *their* will. If it is strong, then we must test their patience. But if we can make this refusal *theirs,* we may yet protect us both."

The Drull was silent, thoughtful. "This is your *kam'ru,*" he said presently, naming the work of advancement. A *kam'ru* would be judged by the Council of Pad'on—three women and two men who had once held the rank of Drull.

J'ten squirmed, embarrassed. The only advancement open to him was to replace Z'lin Ton as Drull. "That is not my intent. I was only pursuing a subject of interest," he said beseeching forgiveness with his eyes. "I won't submit it to the Council without your sponsorship—I misspeak, I will not submit it at all. I wish only to be of service in this crisis."

The Drull sat back in his chair, his folded hands tucked delicately beneath his chin. "The Council will doubtless find your work too practical to be of merit," he said at last. "But it may well have value to me. Tell me your thoughts."

Thackery had nothing to do until and unless the Sennifi answered the repeating contact message, but the respite was a welcome one. With the haste and disorganization that characterized the beginning of the mission, a period of relative inactivity and tranquility was a blessing.

There would have been less confusion had Neale not been so insistent on leading the follow-up mission. Half of *Munin*'s previously assigned crew was already at Cygnus. The remainder was inbound on the packet *Raphael*, on which Thackery had thought to return to Earth. Waiting for the *Raphael* would have added only a few weeks to the timetable and kept the *Munin*'s crew intact. Transferring a handful of key *Descartes* veterans would have sufficiently reinforced the roster for the special requirements of the Sennifi mission.

Judging from what Thackery could glean from shipboard chatter, that had been the Flight Office's original intent. Neale had lobbied for the Sennifi follow-up mission to be delayed until *Descartes* was ready to undertake it, and that *Munin* be assigned to continue the search program assigned to *Descartes*. The compromise which evolved called for a special crew for *Munin*, with *Descartes* to follow her to Sennifi for a reshuffling of crews at the end of the Sennifi mission.

The aging *Munin* was creaky and crowded, but thanks to her recent upgrade, she was as operationally capable a ship as any the Service operated. But the same could not be said of her hybrid crew. The more experienced *Descartes* personnel were given precedence over that portion of the very yellow *Munin* crew which was available. But to fill the gaps, the Flight Office had to turn to such as Koi, drawn from the A-Cyg Archeology staff.

Thackery did not question Koi's ability. She was a far more

highly skilled interpolator than Jael had been (an ability for which Thackery had the utmost respect—from time to time his interpolation instructor would show up in a nightmare, droning, "Every stated fact implies an n-dimensional matrix of related facts"). But Koi's craze phobia had obviously prevented her from having any field experience, making her less than an ideal candidate for the mission.

Nor did Thackery think much of how the chain of command had been juggled. To soothe ruffled feathers, Cormican had been retained as captain. To keep Neale superordinate, as her seniority and experience demanded, the new position of Mission Commander was invented. As near as Thackery could figure it, that arrangement left Neale with the authority to do anything and the responsibility for nothing.

Thackery's own position was an uncomfortable one. As Contact Specialist, he stood between Neale and the five-man strategy team, with a contact leader's responsibility but none of the autonomy that customarily went with it.

Only this time, I understand the rules—

The thought was interrupted by the yelping of the Com tech. "They're answering!" he cried, as Sennifi symbols began to appear on Thackery's screen. Koi quickly paged Neale, then came to stand behind Thackery and watch over his shoulder.

By the time Neale reached the bridge, her chest rising and falling from the exertion of climbing the length of the ship, Thackery had the short message translated.

"'Send full language information,'" he read aloud.

"That's all?" asked Neale, peering at the display.

"I'm afraid so."

"I assume they're talking about our language, rather than asking what we know of theirs."

"That'd be my assumption," Koi offered.

"All right. Do we have a Standard English tutorial bank that's suitable? Something that wouldn't confuse them more than it would help them?"

"I'm not sure," Thackery said. "As far as I know, the first contact has always been in the language of the colony. I don't think it ever occurred to the previous colonies that we have our own language—at least not at this point in the contact."

"It's occurred to this one," Neale said, straightening up and brushing her hair back off her face. "Send an acknowledgment, tell them we're working on it, and then see what you can come up with."

Koi was openly horrified. "Commander, we can't send them a language bank."

"Why not?"

"A language defines a people. With interpolation techniques and implication analysis, I can tell more from a thousand words of a civilization's language than I can from a thousand kilos of artifacts. Even without those tools, they're going to learn a lot about us, and we nothing about them."

Neale was unswayed. "If I were in their position, it would *take* a lot of information to lower my anxiety level. Let's not forget—they're advanced enough to be afraid of us."

"Then give them just enough to talk to us, and make them work for what they can read between the lines," Koi pleaded. "Give them a basic conversational vocabulary, not the whole unabridged." She looked to Thackery for support, but he made his face blank and avoided eye contact.

Neale shook her head. "You forget, we want these meetings, and they apparently don't. I'll agree to screening out technical vocabulary that's clearly beyond their level—AVLO drive and other high T-rating items—but they get everything else. Merry, see that it's taken care of. I'll be in my cabin." Neale rose and left the bridge, leaving Koi wondering what she was up to and Thackery the same about the Sennifi.

It took nearly fourteen hours to transmit a 50,000 word language bank and accompanying chrestomathy in a form and at a speed the Sennifi could accept. The hours of silence which followed were broken at last when *Munin* was hailed from the surface by a voice which was clear, mellifluous, and uncolored by any accent. "This is J'ten Ron Tize," it said. "I speak for Z'lin Ton Drull and the people of the autonomous planet of Sennifi."

"Damn good English for a day's work," Neale said respectfully.

"It has to be synthetic," Koi whispered, "generated through some sort of data processor, their equivalent of the lingua-comp."

"Why?"

"Nobody masters a new language that quickly—"

"We'll see," Neale said, and nodded to Thackery.

"This is Merritt Thackery. I speak for Commander Alizana Neale, the crew of the Unified Space Service survey ship *Munin,* and the United Community of Humankind."

"What the hell is the United Community of Humankind?" Koi wondered aloud.

Neale winked in her direction, a smile breaking through her pensive expession. "We'll see their planet and raise them a federation."

"Merritt Thackery. You have requested an exchange of knowledge."

"Yes," he said. "We believe that we have common interests. We believe that we have a common heritage. Such meetings would benefit us both."

"Merritt Thackery. No meetings are possible without a suitable gesture of friendship on your part."

Thackery looked to Neale. "Ask them what they want," she directed.

"J'ten Ron Tize," Thackery said, turning back to his station. "We understand that our presence may have alarmed you. We are willing to provide reassurance, if you can tell us what would constitute a suitable gesture."

"I can," said J'ten, then paused. "Tell us the location of your home world and of any space habitats with a population exceeding fifty. Identify, both in three-dimensional celestial coordinates and travel time, the location of all spacecraft capable of following you to Sennifi."

Thackery's eyebrows flew up.

"Could have asked for all the colonies," Neale remarked casually.

"We screened out all references to that concept," Koi said, her face showing her shock.

But J'ten was not through. "—Take up a geosynchronous orbit of our specification and maintain it throughout your stay—"

"First-born child of the Commander will be next," Koi muttered.

"Shhh," Neale chided without rancor.

"—Provide us with the design and operating principles of the propulsion system which brought you here. Details for the transfer of information can be arranged. However, we require your decision within thirty minutes. We await your consideration of these requests."

For what seemed to be minutes but was not, silence reigned

on the bridge. "Well, there's one for the books," Thackery said finally.

Neale shook her head, as though rousing herself from some trancelike state of concentration, and turned toward Koi. "See to collecting the information they requested and organizing it in some accessible format. Get what help you can from ship's crew."

"You're agreeing to their demands?"

"Yes," said Neale, unruffled by her accusatory tone.

Koi stared at the older woman, disbelieving. "Someone has to say it," she said finally. "Those demands are outrageous—deliberately so, I'm sure. It's an asking price. We can't accept it—not without haggling first."

"Not for discussion," Neale said curtly.

Koi, stony-faced, would not be dissuaded. "I know that we provide all the colonies with everything the Sennifi asked for, in one form or another—and more. But that comes later, after we've had a chance to size them up and prepare them for the cultural shocks," Koi said. "You're letting them dictate to us."

Silently, Thackery applauded Koi. *How much has Neale been authorized to give away?* he wondered.

"Yes," Neale was saying amiably. "They *can* dictate to us. All we can do is say, 'The price is too high.' It isn't yet. So please get started on gathering that information."

Neale turned then to Thackery, who was belatedly considering adding his voice of objection to Koi's. "Call them back, Merry. Tell them we agree."

J'ten Ron Tize and Z'lin Ton Drull met again at the table under the high arch ceiling of the *sjen*, debate hall, of the scholar complex of T'rnyima.

"This is a large gift they offer us."

"By their measure, a very great gift indeed. It expresses great inner confidence, and great desire."

"Was it your belief that they would refuse?"

"No, though I may be forgiven a measure of hope-without-basis."

"Of course. Will we accept the gift?"

"We dare not. They would see us as in debt to them, and not be content until that debt were satisfied."

"Then I must meet with them."

"I regret the truth of that conclusion."

• • •

"We are pleased by your willingness to make these small gestures," said J'ten Ron Tize. His voice, emanating from the bridge's several speakers, seemed to surround Thackery and the others. "Are you now prepared to make a more tangible guarantee of your good conduct?"

"We show weakness, and they up the ante," Koi said. "As I told you they would."

"Pin them down, Merry," Neale instructed.

Grating his teeth at the nickname—which, absent a timely protest from Thackery, Neale had permanently added to her lexicon—Thackery nodded and touched the SEND key. "Please explain your question."

"We are willing to place envoys aboard your ship to meet with your scholars and answer your questions. You must guarantee their safety. For each of our envoys, two of your number must agree to be our guests on Sennifi while the envoys are with you."

"The correct word is 'hostages', not 'guests,'" Thackery retorted, unthinking.

"Yes," was J'ten's calm response. "I believe you are right."

"Dammit, Thackery, don't editorialize on the air!" Neale exploded.

Thackery's quick finger on the Com controls contained Neale's anger to the flight deck. Visibly chastened, Thackery shrank into his seat to await the next volley of criticism.

"I share your sentiment," Neale said with surprising gentleness. "But our feelings have no place in this. Now, tell them we accept. Make it sound like it's no big deal."

Thackery took a deep breath, which seemed to puff him back up to normal size. "J'ten Ron Tize."

"I am here, Merritt Thackery."

"We understand and admire your prudence, and we're willing to provide this reassurance," Thackery said with fluid sincerity. "We are also ready now to pass on the information you requested earlier, if you are prepared to receive it."

"Thank you," said J'ten. "We withdraw our previous requests, with one exception—that you take up geosynchronous orbit directly above the city from which I now speak to you, known to us as T'rnyima. This will facilitate communications during our visit to your ship. Please prepare to pick up and receive us at this time tomorrow."

One of the techs laughed nervously, and another commented to no one in particular, "They've got *chungas* the size of grapefruit, don't they?"

Thackery was bewildered by the Sennifi's sudden metamorphosis. "Thank you, J'ten. We'll be in touch," he managed to say, then looked wonderingly at Neale and Koi, as though asking for an explanation.

Koi offered only a shrug. Neale appeared satisfied, almost vindicated. "Looks like they're more interested in us than they first let on," was all she would say on the subject. "Good work, everybody. Get some rest, and I'll see the contact team on the rec level in six hours." She left the bridge whistling.

In the *sjen*, J'ten Ron Tize and the Drull of Sennifi stood and faced one another.

"All is as you predicted it would be. Your prescience is unmarred," Z'lin Ton Drull said somberly. "You are clever, J'ten. Perhaps I shall sponsor your *kam-ru* to the Council after all."

"We must be clever," said J'ten, equally somber. "We have little else left."

There were few complexities to the exchange. The experience of the *Tycho* landing obviated any need for isolation procedures, which simplified matters considerably. *Munin*'s gig carried two awks, the sociologist, and the technical analyst to the surface, where a cottage on the grounds of the scholar complex had been prepared for their use. The gig returned with Z'lin Ton Drull and J'ten Ron Tize, who were met by Neale and shown to the adjacent double cabins on the F deck which had been prepared for them. An hour later, all the principals gathered on the edrec deck.

"We greet you as brothers," said Z'lin Ton Drull. "We greet you as travelers asking guidance in an unfamiliar place. We greet you as scholars. We know that you have many questions. We hope that those which we may be able to answer will offer you something which you can fold into the substance of your lives."

He reached up with his right hand and pressed his open palm gently against the side of Neale's head. She did not flinch, for J'ten had forewarned them, explaining the gesture as one which "expresses respect for a fellow scholar's mastery of reason." Following J'ten's instructions, she reciprocated, and then the Drull retreated a few steps to his chair.

A good speech well said, Thackery thought. *I wonder if we can believe any of it.* His eyes followed Z'lin every second, as though by the force of his scrutiny Thackery could pry loose some insight into the stranger. All Thackery had so far were impressions: dignity, precision, self-confidence without ego. Anything else that might be there was masked by the visitor's stoic reserve.

"Since its creation, the Survey Branch of the Unified Space Service has had this as its motto," Neale was saying. "'To teach if we are called upon; to be taught if we are fortunate'. I hope that spirit will prevail in our discussions here. It is also my privilege to welcome you and your people back into the greater community of mankind."

As Neale went on, sprinkling manufactured charm atop a benevolent portrait of the USS, Thackery's attention and gaze wandered. The deck had been made over with flags and tables into a conference hall. He and Neale had been made over as well. The ship's inventory contained no ceremonial uniforms, because the Service had never authorized any such frippery. But at Neale's insistence, a ceremonial uniform had been produced all the same, cribbed from earlier Earth designs and manufactured overnight by a pair of techs skilled with a fabtack. There were even military-style service bars, each segment representing a star system visited, and aiguillettes for the right shoulder.

The idea of the uniforms chafed Thackery's sensibilities almost as badly as the stiff material of them chafed his body. Still, there was nothing to be done. *Be spending a lot of time in it,* Thackery thought, recalling the lengthy Contact Interrogative Plan they had prepared during the craze. There were whole files of queries about Sennifi history, designed to probe for First Colonization clues or knowledge without every mentioning the colonies explicitly. The various science disciplines wanted Sennifi perspectives on the major theories they held dear: evolution, big-bang open-universe cosmology, numbers, space-time relationships, even such basics as conservation and parity. There was a grab-bag of questions from the sociologists and psychologists which would do little more than generate journal fodder: belief in one or more deities, family relationships and structure, concepts of death, sexual behavior—

"—you may begin now." The change to Z'lin Ton Drull's voice alerted Thackery that Neale had finished, and Thackery glanced at his slate for the first question. The session was on.

By the end of three hours, Thackery had posed thirteen CIP questions and Neale nearly twice that many follow-ups. They had received answers ranging from a single word ("No" to "Do you pair-bond for life?") to a fifteen-minute dissertation (on the meaning of scholarship). Z'lin Ton Drull was patient, lucid, and cooperative. Thackery found himself tempted to trust the soft-spoken Sennifi leader but managed to keep his skepticism alive—though not without a struggle.

Then, the Sennifi retired to the quarters that had been cleared for them downship in Contact, while Neale and Thackery hurried upship to the library, where Koi and her team had watched and recorded the session.

"I think we made an excellent start," Neale said twice en route.

But Koi showed no such bouyant enthusiasm. "Positives. We have the Sennifi power structure: the Drull, or 'decision-maker'; Tize, or 'he who sees clearly'; Chen, or 'diligent one'; and Bazi, 'he who yearns'. As the titles suggest, it shapes up as a typical meritocracy. The relative youth of the Drull—about forty, if we converted correctly—confirms the selection procedure he described.

"As for the rest, we can say that they answered, or attempted to answer, all the questions we asked, from systems of measurement to diet.

"Now the negatives. Your charm was wasted on them, Commander. There was neither an immediate response nor a long-term thaw—facial expressions and emotive content were the same from first to last. And, overall, there was very little substantive information—their answers were not very illuminating. That was to be expected, since the first session questions were chosen particularly for their low potential for controversy. But it also means that we haven't yet found their uniqueness, their signature, and until we do we're going to have to tread carefully."

"This afternoon should take care of that," Neale said, unperturbed. "We should begin the colony problem sequence sometime before the end of the session. Break for rats and rest now—back here in one hour."

As the others filed out Thackery held Koi in her chair with

a wordless touch. "I want to check something with you."

"What's that?"

"That the Sennifi didn't ask us a single question."

"What? Of course they did."

Thackery shook his head. "Run it up, please, and check. The only questions that they asked were to clarify questions we'd asked them. They didn't show a tad of curiosity about us."

Koi squeezed her eyes shut as if to shut out distractions. "All right," she said finally. "You're right—"

"Thank you," Thackery said, standing.

"Whoa," she said, reaching out and grabbing his wrist. "There are a lot of possible reasons, and it isn't going to last. What's running through your mind? Why do you think it's important?"

"Can you think of any good reason why the Sennifi didn't take our concessions once they'd won them?"

"Sure. Because they didn't want them. They got the only one they really wanted, which was to park this ship where they could keep an eye on it."

"Maybe."

"No maybe about it. They wanted to test our interest. They were posturing, and we caught them at it. You have a different idea?"

"I can't reconcile the way they treated *Tycho* with them being aboard now. They can't both be honest reflections of what they want."

"They've had almost fifteen years to think it over."

"What I can't stop thinking is, what if that was their real feeling—and this whole exercise is posturing? What if they've just used that time to find a more subtle way of saying no?"

Koi tucked a stray strand of hair behind her ear before answering. "Have you brought this up to Neale?"

"Do you think she'd listen?"

Koi considered. "Probably not, at this point. For that matter, you haven't persuaded me. You can't argue with the fact that they're here, and answering our questions."

Thackery's expression turned dour. "A civilization that will empty a city overnight to avoid contact with outsiders won't balk at a little duplicity," he said pointedly and moved toward the door.

Koi sighed. "Thack—," she called after him, and he stopped

to look back over his shoulder. "I'll keep the suggestion on file. And if I see anything that suggests you might be right, I'll see that you know about it."

Thackery nodded wordlessly and was gone.

It took two hours and the conscious omission by Neale of several opportunities for follow-ups, but at last they reached the first question in the colony problem sequence. It was a simple question, and Neale preempted Thackery's role to ask it.

"Who was the first Sennifi?"

"The question is without meaning."

Neale looked to Thackery for help. "What is the earliest event recorded in your histories?" he asked, stepping in smoothly.

Z'lin Ton Drull's answer could hardly have been more unexpected. "We have no histories."

Neale spent several minutes establishing to her satisfaction that there had been no misunderstanding, that the Drull understood both the purpose and nature of a "history." Once over that hurdle, Neale asked the obvious follow-up: "Why not?"

Z'lin's involved answer consumed the remaining hour of the session, and painted a picture of a society firmly rooted in the present. "When the nature of the Universe is found in cycles," the Drull explained patiently, "what point is there in arbitrarily selecting a starting or stopping point, then tallying up the cycles as if each repetition were unique? It is an unworthy formulation."

Steadfastly, the Drull rejected the idea that life was a progression from some past origin to some future ending. "My entire life has been spent in the present," he said. "I have never left it for a moment."

But, Neale protested, didn't great scholars of the past, now dead, contribute to the present? Didn't what they accomplished shape the present?

"If the creation of a person's mind—an idea, a work of art, a work of music—affects today, exists today, then the creator is still with us. To say that this person died in cycle one thousand or ten thousand is to say that he gave us nothing and is remembered by no one. The mind is only alive in the present, for the present is all that there is."

A Hindu might understand, Thackery thought as he listened. It was clear, however, that Neale did not, or did not want to.

The longer Z'lin explained, and the more reasonable his tone, the closer Neale came to losing the struggle to keep anger off her face and out of her voice.

"Then where did the Sennifi come from?" she asked sharply. "Why are you here?"

"The question is without meaning. We *are* here," the Sennifi leader said simply. "That knowledge suffices."

At that, Neale slumped back in her chair, her body language shouting her frustration, and let Thackery carry the last few minutes of the session alone. When it was over, she launched herself out of the chair and descended on the library.

"Can he be telling me the truth?" she demanded of Koi. "Can that really be what they believe?"

"When you pose questions under these circumstances, you tend to get answers that reflect idealized understandings rather than operational truth—like the difference between Service Protocols and how things are really done. But with that caveat, yes, he probably is telling the truth, at least as he sees it. They are not unaware of time, mind you—they showed that in setting a deadline for us, and in scheduling their pick-up and the upcoming sessions. But that doesn't contradict the likelihood that where we see ourselves moving forward, they see themselves running in place."

Neale threw up her hands in disgust and stalked out without a further word.

Koi sighed and looked to Thackery. "Is she always going to be like that?"

"More or less."

"Then I'll tell you and let you pass it on when the right time comes. I've got two little things that might bear some closer examination."

"Shoot."

She motioned him over to one of the terminals. "You might have noticed that the Sennifi equivalents for 'hour', and 'minute', which are their only quantitative units of time, both follow the rule of formation for words indicating a subunit of a greater whole. Except in the case of 'hour', there is no greater whole, at least not in the data they provided us. It's as if we called the second a milliday but had no unit called a day."

"I see that. Their 'day' is a qualitative term, like our morning or twilight. So?"

She pointed at an expression in the midst of a crowded

screen of numbers. "The length of their 'hour' doesn't match up with any of the natural cycles of their planet, in any multiple."

Thackery frowned. "At the risk of being thought dim, so? Earth's basic time unit doesn't, either. The second is defined as some 9-billion-odd periods of the radiation from a transition in a cesium atom, or some such."

"Now. But at one time it tied into other units that tied into Earth's rotation, and between that and cesium is a lot of political and technological history. There is no system of time that I'm aware of that did not begin with physical constants, usually astronomical rhythms. So this might be a clue to where the Sennifi came from, and maybe even when. I've got somebody checking to see if the Sennifi hour correlates with any Earth rhythms or time-keeping systems."

Thackery was disappointed, and let it show on his face. "What's the other thing?"

"The evacuation of the city of Rijala when *Tycho* was here. We've had a chance to completely review the *Tycho* observations, and explaining how the Sennifi did it has become a bit of a problem. They can't have gone out into the countryside, or the *Tycho* imaging team would have detected them. They weren't in hiding in the city, or the contact team would have found them. And we've found no roads or mass-transit systems linking Rijala with the nearest other cities—which are a good two hundred klicks away in any event. But the telecameras clearly show people were there the evening before and two hours after the contact team's visit. I recommend we ask the Drull about it. The answer should prove interesting."

To no great surprise, Thackery found Neale's cabin anteroom darkened and whirling with stars. He had time to spot and silently name the nine green colony markers before Neale brought up the lights.

"What's on your mind, Merry?"

Thackery took a step forward. "Dr. Koi had some observations we might want to consider in relation to tomorrow's session."

Neale listened attentively, nodded occasionally, as Thackery recapped his conversation with the interpolator. When he was finished, Neale made a sound deep in her throat and traced a fingertip along the line of her jaw.

"Let me make this as clear as I can, Merry," she started slowly. "If we never find out why they brushed off *Tycho*—if we never know why they upped the ante and then folded—if we never discover how they can evacuate a city of fifty thousand overnight—but we get some light shed on the colony problem"—she said each word deliberately, then paused for emphasis—"then I'll go home happy. I won't take the chance of pushing on what might be sensitive ground."

"After today, you still think they're going to be of any help with the colony problem?"

"We're far from finished," said Neale, and Thackery realized that the impatient Neale of an hour ago was gone. "We'll stick to the CIP. But Merry—I do appreciate the way you're staying on top of this." Neale's smile was pleasant but empty, and Thackery, realizing he was being dismissed, took his leave.

But each succeeding session with the Sennifi seemed to chip away at Neale's determined patience. "We're getting answers— but are we getting information?" she asked after one concluded. The question was rhetorical, for everyone within earshot knew the answer was no.

It was Koi who finally identified the problem, seventeen days after their arrival and thirty-one sessions into the CIP. "We've all been asking, 'What's happening here? Why are we getting so little new information?' It's almost as if we're talking to ourselves.

"And that is exactly the problem. We're getting our own language thrown back at us—our concepts, our schema. Z'lin fits the best available Standard English expression to a unique Sennifi thought, and we get an answer which makes sense but has been filed smooth. We learn nothing, and I can't interpolate, because the subtleties are lost in translation."

"Are they doing this deliberately?"

"They can't help but do it, as long as the sessions are conducted in English. They're answering all our questions, and the answers are self-consistent. For instance, their lack of histories was a major disappointment. But their science has a similar present-focus, to the point that the cause-effect relationship is blurred. They see change as the result of a loop of forces, where an effect can be a cause, like a snake swallowing itself tail-first."

"So they're not hiding anything."

"Unless they asked for our language data exactly for this

reason. The best way to find out is to ask them to teach us their language."

The question was put to Z'lin Ton Drull that afternoon. "We would be pleased to teach you our languages. However, you should realize what such a task entails," said Z'lin. "The language in which you first hailed us is called *haarit*. It is a language used for formal communications, and mastering its inflections takes a Chen seven years. Then there is Paston's Language, the *semm, K'nau*—all of which are scholar's languages, all of which are more difficult than *haarit*. Our common language, which you might well learn quickly, cannot express many ideas of interest to us both."

A sad expression touched Z'lin's features, a first. "It was to honor your language's creator and to avoid this problem that I took for myself the challenge of mastering your language. But it is clear my mastery is flawed. I have failed to express myself to your satisfaction. My inadequacy—"

"No," Neale said quickly. "You've given no offense. Your skill with our language is considerable, and the creator is honored. Those who come after us will return the honor by studying all your languages. But we will not concern ourselves with that here." She smiled reassuringly, and let the matter drop.

That session was a turning point in Neale's attitude, and her interest commenced a steady decline. She shortened pre- and post-interview conferences by arriving late and leaving early. Eventually she stopped coming at all, depending on Thackery to keep her on track in the CIP and on Koi for file summaries of the results and analysis.

Before long, she complained that the summaries were too lengthy, too tedious—and Koi reluctantly shortened them. Eventually even the sessions with the Sennifi were affected. Neale canceled one with no explanation, and ended another an hour early. True to the pattern they had set in the first meeting, the Sennifi did not ask why.

The farther Neale retreated from the proceedings, the angrier Koi became with her.

"Is she so set on the colony problem to the exclusion of everything else that she can't see the other questions that need answering here?" she demanded of Thackery.

"Yes," he said simply.

"The issue here is the Sennifi themselves—why they're the way they are. Everything else is ordinary."

"You're preaching to the converted," Thackery said, and gave a shrug that said *it's out of our hands*.

And more and more, the crew of *Tycho* began to talk not of Sennifi, but of the rendezvous with *Descartes* and of moving on.

On the twenty-sixth day at Sennifi, the Kleine transmitter came alive, and so did Neale.

The dispatch told of the spanking-new ship *Eiriksson* and its discovery, on its first craze, of a tenth colony on a planet orbiting 2 Triangulum Australis. The colony was extinct and the ruins crumbling, but there were pictures which showed that the inhabitants had been human. There were also writings, an entire library full of fragile ancient documents. The figure being tossed around was 100,000 years—twice as far back as the Mannheim hypothesis placed the First Colonization. If the date were confirmed, it would mean a lot of rethinking was in order, even if the writings were never translated.

In less than twenty minutes, everyone on *Munin* knew the gist of the lengthy dispatch—except the Sennifi, secure in their cocoon of cabins aft. Within the hour, Neale summoned Thackery and Koi to her cabin.

"Exciting, isn't it?" Neale gushed, waggling a fax of the dispatch.

"Especially for *Eiriksson*," Thackery said carefully, nursing a suspicion of what was coming next.

"Worth a dozen Sennifis," Neale said. "The most exciting find since the Journa colony. Unfortunately, I'm stuck here, playing word games with these sterile-brained—." Words failed her, but her frustration was evident. "But that doesn't mean I can't put in some time on this. So there's going to be a little shuffling of assignments. Merry, you'll take over as our chief representative. My position. I've already cleared the change with the Sennifi."

Thackery nodded, unsurprised.

Neale went on, "Amelia, while the interpolation work's still thin, you should be able to back Merry up."

"Yes, Commander."

"How long is this change for?" Thackery asked.

"I expect until we reach a good stopping point and leave here. Which reminds me, I want you both to give me your estimates of how long it's going to take to complete the CIP.

It strikes me that with the language problem we're facing, a lot of what's left might better wait until a permanent liaison is established. I think we should start steering things in that direction."

"Are you thinking of cutting short our stay?" A faint hint of criticism crept into Thackery's tone.

"It's a possibility I'm considering. This assignment may not be the most efficient use of this ship or its personnel." She turned toward the controls of her projector. "Get back to me with those estimates by this time tomorrow."

Before they reached the doorway, Thackery and Koi were surrounded by stars—only this time, there were ten little green pinpoints.

"Fry her and her hurry," Koi fumed as she descended the climbway toward her quarters. "She can't take us away from here now."

"Sure she can," said Thackery, struggling to keep us. "She wants to go home. With the craze, by the time we get back, ten years' work will have been done on the *Eiriksson* find."

"Fry the *Eiriksson* find, too."

"She's not the first to get caught up in the colony problem," Thackery said. "It's the intellectual challenge of the millenium. I sometimes think that anyone *not* caught up in it—myself included—betrays by that their lack of genius."

"You're quite the apologist, aren't you?"

"I manage."

"So you're not upset by this at all?"

"No. I'm glad the dispatch came."

They reached the crew quarters level and swung off the climbway. "Glad!" she exclaimed.

"Yes, glad—because Neale's been keeping us away from the questions that matter, and now she's out of the way. I've been sitting there watching those two session after session and biting my tongue so hard I think sometimes I'm going to start bleeding from the mouth, because I didn't dare raise anything not in the CIP. There's been something wrong from the first day, and I told you about it then. It's not what the Sennifi've done. It's something they haven't done. From the beginning, something's been missing. *Curiosity.* They give every appearance of having none of their own, and they've done everything possible to extinguish ours."

"What are you getting at?"

"This," Thackery said, opening his cabin door. "The Sennifi have no intention of giving us anything. They have no interest in what we know or in us. They're simply waiting for us to get tired of this and leave. And now Neale has as much as told them that they're very close to succeeding.

"That much I'm sure of. The only thing I want to know now is why. They're hiding something. And I think it's time we started looking in the closets."

READY.

The word appeared silently on Thackery's slate, lying angled on his lap so that only he could read it. It was Koi, two decks upship in the library, speaking into her netlink. Thackery was alone in the conference hall, waiting for the Sennifi. He had insisted on meeting them alone, and Koi had not fought him.

The Sennifi filed in and sat down across the table: first Z'lin Ton Drull, wearing the familiar green robe, and J'ten Ron Tize at his heels.

"Good morning," Thackery said.

"Good morning," replied the Drull. As Thackery expected, there were no questions about the empty chair to Thackery's right. Z'lin simply waited for the first question.

"We've met here forty-six times now, over one hundred fifty hours," Thackery said soberly. "We've asked you hundreds of questions, and you've answered every one. My first question for you today is this: Why should we believe any of your answers?"

WATCH IT appeared on the slate almost immediately, followed by MAKE NICE. YOU STILL NEED A RIDE HOME.

"Whether our answers are sufficiently congruent with your preconceptions to be marked as truth is outside our concerns," the Drull said, his answer as immediate as if it had been re-hearsed—a possibility Thackery was still toying with. "But a scholar prides himself on his scholarship, and true scholarship requires answers without error or deception."

"Would you lie to us if you saw us as a danger to you?"

"You cannot endanger us," the Drull said without bravado.

NON ANSWER. FOLLOW UP.

"Then why are you afraid of us?" Thackery demanded, leaning forward.

"We are not afraid of you." There was no more expression

in Z'lin's face or voice than there had been for a discussion of mineral classification ten days earlier.

Koi noticed as well. EITHER THEY CARRY A GENE FOR POKER-FACEDNESS OR ??? WHAT THE HELL LET'S FIND OUT. STEP ON THEIR FEET SOME MORE——BUT GENTLY.

Inwardly, Thackery smiled. Outside, he was rigid. Where Neale had approached the sessions as though they were audiences with a king or pope, Thackery's demeanor was more akin to a prosecutor quizzing a defendant. "When our first ship, *Tycho,* reached here, you evacuated Rijala to avoid meeting with the contact team. How was that done?"

"The people of Rijala left by the tubes." To Thackery's surprise, Z'lin deferred to J'ten for the rest of his answer. "I know only the means, not the principle. Perhaps J'ten can provide the details you require."

AMBUSHED. HE WAS WAITING FOR THAT QUESTION.

J'ten could and did, launching into a description of an ambitious system of subterranean tunnels carrying magnetically levitated cars and linking the sixty-eight Sennifi cities.

DAMN DAMN DAMN, Koi expostulated. I HATE SURPRISES. A few minutes later she came back with, FOUND CONFIRMATION IN TYCHO DATA. THEY'RE THERE, APPARENTLY QUITE DEEP AND OBVIOUSLY NOT OFTEN USED, SINCE WE HAVEN'T SEEN THE SAME TRANSIENTS IN THE MAGNETOMETRY. STILL CHECKING SOME THINGS. STALL, WILL YOU?

Thackery let J'ten go on, offering more detail than he had use for but providing Koi with the time she wanted. Before long the slate lit up again, and Thackery read it in oblique glances that, although quick, did not escape the Drull's attentive eyes.

PAYOFF AT LAST! TAKING POPULATION OF RIJALA, ESTIMATED TUBE CAPACITY, AND TIME AVAILABLE, EVACUATION COULD NOT BE ACCOMPLISHED EVEN IF THEY STARTED THE MOMENT LAMM DECIDED ON LANDING. SIC EM.

Thackery pounced on the brief pause at the end of J'ten's next sentence. "We detected your Tubes with our instruments some time ago," he said, directing his words to Z'lin. "They could not have emptied Rijala in the time you had available."

"Your work contains errors," Z'lin said, undisturbed.

I THINK WE'VE BEEN INSULTED. STAND PAT. WE'RE ONTO SOMETHING.

"Our work is without peer," Thackery said tartly but could

not immediately decide where to go from there. "There is another problem," he said finally. "Why did you do it?"

"Your intent was unknown. We did not immediately realize that you were scholars. You have since shown both a dedication to knowledge and a willingness to share it freely. Those are the marks of scholars everywhere."

THAT'S A BULLSHIT ANSWER. BUT HOW CAN YOU ARGUE THEIR MOTIVES?

Round to him, Thackery thought. "We're pleased that you recognized those qualities in us," Thackery said. "We've had difficulty with some of the things you've told us, though."

"I'm sorry that my explanations have been inadequate."

"There's still time." Thackery hesitated, collecting his thoughts. "You could begin by explaining on what units your system of measurement is based."

SWEETEST! I THOUGHT YOU'D FORGOTTEN.

"I am happy to repeat what I have said before. The basic unit of time is the *z'su* and of length the *z'von,*" said Z'lin. "Surely—"

BEING INSULTED AGAIN.

"Yes, yes, we understand that much. But on what is the *z'su* based?"

"All valid systems of measurement are based on fundamental physical constants."

GET HIM! GET HIM!

"Yes, of course," said Thackery agreeably. "What constants?"

"I am sorry," the Drull said. "As with the Tubes, I can use these units without knowing the ways in which they are specified by our more technically minded scholars. I will provide answers at our next meeting."

NO! DON'T GIVE HIM A CHANCE TO REHEARSE.

Koi's comments were becoming an annoyance, especially when her urgings were echoes of Thackery's own thoughts.

"Z'lin Ton Drull, we have already compared your units with the fundamental physical properties of matter and with the natural rhythms of Sennifi. There is no correlation. Either you have lied to us, or this is not your home world."

"Our home world is beneath us," said the implacable Sennifi leader. "I have not lied. You are mistaken, Merritt Thackery."

THE HELL IF WE ARE. I CHECKED SIDEREAL DAY, APPARENT EQUATORIAL DAY, MEAN SOLAR DAY, EPHEMERIS DAY.

Thackery reached out and shut off the slate and the room's video monitors, cutting Koi off from events in the room.

"I've been mistaken from time to time, including about you," said Thackery. "But I'm not mistaken about this—in all the time we've been meeting, from the first moment *Tycho* discovered you, you haven't cared to find out anything about us. Yet you claim to be scholars, dedicated to knowledge. How do you explain this contradiction?" Thackery's voice had lost its thin patina of politeness.

And the Drull hesitated. Did a flicker of emotion, fear perhaps, or dismay, slip past the mask of his face? No matter— he *hesitated*. "What little we wish to know of you, we know," he said finally.

Z'lin Ton Drull rose, and J'ten rose with him. "What little we wish to know of you, we know," the Drull repeated. "We see you as you are. We learn of you as true scholars do, not with our mouths but our eyes. Your future and past have no more reality than our own. Your world is beyond our reach. What then should we ask you?" Without waiting for an answer, the Drull turned and walked toward the climbway.

"Z'lin!" Thackery called as the Sennifi began their descent. "One last question! *Why do you want us to leave?*"

Z'lin Ton Drull neither looked back nor answered.

"Freezin' Jesus, Thackery, what did you say to them?"

"Leave me alone," Thackery said brusquely. "I've got to think this through."

"You made them so damn mad they fucking walked out."

"No. I scared them. And the worst thing is that I don't think I'm going to be able to do it again. There was just a crack, but I couldn't break him. He won't let it happen again, either. Damn! Go away," Thackery said as he slipped inside his cabin. "I've got to think this through."

"Do you realize what Neale's going to say when this reaches her?"

"Neale is not the problem," Thackery said, and slammed the door shut.

"There is a disturbance in that one which will not be quelled by empty words," said Z'lin Ton Drull. "This was not planned."

"I acknowledge the failure," J'ten Ron Tize said, his head lowered contritely.

"I do not charge the failure to your scholarship. This one is different. He is not in balance."

"Do you propose that he has the knowledge of the Mark?"

"No, J'ten," said the Drull. "Can you not see it? This one bears the Mark itself."

The lifepod was cramped and smelled of plastic and oil, but then, it wasn't designed for comfort. It was designed to hurl up to four crewmen a safe distance from an ailing survey ship, if possible in the direction of another ship or to the surface of a planet. Thackery had not been in one since Unity, but he remembered enough, and the lifepods were smart—smart enough to let Thackery choose a destination and tell him if it could be reached.

He hesitated but a moment, to try to decide when he had decided. The decision was one of synthetic inspiration, not lockstep reason. Reason said, climb out and walk away. But he had nothing to show for the breach he had created, nothing save proving that even the Sennifi could be badgered to the point of annoyance. Nothing to show—and so something more to do.

With a short, decisive motion of his hand, Thackery slammed down the mushroom-capped firing switch.

A moment later, he and the lifepod were falling toward Sennifi, leaving behind only a circular wound on the hull of *Munin* to mark where they had been.

Though there was no telecamera to confirm it, Thackery knew that the lifepod was arcing around the curve of the planet toward Maostri, a city of fifty thousand. He also knew that alarms were sounding on *Munin*'s bridge, and of that he soon got confirmation.

"Thackery, this is Neale. Acknowledge."

Inside the tiny obloid, Thackery steeled himself against the urge to return to the approval of those who would judge him. There was no point in answering. The lifepod was committed to the gravity well of Sennifi; in a few minutes he would be on the ground. If they wanted him back, they would have to come and get him—and they would, with little delay.

The cabin's air was growing warmer, and Thackery could envision the skin of the capsule glowing a cherry-red. As the air became more heated, so did Neale's insistent calls. Blissfully, the ionization halo soon shut her out.

The blind fall was discomfiting. Though Thackery could imagine the lifepod beginning its intended spiraling descent, he could with equal ease envision it falling unchecked toward the ground. *So this is what McShane and Koi feel.* As anxious seconds ground by, Thackery found himself finally grateful for the company of Neale's livid expostulations. *How long,* Thackery wondered—

And reached Sennifi. The roar of the precontact retros deafened him, and the impact of landing snapped his head sideways. Pain shot through his neck, and he bit down on the soft inside of his cheek. The lifepod was well padded and the harness holding him well designed, but Thackery nevertheless felt bruised from the inside, as though his bones had turned against the soft tissues they adjoined.

Maladroit in his eagerness, Thackery fumbled at the hatch release, and crawled out into the dust of a Maostri street. He looked up to a scene delineated by strong sunlight and sharp shadows.

It was a scene of stillness.

He was in the midst of the city, its buildings rising all around him. Their soft yellow color and rounded lines harmonized with the hills beyond the city, though the material from which they were made was neither earth nor rock. No curious faces peered at him. The street around the lifepod was empty.

Thackery struggled to his feet and called a greeting. It echoed back at him from the flat walls of far structures, but was not in any wise answered. On unsteady legs, he tottered off to find those who had fled at his carriage's reckless approach.

He did not find them.

The longer he searched, the more he denied the obvious; the more the hurt grew. At last, he sank to his knees in a multi-tiered plaza, shaken by the truth. The city was deserted. He could not deny the fact. He could not fathom its meaning. *How did they know what he was going to do—Where he would go— They couldn't have known—*

The drone of the ship's gig as it settled on a high platform at one end of the plaza failed to penetrate to his consciousness. It was a quiet sound that brought him back—the sound of cloth, folds rubbing against each other and sweeping along the ground. Thackery turned and looked up, into the face of Z'lin Ton Drull.

"They were never here," Thackery said.

"No."

"And Rijala?"

"Only caretakers. We have a compulsion for order—it is part of our pretense that nothing has happened." He extended a hand and helped Thackery to his feet. "Do you understand what you see?"

"I think what—but not why. You made us—and *Tycho*—think that your cities were full. Your population has collapsed, and you kept us from seeing it. But you said you weren't afraid—"

"We are not afraid *of* you. We are afraid for you. You know the why as well. You asked why we wanted nothing of you. It is true that we did not wish to place ourselves in your debt, for you would have stayed till you thought it repaid. But my answer then was truthful."

"You already had the answers to anything you might ask," Thackery said with sudden insight.

Z'lin nodded. "We were curious, once. Our curiosity was satisfied."

"How?"

"By whom," Z'lin corrected, and began walking, out of the plaza and down a silent street. Momentarily stunned, Thackery hurried after him.

"I will answer your question now," Z'lin continued. "The *z'von* is based upon the ultimate diameter of the Universe. The *z'su* is based upon its ultimate age. They are logical units, you will agree."

The answer seemed to liquefy the bones in Thackery's body. "What science can give you—"

"No science. The D'shanna are beyond science." Z'lin stopped and closed his eyes. "The D'shanna are the sword that cut us, that opened the wound that never healed. In form, they are as amorphous as the lights one sees with the eyes tightly closed—and as undeniably real." The Drull opened his eyes and began walking again. "They came five times, the last a hundred years ago. They destroyed everything we were, and made us everything we are."

"But how?" Thackery's dry throat turned his question into a rasping whisper.

"They answered our questions."

Thackery grabbed Z'lin's arm and spun him around so they faced each other. "What are you saying?"

"I am near the point at which I will answer no more questions, not even for such as you," Z'lin said calmly. "But this much we owe you—that you understand us. The D'shanna are creatures of light and knowledge, acting in real time yet existing timelessly. In your language, these are contradictions and impossibilities. In the reality of the Universe, they are not."

And then Z'lin smiled, sadly, self-critically. "We were bursting with pride when they came, Merritt Thackery, flush with the certainty of our greatness. We had only just completed the Tubes—had our lives in balance—were preparing to step beyond this planet. We were what you are—and they shamed us. Shamed us like the man who proudly calls on his neighbor to tell of the hut he has built, only to find his neighbor completing a mansion.

"They answered every question we asked of them. Like you, we made the mistake of asking too many."

The picture was suddenly complete in Thackery's mind: avoiding a future known in too much detail to be of interest, tending their slowly emptying cities, playing intellectual games and copying the art of a more vital past. Contact with the D'shanna had marked the Sennifi as clearly as a woodsman's blade marks the side of a tree.

"Why did they do it?" Thackery asked. "Surely they knew—"

Z'lin nodded, too proud to acknowledge his tear-filled eyes. "That was one question we did not know to ask until too late. But I believe I know the answer now." He stared oddly at Thackery, wistful and angry in a single expression. "This is the end, Merritt Thackery. As I have already explained to your commander, we will accept no ambassadors, no membership in your community. You are welcome to try to explain to her why, but she will not believe you." He turned and started to walk away.

"Wait!" Thackery said, leaping to block his path. "Why did you tell me?"

"Do you truly not know, or is it only that you do not know the words to name it?" Z'lin asked. "You bear their Mark, as deeply as we. We share the curse of having known them. Search your memory and you will know the time."

The search was not a long one. *Jupiter* . . .

"What I have told you cannot harm you. Regrettably, it also cannot satisfy you. Perhaps if you search with sufficient vigor, you will find them." Z'lin looked away. "For my part, I pray that you do not."

With that, Z'lin Ton Drull turned and walked off down the sloping street, away from the plaza and into the heart of the dead city of Maostri. Thackery watched him for a long time: a man more alone than he seemed, and seeming terribly alone.

But for all his empathy, Thackery could not quell his growing excitement for long. For he knew what Z'lin Ton Drull had known, knew the reason for the moment of hate in the Sennifi leader's eyes. The D'shanna had left their mark on the Sennifi deliberately, a living trail sign that Thackery could read more clearly than any, an invitation that only Thackery could grasp the import of. He turned away from the specter of Z'lin's dying world and began to walk, first slowly, then briskly, back to the plaza, to the gig.

At long last, his search was over, and there was purpose. For somewhere, the D'shanna were waiting. And he would not disappoint them.

chapter 11

Alliance

The setting was different, but the sight was distressingly familiar. Once again, Thackery returned from the surface of a planet to find himself facing the questions and skepticism of an inquiry board. But there was one change Thackery found ominous: joining Neale and Rogen on the other side of the table was not Dunn, but Cormican.

In the brief time Thackery had known him, Cormican had shown himself to be solid but unimaginative, a conservative ship's captain who liked rules and order. Cormican would have little tolerance for the sort of free-lancing Thackery's trip to the surface of Sennifi represented. Worse, the substitution meant that the only officer who seemed to understand all of Neale's dimensions—and therefore the nearest thing to an ally Thackery might hope for on the board—was gone.

This time it's you she wants, was Thackery's grim thought as he took his seat.

Neale's preamble showed that she, too, had taken note of the parallel. "Well, Merry," she said. "You must like these little sessions, eh? You're two for two now."

"I've been privileged to be involved in two of the most unusual Contacts on the books," Thackery said agreeably.

Neale propped her chin on her folded hands. "You've certainly done your part to make them so, in any case."

There was no winning response to that, so Thackery made none.

"The board has read your report on your——excursion——to Sennifi," Neale continued. "Some of what you said cries out for explanation. Some of what you left out demands explication."

Neale had been rehearsing for the encounter, Thackery observed silently; that sort of thing did not fall naturally off her tongue. "I'll be happy to answer any questions you have, and to amend the report to make it more inclusive."

"The answers will be welcome. The rest won't be necessary. Those portions of your report that are relevant will be incorporated into the overall contact report."

"I see." And Thackery did see, very clearly. *She not only wants you, she thinks she has you.*

"Let's begin with yesterday morning, in the conference room. You deviated from the Contact Interrogative Plan. Why?"

"The CIP hasn't been producing any real results for weeks——"

"Oh? Had the Sennifi been uncooperative?"

"On the face of it, they were being very cooperative. That was the key to their strategy——"

"Z'lin Ton Drull disclosed their strategy to you?"

"Not in so many words. But it's obvious in retrospect——"

"Let the board decide what's obvious and what isn't. You're here to answer questions, not to make judgments."

It'll take more than interruptions to get me to blow up in front of the others, Thackery thought determinedly. "Dr. Koi and I had identified anomalies which I believed were potentially more profitable than continuing lockstep with the CIP——"

"Measurement systems and the evacuation of Rijala."

"The presumed evacuation of Rijala," Thackery corrected.

"And on whose authority did you take up those issues during yesterday's session?"

"On my own as Contact Specialist. After the Commander removed herself from the conduct of the negotiations, I believed I was within my authority. The Commander might recall that she was the first to raise the possibility of modifying the CIP." Thackery looked steadily at Neale, but his words were meant for the rest of the board.

"But you made no effort to confirm these 'beliefs.'"

"No."

"Nor did you rethink the wisdom of your decision when it became obvious that your manner of questioning and the questions themselves were disturbing the Sennifi."

"That reaction was what I was most interested in."

"Ah—then you intended all along to force the Sennifi to break off negotiations." She did not give Thackery a chance to defend himself, moving briskly to another question. "Now, according to your report Z'lin said the Sennifi system of measurement was based on"—she paused theatrically and glanced down at her notes, and a hint of sarcasm crept into her voice—"the ultimate age and diameter of the Universe?"

"Yes."

"And you found that significant?"

"Yes. It's consistent with the linguistic forms. And it tends to support the rest of Z'lin's account."

"Did you trouble yourself to discuss this with Guerrieri?"

"Why should I have?"

She smiled faintly. "He would have reminded you that his fellow astrophysisicts long ago determined that the Universe is open, without any 'ultimate age' or 'ultimate diameter'. Perhaps you're aware that Earth civilizations once used a calendar based on the years since the birth of Christ and a measuring system based on the length of an Egyptian carpenter's forearm. Do you think those facts prove the existence of a Garden of Eden, or that the Pharoahs were gods? Your credulity would be heartwarming if you were a child, but you're not."

Neale was just warming up. "That goes for the rest of Z'lin's little allegory, as well. I don't have any trouble accepting that Z'lin told you what you report. I have trouble with how readily you apparently accept it. The one positive outcome of your little expedition was that it showed us what arational mystics the Sennifi are. You seem to have uncovered one falsehood one moment and swallowed an even bigger one the next."

"The Sennifi were lying to protect us from an experience that debilitated their entire society."

"That being Contact with these D'shanna."

"Yes."

"You have no evidence that they're any more real than the angels and devils of our own mythology. What's more, you can have no evidence."

"The evidence is the Sennifi themselves. And what the D'shanna did to Sennifi, they may have done to Earth. If you're looking to explain why the FC civilization disappeared, that possibility has to be given some consideration."

Neale sat back in her chair and nodded her head sagely. "Now I think we begin to see why you're so eager to have us believe Z'lin's story. That would make you the author of the new paradigm, wouldn't it? The Thackery Theorem topples the Mannheim Hypothesis from the throne—"

It was Thackery's turn to interrupt. "Not everyone thinks the way you do. I've got no personal attachment to this idea."

"No? Should I remind you that you were talking about second-species intervention a year ago, when we were outbound on *Descartes?* Tell me this, Merry. If we did believe you, what would you have us do?"

"Look for the D'shanna."

"I see," Neale said slowly. "You'd have us commit the precious resources of the Service to searching for beings which you cannot even demonstrate exist, much less tell us anything useful about. And in your defense all you can point to is the unimpeachable testimony of the Sennifi."

Thackery said nothing. There was no point.

"As it happens, there are simpler and more sensible explanations available," Neale said. "It seems that 2 Aquilae is a slightly variable star, now in the active part of a roughly thousand-year cycle. I'm assured that the hard radiation flux at the surface is sufficient to contribute synergistically to a decrease in fertility. Of course, the Sennifi's naturalistic medicine offers them no means of understanding that, much less coping with it. So it's no surprise that they evolved a face-saving explanation for their loss of virility."

"Is that the explanation you intend to forward to the FC Committee and the Flight Office?" Thackery asked, scowling.

"It is."

"Permission to file a minority report on the Contact."

"Denied."

And with that, it was over. Rogen and Cormican had not said a word—it was as if they were merely props for Neale's little stage show. All that remained was to wait until the reviews appeared. And Thackery was more certain than he wanted to be about just how his performance had been received.

Outside, Koi was waiting for him. "How bad was the flaying?" she asked as they started downship together.

Thackery pursed his lips. "I'd say she took off about the first five layers of skin."

"Ouch," Koi said, and fell silent until they reached the privacy of Thackery's cabin. "So she didn't believe you."

"She believed me. She didn't believe Z'lin."

Koi sighed expressively. "I thought as much."

"What's all this about radiation, anyway? You never mentioned it."

"She didn't get it from me," Koi said defensively. "She called in the science team one by one last night and asked them if they had found anything that could account for a population decline on Sennifi."

"So does it?"

"If that's all you look at, yes. Look, it's a little hot down there. *Tycho* picked up on it during their landing, too. Now, you can graph those two readings as two points on an upward curve, or as two slightly different peaks of a shorter cycle. If it were the first, we'd see a whole pattern of effects, one of which could be a decline in fertility. But that's not what we see."

"Didn't you explain that to Neale?"

"She has a flexible standard for evidence. When she doesn't want to be convinced, the standard is very high. When she's eager to believe, the standard is low. I'm afraid nothing I could tell her would help your case."

Thackery shook his head. "I guess I knew that without asking," he said glumly. "I was hoping that she was doing this as a way of appropriating the credit for herself."

"I think you've presented her with something she's not conceptually equipped to deal with."

"What about you?"

"I don't know," she said. "I have to be generally sympathetic. I started you off on this. But she's right. It's just a story. Extraordinary claims—"

"—require extraordinary evidence. Yes, I know all that." He paused and looked at the floor. "I also know that Z'lin's story is at least essentially true."

"Why?"

He hesitated before answering. "Because of something I didn't put in the report. I think I had a brush with the D'shanna myself, ten years ago."

"Tell me."

"I've only ever told one other person, and afterward I wished I hadn't."

She reached out and touched his hand. "I won't give you reason to feel that way."

"I guess I know that, too, or I wouldn't have brought it up." Somehow the memory seemed clearer, sharper, as he retold it this time—if he looked away from her and off into the dark corners of the cabin, he could almost place himself back in the Panorama, and recapture the rush of feeling as the shield rolled back to reveal the face of Jupiter.

"I know my experience doesn't exactly parallel what Z'lin said. I didn't see any D'shanna. No one spoke to me. But I had an overwhelming sense of Contact with alienness. I saw everything differently, more intensely, more emotionally. What happened to me was all out of proportion with anything that came before or after."

"And that's why you joined the Service?"

"Yes. It's shaped every important choice I've made for ten years. Jupiter changed me, Amy—it pushed me sideways, and I've been out of balance ever since, without ever understanding how or why. Even Z'lin could see it, and knew I would understand. I don't think he would have told me what he did, except for that."

"You sound as though you're carrying a grudge."

"Don't I have reason to, as much as the Sennifi do?" he demanded, pulling his hand away and retreating across the compartment from her. "My life was in perfect order, and they made it a disaster," he continued, his back to her. "I've been miserable since I first set foot on a survey ship. I'd have gotten out at A-Cyg if there were any point to it. But there's nothing to go back to. The chance I had is already long gone." He turned back to her, and his features were contorted by his anger. "Who has a better reason to find them?"

"I'm sorry—"

Thackery blew a long breath through pursed lips. "You've got no reason to be."

"I was going to say I was sorry I couldn't help."

"You did help. I would never have gone to the surface if you hadn't noticed what you did."

"I'm not sure I did you a favor. D'shanna is a Sennifi word—"

"From the *haarit* language."

"Have you had time to analyze it?"

"No," he said.

"I have," she said. "It means, first order, *life stealers*—second order, *implacable enemy*—third order, *totality of evil*. These are the things you want to go hunting?"

His face reflected his childlike helplessness to control his own compulsions. "I have to, Amy. I have to."

"But Thack—if you're right, then the Sennifi may know the answers to all the puzzles we've been trying to decipher. They may have the solution to the colony problem."

Thackery nodded vacantly. "The very highest class of scholars knows. Z'lin Ton Drull knows, I'm sure of it."

"Then *this* is where we should be. We need to stay here and persuade them to help us. Hell, we should move the whole Data Analysis Office out here."

A tolerant smile played across Thackery's lips. "We could fill their skies with ships, and I don't think they would ever tell us," Thackery said, shaking his head. "I don't think we have any leverage with them whatsoever. I don't think we could bribe them, or threaten them, or punish them enough to get them to share what they know. They are an extremely moral people, and they would view it as an extremely immoral act. They simply would not do it."

"What if we went in and seized their records? Took over their scholar complex and their libraries? We could dig it out of there on our own."

"And thereby demonstrate what *our* moral stature is? No, Amy, you've missed something. The whole function of the scholar's languages in their society is to insulate the knowledge from all but a few. The concept of the D'shanna, of a star-spanning civilization, of the beginning and end of the Universe, can't even be expressed in their common language. Without their willing help, a hundred interpolators working a thousand years wouldn't have a prayer of sorting through—"

"Damn it, Merritt, if they know what happened to the FC civilization, we have to try!"

Thackery shook his head slowly and emphatically. "It's better that Neale and the others don't believe Z'lin's story, or they'd probably do exactly what you say. No, Amy. If the Sennifi know, then the D'shanna also know. I intend to hear it from them."

For three days, Thackery remained in purgatory, hearing nothing from Neale about the specifics of his ultimate fate. He spent most of that time with a slate, searching the contact records from the other colonies in the faint and ultimately fruitless hope of finding some evidence to corroborate his story.

The remaining time he whiled away as pleasantly as possible with that portion of the *Munin*'s crew who were willing to be seen with him. The division was, with one exception, along operations-scientific lines. The science team insisted on regarding him as some sort of hero; the command crew, as some sort of pariah. The exception to the rule was Kellerman, the planetary ecologist, who saw the elevated status which came with being Neale's new favorite as a license to sneer down at the less fortunate.

Throughout Thackery's term in purgatory, there was a steady flow of Kleine traffic back and forth with A-Cyg. Unfortunately, Thackery was neither a party to it nor privy to its contents. Doubtless, most of the dispatches concerned the Sennifi; a large fraction of the rest, the imminent arrival of *Descartes*. But just as certainly, some of it had to do with Thackery himself.

Sentence had still not been pronounced when *Descartes* dropped out of the craze a few light-hours away. The rendezvous and the expected crew transfer to follow quickly became the primary topic of conversation, even among those not expecting to be affected.

It was Guerrieri who came looking for Thackery with the news. He found him curled up in a chair in the edrec room, all alone watching a recording of a pre-Restoration absurdist drama about a family facing a New Ice Age.

"Have you heard?"

"Heard what?"

"Descartes will be alongside in an hour."

That interested Thackery enough to press the PAUSE button. "Have they posted crew assignments yet?"

"No. Do you mean they haven't told you yet what they're going to do with you?"

"They haven't. But that doesn't mean I don't know. Neale's going to continue on with *Descartes,* and I'm going to be sent back with *Munin.*"

"Well—at least you won't have to deal with her anymore."

"You will. You'll be going over to *Descartes.*"

Guerrieri admitted sheepishly, "That's kind of what I'm expecting. I haven't had any problems with her, though. You've been kind of like a lightning rod—kept the rest of us safe."

It was clearly meant as a joke, to relieve the astrophysicist's embarrassment over what would in all likelihood be a very final separation. "Glad to have been of service," Thackery said in similar spirit, but his mind was elsewhere. *I don't know how to say good-bye to you, Derrel. We've skirted around the fringes of friendship, and I don't know what that calls for. But there's someone else to whom I know just what I want to say—*

"Where are you going?" Guerrieri asked, making Thackery aware that he had risen from the chair.

"To see Neale. To say all the things I bit my tongue over at the inquiry."

"Aw, Thack, why bother?"

"Because this is my last chance. And because I've got nothing to lose."

When Neale's cabin door opened, Thackery was pleased to see by her tousled hair and reddened cheek that his page had roused her from sleep.

"Tell me, are you incapable of learning shipboard etiquette, or do you just think it's all a bore?" she asked icily.

"I want to talk to you."

"Well, whatever Merry wants, Merry gets. Come in, come in," she said sarcastically, stepping aside and gesturing with a sweeping motion of one arm. "What can I do for you?"

"You can stop calling me Merry, for one thing," he snapped. "My name is Merritt Thackery. I'm not your son, or your pet, so if you want to address me you'll use my given name and not invent new ones for me."

"Forgive me—I didn't realize that you were above nicknames," she said, closing the door behind him.

"My friends are welcome to call me Thack."

"And of course, you don't count me among them."

"You're damned right I don't."

"Trying to display all your social failings, *Mr. Thackery?* Your attitude's a bit lacking in command respect. If I were a disciplinarian like Cormican, I might be tempted to—"

"You've given up the right to respect by your conduct here."

Neale laughed. "My conduct here? Which one of us stole a lifepod and made an unauthorized contact landing?"

"I didn't ask for this post, and I wouldn't have picked myself for it. You chose to leave a better man back at A-Cyg. If you're not happy with my performance, you have only yourself to blame. Not that you're very good at accepting blame. You ducked responsibility for what happened at Gnivi."

"As your beloved mentor Mark Sebright took pains to point out to me, when a survey ship is in-system the Contact Leader is in charge. The blame for those two perfectly preventable deaths fell exactly where it belonged."

"Is that why you enlisted me to help pressure him into an early landing? You were thinking about your career then and nothing else."

"You didn't have to say yes. And what do you claim to have been thinking about? The greater good of mankind? You were being just as self-serving as you say I was."

"True. And I'm honest enough to admit it, and have conscience enough to regret it."

"Oh, I see! *That's* where you acquire your moral superiority—by wringing your hands after the fact. Now all we have to decide is where you lost your judgment. I hear you're still pushing your D'shanna fantasy downship. Tell me, how long have you known you're the only one gifted with the wisdom to point out our errors and save us from ourselves?"

"Dammit, I only want a fair hearing—"

"You had it. And if you keep identifying yourself with this nonsense, you just may invite a psychological evaluation and a fitness review."

"Is that how you've decided to get rid of me?"

"I have no interest in 'getting rid of' you. You haven't proven yourself particularly useful, but that's hardly the basis for a vendetta."

"I'm no use to you because I've found out what kind of person you are—a selfish, amoral opportunist—"

She smiled slightly. "You need to be getting more sleep—fatigue is making you testy."

"—who doesn't belong in command of a survey ship."

"I agree," she said, nodding gravely. "As does the Flight Office, you'll be pleased to hear. You see, Merry, I've been appointed to fill a vacancy on the FC Committee."

Thackery's eyes widened in dismay. "What?!"

"I knew you'd be pleased. Of course, I can't discharge that responsibility and hold down a full-time ship billet at the same time. So I'll be returning to A-Cyg in *Descartes*."

"But *Descartes* is continuing on—"

"Oh, no, that was before this news. Now it's *Munin* that's

continuing on. Oh, and Merry—you'll also be pleased to know I recommended you for Contact Leader, and the Flight Office found that agreeable. So you're staying with *Munin,* along with Commander Cormican and Dr. Koi and the rest of the science team—now the survey team. Except Kellerman, of course. You do have one body to spare, and I'm going to need a new executive assistant."

"No!"

"Oh, yes. Oh, you'll want to know that the clock goes back to zero for you. It'll be a three-year tour contract, with no allowance for your time on *Descartes.* It's only fair. Most of the crew is new, and we can't let one or two individuals dictate the timetable of an entire survey ship, can we? I hope you enjoy your new assignment, Merry. I know I'm going to enjoy mine."

The encounter left Thackery shattered and emotionally empty. Eventually he found himself standing outside the closed door of the science lab, without quite knowing why and without the will to either leave or enter.

Then the door opened and he was nearly run down by Barbrice Mueller, the young technoanalyst.

"Mr. Thackery," she said in surprise, and sidled past, leaving the door open for him.

At the mention of his name, Koi glanced toward the door from her station. Seeing the look in Thackery's eyes, she left her work without a word.

"She did it to me again," he said helplessly as she joined him.

"Let's go to my cabin," she urged, and he followed her suggestion docilely. Once there, he sat round-backed on the edge of her bed, staring down at the floor.

"You went to see Neale?"

"It was like arguing with Andra—and I never won those, either. I never even reached her." He craned his head and found Koi, still standing, by her desk. "I don't think I inhabit the same world as people like that."

"Unfortunately, you do."

"No, I mean it. It's like there are two realities. In one, I screwed up at Gnivi and broke all the rules at Sennifi. In the other, I distinguished myself at both places and earned promotions."

"History belongs to she who writes it."

"But she had me set up. With the stunt I pulled, she didn't even have to work hard to do it. Now I'm going to be Contact Leader on *Munin*."

Koi showed no surprise at the announcement. "Her priorities have changed."

"But after tearing me to pieces in front of Cormican, to transfer me to his crew—"

"She probably managed to make it look like the Flight Office's doing. Look, she's not doing you a favor. From her point of view, this is a better way to get rid of you. She can go back to A-Cyg and enjoy the fruits of your success, while making sure that you're not around to compete for the credit. And if she publishes a second-species proposal, it'll be all hers."

"I thought you said she couldn't cope with that idea."

"She adjusted quickly. I did some poking around in her netlink's activity register. She's been looking into the whole history of the idea, back to Von Daniken himself."

"I don't understand. When I talked to her about this once before, she laughed it down, called it wishful thinking. Are you saying she believes me?"

Koi's voice was gentle, soothing. "Maybe she believes you despite herself. Maybe she's finally decided that the colony problem won't be solved in her lifetime—which means that she wouldn't be proven wrong in her lifetime, either. There are no serious second-species theorists. If she could pull something sound out of that psuedoscientific mishmash, that'd establish her as someone of substance on the committee. Or maybe she plans to write the definitive refutation of the second-species hypothesis—which might accomplish the same thing. Whatever her plans are, she's going to make sure that you're not around to gum them up."

He shook his head despairingly. "I understand what she's doing to me. I expected it, or something like it. But she's hitting at you, too—why? Because you weren't smart enough to keep your distance from me? She's got no right to put you where you're going to have to go through the craze time after time."

Koi took a step toward him and tentatively stretched out her hand. "Don't be angry with her about that."

"I can't help it."

"No—I mean it. I requested the assignment."

Beyond surprise, Thackery mustered only a feeble "Why?"

"The drugs make the phobia manageable. I think I can cope with it."

"But why even try?"

"I want to go where you do."

"I don't understand."

She came and sat beside him, and he let her take his hands in hers. "Thack—I don't know how to be shy about either part of this. Professionally, I find the possibility that you're right more interesting than the probability that you're wrong. And personally, I like you. I think you need an ally, a friend— maybe a lover. I think maybe I could be all three."

He wanted to warn her off, to make her understand how twisted and pointless his relationships with women had been. *They all wanted something from me—Andra, Diana, Neale— always wanted something more and gave so little back. I don't even know you enough to know what it is you want. How can I trust you? How can I trust any of you?*

But he also wanted her to hold him, to let her pull his head down to her shoulder, to have the comfort of her arms around him and her warmth close by. And in the end, that urge was stronger. He reached out to her, and found her embrace a better refuge than solitude or bitterness.

Only after the anger and frustration had drained from him did the embrace turn sexual. It did so fitfully, each of them self-conscious, neither of them certain that they were ready to face that complexity so quickly. Not surprisingly, they were awkward with each other, tentative and unsure. But for all that, their lovemaking was also tender and affectionate, a combination Thackery found he preferred over the memory of other more practiced partners. By the time they lay snuggled against each other afterward, her head resting on his chest, the self-consciousness was gone.

"What do you really want?" she asked, almost in a whisper. "If you were making all the decisions, what would you give yourself?"

He did not hesitate. "Operational command of a ship—so I could follow the trail wherever it leads."

"Then work on it," she urged him. "Figure out what angle will get them to go for it."

His finger traced its way lazily down to the warm hollow at the base of her spine. "Ships are too scarce, and they're always going to be scarce. They'll never turn one over to me."

"No, of course they won't," she said, rolling over and propping her chin on her hands to look at him. "But they might commit one to a new strategy, if they thought it had potential. They're looking down the road to Phase Three, and I can tell you on good authority that they have serious doubts whether they'll be able to muster the ships and crews it will require. If you can make them believe you can make the search more efficient, they'll listen."

"But what I want to do would probably be less efficient—taking a ship out of the comprehensive search program to chase down loose ends."

"That doesn't matter until after the fact. Look, if the billet you want doesn't exist yet, you have to try to get them to create it. You've got three years by our calendar, seventy or more by theirs to make your case, and then we'll be back at A-Cyg and you can try to claim a place in whatever's come of it."

"But three years wasted—"

"They won't be wasted. There's a lot to do."

He nodded and kissed her forehead. "I just wish I could somehow get my version of the Sennifi Contact into the record."

"Already seen to," she said with a mischievous smile. "It's part of the anecdotal sociology file in the scientific dispatch. Neale won't catch it, and the Analysis Office won't make much of it—but it'll be there when you need to go back and point to it."

Cocking his head, he gazed at her fondly. "You're really looking after me, aren't you?"

"I'm going to try," she promised. "I'm going to try."

chapter 12

The Lesson of Delphinus

Though he had been aboard *Munin* nearly two months, Thackery had never been in Cormican's quarters until called there the first morning out from Sennifi. He found the compartment spartan, practical, and uncluttered, more a place to sleep and bathe than a personal living space. That reflected the long hours required by the man's command style, which was to make individual contact with every member of the operations crew at least once in the course of a four-shift, 24-hour cycle.

After admitting Thackery, Cormican retreated to the doorway to the bathroom, where he resumed shaving his stubble-darkened jowls. "I don't make a habit of going out of my way to have private conversations on professional matters," he said without preamble. "If I can't say what I have to in front of anyone who might be around, I figure I probably don't need to say it at all. But I thought we should get a few things settled before any more time passed. You've got a lot of experience, Merritt, a lot more than me, but the fact is, you don't seem to have picked up any good sense along the way."

"Go on."

"The fact is, I don't believe in heroes, and I've got no time for grandstanders. People in positions of authority don't have more freedom than the people they supervise, they have less. That's the price of responsibility. The more there is at stake, the more cautious you have to be. Am I coming through?"

"Yes."

"Good. Then you understand that I'm not impressed with results. What I mean is, they won't keep me from looking at what was done to get them and sounding off if I don't like what I see. As far as I'm concerned, there's always more than one way to achieve a goal, and I expect you to take the path of least risk. Clear?"

"Very."

"Now, this business back at 2 Aquilae—you did make a breakthrough, but we'd eventually have found out what the Sennifi were all about some other way, without stretching the Protocols past the limit. I'll tell you this, I'd damn well not have let you off with a verbal reprimand. I'd have paid off your contract and sent you packing. But that's past and this is present, so I'll say no more about it. That goes for the rest of your disagreements with Commander Neale. I'm not an appeals court. I can't change any of her decisions, and I'm not interested in hearing arguments on why I should try."

"I didn't intend to offer any."

"Good. You make sure you understand this—you pull that kind of stunt under my command and you'll find yourself on a nice desert planet with a canteen and a canister of protein paste, waving good-bye as we craze. I won't have it, you understand? I won't have it. By the Protocols, Concom Thackery. And if you get into a gray area, you come tell me what you're going to do and why. No surprises. I hate surprises."

"By the numbers," Thackery acknowledged.

"All right. I've had my say. Now you take your shot, and make sure you get it all, because I don't want to be sorting this out halfway to Deneb."

Thackery shook his head. "I don't have much to say. What you described is exactly how I want to work. I should tell you I intend to make rehearsal landings at the first opportunity, on worlds where the risk is minimal. There's a big difference between training and reality, and I want the contact team to know that right up front. I also want them to learn the limitations of orbital surveying. You have any problems with that policy?"

Cormican twice ran his fingers back through his thinning silver hair as he considered. "No. That seems prudent," he pronounced at last. "Fact is, if it goes well, I'd like to see if we couldn't get everybody down at least once in the course of this mission—techs, awks, the whole crew. Seems to me that standing on an alien planet ought to be part of the payoff for giving up a normal life. We ought to send them all back with at least one good story for their descendants, don't you think? And I'd hate to see anybody get the idea that the survey team is better somehow, that they get all the privileges and perks. What do you say to that?"

Thackery did not welcome the prospect of looking after what amounted to tourists, but it was too early and the ground too soft for a pitched battle. "I say the gig is rated for six people," Thackery said, "which is two more than we'll routinely take to the surface. Those seats are at your disposal."

"Good. Maybe we'll be able to work with each other after all."

"I hope so."

Munin's first stop was 26 Sagittae, a cool red M-class dwarf too dim to be seen even from A-Cyg without optical aid. By the time she came out of the craze there, Thackery had completed what he expected to be merely the first installment of a continuing series of theses and position papers, this one an overview entitled PHASE III ALTERNATIVES: THE CASE FOR SELECTIVE SURVEYING.

On the bridge to supervise a priority dispatch of the paper, Thackery was among the first on board to learn from the update dispatch that while the ship had been out of touch an eleventh colony had been added to the human community. At the earliest opportunity, he and Koi curled up together on his bed to review the Liam-Won contact report.

"All I've heard was that it was the *Edwin Hubble*," she said, tugging at the slate he held so that she could read its display.

"The colony's on a free-water planet orbiting 85 Monocerous."

"What kind of spectrum on the primary?"

"F5 III."

"That's right on the Galactic equator," she said, noting the celestial coordinates.

"A very popular choice this season. So is Gnivi. So is Sennifi."

"Actually, that's seven colonies in or near the plane of the Galaxy, with only two colonies each in the whole northern and southern galactic hemisphere," she mused. "There might be a case there for focusing the Phase III search in the plane, maybe pulling ships out of the Boötes and Eridanus octants."

"Tech rating of 3.1," he read. "Another Bronze Age civilization."

"That's four in that range."

"Another very popular model. Yelp if you see anything new—I'm beginning to think I've seen it all before."

They scanned the remainder of the summary at a fairly fast scroll, then laid the slate aside and reflected.

"What's your gut feeling?" Thackery asked. "Have we found most of the colonies, or just scratched the surface?"

"It would be easier to say if we had any idea what the FC starships were like."

"Is that the only answer you're going to give me?"

"No. That's the excuse that comes before the answer. I suspect we've found almost all of them. I've always thought of forty light-years as about the outside limit for most of the possible non-AVLO technologies, and most of our ships are pushing that now."

"And when we've found them all and we still don't know any more than we do now—"

"I thought you were counting on the D'shanna sorting it all out."

"You don't expect me to not think about it until then, do you?"

"If you're so jaded about having a live, warm woman in your bed that you're so easily distracted—"

A sharp poke in the ribs interrupted her teasing. "Don't you know, I'm attracted to you for your brains, not your body?"

She sat up, shucked off her blouse, and struck a pouty, bare-breasted pose. "Really?"

That precipitated a forty-minute interruption that was as much playful as passionate.

"I was serious, though," he said when they settled back into a more restful embrace. "How much more do we really know now than we did just after *Jiadur* reached Earth? Not a hell of a lot. In fact, the problem's worse now than it was then. Every colony we find makes it that much harder to believe that the FC civilization just up and vanished. The farther each new colony is from Earth, the harder it is to explain how they accomplished the colonization. I think our search has been too narrow in scope. The answer has to lie outside ourselves."

She shook her head. "I can't agree. The difference between one colony and ten is incremental. But the gap between a planet-bound civilization and an interstellar one is several orders of magnitude. You're just experiencing a kind of delayed incredulity. If the Forefathers could do it once, they could do it a dozen times. If they could reach Journa, they could reach Sennifi."

"Whereupon they abandoned any traces of the level of technology required to get them there."

"You mean that the colonies lack spaceflight capability? What point was there in retaining it once they reached a suitable planet? And they wouldn't have had the technological base to sustain it. There's a limit to how much you can bring with you, even in a starship the size of *Jiadur*."

"If they had starships at all."

"What do you mean by that?"

"Just that I don't find any of the alternatives convincing. If they used small slowships, then how did they manage to live long enough to start colonies this far out? If they used generation slowships, then why haven't we found at least some remnant or wreckage of something that large? And if they used fastships, why isn't that level of technology reflected in the colonies they founded?"

"The colonies *had* to fall back to a simpler lifestyle. You can't expect them to start their new society at the same level as the one they left."

"Of course not—but it's been thousands of years since then. The knowledge base that they brought with them should have put at least some of the colonies on our level by now."

"That's a fair argument," she conceded.

"Here's another. Consider it from the point of view of the FC civilization. How many ships did they send out? How many *could* they before we have to think that, glacier or no, they'd have to have been so large and so powerful as to necessarily leave some traces? There's another variable that's even more disturbing. Did every ship survive to start a colony? Highly unlikely. Then is there one colony for every ten ships that set out, or one for every hundred? That gets us into some very difficult numbers."

"So let's hear some answers."

"I'm only good at the questions," he admitted. "That's why this whole thing is going to make me crazy."

• • •

26 Sagittae offered only a pair of small moonlike planetoids, suitable for rehearsal landings but of no other value. Thackery went on both landings, nominally to supervise the command crew hitchhikers. His real purpose was to flesh out his Service record as favorably as possible; each landing was entered as a discrete item, while he received no specific credit for directing a landing in which he did not take part.

So he continued the practice in the next system and the next, stretching the definition of a suitable planet from min-E to E-1 and even E-2 where necessary. Hard work and Koi's company made the time go fast. After each craze, he would send out the latest addendum to his growing treatise on high-probability searches. Only once was there any explicit response, and that was a copy of another paper refuting most of the points in Thackery's last exposition. He shrugged it off and proceeded to refute the refutation.

As the count on his personal scorecard climbed into double figures the worlds he had seen and walked all began to merge together in his mind. Was the patterned tundra ground they briefly mistook for evidence of human engineering on 27 Sagittae-5 or 5 Serpens-5? Was it 61 Aquilae-6 which had the great white kaolinite plains? Where was it that Barrister nearly put us down in a bog?

Only Thackery's growing collection of memorabilia kept the record clear. There was one object from each landing: the Gnivian fertility icon, a scrimshaw-like mosaic tile pried from the plaza on Sennifi, a spike-leaved flower (encased in a block of clear preservative) picked on 12 Vulpeculae-6, a chunk of glittery itacolumite from 26 Sagittae, and more—each with the standard A.R. date on which he acquired them engraved on the underside.

They were his memory crutches, without which he doubted he would remember in detail much more than the two contact landings. Rehearsal landings and survey landings alike were, by necessity, made on worlds which fell into a narrow range of all possible worlds. He was not geologist enough to read a planet's morphology and see not just a landscape but an un-folding drama, nor biologist enough to see in each organism a unique natural history and ecology. He knew that those things existed, and learned of them through the team, but even so, the worlds without man made little impression on him.

Until 61 Delphinus-5.

Afterward, Thackery blamed himself. He had not conducted the time-consuming prescribed inspection of his E-suit after each decontamination procedure. In retrospect, he knew that the right glove had gone on too easily as he dressed for the landing on Del-5. That was the telltale sign of a degraded binding ring. That should have been all the warning he needed.

But the string of unremarkable landings on forgettable worlds had made him casual about safety and contemptuous of the risk. After sixteen planetfalls, he had come to regard the descent and ascent as the only potentially dangerous part of the landing ritual.

Del-5's largest continent had a drier climate than might have been expected on a planet four-fifths covered by water, but a range of rugged, geologically new mountains along the eastern coast stripped most of the moisture from the prevailing sea breeze. Nevertheless, the interior savanna was home to a variety of simple lifeforms, some plant-like, some animal-like, and some of uncertain classification.

The most interesting of the last group were the colorful, lichen-like autotrophs which clung to the near-vertical surfaces of crumbling volcanic dikes and sills throughout one 500-hectare region. What made them interesting was that they were motile, migrating slowly across the barren rock in the course of each day, trying to avoid being caught in the shadows.

Though a full study of Del-5's ecology and of the autotrophs' niche would have to wait for later visitors, Norris was set on adding one of the creatures to *Munin*'s storehouse of geological and biological samples. Capturing one for examination meant a bit of rock-climbing, however, since the most accessible ground the team spotted while scouting in the gig was some sixty metres up on the side of a well-weathered scarp.

It was Thackery who volunteered to accompany Norris on the hunt. Together they went scrambling up the sloping talus pile of rock litter to the bottom of the sunbattered rock face on which the creatures were arrayed. The talus was composed of fine bits of weathered quartzite, banked to the limit of the local gravity, and the climbers started minor landslides with each step.

When they reached the top, Guerrieri moved in with the gig

and maneuvered it so that its wedge-shaped shadow fell over a cluster of some twenty of the autotrophs. Those in the middle of the shadow simply froze where they were, while those farther out began to move toward the sharply defined edge of the shadow. With Thackery and Norris directing, Guerrieri eventually herded three of the creatures down within reach of the long-handled specimen scoop, and Norris swept two of them into the scoop's pouch with a single practiced motion.

Then it was back down the slope to where they had left the back-pack sized Specimen Preservation Unit. All that was left to do was transfer the specimen from the scoop to the holding chamber of the SPU, wherein a blast of liquid nitrogen would render the specimen ready for examination. For fast-moving organisms, the scoop could be attached directly to the SPU. But when the specimen allowed, it was decidedly simpler to open the top of the SPU chamber and place the specimen inside by hand.

Using the latter method, Norris quickly transferred one of the autotrophs. But the second specimen resisted, clinging by some means to the inside wall of the scoop like a cat with its claws dug into a bed. Watching the struggle with some amusement, Thackery suddenly noted movement at the lip of the SPU chamber as the first autotroph began to crawl? glide? wriggle? over the edge.

"Trying to get away," he warned.

The two men reacted with incompatible responses: Thackery reached out to brush the creature back into the chamber, while Norris reached out to slam the chamber's lid shut. Having seen the motion first, Thackery's reaction was the faster but also placed his hand in peril. He snatched it away as the lid came down, but not fast enough to keep the tip of the middle and index fingers of his right glove from being pinched between the metal edges.

The thin, flexible fabric showed the strength for which it was reputed, and did not tear. Instead, the wrist ring of Thackery's glove popped loose, and the glove was left dangling from the seam of the closed lid, while the skin of Thackery's right hand felt the warm sunlight and gentle breezes of 61 Del-5.

It was a matter of only five minutes to free the glove, call the gig down, and retreat to the safety of its flight deck. There Connolly bathed both the bare skin and the glove with a powerful cell-disrupting antiorganic. The chemical caused a burning sensation which grew steadily more intense until washed away under a water jet a short time later.

"That antiorg will kill off the first layer of your epidermis, along with anything that might have climbed on for a ride, so you might feel just a little itching a few hours from now," Connolly advised him as he fitted the glove back in place. "If the itching is bad, or you get any other symptoms, don't be slow about telling me."

Back on board *Munin,* Thackery experienced the itching as predicted—a gnawing, maddeningly irresistible sensation that he responded to with scratching. But he made no point in mentioning it to Connolly or even Amelia, since it seemed a nuisance he could tolerate until the irritation passed.

But by that evening, his right hand had begun to puff up, and several other spots to itch: the fingers of his left hand; several patches on his right forearm; an area low on his left cheek, near the jawline. The moment he became aware of the new outbreaks, Thackery went searching for Connolly.

"Could I be having an allergic reaction to the antiorganic?" Thackery asked, holding his swollen hand up for the biologist's inspection.

"No," Connolly said, his voice and expression betraying his concern. "You were tested for it when you signed on. We'd better get you isolated."

Very shortly thereafter, Thackery was ensconced in cabin F5, which was equipped with the special ventilation, door seals, and other facilities needed to turn it into a negative-pressure Level II isolation chamber. Following Connolly's instructions, Thackery took skin scrapings and blood and urine samples and passed them out through the small double-doored transfer lock. Later, dinner was passed in to him the same way.

"No matter what this turns out to be, the best thing you can do for yourself now is rest," Connolly advised via the shipnet. "You just rest while we look into this."

As usually follows such prescriptions, Thackery slept poorly. By morning, his fingers resembled fat sausages, and he could not bend them enough to make a fist. The skin over the swollen areas had begun to harden into a scabrous crust, and as he tried to wash and dress, the crust split open and oozed a watery fluid. Connolly demanded samples of the crust and the fluid as well, and took them without offering either information or encouragement in return.

For those Thackery had to depend on Koi, who kept an open line between her cabin and his prison and used it as often as her schedule allowed.

"You can beat this," she assured him. "You're going to be all right."

Thackery wondered if she believed it. He himself was not so confident—it was his body that was under attack, his body that was changing hour by hour, his body that was being violated in unpleasant and unpredictable ways. A survey ship's lab wasn't equipped to be a medical research facility, and Connolly wasn't trained as a medical researcher. Lying alone in the room, regarding his affliction with both disgust and dismay, Thackery remembered the hated gnotobiotic screening back at Unity.

Like issuing a warrior a paper shield and a rubber sword and saying, Sorry, best we can do for you.

No new outbreaks appeared, either on Thackery's body or among the rest of the survey team, but as the day wore on those which were already underway brought increasing misery. Presently Thackery began to pester Connolly for something to reduce the swelling, to end the itching, to blunt the growing pain.

"You've got active antibodies in your bloodstream for anything we already know how to treat," was the unencouraging answer. "I can't give you anything else until I know what I'm trying to fight."

By the end of the second day, the crusting skin on Thackery's right hand had oxidized to an ominous black, and the other patches had begun to darken as well. The sores seemed to be drying out; each new crack no longer bathed his hands in slippery fluid. But all the same, his hands were nearly useless.

That evening, Connolly came by and joined Thackery in the isolation cabin, taking no special precautions to protect himself.

"This must be good news," Thackery said hopefully.

"It is," the biologist said with a cheery smile. "This problem is not an infection. There are no active Del-5 organisms in your system or on your skin. So we don't have to keep you here any more."

"Wonderful," Thackery said, and held up his hands. "What about this, then?"

"Ever had toxin dermatitis?"

"No."

"You've got it now. Your body is reacting to an alkyl produced by one of Del-5's single-celled inhabitants. We found them by the millions on the rock crawlers."

"A poison?"

"Looks like an internal product or structural element rather than a defense mechanism. The antiorg pops cells like balloons, which is how you got exposed to the compound. From there on, it's just a bad match between its biochemistry and yours. Which we can do something about now. Roll up your sleeve."

But the freedom to leave F5 meant less than it might have. With his hands as they were, he could not negotiate the climbway, and so was restricted to F deck. He could not make love with Amy, and he would not let her make love to him, would not accept her willingness to give without receiving, for he projected onto her the revulsion he felt at the sight of himself.

That was the worst part: the constant reminder of vulnerability, of mortality, represented by the repellant disfigurement he carried everywhere with him. *For what?* he demanded of himself. *Why am I taking these risks?* His own attitude shamed him, and he would not talk about the feelings with Amy. Instead, when she came downship to see him he found himself talking about a world she had never seen: Earth.

Munin was ten days into the craze before the black scabs began to break away, revealing large patches of a fragile-looking reddened skin which wrinkled strangely when he moved. In time the red blotches became white, the skin thickening into keloids like those of a burn victim. Hair would never grow there again, nor would his normal, lightly tanned coloration return. But at least there was no longer any doubt that he was going to recover.

In retrospect, the Del-5 episode ended relatively well. The discomfort and disability were temporary, the disfigurement minor. Thackery's worst fears were not realized. He had not infected the crew. He had not died.

But he was left changed, all the same.

Thackery was sure that Koi would notice—sure that, as close as they had become, she could not avoid noticing. That was the best way. He wanted her to notice, and understand, and accept, so that he never need to defend it, so that it would never be an issue between them. It did not happen that way.

The last night of the craze, he and Amy sat arm-in-arm among a dozen so sprawled in chairs and on the floor of the edrec deck. A clear-voiced awk named Johnna had coaxed Guerrieri into bringing his dulcimer and his music upship for an informal concert. Since neither knew the other's repertoire, they took turns singing old ballads and new chanteys, songs of Earth and lost lovers, of selkies and starships. When Guerrieri played alone, there was a reverent silence as the scythe-shaped hammers flashed in his hands and the steel strings rang.

Presently a tech named Kemla joined them, offering what seemed to be an endless treasury of quaintly bawdy songs in a sonorous voice which made up with enthusiasm for what it lacked in training. Norris absented himself for a few minutes, returning with an accompanist's Keytone on which he displayed unexpected skill. The rest, including Thackery and Koi, contented themselves with joining in whenever the chorus of a given song permitted, at first tentatively and half-throated, later confidently and vigorously.

Whether it was the songs themselves or the spontaneous, familial way in which they were shared, Thackery was drawn under their spell. It was one of the songs sung by Johnna that stayed with him the longest, a wistful century-old wish-song with a haunting melody and a poignant vision:

> Give my children wings, but not the ghosts of wings
> I have found in the words of the dreamers
> Let them fly away to a world so far away
> from the fools and the cruel and schemers
> Give my children life, a vast eternal life
> And a universe teeming with wonders
> Continents and skies, a million different skies,
> Full of rainbows and snowflakes and thunder...

Lying in bed with Koi afterward, Thackery was suffused with an uncomplicated sentimentalism that brought him to the brink of whispering *I love you,* words which to him carried such a burden of risk and commitment that he had never before used them. But Koi's mind, he soon learned, was occupied with very different thoughts.

"I can't find your new dispatch anywhere in your personal

library," she said as she snuggled on his shoulder. "Haven't you been working on one?"

"What are you doing poking around in my library?" he demanded, pulling away.

She sat up in bed and turned to face him, making no effort to cover up. "You always have me review your work, and we reach 29 Sagittae tomorrow. I thought you'd just neglected to transfer it to my library."

"I'm not working on one."

"I figured that out by now. It's not too late. I can help you. We can have something ready before we're finished in this system."

He shook his head and avoided her eyes. "I don't think I'm going to be doing any more of them."

"Having trouble hitting your stride again? I said I'd help—"

"No. It'd be a waste of your time and mine." He looked up and met her questioning gaze. "I don't know what I was think-ing—what kind of Messiah complex I had. I'm never going to get a chance. My papers come in at A-Cyg six, eight, ten years apart—they aren't going to make any impression. I'd have to be there, fighting for what I want when the opportunity came up—if it ever did."

She cocked her head to one side and studied him. "So what do you plan to do instead?"

He reached out and enfolded her hands in his. "Leave the Service. Go back home, with you. With you there it wouldn't matter how much it'd changed."

She reclaimed her hands. "What's happened to you?"

"Nothing's happened. I've just reevaluated my priorities. I've realized that I'm a fool to take time away from being with you for a long shot."

"That long shot is part of why I'm here to spend time with."

"I know that. But we have more going for us than the D'shanna, don't we?"

"We do—but that doesn't mean this isn't a problem for me."

Thackery sighed. "Amy, I've never really been sick before. I didn't like it. What if I'd inhaled the Del-5 cells, or ingested them? What if that alkyl had had a chance to work on my digestive tract, or my lungs, instead of my hands? I'd be dead now. I had a good reason to think about how I was spending my life. And I decided that the next chance I have, I'm going to take some time for myself."

"But the D'shanna—"

"Let someone else find them," he said, more harshly than he intended. "Let someone else worry over it. I've done my part, and more. It's time I was a little selfish. It's time I stopped taking silly risks, like the Del-5 landing."

"How was that a silly risk?"

"I had no good reason to be involved. I didn't contribute anything unique, or do anything that others couldn't have done."

"So what, then? Are you going to stop making landings because of what happened?"

"Yes."

She looked at him with surprise. "You're afraid."

"I'm afraid of losing you. I haven't had that much happiness, Amy. You can't blame me for wanting to hold onto what I have."

"If you had died, you wouldn't feel the loss—I would. Only the living grieve and regret. The dead are spared the necessity. Look, Thack—you'll lose a lot more by living afraid than you would by dying."

"Like what?"

"Like me." She patted the medpump strapped to her bicep. "I'm not out here filling my veins with drugs every time we craze so that you can have a convenient playmate. If my being here for you has made you so comfortable that this is the result, then I'm not doing right by either of us."

"What are you talking about?"

She laid down with her back to him and pulled the sheet up over her shoulder. "I'll move my things out as soon as I talk to Barbrice about moving in," she said, naming the surveyor who had been enjoying a single cabin.

"Dammit, Amy, I love you! I don't understand what you're angry about!"

"I'm not angry, Thack. I'm disappointed. Love isn't something that you drop out of life to enjoy."

"Look, I didn't mean—"

She rolled over to face him. "Yes, you did. And it isn't the way I want to live, or to see you live. I love you, too, Thack. I just can't do it the way you want me to."

"I don't know why you're doing this."

"If you did, I wouldn't need to."

Thackery knew there was no point in arguing. Koi was not negotiating to gain concessions, or asking to be dissuaded, or inviting Thackery to plead. That was not her way. She had made a decision, and anything he might have said had already been taken into account.

chapter 13

Recall

As Koi slept, as Thackery lay in the darkness and listened to her breathing, as *Munin* sped onward through the AVLO night, far away in the Lynx octant the Pathfinder *Dove* was dying.

The trouble began in a field coil, one of forty arrayed in a ring around the *Dove*'s drive halo and linked by dozens of thick cables to the fore and aft field radiators and to the deck grids which provided the ship's gravity. The coils were where the flux built up, each an instant later than one neighbor and an instant earlier than the next. That rigid sequential pattern smoothly induced the multiplier effect—forty coils behaving as though they were fully energized, even though only a single coil was at any given instant. It was from that illusory energy that the illusory mass of the drive's phantom gravity well proceeded.

Each coil was a complex structure of insulated wire as fine as hair and fast-response capacitors as massive as logs, linked by a microprocessor controlled bank-switching system which assured that, picosecond to picosecond, the accumulated charge was in balance. Unless electrons could be considered exceptions, there were no moving parts in the entire 200-kg mass of each coil.

But that did not mean that there was no wear. The AVLO-D coils, unlike those powering later survey ships, were not chilled by exposure to space to superconducting temperatures, and so the fine niobium-zirconium filaments were subject to

Joule heating each time the drive was used. Of course, the alloy had been chosen with that in mind, and no detectable damage resulted from the subatomic stress.

But that did not mean that there was no damage. With each flux cycle, random microscopic hot spots were created at the sites of tiny metallurgical imperfections. Over time, the imperfections grew to flaws, and the flaws to actual breaks. Even that had been foreseen, for the bank-switching system simply readjusted the coil's output to a slightly lower level, the central controller brought the other coils down accordingly, and the drive continued to operate, albeit at a fractionally lower efficiency.

What the engineers who built the drive did not anticipate (and could not have been expected to) was how long the Pathfinder *Dove* would remain operational and how often its drives would be called on to hasten it to one or another new destination. In carrying out the fault-test modeling to twenty-five craze cycles, they were confident that they were providing at least a twenty-cycle margin of safety.

But that margin had been reached and substantially surpassed long ago. Two major overhauls, five tear-down inspections, and three hundred eighty-one years after it was first placed in service, thirty-eight of the forty original coils were still in place. When Commander Dylanna Lapedes, the first Journan to achieve command rank, pronounced the survey of 61 Canum Venaticorum complete, it was those coils which responded to the gravigator's call and started *Dove* smoothly on its way.

And less than an hour later, as *Dove* reached a velocity of some 100,000 kilometres per second, it was coil Twenty-Eight, built in a Copenhagen assembly plant and installed on-orbit by the grandson of a New York street merchant, that failed.

It failed suddenly and spectacularly, with blue-white gigawatt arcs dancing inside the cylindrical housing, leaping from one subassembly to another. Within seconds, the superheated gases generated by burning insulation and vaporized wire filament exploded outward, and the starboard half of *Dove*'s drive halo became an inferno. The skin of the ship bulged, then split open in a great tattered rent. An instant later, the conflagration was out, deprived both of spark and oxidizer by its own violence.

The pressure vessel which comprised the climbway and the adjacent living spaces had not been broached, and though everyone aboard *Dove* had been killed. There was still light, and air, and food, and those systems not dependent on the drive still functioned. But *Dove* herself was mortally wounded, and the velocity at which she was moving condemned her crew to death.

For without the protective bow wave of the AVLO drive, the smallest bit of space flotsam would strike *Dove* like a bomb, turning the energy of *Dove*'s own motion against it. Neither the gig nor the lifepods, their hulls and propulsion systems equal only to the modest demands of in-system flight, offered any hope of escape. And the cometary cloud belonging to 61 Canum Venaticorum lay but a few minutes ahead. Under the AVLO drive, the cloud was a triviality, a tissue of microscopic dust and infinitesimal ice crystals. With the drive destroyed, the cloud was an impassable mine field.

There was enough time only for a brief final dispatch, transmitted by the tortoise of radio rather than by the rabbit of the drive-dependent Kleine, and for a few hapless tears and desperate prayers.

For a long minute it seemed that luck had favored *Dove*. Then a kernel of icy dust no larger than a pinhead intersected *Dove*'s trajectory. The energy of the collision sheared off half the forward radiator and shattered the bridge deck. *Dove* began to slowly tumble end for end, its atmosphere and crew spilling out through its wounds. Then, disemboweled and beheaded, the aging Pathfinder finally died.

Dove's last transmission was first received by the survey ship *Edmund Hillary*, some twelve light-years away in the same octant. The transmission was not a plea for help, for Commander Lapedes had known, and *Hillary* was forced to acknowledge, that *Dove* and its passengers were beyond helping. All *Hillary* could do was speed the news of its destruction to A-Cyg, Unity and the rest of the fleet.

By that time *Munin* had finished its work at 29 Sagittae and was more than halfway to its next destination. Deafened by the craze, *Munin* did not catch Hillary's dispatch. Consequently, it was not until they regained their senses inbound to the next system that they learned of *Dove*'s fate.

The news came in a Priority command dispatch, which Cormican shared over the shipnet a half-hour after it was brought to him:

To: Russell Cormican, Commander
USS 3 *Munin*
From: Berylina Maggis, Director
Flight Office, Unity
Classification: Commander's Discretion

You are hereby directed to discontinue your current operations and effect the return of *Munin* to Advance Base Cygnus. Your immediate acknowledgment of and compliance with this directive is required.

The Technology Office evaluation of the circumstances surrounding the loss of USS 4 Dove concludes that said incident was related to catastrophic failure of AVLO-D drive S.N. 101-044. This failure has been judged to be non-anomalous and all similarly equipped vessels are considered AT RISK. All due discretion is recommended for your return, including restricting drive output to 30 degrees or less and continuous monitoring during the acceleration and deceleration phases.

Appended find copies of the relevent accident report, accident inquiry, and technical evaluation.

"Personally, I don't see any reason we couldn't complete a survey of this system," Cormican concluded, "but the orders don't seem to leave any room for that. I've asked the gravigation and engineering staff to conduct a full diagnostic test of the drive. They have advised me that will take most of the rest of the day, so I am tentatively scheduling us to begin the acceleration phase of our trip back to A-Cyg for ten tomorrow morning.

"I'm as sorry about this as you are, but it does seem the prudent thing to do. I haven't been told how your contracts will be handled, but be assured I intend to make a case with the Flight Office that our return be considered end-of-tour and that everyone receive a full payout. Thank you for your attention."

Thackery was alone in the survey lab when the announcement began, and afterwards headed upship to find someone to talk to about it. He found that a half-dozen of the crew had already gravitated to the edrec deck, and a loud and multifaceted discussion was already underway. Thackery joined the gathering and listened.

"But, good Christmas, a thirty-degree slope—," one of the awks was saying, "It'll take us ten days just to craze."

"Ron's already worked it out—fifty-seven days back to A-Cyg."

"See? That's got to be the slowest leg anybody's run since *Pride of Earth* went out."

Connolly said, "It'll make it tough on Amy—running that long in the craze with an iffy drive to think about."

"I heard that," Koi called as she stepped off the climbway to join them. "Don't listen to him, folks. I happen to know he's been holding a tranq pump in reserve for himself."

There was laughter, and she came and stood by Thackery, close but not touching, friendly but reserved, just as she had been since moving out at 29 Sagittae. "What do you think?" she asked quietly.

"I really don't know yet." He expected her response to be *You should be happy—here's your chance to go home early,* or *how did you arrange it?*

I don't want to go home, he was ready to answer. *Not now. Not alone.*

But all she said was, "I feel bad for *Dove*'s crew. They had a little more time to think about what was coming than I'd like to have." And then she moved off to sprawl in an empty chair opposite from where Thackery stood.

Thackery did not, in fact, know how he felt, which was why he was listening, and not talking. He was somewhat surprised that most of the others seemed to be taking it as an interruption, a bureaucratic annoyance, rather than as a respite or an early furlough. Gwen Shinault, the senior tech, was actually angry.

"This is totally unnecessary," she proclaimed loudly. "If they would just let us program the controller to shut the drive down instead of trying to juggle an unbalanced flux, there'd be no need to recall us. If *Dove*'s controller had been wired that way, I'd wager she'd still be in one piece."

"And stranded way the hell out in Ursa Major."

"I'll make you a bet you won't take that *Dove*'s crew'd have been glad to have that choice if someone'd offered it."

The loudest part of the conversation shifted to another part of the room. "What do you think they'll do with *Munin?*"

"You mean if we get it back?"

"Oh, hell, we'll get back," said one of the awks cheerily. "I'm with Gwen. I wouldn't have second thoughts about ignoring the directive and just continuing on."

"You're not smart enough to have second thoughts" was the response, to general laughter. "They'll scrap her, of course. What else can they do?"

"Why not replace the drive?"

"If you ever wondered why you're still an awk, it's because of bone-headed statements like that one. Why do you think the Pathfinders still *have* AVLO-D drives? They're building *Cygnus* with an AVLO-M, for crissakes. If replacement was a workable proposition, it'd have been done a long time ago. Bennie's right. The only thing to do is scrap her. She's expendable."

No, no, no—not if I have anything to say about it, Thackery thought with sudden elation. He tried to catch Koi's eyes, but she was looking in another direction.

Just as well, he thought, catching himself. *It'd be wrong to say anything. She's made clear she's not interested in being won back—not that I ever "won" her in the first place.*

With a nod of acknowledgment to those who noticed him leaving, Thackery slipped away and headed downship, his thoughts still racing.

She'd only think you were doing it because of her, anyway, and there'd be nothing gained from that. That's not the reason. That never was the reason. I have to do it for myself.

He reached D deck and hastened along the short corridor to his cabin, where he took up his slate and curled up in the only chair.

No. That's the wrong reason too, he thought as he accessed the ship's library. *I have to do it because I'm the only one who can. I'm the one who knows. I'm the one who sees. If I don't do it, no one will—which just maybe is what she was trying to say.*

There was no desk in the putative office of the Cygnus liaison of the Committee on ReCreation of First Colonization

Planning, making Thackery wonder briefly if he had been led merely from one waiting room to another. Then a short, slender man swathed in a silky amber wrap rose from a chair facing the greatport and turned toward Thackery.

"Mr. Thackery. I'm Eloi Zamyatin. I'm very pleased to have the chance to meet you." The liaison extended his hand palm-up in the Daehne gesture of greeting that was current at A-Cyg, then settled back in his chair.

"Why is that?" Thackery asked, choosing a seat opposite the director.

The question both surprised and discomfited Zamyatin, suggesting Thackery had broken a rule of etiquette either by questioning the compliment or by not responding in kind. "Well, of course, your name is all over the contact records for this octant," Zamyatin stuttered. "You have quite a reputation here."

"Good or bad?"

"That's a matter of some disagreement," Zamyatin said, regaining his poise. "You seem to polarize opinion rather sharply. As a matter of fact, your Sennifi Contact is the model for a decision-making simulation in the Command training curriculum, and it almost always generates an animated discussion. I would have known you in any event, of course—you fairly papered this office with your proposals and theses during your last tour."

"Have you read any of them?"

"Why, yes, one or two."

"Then you already have a pretty good idea what I'm here for."

"Your argument, as I understand it, is that we need experience with a selective search mode before we are forced into such a strategy by the sheer numbers of candidate stars in Phase III."

Thackery nodded emphatically. "Let me put some specifics on the table. The census of the galactic disk tells us we're looking at over four thousand stars in the Phase III, 50-to-75 light-year, shell. That's two and a half times as many systems as in Phase II. Even with the forty survey ships we've been promised by the Procurement Office, it'll take a minimum of four and a half centuries to complete a comprehensive survey."

"And so you are arguing that we should give up our commitment to a comprehensive survey."

"As someone who has been out there, I can testify that

there's no need to survey most of those systems. We've already surveyed more planets than we can reasonably exploit in the foreseeable future. The Analysis Office has a tremendous backlog of Phase II data, and even the most interesting discoveries aren't yet scheduled for a follow-up visit. Use of high-probability search criteria is incomparably more realistic."

Zamyatin nodded thoughtfully. "These are Planning Office decisions, of course, not Committee decisions. Nevertheless, I agree completely that to conduct Phase III the way we've conducted Phase II would be either unacceptably expensive or take unacceptably long. You may not be aware that the Planning Office is already leaning toward another solution. We now have a compact AVLO drive. More importantly, we have the Kleine. Those two facts mean that robot probes are now feasible. The Kleine makes the necessary remote monitoring and teleoperated systems possible."

"So the decision has already been made?"

"Tentatively. We'll build perhaps a hundred robot probes with teleoperated landers, and only a few additional survey ships. The robot probes will perform the comprehensive search, and the crewed survey ships will follow up on the most promising finds, be they colonies or organisms or something else of significant scientific interest. The result should be a more efficient search in a substantially reduced time frame. You see, technology has changed the strategy."

Thackery was dismayed but undaunted. "Have any robot probes been field-tested yet?"

"No. I believe the first ones are under construction now at Advance Base Lynx."

"Then there's no assurance that they'll be able to perform as required. You're talking about an extremely complex system and an extremely difficult task."

"That is why the decision is still considered tentative," Zamyatin admitted, "and why none of the Cities-series survey ships have been cancelled. But I have no doubt that our engineers will eventually be able to make the probes perform as required."

"Eventually, I agree. But the fact is that if you're only just getting around to building the first operational probes, there've been problems already. And there's a real possibility that you'll be looking at starting Phase III with survey ships alone."

"I admit to some finite possibility that may happen. But the point is moot. I strongly suspect that your high-probability strategy consists of educated guesses hidden by a smokescreen of interpolation. And even if I felt differently, there are no ships available to test your theories."

"There's *Munin*."

"*Munin* is to be deactivated. The Flight Office has decided that the risk of continued operation doesn't justify the gains. *Cygnus* is ready, so there'll be no loss of coverage in this octant. And the cost of the kind of thorough overhaul that *Munin* needs is so close to the cost of building a new ship that there's no sense to it. Look, the ship is a bloody Pathfinder, for goodness' sake. Let her rest."

"Who owns *Munin*?"

"Well—the Service, of course."

"Not the Flight Office specifically?"

"No—the Procurement Office assigns each ship to one command or another as they're completed."

"So what the Flight Office is saying is, this ship has no utility for us in our present search strategy."

"They haven't scrapped it, no, if that's what you mean. But it's only a matter of time."

"Requisition it."

"What?"

"How did you get the deepyachts the Committee uses for colonial visits?"

Zamyatin bobbed his head. "We do operate a few ships for our own purposes, you're correct. We prefer not to depend on the Flight Office for transportation. But what makes you think that we would be any more willing to assign valuable personnel to a ship as unreliable as *Munin*?"

"I have it on good authority that the drive controller can be modified to assure that a *Dove*-type failure doesn't result in the loss of the ship."

"I've heard some discussion of that option. But it doesn't meet the Flight Office's safety criteria. The crew could be stranded for twelve to fifteen years until a rescue mission reached them."

"The Flight Office won't be operating *Munin*."

"You're still asking us to assign valuable personnel to a highly speculative and unnecessarily risky enterprise."

"There's no need to assign anyone. She can be crewed by volunteers—starting with me. My tour contract has been fulfilled. I can go where I please."

"I understand Flight would like very much to have you for *Cygnus*."

"They're not going to get me, regardless of your decision."

"Um. A commander doesn't make a crew, though."

"There are others who'd be willing to go. Post a notice of opportunity. Put *Munin*'s name and mine in it."

"And I'm sure there'd be many applicants—I said you had a reputation. But most of them would be kids eager for any billet and not really equipped to evaluate the risk."

"I wouldn't object to restricting the notice to vets."

"Of course not—that'd put you in a position to coax your crewmates into going out with you instead of *Cygnus*. That'd make us popular with the Flight Office."

"If I had the right people, I wouldn't need the full complement of twenty."

"How many do you need?"

"If they were the right people—twelve. A three-person Strategy Team under my direction, and a seven-person operations crew under a competent Exec like Gwen Shinault."

"I see." Zamyatin rested his chin on his steepled fingers. "Concom Thackery, there remains a rather delicate issue I was hoping to avoid getting into—"

"Say it plainly."

"As you wish. Even if we were agreeable in principle to this kind of exercise, nothing you've said argues very strongly that this is the right time or, to be painfully blunt, that you're the right person."

Thackery gazed steadily at his host. "Mr. Zamyatin, what year were you born?"

"Why—'24."

"Do you mean 424?"

"Well, of course."

Thackery laughed lightly and smiled tolerantly. "Mr. Zamyatin, when you're talking to a vet, you automatically give the century as well. I was born in A.R. 163. I've been a contact linguist, an aide to Committeewoman Alizana Neale, and a contact leader. I've completed two survey tours and taken part in sixteen landings. I've been in the middle of the first Contact with the Gnivi and the first productive Contact with the Sennifi.

Now, who do you think has a better perspective, someone who's lived Service history, or someone who's read about it?"

"That's not relevant—"

"It's the *only* thing that's relevant. You have no concept of how badly the Service needs to begin finding final answers. Why do you think we've been so compulsive about a comprehensive search? Why do you think pushing back the frontier has been given priority over everything else?"

"But look at how successful that policy has been."

"Successful?" Thackery snorted. "There hasn't been a single fundamental discovery in two-hundred fifty years, not one. And the way we've gone about it has something to do with that record of failure. We've been so single-minded, we ended up narrow-minded as well. We need to break out of the sterile thinking that's dictated strategy up till now and try something else—anything, so long as it creates new possibilities and lets us start thinking in new patterns."

"In essence, you're asking for a ship and a free hand."

"And I've given you more than enough reason to approve the request."

"Concom Thackery, I don't have the authority to make that requisition."

Thackery exploded out of his chair. "Then why am I talking to you?" he demanded. "Tell me who does so I can get on with this."

"The Chairman of the FC Committee has authority over all nonstandard research and flight activity related to the colonies."

"So who is it, and where can I find them?"

"The Chairman is on Liam, in the Lynx octant. But surely you know who it is."

"If I did, would I ask?"

"Why, I assumed since you served under her—the present Chairman is Alizana Neale."

Thackery stared and his face went slack. He dropped heavily back into his chair, covered his eyes with one hand, and let out a long, frustrated sigh. "Of all the—"

Unexpectedly, Zamyatin broke into a broad grin. "I can't take this any further. Concom Thackery, please relax. *Munin* is yours."

Thackery shot the Director a poisonous look. "Then what—"

"In truth, you had it when you walked in," Zamyatin said

quickly. "Someone else filed this same request yesterday, so I had already run it up through channels to find out what the policy would be. Chairman Neale contacted me personally with the answer. She said that if you were involved, you were to be allowed to have *Munin*, but to make you sweat a little first. She said to make sure you really wanted it. There's a message, too—" he paused and glanced down at the slate lying beside him. "'I've been unable to prove you wrong. Now see if you can prove me wrong.'" He hesitated, then added timidly, "Does that make sense? I hope I didn't take this too far—"

"No. No, it's all right," Thackery said distractedly. "You were just doing what she wanted. You said someone else had made a request—"

"She's probably outside now. I told her I'd have an answer for her this morning."

It had to be Koi, and was. Ignoring Zamyatin at his heels, he guided her by the elbow out into the corridor.

"What were you doing there?" she asked when they were alone.

"The same thing you were. I didn't do it to get you back," he said.

"I know," she said.

"But I do want you back."

"I want to come back—as long as you understand that it's because of what you are, not because of what you did. It doesn't matter what they decided. It matters that you tried."

"I understand," he said.

"So what did they decide?"

He grinned. "They said yes."

She took his hand. "Then come on—let's go see if we can find an appropriate way to celebrate."

"My preference will depend on which bit of good news we're celebrating," he said, starting them toward the lifts.

"Let's be creative and try to cover both."

Koi was in her shower and Thackery relaxing by the apartment's greatport when the knock came. Reluctantly, he disengaged both eyes and mind from the star fields of Sagittarius and the heart of the Galaxy hidden therein, and went to the door.

"Hey, Derrel," Thackery said on seeing the caller.

"Hey, yourself," Guerrieri said, stepping inside. "Is this

where the Merritt Thackery Travel and Tour Company hangs its hat nowadays? I couldn't get an answer at your place or find you around the Planning Office, so I tried a long shot."

"Just visiting."

"I'll bet." He nodded toward the greatport. "Haven't you seen enough of that for a while?"

"I was doing some thinking."

"You've got a lot to do, from what I just heard—congratulations."

"Thanks."

"So where are we going?"

"We?"

"Were you planning to leave without me?"

"You're senior on the *Munin* survey team. You're probably a lock to move over to *Cygnus* and become Concom."

"Too much responsibility," Guerrieri said with a shrug as he settled in the upholstered pit by the greatport. "Besides, I told you once—you're a lightning rod. I like to be around to see the fireworks. That is, if you'll have me," he added, with a raised eyebrow.

"I could use a good dulcimer player."

"You forgot to list it in the Notice of Opportunity. So where are we going?"

"I don't know," Thackery said, joining him in the pit.

Guerrieri laughed in a friendly way. "I thought you'd have it all figured out."

Sighing and stretching out his legs, Thackery said, "The temptation is to go back to Sennifi."

"Sure. But Z'lin Ton Drull is long dead."

"More importantly, the D'shanna are finished there. They won't be coming back."

"They didn't succeed, though. The Sennifi are still holding on, even though they still refuse any help or contact."

"I've been wondering if maybe the D'shanna did accomplish what they wanted to. Maybe they didn't need to completely wipe out the Sennifi."

"What do you mean?"

Thackery frowned. "The Drull told me that they were on the verge of space travel—'preparing to step beyond this planet' was how he said it."

"And after the D'shanna came they gave it up."

"Exactly."

"So?"

"So all three of the extinct colonies were technologically advanced. Every one of them grades out on the Journa-Sennifi level—tech ratings over six."

"I'm no expert on FC analysis, but you can't be the first one to make that discovery."

Thackery shook his head. "It's one of the most elementary correlations."

"Is there an elementary explanation?"

"A good one," Koi said, appearing at the bathroom door wearing a fluffy torso wrap and nothing else.

"There she is," Guerrieri said. "Hello, Amy."

"Hello yourself." She came and sat behind Thackery on the edge of the pit, keeping the wrap secure with one hand and playing with Thackery's hair with the other. "About the extinct colonies being advanced—only a fairly advanced civilization leaves enough of a stamp on the environment. The 6.0's and above build the large permanent structures that tell us a hundred, a thousand, ten thousand years later that they were there."

"So the assumption is that there probably were other extinct colonies on some of the planets we've surveyed?" Guerrieri asked.

"Yes," Thackery said. "Which will remain undiscovered until we put an archeological team down on every livable planet to look for middens and graveyards."

"That *is* a good explanation."

"I know. And probably the reason why nobody's ever gotten very exercised over the fact that all the extinct colonies were advanced."

"There's a 'but' or 'until' rattling around in there somewhere."

Thackery nodded. "If you don't assume that we missed some extinct primitives, if you turn it around and think of it as all the advanced colonies are extinct—"

"And then there's room for another explanation."

"Like maybe the D'shanna picked off all the colonies on the verge of acquiring space technology."

"After having done the same thing to the FC civilization—," Koi said slowly. "Why didn't you mention this before?"

"It came to me while we were making friendly," he said,

craning his head to the left to look up at her. "I didn't think it was the right time to bring it up."

She gave the top of his head a sharp, playful slap while Guerrieri looked on, amused. "And I thought I had your full attention. You're hell on a woman's ego, Thackery."

"Just think of yourself as an inspiration to me."

"I'd give you my full attention," Guerrieri volunteered.

"Mind your fantasies," Koi said good-naturedly, and directed her attention back to Thackery. "And you, you mind your thoughts."

"Yes, ma'am."

"Don't call me ma'am," she said, slapping his head again. "We'll need to find proof—evidence they interfered with the other colonies."

"I'd rather find them."

"To do that, we'll have to find an advanced colony before they do," Guerrieri said.

"We were only a hundred years behind them at Sennifi," said Thackery.

Guerrieri's expression darkened. "Slow down a moment— I thought the D'shanna knew everything. What chance do we have to find a colony ahead of them?"

Koi shook her head. "All they had to do is be able to make the Sennifi believe they knew everything—and I don't have to remind you how gullible even Galactic Age humans are. If the D'shanna were everything the Sennifi said they were, the name for them would be God."

"More aptly Satan, when you remember what they've done to us," Thackery said with an edge to his voice.

Koi began to rub his shoulders soothingly. "The nearest extinct colony is 7 Herculis, in the Boötes octant."

Reaching up to clasp her hands, Thackery said, "I was just thinking that very thought,"

"So when do we leave?" Guerrieri asked.

"As soon as Shinault has *Munin* ready and I have a complete crew."

"Good," Guerrieri said as he stood. "Then I've got some time to see to some business. Watching you two is hell on a single man."

chapter 14

Antinomy

Munin's new crew shaped up much as Thackery had projected.
The strategy team was composed entirely of *Munin* veterans:
Koi, Guerrieri, and Barbrice Mueller. Challenged by Thackery
to make good on her boasts that *Munin* could be made safe,
Gwen Shinault accepted the Exec position, and brought with
her two *Munin* techs—astrographer Joel Nunn and gravigator
Elena Ryttn. The remaining five slots, four awks and one tech,
were filled from the base's QCAN list.

Within three months, *Munin* was orbiting 7 Herculis-5 and
the strategy team on its way to the planet's surface. As Guerrieri
guided the gig down to the landing site Thackery and the others
could see that the dome of the city had collapsed and lay in
the streets with the rubble of the buildings on which it had
fallen. Both suns were in the sky, the yellow subgiant high in
the southwest and the small reddish dwarf low to the eastern
horizon. Their rays created overlapping and discordant shadows
on the manscape.

Twin air skiffs, small agile craft with the Analysis Office
logo on their V-tails, sat at the north end of the tarmacadam.
A reception committee of one waited for the visitors at the
edge of the field, wearing an E-suit against the sulfurous smog
which now tainted a once-breathable atmosphere. Inside the
suit was a young research aide with a shock of almost white
hair, an affable grin, and the name Kevin Jankowski.

"Welcome to 7 Herculis-5, Commander Thackery," Jankowski said, almost shouting as though he needed to be heard through the E-suits without benefit of the transducers.

"Thanks for coming out to meet us."

"Well, you almost have to have a guide to find your way through the city to our hidey-hole. I'm afraid we haven't put very much effort into making things ready for visitors. Which reminds me—I hope you don't have any heavy gear that you need transferred to the Annex. Our only ground transportation is a crane-and-cargo wagon we use for excavations, and it's out of action until our mechtech can nurse it back to life."

"Just a couple of portable netlinks for now," Thackery said, nodding at the small cases being carried by Koi and Mueller.

"Okay, then—let's head on in."

The steel ribs of the dome still arched over the city, but most of the material which had spanned between them was gone, like an umbrella stripped of its fabric. Only near the ground, where the curvature of the dome approached vertical, did the clear panels and their supporting structures still stand.

"The dome was added after the city was built?"

"That's right—sometime during the early phases of the volcanic episode that transformed the atmosphere. It isn't completely over, by the way. We get a little quake about once a month, and there've been two sizable eruptions in the midlatitudes in the last year."

"How long ago was the dome built?" asked Mueller from behind.

"About six thousand years. But our surveys have turned up earlier habitations all over this area. They were here a long time before that."

"Anticlinal valley," Guerrieri said, craning his head to look at the parallel ridges a few kilometres to the northwest and southeast. "Probably pretty fertile at one time. Topography doesn't seem to have been much influenced by the volcanism."

"That's right, too," Jankowski said. "This region never got more than a bit of a dusting of ash. But going by the Wenlock—that's the name of this city—going by the Wenlock records, we've found and excavated parts of three other cities that were hit a lot harder."

"If they'd known how to make synglas, that'd still be standing," Koi said with a nod toward the dome.

"Probably so," said Jankowski. "Still, their plaz wasn't bad. We think it took a pretty good earthquake to bring the dome down."

Jankowski led them into the city by means of a hundred-metre long tunnel through the base wall of the dome. The tile-like floor of the tunnel was masked by a thick coating of windblown and foot-tracked dust and ash. Grooves five centimetres wide and equally deep encircled the passageway at three points, marking where airseal doors, now permanently retracted, had once separated the city's atmosphere from the planet's.

"We call this the Anjur Gate," Jankowski advised them. "There's twenty-six gates in all, spaced about a third of a kilometre apart. The whole area enclosed by the dome is just a shade over seven square kilometres."

When they emerged and looked back, they saw that the tunnel had brought them through a terraced earthen bank which climbed at least fifty metres up the inside wall of the dome.

"That was apparently their last major engineering job, moving their agriculture indoors," Jankowski said as he followed their gaze. "They took the base material from the western cliff and the topsoil from the river's flood plain."

"I don't understand," said Mueller. "There's a fair amount of flora in the valley even now—"

"All native. Their basic food crops—"

"Do you know what they were?" interrupted Thackery.

"Artificially selected variants of *Triticum*, as on the other colonies. Actually, they had bred the parent material into four distinct subspecies, one of which apparently could be raised in aquaculture. The terraces were just part of the agricultural system. There's a square klick of tanks one level down."

"Down? That'd be some engineering job."

Jankowski's grin was clearly visible through the Synglas faceplate. "Just because they're dead doesn't mean they weren't smart. Sir, could we keep moving? Dr. Essinger instructed me to bring you in directly. I'm sure there'll be plenty of time to see everything later—"

"Of course."

Jankowski led them through a maze of short streets lined with low buildings. The streets branched diagonally from one circular courtyard to another, and the view down almost every street was blocked off by the three- and four-story structures which occupied the center of the courts. The structures were as different from each other as a slender spire of steel, a marble colonnade, and a great bronze sculpture of a beclawed bird of prey.

"They made very good use of their space," Mueller commented as they passed through one court. "This street plan makes the city seem much larger. Every major artery has a focal point, every vista terminates in the foreground instead of running to the horizon. That reduces the confining impact of the dome."

But for all its praiseworthiness, the Wenlock handiwork bore everywhere the stamp of decay: the spire corroded and listing, two columns from the colonnade lying on their sides in pieces, the thin wings of the bird eaten through in a hundred places. The streets they took were littered with debris. Many others were blocked by twisted metal and tumbledown masonry.

"This isn't what I think of when I hear the word 'ruins,'" Koi said to Thackery. "I think of the Acropolis, or Stonehenge, or Chichén Itzá. Not rusting girders and shattered glass and broken concrete. This is what I think of when I think of war."

"The only war here was the one they fought against the planet itself," Jankowski said, overhearing and dropping back beside them.

"Are you people confident that that's what killed off the Wenlock?" Thackery asked. Koi caught the faint hint of worry in his voice.

"Just look around you," Jankowski invited as an answer. "Look at what they were up against. I'm continually amazed that they lasted as long as they did."

The 7 Herculis Research Annex occupied four contiguous homes on the Avenue of Flames, in a section of the city left virtually untouched by the travails of the rest. The entrances to the Annex had been replaced with lock chambers and the outer walls and windows coated with a sealant, together rendering the buildings a controlled environment.

But inside, the Wenlock presence remained strong. Ramps, which the Wenlock seemed to have preferred over stairs, linked the lower level with the upper. The architecture was open and flexible, the interior screen walls little more than columns, the doorways wide Tudor arches spanned by tautly stretched panels of patterned fabric. Thackery was brought up short by the sight, set into the masonry floor of the entryway, of the imprints of five human hands.

"They're in all the homes," Jankowski said, placing his helmet on a nearby rack and beginning to strip off his E-suit. The others removed their helmets and tucked them under their arms. "Since in most of the homes the prints were all made at the same time, we think it was part of a ceremony associated with moving in. Sometimes you find a print filled in, or a new print added. Whatever other meaning they may have had, they sure make taking a census easy."

"How many lived here?" Thackery asked.

"About eighty-five thousand, peak. That may sound like a lot, considering how small Wenlock is, but there are lots of urban areas on Earth with higher population densities. And as your aide there noted, they did know how to make good use of space."

"Barbrice Mueller," Thackery said, realizing that he had been deficient about introductions. "Where to now?"

Jankowski stepped out of his suit and hung it beneath his helmet. "If you'll go up that ramp, you should find Dr. Essinger in the first alcove to the right at the top. I'll take the others to the room that's been cleared for you."

"That's fine."

The rampwell had been turned into a small gallery, hung with framed faxes of Wenlock portraits labeled with the grid numbers specifying where they had been found in the city. As Thackery climbed, he lingered briefly to study each. The Wenlock had clearly disdained artistic license, even in the service of self-flattery: The faces that stared out at Thackery bore the lines, flaws, and scars which made them unique, and made them human.

Dr. Essinger made no effort to hide his unhappiness with *Munin*'s presence. His greeting to Thackery was polite at best, and his mouth was puckered by annoyance.

"I really don't see why we should be expected to put up with a continuous stream of sightseers, and not get any work done. It's bad enough dealing with the ones who come on the packets. Now the sightseers have their own ships," the research director complained as they sat down on the woven bench facing him. "I thought for sure when Higuchi found his second colony that we'd be rid of the interruptions."

Thackery started. "Commander Higuchi of the *Edmund Hillary?*" he asked.

"How long were you in the craze?" Essinger demanded, squinting at him. "Of course that's who I mean. Is this a surprise? Do you mean to say you don't know about 16 Herculis?"

"We came from A-Cyg," Thackery said. "We're nineteen years out of sync."

"Well, you could at least review your damned library updates when you come out," Essinger muttered. "Yes, *Hillary* found another colony, on 16 Herculis, five years ago."

"Extant?"

"No, extinct, like this one."

"What's the tech rating?"

"Six and a half, preliminary," Essinger said grudgingly, then seemed to perk up. "You know, *Hillary's* already moved on, and the 16 Herculis field team hasn't been sent out yet. If you went out there now, you'd have the jump on everyone. It's not even ten lights from here."

"We appreciate the information," Thackery said. *But not the suggestion.* "You can be sure we'll go over the 16 Herculis contact report carefully. But we have things to take care of here before we go anywhere else."

Essinger peered narrowly at Thackery. "What exactly is your status? How much help are you expecting from us?"

"We're trying to establish criteria for a high-probability colony search program. Within that objective, we've been given a fairly free hand. As far as help from you, we'll be doing our own field work. I don't think we're going to be in your way."

"No digging," Essinger warned. "You do any digging without my authorization and the supervision of our chief archaeologist and I don't care who you are, we'll bundle you back on your gig and send you home. We've got responsibilities here, you know. We're the ones who're accountable."

"I doubt we'll be doing any digging. We're most interested in the last days of the Wenlock, so we'll be working right here in the city."

"What the hell are you looking for?"

"Evidence to support or refute a theory."

"I'm not an idiot. I figured that much out. What kind of evidence?"

"We'll know it when we find it," he said.

"Wonderful," Essinger said in a voice heavy with sarcasm. "You know, this is my third rotation here. I've seen all kinds of people come out from the Planning Office and the FC Committee who thought they just had to see it themselves, or had some pet idea that they just had to check out personally. Do you know what? They didn't find a damn thing they couldn't have gotten from our reports."

"Are you trying to say that we're not welcome?" Thackery asked, raising one eyebrow questioningly.

"Since you bring it up, that's exactly what I mean," Essinger said gruffly. "I can almost understand that the Analysis Office has trouble saying no to the Committee. But I don't know why they can't at least protect us from our own. Unless maybe this is actually some sort of inspection visit? If so, you'll soon see we're not out here partying. This is hard work, and we're working hard."

"We're not here to check up on you."

"No? Then, frankly, I don't know why you just didn't stay on A-Cyg and consult the Analysis Office. They know everything we know. We're not holding anything back."

"You've done nineteen years' more work while we were in the craze," Thackery said pleasantly. "That's why we came."

"You wouldn't have had to come here to jump ahead. You could have gone to A-Boo, or even to Earth. No, you're not telling me everything."

"It's not our job to tell you everything," Thackery said calmly. "But as long as we're here, it's part of yours to tell us everything we want to know. So why don't you put a lid on your professional pique, and tell me about this earthquake that supposedly finished off Wenlock."

Thackery found Koi alone in a small room on the second level of the next house, sitting crosslegged on the floor with a portable netlink on her lap. She looked up and her face brightened as he entered.

"Where are the others?" he asked.

"Got an invitation to lunch. I decided to wait for you."

"Thanks. Is this our workspace, or our quarters?" Thackery asked, surveying the bare walls and floor.

"Both. They're going to try to dig up some spare foldaways and a table or two. Did you find out anything?"

"I found out the Universe didn't stop while we were en route."

"I know. I was just looking over the library update. Pull up a piece of floor," she invited with a sideways jerk of her head.

There were, in fact, two new colonies. Three years before the 16 Herculis find, the *Francis Bacon* had discovered an active agricultural settlement on 66 Tauri-7C, a satellite of a brown dwarf orbiting an F-star in the Hyades. Though Essinger hadn't thought it important enough to mention, Shinn was the first human habitation, FC or otherwise, to call a secondary satellite home. It was also the first find in the Perseus octant since Journa.

Thackery stretched out his legs and leaned back against the wall. "You know, considering that I've spent nine-tenths of the last two hundred years in the craze, it's perfectly reasonable that every time I come back down to normal time a new colony's been found—"

"Life goes on."

"—but damned if it doesn't make me feel like I'm always behind and never going to catch up. I thought you said the list was about complete."

She shrugged. "Thought it was."

"So now we have eight colonies in the northern hemisphere and five in the south."

"Baker's dozen."

"What are you so cheerful about?"

"Just eager to get to work," she said, kissing him on the ear. "Did Essinger have anything substantive to say?"

"I asked him about the earthquake. All the evidence is indirect. No firsthand accounts."

"You sound relieved."

"Maybe I am, a little."

"The D'shanna don't have to be responsible for all the extinctions. There can be colonies that failed without their help."

"I know. But if the D'shanna weren't involved, then we won't find out any more about them here, or get any closer to finding them."

"True enough. But from what I've seen already, we're going to have to make a hell of a case for ourselves to convince anyone the earthquake wasn't responsible."

"But wouldn't an earthquake strong enough to bring down

the dome have damaged these buildings as well?"

Koi took a moment to consider before answering. "That depends. If the dome wasn't designed to damp out harmonic oscillations, it could have been the first thing to go. Just like soldiers aren't supposed to march in step while crossing bridges. It may have been checked out already. If it hasn't, I'll see to it. By the way, are you hungry? I know they're not waiting on us, but we're probably welcome anyway."

"What I really want is to get a good picture of Wenlock in my mind. What do you think?"

She set the netlink aside and started to scramble to her feet. "I think we should go get Jankowski and have a look around."

They found Jankowski sitting with Guerrieri and Mueller in the small dining room of the fourth house, laughing with them over some story Guerrieri had just finished telling. "Sure thing," was Jankowski's reply to their request. "Just let me clear it with Dr. Essinger, make sure I'm not needed anywhere else."

While he was gone, Thackery and Koi had time to share one of the sugary wheatrolls sitting in a basket on one of the counters.

"Do you want us to come with you?" Guerrieri asked.

"No. Dr. Essinger isn't too happy with our presence, so I want us to become as independent as possible. Spend the afternoon poking around here. I want to know where everything is and who to see about getting it. If you have time, you can change our 'links over to the local frequencies, too, so we can access their files directly."

"Will do," Guerrieri said with a nod as Jankowski returned.

"Any problems?" Thackery said, twisting toward the young archaeologist.

Jankowski shook his head and grinned crookedly. "No. In fact, he was looking for me, to tell me that I'm assigned to you until further notice."

"A combination guide and keeper?"

"I guess. You ready? We'll lose the light of the primary before too long."

"Then let's get going."

The dividing line between the relatively well-preserved buildings at the rim of the city and the ruins at the center was a sharp one. Jankowski led them down streets which had obviously been cleared of their rubble, for brightly colored, numbered stakes projected from the pavement at regular intervals, marking the corners of the excavation grids. The buildings on either side were battered-looking, with collapsed roofs and bulging walls.

"We've got two teams working, one here in Wenlock and one in Werno—that's the city about two hundred klicks southwest," he said. "I'll take you to the local site first, and then over to the artifact warehouses."

"How long have you been out here, Jankowski?" Thackery asked.

"I'm in the second year of a five-year rotation. I'm afraid that makes me about as junior as can be on the staff here—most of the others have been here at least two rotations. There isn't much turnover in the colony Annexes, especially in Boötes—retirement or death, that's about it. I replaced a senior archaeologist who was killed in a cave-in over in Wynea. Of course, there'll be a lot of new faces if the Office ever gets around to putting together the 16 Herculis followup. I think five of the staff members have applied for it."

"So where are you from?" Thackery asked.

"Oh, A-Boötes, of course. First generation native. My father was born on Earth." He laughed. "My mother was born on a packet, during the craze. Called herself a 'tweener."

Stopping at an intersection with an uncleared street, Koi picked up a palm-sized fragment of plaz and turned it over in her hands. Though the edges of the fragment were ragged, they were not sharp, and there were no fracture lines through the body of the fragment.

"What's this made of?" she called to Jankowski.

He stopped and came toward her. "I'm not a chemist, so my answer may not satisfy you. If it contained more silicon and calcium and had a less ordered structure, we'd call it glass. There's also a surface coat, a long-chain polymer coating a few tenths of a millimetre thick—like a plastic. That's why we call it plaz—a slightly bastardized acronym for polymerized glass."

Koi tried to flex the fragment, to no noticeable effect. "Ugly coinage—good engineering."

"Good chemistry, actually," said Jankowski with a grin. "The Wenlock were crummy engineers. Just try one of their flush toilets if you need proof."

• • •

Since the archaeological work had begun nearly a half-century before, three of Wenlock's seven square kilometres had been fully excavated, and the collection of artifacts had long ago reached the point of diminishing returns. There was a houseful of skeletons, bagged, tagged, and lying in stacks; thousands of 24-page pamphlets Jankowski called chapbooks, diligently sorted and cataloged but untranslated; an enormous variety of small machinery and housewares, from a wishbone-shaped razor missing its blade to a kitchen canister which still held several hundred grams of caked einkorn flour.

"We photograph everything with a pan camera, holo and high-res," Jankowski explained, "and then there's not much else we can do with it except store it in the event that somebody somewhere decides they have to see the original."

"How often does that happen?"

"Not very. Considering the time problem, they just about have to come here. I understand we've had about one on every packet, and the packets come every six months. Most of them take care of their business during the two-week layover and go back on the same packet. This isn't exactly Vacationland, as you may have noticed."

"But you like it here?"

"Oh, sure. It's——." His gaze wandered as he searched for the right words. "I guess it's the way everything these people did became intertwined with this planet that fascinates me. I'll give you an example. There used to be a native plant—I say used to be because we haven't been able to find any living specimens—which had bioluminescent nodules that it used as part of its reproduction strategy, the way Earth plants use flowers to attract insects. The Wenlock grew it in those long channels you've seen along the face of the buildings, like window boxes, to light the streets at night. And they copied the chemistry to use in their own homes in the cold-light lamps."

"You don't see that kind of synergy on an Advance Base," Koi said with an understanding smile.

Jankowski nodded. "The last Wenlock died before the first pyramid was built. I can hold in my hand the skull of a man who lived before Greek culture named the constellations. I guess I feel more in touch with my human heritage here than I do anywhere else. Being here makes time real for me. Do I sound crazy?"

"No," Koi said and patted his arm through the suit. "Not at all."

Jankowski's guided tour consumed nearly two hours. Toward the end, Thackery became less and less communicative, with fewer and fewer questions and less to say about the answers. By the time the trio started back toward the Annex, Thackery had withdrawn completely. Even the voluble Jankowski seemed to notice, and took the cue to be silent himself. Then, as they left the collapsed roofs and bulging walls and blocked streets of the center city behind, Jankowski came up alongside Thackery and touched his elbow.

"Did Wenlock bore you or disappoint you?" he asked.

The question recalled Thackery from his inner retreat. "I've insulted you somehow, haven't I? Please don't take my lack of enthusiasm personally, Kevin," Thackery said. "It has nothing to do with Wenlock, and certainly nothing to do with you."

"I'm not insulted. I'm just wondering if there isn't some way I could have spent your time better."

"You showed us exactly what I wanted you to. It's not your fault if what we saw didn't satisfy our need. You know what we're here for?"

"Generally."

"If you do, then you know that we're looking for what no one else has seen, or what they saw and didn't think important. We're playing a guessing game, and we're dealing with impressions. We can't have them if we don't go out and see things firsthand."

For a time, no one said anything. Jankowski made a halfhearted game out of kicking a pebble-sized chunk of masonry ahead of him as they walked on.

"Kevin, you have a good feel for these people—," Koi began.

"I think so."

"Since you've arrived, have you seen any sign that they considered returning to space to avoid what happened? Any evidence that they had kept that capability or could have stretched themselves to reacquire it?"

Jankowski stared intently at the ground before him as he thought. "No. They were tip-top farmers. They were pretty good chemists. They were fair breeders—they created varieties of *Canis* for everything from food to draft animals to pets. But the kinds of technology required for space travel, the metallurgy, the electronics—no. They just hadn't taken things in that direction very far at all. I don't guess that's what you wanted to hear," Jankowski added apologetically.

"No, we want honesty above all," Thackery said.

"I know. I just wish I could be more helpful to you." Despite his helmet's faceplate, Jankowski's frown and furrowed brow were evident to both Koi and Thackery. "If it's oddities you're looking for, about the best I could do is take you out to see the delta-wing at Site 241."

Thackery perked up noticeably at that. "Wing as in aircraft?"

"Sort of. It's just a name, really, for about 300 kilos of metal—"

Koi was frowning. "I've been over the archaeological reports pretty thoroughly—"

"You won't find it there. Frankly, it's a bit of an embarrassment, not being able to explain it. Every dig has its little mysteries, as Dr. Essinger says. But don't let me lead you on— it's not a real aircraft, just shaped like one—"

Thackery would not hear Jankowski's qualifications. "I want to see it. Is it back at the warehouses?"

"No, it was left *in situ.*"

"Where?"

"North of Wynea. We'd have to take one of the skiffs—"

"What's the problem, do we need a pilot?"

"Oh, no, I can fly it—"

"Then take us there."

The primary sun had set by the time they reached Site 241, but the dwarf provided a bright twilight in the great pit. Thackery was out the door almost the moment the skiff landed on the barren volcanic plain, and Koi was not far behind.

"They found it about eight years ago, during an aerial scan," Jankowski said as he joined them on the rim of the pit. "But you see what I was trying to tell you. It's not really a plane. It's just a skeleton of something that looked kind of like one."

Thackery had already come to that unhappy conclusion. The artifact consisted of three S-shaped ribs of bluish-tinged metal, each a few centimetres across and perhaps thirty metres in length. All three ribs came together to form the "nose" of the plane. Two of the ribs, one reversed from the other, lay flat on the floor of the pit and formed the outline of the "wings."

The third rib, partially supported now by a truss added by the excavators, swept up and back along the centerline of the "fuselage" to form the leading edge of the "tail." A conical piece of the same bluish metal reinforced both the triple joint and the suggestion of an aircraft nose.

"This is all that was found?" Thackery asked, his disappointment evident.

"Oh, no. But all the small artifacts were removed and stored. I think there were over a hundred of them, all found within the area marked out by the boundaries of the wings."

"What kind of artifacts?" Thackery asked, more from reflex than real curiosity.

"Metal. Little things, the size of your palm or smaller. Pieces from some kind of machinery."

Koi asked, "Can we go down in the pit?"

"Sure. There's some footholds cut in the wall at the far end."

"I'll pass," Thackery said, and sat down where he had been standing.

When the others reached the bottom, Koi went first to the nose and examined the joint there, then stood and walked toward the back, running her gloved fingers along the spine-like center rib until it was too high for her to reach. "Why did they stop digging?" she wanted to know when she straightened up.

Jankowski frowned. "They went all the way down to the A level. You can see by the ash layers in the wall of the pit all the episodes of volcanism. Ash, pyroclastic flow, tuff breccia, ash again, basaltic lava—we're standing on what was the valley floor when the Wynea lived here."

"So we're looking at the whole thing? There's nothing buried?"

"No."

"And no other structures in the area?"

"No."

"Anything else like this on the whole planet?"

"Not that we've found."

"So what do your bosses think it is?"

"A range shelter."

Koi regarded him dubiously. "Really?"

"They modeled the prevailing wind patterns in the valley prior to the volcanism and found that the small end faces upwind. If you span the area between the center rib—think of it as a ridge pole—and the ground ribs with fabric, like they do with the arches inside their buildings, you'd have a good-sized protected volume inside."

Thackery called down into the pit, "You almost finished, Amy?"

"Almost," Koi answered. "Why aren't you sure?" she asked Jankowski.

"Mostly the fact that we haven't found any more of them yet—though Dr. Essinger expects to, eventually. 'Find one, it's an oddity—find two, it's a commodity' is how he says it."

"And that's why it hasn't been included in the Annex's reports?"

"You have to understand that everything we find spends some time on the Interim list before any report is filed. This one's just been there a little longer than usual."

"Because you can't find another?"

"I guess. And because of the way this one was found. It was solid pyroclastics and lava right down to the spine—and then nothing, right down to the original valley floor. The other artifacts were just lying on the A level, on the floor of the shelter, as it were."

"There was a cavity in the deposits?"

Jankowski nodded. "The center rib was part of the roof of the cavity. Whatever the fabric was, it was apparently strong enough to hold out the lava until it cooled—which the other fabrics we've found indoors wouldn't have. Dr. Essinger would like to find a sample of it before he closes the books."

Koi looked up to where Thackery sat on the lip of the pit. "What do you think?"

His face devoid of interest, Thackery clambered to his feet. "If you folks can get out the way you got in, I think it's time we headed back."

"You *are* disappointed, no matter what you told Kevin," Koi whispered to Thackery when they were alone that night, squeezed together onto a one-person foldaway in a test of both agility and companionability.

"I'm just afraid you're right—that the colony failed without any help from the D'shanna."

"Did you ever really expect anything different?"

"All the way over to Site 241, I was thinking that Sputnik

followed Kitty Hawk by only about fifty years. If the Wenlock had achieved flight, then the D'shanna would have had reason to come here."

"Kevin tried to tell us it wasn't a plane."

"And I wouldn't listen, I know. Well—there's two new colonies waiting for us. Essinger says we could probably beat the followup mission to 16 Herculis. Or we could go all the way across to the Perseus octant and drop in on the Shinn."

"Or we could always just get into *Munin* and go out to the rim of the Galaxy, and come back a few thousand years from now when somebody else has sorted it all out."

"Don't think the thought hasn't crossed my mind."

"I was joking," Koi said, pulling away from him. "Besides 16 Herculis, there's still Ross 128 and 2 Triangulum Australis. And I'm not ready to write off this planet yet."

"Oh, we'll stay a while yet. But I can't see much reason to hope for anything."

"Do me a favor?"

"What's that?"

"Don't be with us like Neale was with you at Sennifi. Let me tell you when I'm finished, and not the other way around."

His smile was rueful. "Sorry."

"You haven't done it yet," she said, and kissed him. "I just want to make sure you don't."

A night's sleep seemed to restore Thackery to his former state of enthusiasm and optimism. He was the first up of the *Munin* team, and had cleaned and inspected all four E-suits by the time the others dragged themselves down to breakfast. "I've asked Kevin to take us out to the Werno dig," Thackery told Koi when they settled at a table.

Her face wrinkled unhappily. "Why don't you take Derrel, or Barbrice?"

"Why, what are you going to do?"

"I want to look a little more into this business of the 241 artifact. Besides, we don't want the others to think that the only way to get to go on a field trip is to sleep with the boss."

"You think they might think that, eh? Then I guess I'll take Barbrice."

Koi glowered threateningly, then relaxed into a smile. "That's all right. She's gay."

"Figures. Listen—there's no need to get hung up on the 241 artifact just because I was for a while."

"No danger," she said cheerfully. "We'll see you in a few hours."

Now that she knew it was there, Koi had no trouble extracting the data on the 241 artifact from the Annex's Interim files. The abstract contained a variety of information which Jankowski had not provided, including one intriguing fact: an assay showing that the ribs were made of tantalum-niobium alloy.

That one discovery made the range shelter idea fallacious on its face. Tantalum and niobium were both refractory metals, relatively rare in the crust of 7 Herculis-5—in fact, the orbital assays suggested that the source minerals, tantalite and samarskite, were even less common on 7 Herculis-5 than they were on Earth. Abundance aside, together tantalum and niobium made an alloy with outstanding corrosion resistance, high-temperature stability, and tensile strength—hardly the alloy of choice for something as mundane as a shelter.

This wasn't part of their working technology, she thought triumphantly. *And Essinger must realize it too. That's why they haven't said anything. He's in no hurry to look stupid.*

After a few minutes of further checking, Koi confirmed that except for Site 241, no tantalum-niobium artifacts had been uncovered anywhere on the planet. That might have been of minor significance, except for the level of skill the Wenlock had evinced as chemists.

For tantalum was resistant not only to ordinary atmospheric corrosion, but to acids and alkalis as well, even to highly reactive fluorine. Had tantalum been available in quantity from some local deposit or ore, now hidden from the surveyors by layers of ash and lava, the Wenlock would surely have found a variety of uses for it. But even in those applications where its properties would have been valuable—surgical instruments and implants, cutting tools, chemical equipment—the Wenlock had employed more conventional alloys, such as iron-chromium steels.

This isn't proof, she told herself sternly, trying to constrain her deductive leaps. But there was no resisting the central conclusion: *Whatever the 241 artifact is, it wasn't made on this planet.*

Koi turned next to the photographic records of the artifact.

"Model," she instructed the netlink, and a three-dimensional solid graphic replaced the actual image.

"Hold foreground and abstract," she instructed, and the pit vanished from the display.

"Rotate left and down. Stop. Draw," she said, and touched a stylus to the screen to trace a line closing the double-S base and another vertically from the back end of the center rib. *That looks good—*

"Fill, using Class A aerodynamic parameters," she said, and the skeleton acquired flesh.

"Rotate right and up."

The modeling program obediently complied, and Koi sat back in her chair and steepled her fingers against her lips. On the display before her was a persuasive side view of a high-tailed, delta-winged aircraft.

Aircraft? High tensile strength—high melting point—high corrosion resistance—just like you'd need for—

"Evaluate: atmospheric entry, multiple-skip aerodynamic braking, unpowered descent to flight-normal altitude."

NOT POSSIBLE UNDER CURRENT PARAMETERS.

"Modify."

As she watched, the trailing edge of the wing lengthened, the fuselage tapered to a point at the base of the tail, and the vertical stabilizer grew larger. The changes affected only the portion of the shape which the modeling routine had created; the three tantalum-niobium ribs remained unchanged.

MODIFICATION COMPLETE.

No, not an aircraft—a goddamn spacecraft. A winged reentry vehicle. These people found the skeleton of a goddamn transonic spaceplane sitting under eighteen metres of pyroclastics in the middle of nowhere on a colony planet and didn't even know what they'd found.

"Save model," she said grimly, and folded the netlink's display flat against the controls. *There's one big problem, Amy dear. The Wenlock couldn't have built it. The D'shanna, at least Merritt's D'shanna, wouldn't have needed it.*

As far as Koi knew, that left only one possibility. And that one was so fantastic that she could scarcely bear to entertain it.

Guerrieri did not share her enthusiasm, and was loathe to share her conclusion.

"That's not a spacecraft—it's a shell," he complained when Koi showed him the model.

"That's what I want your help with—filling it."

He shook his head. "You're as bad as the paleontologists who reconstruct an entire skeleton from half a jawbone."

"This 'jawbone' has a melting point of over 1600 degrees Celsius, a perfect airframe profile, and an extremely suspect genealogy."

"But it's still just a jawbone. Don't you realize how complex even a dead-stick glider is? Where's the load-bearing stringers and truss spars? Where're the control surfaces? Where're the avionics and navigation packages?"

"Some of those may be in the Annex warehouses. That's why I want you to go out there with me and look at the rest of the Site 241 artifacts."

Guerrieri sighed expressively. "You won't let me rest until I say yes, will you?"

"Nope. Best you surrender now."

Guerrieri raised his hands over his head. "I'll get my E-suit."

The 241 artifacts were together in one storage crib, the smaller ones individually bagged and filed, the larger ones individually boxed and stacked. Each object and container bore a glittery scanstrip, on which its file number and the location in which it had been found were encoded.

Inside the containers, Guerrieri and Koi found an array of metallic objects which might have come from an exotic hardware shop. Nearly all had moving parts—bits of tubing with integral flutter valves, variable-angle Y-connectors, pinless shear hinges, interlocking mushroom-shaped anchors. Yet the artifacts bore little evidence of use or wear, and their surfaces gleamed the same burnished blue-silver as the larger pieces still at Site 241. Guerrieri shook his head as he turned one over in his hand.

"Barbrice would be a lot more use to you with these than me," he said, wearing an almost comic expression of befuddlement.

"She's with the boss," Koi said with calculated offhandness. But her mind was busy. *You know Thackery in a way she doesn't—better maybe even than I do. You share a survivors' bond, from* Descartes *and* Gnivi—*it's why you came on this tour, whether you realize it or not. You knew him before the*

D'shanna took hold. You may be the only one who knows whether he'll be able to give them up.

"Lucky her," Guerrieri said, returning the object he held to its envelope and reaching for another. With Koi looking on but saying little, he continued that process for more than an hour, even to uncrating the larger objects, though they proved no more illuminating than the small ones.

"I've seen enough if you have," Guerrieri said when he had repacked the last case.

"I'm done," she said agreeably. She did not mention that she had visited the storage crib electronically that morning, using the archival recordings of each object which Jankowski had mentioned. *It's different when you hold them in your hand. More real—more convincing—I hope.*

"Can we head back now?" Guerrieri asked.

"Sure, if you promise to spill your thoughts on the way."

"I was afraid you'd expect that."

"Why?"

Guerrieri closed the warehouse door behind them, then stopped to turn up his suit ventilation and thereby dispel the fog that had formed on the inside of his faceplate. "There's not much question that they go with the big artifact, and with each other," he said as they started off down the street toward the Annex. "And they're mechanical, structural—they were clearly meant to do things. But they don't *make* anything. I don't know what else I can say."

"That may be enough."

Guerrieri shook his head. "Don't you understand? It's still just bits and pieces. Where's the rest of it? Unless your picture of what happened here includes street thieves and chop shops?"

"Hardly."

"Then what happened to the structural material? The control surfaces, the spars, the stringers, the skin?"

Inwardly, Koi smiled. *That's the first step—now you want to know what happened to something that two hours ago you said didn't exist.* "It's gone."

"Gone where?"

"Into the ground."

"What are you talking about?"

"The artifact was buried in basaltic lava. Even three miles from the nearest vent, that lava had to be a thousand degrees Celsius. The heat destroyed everything except what we've seen—everything that wasn't made of tantalum-niobium."

"You're saying it survived the heat of a free-fall reentry and then was destroyed by the lava? That's nuts."

"Not at all. The nose cap and wing leading edges are the only areas which experience temperatures in the thousand to fifteen hundred degree range. All the other surfaces see less than a thousand degrees—most less then five hundred, and that only for a few minutes. But the lava would have taken days to cool. I ran the numbers."

"And by the time it does, the rest of the spacecraft is gone—leaving the cavity the dig crew found," Guerrieri said slowly. "So what did they use, then? What was the magic material?"

For an answer, Koi bent down, picked up a fragment of plaz, and handed it to him.

He ignored it and stared at her. "A glass spacecraft?"

"I wish it were that simple," she said with a shake of her head. "That isn't glass. It isn't even almost-glass. There's almost no silicon, almost no calcium, almost no sodium."

"So what *is* in it?"

"Oxygen and hydrogen, in a ratio of 8 to 1 by molecular weight and 1 to 2 by molecular count. And a few minor impurities—"

"Oxygen and hydrogen—that's water."

"Arranged in a long-chain tetrahedal crystal structure, with each oxygen atom bound to four hydrogen atoms."

"Crystal structure—," Guerrieri gaped at her. "That's ice, goddamnit. What the hell are you trying to tell me? That's ice, goddamnit all."

"That's what I'm trying to tell you."

Guerrieri's protests ceased then, and he took a seat in the doorway of a ruined Wenlock home. "You choreographed this all very nicely," he said in a subdued voice.

"Thank you."

He looked hard at the piece of plaz in his hand. "I assume you ran through all my immediate objections yourself."

"I went through a lot. I probably have you covered."

"Not conventional Ice-1, of course. You're talking about a metastable polymorphic form."

She nodded. "Just like diamond is a metastable form of carbon—and as unlike the parent material as you could ask for. I'm glad I don't have to give you a course in chemical polymorphism."

"Oh, no—I spent a long night sweating over the phase

diagram for water back in my Institute days." He turned the plaz over and over in his hand slowly. "I can tell you this, nothing like this was on it."

"Call it Ice X. Or maybe the impurities are important, and we should call it an alloy instead. We need to put a good X-ray crystallographer to work finding out."

"It's just possible. Just barely possible. Which means that maybe the Wenlock did build spacecraft after all—at least one."

"No," she said firmly. "This is not a Wenlock artifact."

"Then what?"

"You know what it has to be."

Guerrieri let the plaz slide from his hand to the pavement, and cocked his head to stare at her. "Please be gentle with me. My head hurts already."

She smiled at his joke. "I'm trying, but it isn't easy."

"You're going to make me say it, aren't you? That this is an FC spacecraft?"

She came and crouched before him, at his eye level. "What if Mannheim were just just a little bit wrong? What if the FC civilization existed not during an interglacial stade, but during one of the glaciations? Couldn't an inventive culture deprived of what we consider the crucial metals develop an entire technology based on what *was* available to them?"

"A technology of ice?"

"That's one pretty remarkable product of it lying there by your feet."

"It's a long way from a city dome to a starship."

"It's a long way from a DC-3 to an orbital shuttle—but it's a straight line. Earth only has knowledge of one kind of technological society. That makes it hard to judge the limits and capabilities of other kinds."

"A ship this size couldn't carry enough fuel to go from planet to planet, much less star to star. It couldn't even carry consumables for the six or eight people who could fit in it."

"It wouldn't have to, any more than the Munin's gig has to. Not if the 241 was a parasite lander attached to a much larger starship."

Guerrieri just looked down at his feet and kept shaking his head.

"The point is, we don't know what's possible, because we've never thought like this."

"And the crew—or should we call them passengers?"

"Call them colonists," she said. "They could have been dropped off in small groups as the mother ship flashed through each system at five or eight or ten percent of c."

Guerrieri pulled himself to his feet. "Let's walk," he said, and started down the street.

They went several blocks before Guerrieri spoke again. "I'll say this, you've certainly managed to break out of the straight-jacket of conventional FC theory."

"Why, thank you," she said, answering his wry flattery with false gratitude.

"You've also connected a very few facts with a great deal of speculation."

"I know. But that's the way I've been trained to think—to see what isn't there from what is."

"True enough. I'm just not used to hearing it on this scale."

"I'm not used to doing it on this scale."

"I suppose not. So you're not claiming to have solved the riddle of the Sphinx—"

"No, of course not. I'm saying it bears looking into—especially since conventional theory has been at a dead end for two hundred years."

"You'll get no argument from me on that," Guerrieri said. He took the next few steps more slowly, then stopped. "Do you know what happens if you're right?"

"Yes."

"You have a lot of questions to answer. But you may also have answered a lot of questions. Why the FC civilization disappeared. Why the colonies don't reflect their founding technology. Why their populations are still relatively small. Why some colonies are on less-than-desirable worlds. Even why they forgot their origins. And you've done it all without resort to the D'shanna."

"You sound more amenable to the idea than you did a little while ago."

"I sound that way because I feel that way. But, Amelia—I'm not the one you have to convince. And I don't much want to have to be the one to tell him."

"You won't be."

"I never knew exactly how it was we were supposed to find the D'shanna. But this I know how to check. There are things we can do to either prove or disprove your scenario. We have something tangible to look for."

"That's what I hope to make Thack see."

Guerrieri nodded thoughtfully. "What if he won't listen?"

"Is that what you expect?"

"I don't know what he'll do."

"I think he'll listen," Koi said without conviction.

"I hope so. But if he won't?"

Eyes downcast, she did not answer immediately. "I'll have to think about that," she said, and turned away toward what passed for home.

Jankowski, Thackery, and Mueller returned from Werno in late afternoon. Though burning to unburden herself, Koi waited until after the evening meal, when the team returned en masse to their quarters.

"I found out some things today that I think we need to deal with, as a group and in terms of our objectives on this tour," she said, pulling the fabric wall over the entry arch to provide a privacy that was more illusory than real. "Is this a good time, or should we schedule a team meeting for sometime tomorrow?"

Thackery stretched out on one of the foldaways. "Now is fine with me. Anyone else have any firm plans? Derrel, you didn't plan any erotic assignations for tonight, did you?"

"No," Guerrieri answered with a crooked grin.

"Go ahead, then, Amy. The floor is yours."

It took Koi the better part of an hour to lay out the facts, the inferences, and the speculations for Thackery and Mueller. Guerrieri concentrated on watching Thackery, his expression, his body language, the little eyebrow flicks and absent-minded finger play that might provide the cues to his thoughts. He was less concerned about Mueller: after the first few minutes, she had pulled a netlink onto her lap and from that point on divided her attention between the display's images and Koi's words.

When Koi finished, there was silence as everyone looked to Thackery for his response. Staring down at the middle of the floor, and thereby avoiding their eyes, he swung himself up to a sitting position, and then shook his right arm and grimaced.

"Damn thing fell asleep," he said. The uneasy laughter emphasized the tension rather than dissipating it. Thackery grinned ruefully and looked to Mueller. "Barbrice, you've been busy there. Any thoughts?"

"While I was listening I skimmed the 241 archives. The artifacts are definitely anomalous." She pursed her lips, then shook her head. "I can't comment on the rest."

"Derrel? Are you up on this? You have an opinion?"

Guerrieri pursed his lips and thought a moment. "About all I can say with confidence is that we wouldn't have done it this way. But then, we didn't do it."

Thackery turned to Koi. "I guess we know what you think."

"We've discovered some very exciting evidence that could lead to a final solution of the colony problem," Koi said. "On the other hand, we've found nothing to support the notion that the D'shanna have been here or had anything to do with the loss of this colony."

"Tell me, why didn't the permanent staff pick up on this?"

"I can answer that," Mueller said. "The technoanalysts finished their work here more than a decade ago, before the 241 dig took place. The staff now is composed almost exclusively of ethnologists."

"Besides which, Dr. Essinger's handling of the find shows he knew there was something different about it," Koi added.

Thackery scratched the crown of his head, then clapped his hands together once and interlaced his fingers one at a time. "I'm sorry," he said finally. "I can't go along with that."

On hearing that, Koi hooked her hands behind her neck and bowed her head, missing a sideways glance of sympathy from Guerrieri.

"I'm absolutely delighted by what you've found out about the 241 artifacts," Thackery went on. "I have no doubt that the plaz material could be used structurally in a winged vehicle, be it aircraft or spacecraft. And whether the plaz is Ice-X or some other metastable polymorph doesn't really matter in that context. The fact is, you've made a very plausible connection between Wenlock technology and a set of anomalous artifacts. But the rest of what you say is positively Byzantine. I don't really know why you went to the trouble."

That brought Koi's head up and a cross expression to her face. "The Service spent a lot of time and money training me to think synthetically. That's what interpolation is all about."

"And you're good at it, no doubt about that, Amy. But you're a long way out on a very skinny limb here. On the other hand, you *have* convinced me of two things—that the D'shanna *were* here, just as we expected them to have been. And that it's pointless for us to stay on 7 Herculis any longer. They were here, but it's been six thousand years, and the trail is too cold to be of any use to us. But we now know where to look for them—on a world rich in refractory metals. We know their signature—tantalum."

"You think the 241 artifact was a *D'shanna* ship?" Koi asked, making no effort to mask her incredulity.

"Absolutely," Thackery said, coming to his feet. "Just think what a powerful motivator the decades of unending volcanism, the destruction of the other cities, would have been, what a spur to space. Escape, escape—that's what the Wenlock had to be thinking, how can we escape? That's when the D'shanna came. That's when they showed them how to make plaz and to put this protective dome overhead. The earthquake finished off the Wenlock, all right. But it was the D'shanna who made sure they were still here when it hit."

Koi said nothing, but her expression spoke volumes about her disagreement.

But Thackery seemed not to see it. "Have you talked to any of the Annex staff about this?" he asked.

Koi looked at Guerrieri, who shook his head. "No," she said.

"Don't."

"We have to at least alert Dr. Essinger to what he has here," Koi protested.

"Why? He's been sitting on this for eight years. If he hasn't the wit to figure it out for himself—well, let him wonder why we left so quickly. We owe him nothing."

"So where to, then?" asked Guerrieri. "16 Herculis, to look for another iceship?"

"No," Thackery said, shaking his head. "Now that we know for certain that the D'shanna are bound by conventional technical limits, we know we have a real chance of finding them. We know they couldn't have swept through the Local Group and killed off all the colonies in a few dozen or a few hundred years. I've thought all along that we're catching up with them. Now I'm wondering if we already did."

"What do you mean?"

"Dove. Where was *Dove* when she was destroyed?"

It was Mueller who answered. "In Ursa Major, headed for Talitha."

"Then that's where we're going. And when we get there,

don't be surprised if we find both a colony and the iceships of the D'shanna."

A short time later, with Mueller poring over the 241 archives in detail and Thackery the astrography file on the Ursa Major moving cluster, Koi slipped away. Guerrieri followed her to a darkened second-floor terrace which looked out onto the moon-lit ruins of Wenlock.

"Well?"

"Do you want to say you told me so?" she asked irritably. "Then do it and be done."

"You didn't press him."

Koi scowled. "You weren't much help, either."

"My advice to him has to be more conservative than my brainstorming with you."

"I suppose," she said wearily. "This is just the first round. If I'm right, there'll come a time when I can prove it and he can accept it. I can wait until then. I'm asking you to wait, too."

"He sounded like Neale used to—the secrecy, the single-mindedness."

"He isn't like that."

"Do you think so? Do you really think so?"

She looked at him with an uncharacteristic look of help-lessness in her eyes. "I have to."

Guerrieri's mouth was a thin line. "I wish I could," he said, then hesitated before continuing. "When I thought he was right about the D'shanna, I admired his dedication. Now that I think he's wrong, I'm beginning to wonder if the right word isn't obsession."

Then he saw what his words had done to her, and remem-bered that for her, matters of human as well as cosmic scale were in the balance. He could not take back the words, but he could hold her, and he did—and wondered for the first time if there were any way the flight of *Munin* could end well for all aboard her.

chapter 15

In a Dying Place

Three days out from 7 Herculis, the first defection took place. The occasion was a pre-entry briefing on *Munin*'s destination star, the setting the C deck wardroom. The audience included not only Thackery and the strategy team, but Shinault and Joel Nunn, the ship's astrographer, as well.

Nunn stood in the midst of the astroprojection, the stars like a halo of fireflies around him, as he spoke to the darkened room which hid his audience. "The Ursa Major Moving Cluster is the nearest star cluster to Sol, only slightly more than half the distance to the Hyades. The nearest members are some sixty-five light-years from Sol, and the cluster is scattered over an elliptical volume of space some thirty light-years long and eighteen light-years wide."

A touch of the control wand displayed the nineteen members of the cluster in bright green. From where she sat, Koi could see clearly how several members formed most of the Big Dipper: Merak and Phad, Megrez and Alioth, and the triple double Mizar and Alcor. Only Benetnasch, the tip of the Dipper's handle, and Dubhe, the northernmost of the pointer stars, remained white.

"The cluster members all share a common proper motion eastward and south toward Sagittarius," Nunn went on. "Talitha is not considered a member of the Cluster, but it is a member of the larger Ursa Major Stream which occupies a region of space several hundred light-years across, and which includes Sirius and 1 Ophiuchi."

Another touch on the wand, and Talitha brightened as though it had gone nova.

"Talitha *is* part of the Ursa Major asterism, marking one of the front feet of the Bear. At a distance of fifty light-years, it lies right on the Phase II boundary, and consequently was the most distant system *Dove* was scheduled to visit. Like the members of the Cluster, Talitha—or 9 Ursae Majoris, in the Kalmar system—is a main sequence star, spectrum A7, luminosity about 11 Sol. There's a dwarf binary companion at a distance of about 70 A.U., with a period of more than six hundred years. With that separation, the presence of the companion probably doesn't rule out a stable planetary system, although the A-Lynx observatory has been unable to establish that one is present."

"Thank you, Joel," Thackery said, sitting forward in his chair. "Does anyone have questions?"

"Is this trip necessary?" Guerrieri said under his breath. Koi heard and shot him a venomous look, but Thackery seemed not to notice either the comment or the rebuke.

"That'll be all, then, Joel. Thank you," Thackery said, and took the astrographer's place as the lights came up. "The fact is, none of the Cluster stars have been surveyed, and very few members of the Ursa Major Stream. Yet as one of the most striking constellations as seen from Earth, Ursa Major was certain to have attracted the attention of the FC planners. No colonies have been found among the nearer, unassociated stars— in fact, Ursa Major lies at the center of the largest region of apparently uncolonized space."

Thackery touched the control wand, and a standard plot of the northern octants appeared. "Please note that if you draw a line from Journa to Ross 128, and another from 7 Herculis to Liam-Won in Monoceros, the lines cross here, in Ursa Major. These are some of the reasons I expect to find a colony in this region. It may not be orbiting Talitha. Even though I'm optimistic, I want you all to realize that Talitha's only a starting point for what could be a long search. 5 Ursae Majoris, the brightest cluster member and thereby a likely candidate in its own right, lies seventy light-years out. If we come up empty at Talitha, 5 UMa will be our next stop."

"I can't listen to any more of this," Guerrieri muttered, this time loudly enough to be heard. He threw down his fax of the briefing agenda, folded his chair back into its bulkhead recess with a clamor, and stalked from the compartment.

Thackery knit his eyebrows in puzzlement. "What's the matter with Derrel?"

"I'll find out," Koi volunteered, and hurried away before her offer could be refused.

She caught up with Guerrieri three decks downship, as he was about to enter his cabin. "What the hell was that display all about?" she demanded, grabbing him by the arm.

Wordlessly jerking free of her grasp, he turned away and slipped through the doorway. Uninvited, Koi followed and closed the door behind them.

"Now explain," she demanded.

"I don't think you're in a position to demand explanations from me." He sighed weightily. "I wish Thack'd come, instead of sending you."

Koi sighed and settled on the edge of the unmade bunk. "You may still get a chance to explain it to him—he didn't send me," she said. "I came down here to let you vent gas at me, so maybe you wouldn't feel the need to do it at him."

Guerrieri snorted and shook his head. "If that was all I wanted, I could have stayed upship and said my piece there."

"Then what is it?"

Before answering, Guerrieri pulled his dulcimer case from its storage niche and began to undo the latches. "I just cannot sit there smilingly while he goes on and on about the inner thoughts of FC planners and the secrets of Ursa Major," Guerrieri said. "This trip is a complete waste of time. We should be on our way to one of the colonies, not heading as far as possible away from them."

"We agreed we were going to be patient until we had more evidence."

"I said nothing of the sort. The only promise I made was to myself, to bite my tongue until it hurt too much to keep doing it. Well, it's hurting pretty good now. Haven't you been talking to the rest of the crew?"

"What do you mean?"

"Maybe they think you're too close to him, they don't dare ask. That's not the case with me. I must have had four or five people already question why we're going to Talitha. It's still polite, like they're curious about something that just hasn't been explained to them. But it'll get worse. They know that something's changed—he's drawn inside himself, like he doesn't see us anymore. Don't tell me you haven't worried about it yourself."

"Aren't you being a little hard on him—"

"Did you read his 7 Herculis exit dispatch? There isn't a word in it about the iceship or the tantalum signature. Who's going to collect the evidence, with us here and no one else even having had a chance to hear your ideas?"

"When I talked about waiting for him, I didn't mean a week. We aren't facing any deadlines."

Guerrieri stopped in the middle of removing the instrument from its case to stare at her. "What do you mean?"

"I mean it doesn't make any difference whether the colony problem is solved two years from now, or a hundred years after I'm dead."

"Of course it matters—"

"Not to me."

Guerrieri's gaze narrowed. "You're afraid."

"There's nothing for me to be afraid of," Koi said, stiffening.

"Sure there is. What if you get the evidence and he still won't listen? Or maybe worse, what if you have to force him to realize he was wrong and you were right? How's he going to react to that?"

I don't know, she thought unhappily. But she said nothing.

"You've got to push him," Guerrieri said, his tone changed from demanding to coaxing as if he sensed her ambivalence. "You're the only one who has any real influence with him."

"I won't use our relationship that way."

He scowled. "You mean you won't risk your relationship."

"That's not why."

"Then tell me what the reason is."

Oh, there's a reason, she thought, *a good one.* But all she said was a curt, "None of your damn business."

"Fine," Guerrieri said, turning his back on her and setting up the dulcimer on the desk. He lowered the working surface to a comfortable playing level and reached into the case for his mallets. "Just as long as you realize that I'm not going to tiptoe around him any more."

There was no point in her staying: Each had said what they had to say, yet left the other unconvinced. She walked out with the sound of steel strings in her ears, conscious that Guerrieri's usually precise mallet strokes were marred by the ragged edge of his frustration.

The wardroom was empty when Koi returned there, so she continued upship to the cabin she and Thackery shared. There she found him stretched out on the bunk, hands folded behind his head and one leg hooked over the other.

"Did you folks finish?" she asked.

"I postponed the briefing to tomorrow morning. With half the strategy team missing, there didn't seem to be much point in continuing. What's the story with Derrel?"

"Mostly impatience, I think."

"He has doubts about what we're doing."

She admitted, "If he were calling the shots, we wouldn't be going to Talitha."

"If he wanted to call the shots, he should have signed on a different ship," Thackery said harshly, and closed his eyes.

"You two go back a long way together," Koi said, surprised by his tone.

"True but not relevant," Thackery said, opening his eyes and propping himself up on his elbows. "So what do you think I should do about him?"

"Does something need to be done?"

"If he keeps challenging me in front of the crew, it will."

Cautiously, Koi asked, "What are the options you're considering?"

"Going to A-Lynx and releasing him from his contract. I wish I'd left him in Wenlock," he said bitterly.

Koi stared at Thackery curiously. "Did you come downship after us?" she asked with sudden insight.

He nodded wordlessly.

"Ah," she said, understanding. "How much did you hear?"

"I was a few minutes behind you." Thackery sighed. "I heard enough to be grateful to you for supporting me. And enough to know that I can't count on him anymore."

"Because he thinks for himself? Come on, Thack. Isn't that why he's here, to provide another viewpoint? If not, then what do you need the rest of us for?"

"Are you siding with him?"

"Do I have to choose sides? Look, I've got a better option than leaving him at A-Lynx. Why don't you talk with him?"

Thackery lay back and looked away. "No."

"You're making more of this than it is."

"Am I?" Thackery said, sitting bolt upright. "He doesn't believe, Amy. He wants us to turn back. He tried to turn you against me. Isn't that enough? It's almost as if he wants us to fail."

"I think he wants very much for us to succeed," Koi said, as soothingly as she could. "Talk with him, Thack. This isn't personal. It's professional. You should still be able to talk about it."

Thackery shook his head emphatically. "No. I see no reason to give him a free shot at me. If he continues to be a problem, then I'll have to do something. But until then, he can talk to the freezin' walls."

"Barbrice?"

The technoanalyst looked up from her lunch to see Guerrieri at her shoulder. "Yes?"

"Come by my cabin when you're done there."

"Sir?"

"We need to talk," Guerrieri said soberly. "As soon as you're finished, all right?"

Far from certain that it was, she echoed, "All right." A few minutes later, she followed him downship.

"I feel very uncomfortable doing this," Mueller said nervously. "But I thought you should know."

"Go on," Thackery said, resting his folded hands on his knee.

"At first I thought he was going to try to lean on me for favors. Not that he has a reputation for that, but he seemed so—imperious, like he knew he was senior to me and he wanted me to remember it, too."

"So did he ask you for—favors?"

"No. He asked me how I felt about the mission."

"And you said?"

"I told him the truth—that I'm very happy to have been picked and have a chance to be part of this special project. Then he asked me what I thought about Talitha, about our chances of finding anything there."

"And?"

"I told him I was very hopeful, that the way you had figured out what happened at 7 Herculis had given me even more confidence in you. Then he said, 'There are some things I think you should know about Commander Thackery.'"

Thackery listened impassively as the young surveyor recounted the rest of her conversation with Guerrieri. Twice, when she became embarrassed at repeating Guerrieri's catalog of unflattering anecdotes, he calmly encouraged her to continue. Otherwise he was silent.

". . . that you couldn't work with either of your commanders, and that the main reason you were given *Munin* was that it was a convenient way to be rid of you, that the Analysis Office didn't take you seriously and that I shouldn't either," she concluded. "That's when I walked out."

Eyes downcast, Thackery rolled a touchscreen stylus between his fingertips. "You're right—I should know. And I thank you."

Her worried eyes flitted from one focus to another. "Will he know I told you?"

"I'm afraid he probably will. But I can protect you from any repercussions. And I want you to know that I appreciate your loyalty, and I'll remember it."

She smiled a nervous smile. "That's not necessary, Commander."

"But it is appropriate," he said. "You can go now, Barbrice. I have some things to think about."

For the showdown, Thackery chose the more formal surroundings of the ship's library over the informality of his cabin. Guerrieri entered with his face cast into an emotionless mask, but his eyes were wary and alert. "You wanted to see me?"

"Close the door," Thackery said with a nod.

"Oh—this is going to be one of those," Guerrieri said as he complied. "Should I stand against the wall, or would you prefer a moving target?"

"Just sit down." Thackery waited until Guerrieri was settled, then continued. "I understand you're having some trouble with what we learned at 7 Herculis."

"I'm having trouble with what *you* think you learned there."

"Tell me."

"Gladly. Amy did a beautiful little piece of work pulling together the threads of what happened at Wenlock. She may have done enough to start a revolution in FC theory. But you've twisted around her findings so they support your notions instead, brainwashed Barbrice into believing you, and intimidated Amy into backing off on her own discovery. On top of which, you've committed *Munin* to the least profitable search possible—nothing more or less than the kind of plodding, random survey we did on *Descartes*. We should be looking for Amy's iceships, not your D'shanna."

"I thought you were with me on this. I thought that's why you were along."

"Then I left you with a misimpression," Guerrieri said, regarding Thackery with a level gaze. "I came not so much because I thought you were right, but because it seemed right to be going where you were going."

"So you never believed in the D'shanna?"

"As an influence on the Sennifi, yes. As a galaxy-roaming superspecies trying to impose quarantine on human settlements, no. If the D'shanna are so afraid of letting us have spacecraft, explain why they let the Journans build *Jiadur*. Explain why they let us build *Pride of Earth* and the Pathfinders and all the ships that came after."

"*Jiadur* was a fluke. There was no evidence they were going to do such a thing until it was done—it happened in a span of forty years. As for us, they did stop us—the first time. They just didn't do a thorough enough job to keep us from having a revival."

"It doesn't wash, Thack. We've been all over the map now for four hundred years. If they were sharp enough to get to Sennifi and Wenlock at the right time to castrate them, they have to have taken notice of our 'revival' by now. Why are they leaving us alone?"

"We *have* attracted their attention again—that's why this is so urgent. Look at what happened to *Dove*."

"*Dove* had a freezin' *drive* accident, for life's sake. We have her own captain's word for that. There's no ambiguity in her last dispatch, nothing about any external causes. Why do you have to keep bending and stretching the truth?"

"Why is it so important to you that I be wrong?"

Guerrieri sighed. "It's not important to me that you're wrong, but you *are* wrong. The 7 Herculis and Sennifi civilizations died of natural causes, and so did the FC. I know it's not as dramatic, but goddamnit, that's the way it is."

"If I'd known you weren't committed to the mission, I don't know if I'd have picked you—"

"If I'd known that was the only reason you picked me, I don't think I'd have volunteered. Have you looked around yourself lately? You and I are the only ones of our generation on board. We're the vets now, Thack. You never quite let me close enough to be your friend, but we still share something that no one else on board understands, not even Amy."

Seeing Thackery's blank and uncomprehending expression, Guerrieri continued in a softer, sadder voice. "Or am I the only one who feels it? Am I the only one who remembers Rajesh and Queen Maud Land, or crowding into *Tycho*'s library to get our black ellipse? Am I the only one who remembers Mike and Jael? Damn it, I'm the last person you know from home."

"That has nothing to do with Wenlock, or Talitha—"

"It has to do with how you've stopped listening to us since the Analysis Office put us over us."

"I haven't stopped listening to you," Thackery said defensively. "Damn it all, I was counting on you—you, and Amy, and Barbrice. That's why this hurts so much."

"Then why bring us to Ursa Major? Why not follow up what Amy found? Why not look for the iceships on other colonies?"

"We *are* looking for the iceships. That's why we're on our way to Talitha."

"Not the D'shanna, damnit—the FC. We know *they* existed."

"I'm not interested in beginnings," Thackery said stiffly. "I only care about the endings."

Guerrieri stared. "Since when?"

"Since Sennifi."

"So you'll look for the D'shanna to the exclusion of all else, no matter what else we might find or where else the markers might point."

"When we find the D'shanna, we'll get the answers we need, and more."

"More? Like revenge? What would you do if you should find them? How would you settle your list of grievances?"

"I'm not afraid of them. They didn't make war on the colonies. They manipulated them. All we have to do is find them and expose them, and we'll eliminate their power."

Guerrieri shook his head. "No. No matter what you had in mind, *Munin* was sent out to try to pave the way for Phase III. When you get back to that responsibility, I'll work harder for you than anyone. But I have no intention of contributing to this exercise."

"Are you on strike, then?"

"Call it what you like."

Thackery studied his hands as he considered. "I think you've come up with a workable solution," he said at last. "You're restricted from the bridge and the survey lab. You'll be locked out of sensitive files in the library. And I'll instruct the rest of the crew to treat you as though your clearance has been dropped from Active to Non-Service."

"You haven't the authority to do that."

"If you'd prefer, I think we could manage to lock you into Level II isolation in F-5 for the duration. As far as you're concerned, that should be authority enough."

"You'd go that far to insulate yourself from criticism?"

"I'd go that far to protect myself from an unpredictable threat to my command and this ship."

"Locking me away won't be enough."

"You're the only one who seems to find what we're engaged in intolerable."

Guerrieri shook his head. "I'm the only one who's spoken up."

"Who, then? Who else?"

Guerrieri only smiled. "You'll hear from them, eventually."

As near as Thackery could tell, the pronouncement about Guerrieri sent a ripple of surprise through the ship, but created no real disruption. It could have been worse, except that Derrel himself respected the lines Thackery had drawn, apparently unwilling to sacrifice all his freedom to principle. As for the rest of the strategy team, Barbrice seemed more than willing to shun the new pariah. Even Amy had little to say, save regret that the split had become necessary. Though caution was still in order, it seemed the crisis had been averted, the disrupting influence banished.

From Guerrieri's perspective, the situation was very different. Being an outcast from the strategy team actually raised his status with the regular crew, with whom he began spending his time. Taken into their confidence, he learned the true depth of their misgivings. Thackery still had his defenders, but even they yearned for clearer explanations and more concrete goals. Among the others there were one or two vocal detractors, and the rest were nervous, full of disquiet. As though placed on probation, Thackery was being watched closely, his every order analyzed and dissected, almost as though the commander's paranoia were feeding back on itself in self-fulfilling prophecy.

Guerrieri did what he could to put minds at ease, even to expressing more confidence in Thackery than he was sure he felt at the moment. But even as he did, he knew that he would not be able to keep the lid on. Unless Thackery regained their confidence, truth, half-truth, and rumor would simmer and bubble until they boiled over into fear.

And what a frightened crew might do, Guerrieri did not want to consider.

One week after Guerrieri's demotion, Thackery and Koi were cuddling together, using each other as excuses not to rise and begin the day.

"Can we talk about what happens after Talitha?" Koi asked, her head resting in the crook of his arm.

"That depends on what we find there."

"What if we find nothing?"

"As I said the other day, there are some excellent candidates for colonies in the Ursa Major Cluster."

"All of them well beyond the Phase II boundary. I don't remember anything in the expedition Protocols that would allow us to take *Munin* out there."

"There isn't that much of the Phase II zone left unexplored to test our ideas in. I'm sure the A.O. expected us to go beyond fifty lights."

"If so, wouldn't they also have expected us to do it in the Cygnus octant?"

She felt, rather than saw, Thackery's slight shrug. "If we bring them back what they wanted, they won't care where we've been."

"Even so, I think we should use the Kleine to get explicit authorization before we leave Talitha."

"Uh-uh. I won't give them the chance to say no," Thackery said, gathering her in closer to him. "I won't let the Committee or some A-Cyg bureaucrat stop me when I'm this close."

"Is that why you sent the dispatch you did from 7 Herculis?

You hardly told them anything—"

"Because I want to get there first. If we'd told them every-thing, they could have diverted *Newton* or *Hubble* from their A-Lynx missions. It isn't enough to be in the right place. It has to be the right person, with the right understanding—or all we'll have is another fiasco like *Tycho* at Sennifi."

Koi said nothing, and rolled on her side to turn her back to him. Thackery took it as an invitation to cuddle spoon-fashion, and reached around her to cup one of her breasts in his hand. He expected her to wriggle her buttocks against him, the next step in one of their patterns of foreplay. When she did not, he slid his hand down her belly toward the apex of her thighs. Just as his fingertips reached fine, downy hair, she turned again, this time onto her stomach, arms wrapped around the pillow on which her chin was bolstered. Puzzled, he drew back and propped his head on one elbow.

"What are you thinking?"

"That you once made me an offer I wish you'd make again," she said. "I probably should have taken it the first time."

"What are you talking about?"

"About going back to Earth with you."

Even before he responded, she could sense his withdrawal.

"That's not possible now," he said.

"Isn't it? When we're finished at Talitha, we could go back to A-Cyg. Derrel could be released from his contract, and you and I could take some time for ourselves. I'd like you to show me Earth. What Jankowski said about heritage struck home with me."

"This is too important to go waiting."

"To me, you're more important. We're more important." She hoped against hope that he would respond in kind.

Thackery said nothing for a time. "You sound like you don't think we'll find anything at Talitha."

"I don't think we will."

"And you want us to turn around and leave empty-handed?"

"I want to get you out of the Service while you're still a whole person, while I can still see the person I saw at Sennifi," she said, sitting up and facing him. "Don't you see what you're doing? Keeping secrets from the Planning Office—exceeding your authority—taking every disagreement as a betrayal—what's happening to you?"

"That's not the way it is at all."

"It *is*. Open your eyes, Thack. Look at yourself."

"He meant you, didn't he? You're the one he was talking about."

"What do you mean?"

"Derrel. He said there were others who agreed with him. I didn't think he meant you. Everybody wants to keep me from going on farther into Ursa Major. Don't you realize that that only makes me more determined?"

"We're your oldest and best friends—"

"That's why I can't believe you. You wouldn't do this, unless you'd been influenced by the D'shanna. I may have been wrong about Wenlock. They may still have been there. If we hadn't left when we did, they might have gotten to me, too. Where did you two go that day? Think about it. Try to remember anything strange that happened—"

Koi bounced angrily out of bed. "That's just perfect," she said as she began to pull on her allovers. "You've now got anyone who disagrees with you or does anything to interfere with you working for the D'shanna."

"Amy—it's not personal. It doesn't change how I feel about you," he said pleadingly. "I just can't let myself be influenced by what you say about the D'shanna and Ursa Major. Not when you could have been influenced by them. It's my fault, Amy. I wasn't careful enough about security at Wenlock. I assumed the staff there was on our side, but maybe they weren't. I don't know whether they worked through Jankowski, or Dr. Essinger, or both—we don't know enough of how they work, only the results. This is a whole different kind of contamination problem, and I didn't think it through."

Hooking the closures on her clothing as she went, Koi headed for the door. "The only part of that I can agree with is the last—that you haven't thought it through," she said tartly.

Thackery looked at her plaintively. "I don't understand what you want from me. Once you left because you said I was being too selfish. Now I'm doing what you asked and you're leaving again."

Koi sighed and regarded him sadly. "You still insist on trying to understand me in terms of Andra and the others. I'm not like them, Thack. I don't want anything from you. All I ever wanted was for you to be true to your best qualities. And more and more these weeks, you haven't been."

• • •

But even as Koi left the cabin and headed downship toward deck E and Guerrieri, the end of the mission was beginning.

It began with a dimple, which appeared on the mass detector at the gravigator's station on the bridge. The dimple was the footprint of an object ahead of them—the space-time distortion caused by its mass, which the detector noted, measured, and reported to its caretaker, Elena Ryttn.

"Mass-touch," Ryttn said aloud, alerting the others on the bridge. The navcom was already deciding whether the object was small enough to be swept aside by *Munin*'s bow wave, the protective cocoon created by the AVLO field. If not, the navcom would adjust *Munin*'s course. No human intervention was required. On any survey ship other than Merritt Thackery's *Munin*, no human notice was required.

"Astrography," Gwen Shinault called across the bridge to another tech. "Verify and identify."

"Verified," Nunn answered. "Masses about ten to the twenty-first tonnes—a Mercury-class planetoid. True space velocity—whoa, this can't be right."

"What can't be right?" the exec demanded.

"The damn thing's pushing two-thirds of the speed of light."

Shinault was frozen for an instant by her astonishment. Then she shook her head, as one might kick a balky machine, and reached for the shipnet controls. "Commander Thackery to the bridge," she paged, then crossed the bridge to the communications station. "Can you get anything else?"

"Not while we're in the craze."

"Whatever it is, we'll be right on top of it in about six minutes," Ryttn announced. "It's crossing right in front of us—angle to our bow of about thirty-five degrees."

Thackery appeared at that moment at the top of the climbway, still bearing the dishevelment of sleep. "What's up?"

"We're about to overrun an object of planetary mass with a space velocity of .6c."

There was only a moment to weigh the options; *Munin* and the mystery object were moving too quickly for long deliberation. "Navcon, let's get out of the craze," Thackery said, settling in at his station.

"We'll be by her before we regain our senses," Ryttn warned.

Thackery shook his head. "Maximum braking—fifty-degree slope. Let's rattle the dishes."

"But the safety restrictions limit us to thirty degrees—" the tech at the gravigation console protested.

"Do it," Shinault said. "I altered the controller at A-Cyg. We won't lose the drive."

The tech's face was ashen, but he turned back to his console and began the procedure that would bring *Munin* back into normal space. The astrographer and comtech stared at each other in disbelief, all their doubts about Thackery brought to the forefront. Only Shinault seemed sanguine about stressing *Munin*'s drive with maximum flux.

"All stations, alert for high-G transition," Shinault announced over the shipnet. "One minute."

Throughout *Munin*, crew members scrambled to find comfortable positions to be in when the nearly doubled gravity induced by the AVLO braking hit. Those who were close enough to do so crawled into their bunks.

"Begin braking," the gravigator said without enthusiasm, and almost immediately the whine of the inductors jumped an octave. *Munin* shuddered, a new and unpleasant sensation, and then settled down into a harmonic vibration which would have been strong enough to make limp fingers dance on a countertop, except that the increase in G-force which came with it precluded such gymnastics. Aft, the drive's dissipators crackled as they bled off the energies racing through the coils of the core.

The noise from the climbway shaft and the shaking went on for nearly five minutes. To Thackery, thinking of their enigmatic quarry, and the bridge crew, thinking of *Munin*'s ancient drive coils, the time seemed much longer.

Then finally, blessedly, space reappeared.

"You can back her off to thirty degrees now," Thackery said, and the gravigator gratefully complied.

Radar, laser ranging and communication, telescanners, and Kleine transceivers all looked toward the unknown object. The energies they captured carried back confirmation that Thackery's first instinct had been right.

"Regular profile—no rotation—comes up almost like a ship." The astrographer stopped, puzzled. "It's accelerating— very high delta vee. Crossing our bow now. Sweet life, it is a ship!"

"On the window," Thackery snapped, and the telecamera view came up on the central bridge display. The other ship was a point of light, skimming across the star field a hundred thousand klicks ahead of *Munin*.

For a moment, Thackery locked his eyes on the dancing, indistinct image as his mind raced. *D'shanna—FC—which are you?* Then he saw what most of the others had already seen, the only real information which could be gleaned from the display: that the image had the hourglass profile of a survey ship.

"What the hell is another Surveyor doing out here?" Thackery expostulated. "What's their transponder identification?"

"It's probably *Lynx*," Shinault said. "She could be out here by now."

"Or it could be Higuchi in *Hillary*. He may have learned at 16 Herculis what we did at Wenlock." Thackery made a growling sound deep in his throat. "Goddamnit, if they beat us to Talitha—see if you can figure out where they're coming from."

"No transponder identification," the comtech reported.

That was a puzzling development, since every Service vessel used its Kleine to continually relay position information to the Flight Office.

"With that apparent mass, it has to be running under AVLO drive—which means it has to be one of ours," Thackery said, and gestured at the screen. "Can't you give me something better?"

"Not at this distance."

"There's no hull markings on survey ships anyway," Shinault reminded them. "About all we could tell is what series she belongs to."

Thackery nodded. "Navcon, let's go after her. A thousand klicks isn't too close."

"If I can," said Ryttn.

"What?"

"Her acceleration profile—it's steeper than an L-series drive. Fifty-seven degrees."

"Maybe it's a robot probe, with the AVLO-M," said a new voice. Thackery twisted in his chair to see Koi emerging from the climbway.

"Amy—I'm glad you're here."

"I'd have been here sooner, but it's a little hard to negotiate the climbway in two G's."

"Things have been a little hectic up here."

"Is that your excuse for risking everyone's life?"

"The best intercept was to drop down as quickly as possible. If we'd kept to the Flight Office limits we'd have been hours getting back to them. And the way they're accelerating, we might not have gotten back to them at all. And I wanted to get our scanning capacity back as quickly as possible."

Koi studied the telecamera view and the superimposed navigational plot. "Can't we catch it?"

"That may depend on whether it wants to be caught."

"I have a new delta vee," Ryttn sang out at that moment. "Her acceleration curve is flattening out."

Koi pursed her lips. "Looks like she wants to be caught."

As the minutes slipped by, *Munin* first matched the trajectory of the mystery ship, then began to slowly narrow the gap between them. The two vessels raced on in tandem for more than an hour with *Munin* shouting entreaties and the other vessel answering with silence.

"Why wouldn't they be responding?" Thackery wondered aloud.

Koi shook her head. "No transponder, no radio, no Kleine—it's hard to believe they could all be out."

"Can't you give us something sharper?" Thackery called across to the comtech.

The comtech threw up his hands. "I can correct for blueshift, but I can't correct for the smearing of the image, even with computer-guided optics," he said apologetically. "A survey ship moving at these velocities isn't exactly the ideal telecamera platform. If you want better resolution, you'll either have to get much closer or talk them into slowing down."

"New delta vee," called Ryttn. "She's starting to decelerate."

"Let's do the same. Bring us up alongside, in parallel," Thackery directed.

With painful slowness, the telecamera view gained focus and detail. As it did, the bridge crew saw that the ship that grew to fill the display might have been *Munin*'s twin—the double bell of the field radiatiors fore and aft, the rounded bulges of lifepods protruding from the hull amidships, the seams of the gig bay.

"Pioneer class," Shinault muttered.

"No—look at the open gridwork at the lip of the drive radiators," Koi said. "Pioneer-class Surveyors didn't have that. That's a Pathfinder-class ship."

"There *are* no other Pathfinders," Shinault protested. *"Munin's* the only one."

Both women were right, so the argument ended there, in impasse. The celestial pas de deux ended with the ships crawling to a stop a mere thousand kilometres apart, their hulls reflecting red starlight from an M-class giant less than half a light-year away.

"Still nothing?" Thackery asked the comtech.

"Nothing the whole length of the electromagnetic spectrum," was the answer. "Not even infrared. She's stone cold."

At that, Thackery's expression turned grim. "Gravigation, take us over top of her. Dead amidships, and close."

As *Munin* turned toward the other ship and began its deliberate approach, the angle of view changed with painful slowness. The only indicator of their progress was when, by degrees, one set of lifepods disappeared out of view on the lower side, while the second set came into view on the upper side.

Only when *Munin* drew closer and moved to pass over the motionless vessel did the angle change more and more rapidly, bringing into view the far side of the ship and a sight that sent a chill through everyone who saw it. For the hull of *Munin's* companion was torn open from above the bridge to the drive core below D deck, the edges of the aluminum honeycomb skin curled back like paper in a fire. A dark maze of twisted metal was all that remained of the upper decks exposed by the wound. Once that sight impressed itself on the stunned surveyors on *Munin,* there was no longer any question about their companion's identity.

"My God," Ryttn said, rising from her chair on unsteady legs. "It's *Dove!"*

chapter 16

Summit

For a long minute after Ryttn's pronouncement, no one spoke. The words froze them in place, staring at the screen as though to force the dissonant evidence to either vanish or harmonize.

Ryttn brought folded hands to her mouth as though praying, and her eyes showed the fear they had heard in her voice.

Shinault frowned, and her gaze flashed angry challenge.

Koi's face was slack with shock, as though her mind were too fully occupied with constructing an explanation to trouble itself to animate her features.

Nunn was radiant with wonder, and wore a hint of a foolish, delighted smile.

Thackery bit at his lower lip, his heart full, his eyes brimming.

Shinault was the first to find her voice. "That's crazy. Her drive was destroyed—how can she maneuver?"

"We saw her maneuver, therefore the drive wasn't destroyed," Koi corrected. "The damage must have been repairable. Communications are still out—"

Then suddenly everyone was talking at once.

"Repairable? Look at her—"

"There's nothing left of the bridge—"

"The ship can be run from the survey lab—"

"There must still be at least some crew aboard, downship, in the lower decks—"

"No," Thackery said sharply. "You're not thinking clearly. We've made three crazes since we heard about *Dove*. It's been more than fifty years since the accident."

"Someone has to be aboard," Ryttn insisted.

"Yes," Thackery said. "Someone. But not a Service crew. Something else."

Koi stared at him uncomprehendingly, and Thackery answered the stare with a tight smile. "Elena, hold station with *Dove*, five hundred metres away and facing the damage," he said, then toggled the shipnet. "Barbrice, to the dress-out compartment, ASAP."

As the page echoed back up the climbway to the bridge Thackery pushed back the mike wand and stood. A moment later he was gone, the climbway vibrating from descent. He was halfway downship before what he had said penetrated to Koi's consciousness.

"No!" she cried out in sudden anguish. "No, you can't!"

Mueller was already in the dress-out compartment when Thackery reached it. "I'm going across to *Dove*," he said, opening one of the storage bins. "I'll need an E-5, helmet camera, light pack, and maneuvering unit."

"Yes, Commander," Mueller said, turning away and opening the equipment rack.

By the time Koi arrived with Guerrieri in tow, Thackery had donned the white double-layer E-5 suit, and Mueller had the rest of the components laid out and waiting for him.

"Thack, how about letting me go on this one?" Guerrieri asked. "Your skin's too valuable, hey?"

"No," Thackery said curtly.

"Thack—you know the EVA Protocols specify pair work."

"No."

"Merritt—please," Koi said. "There's something very wrong about that ship being here. Don't go."

"Did you tell him about *Dove?*" he asked with a nod toward Guerrieri.

"Yes—"

"Then you've forfeited the right to ask that of me."

Koi's eyes flashed anger. "Damn it, Thack, this isn't a schoolyard fight over who makes the rules. Don't you realize that if something happens over there, there's nothing we can do to help you?"

"Do you think it's an accident that *Dove* intercepted us, that we've been diverted from Talitha? Don't you realize? It's me they want. Ever since the Drull warned me about them, they've been trying to stop me. They're waiting for me. I won't disappoint them."

With a sudden movement, Koi looked away, as though avoiding the sight of him.

He took his helmet from Mueller, tucked it under his arm, and took a step toward Koi. "I have to do this, Amy," he said plaintively. "If I don't, then the last ten years don't make any sense at all. I have to do it."

"Why?" she demanded. "Who are you trying to impress this time? Who do you think expects this? Andra, or Sebright, or Z'lin Ton Drull? You don't owe them—"

"No," he said softly. "This time, it's for me."

When he and Mueller were gone, down into the gig bay to the small personnel airlock, there was silence in the dress-out compartment.

"They have a stronger hold on him than I do," Koi said finally. "I guess I always knew that."

"He'll be all right," Guerrieri said, touching her arm solicitously.

"Sure," she said bravely. "But would you suit up anyway, and stand by here? In case—"

Guerrieri nodded his agreement. "Amy—I don't understand."

"What?"

"Why you wanted to stop him. We were wrong, Amy, and he was right. Nothing else can explain why that ship is out there."

She cast her gaze downward. "Because I'm afraid," she said softly. "Because I'm afraid he's right, and because I don't know what's waiting for him. Nothing more or less than that." She hesitated a moment, then headed for the climbway. "I'll be on the bridge."

The video from Thackery's helmet camera shared the bridge display with the output from *Munin*'s own electronic eyes. From one point of view, Thackery was a solitary white figure growing smaller and smaller as it jetted away; from the other, *Dove* was a dark, ominous metal corpse looming up ever larger against the backdrop of stars.

"Switching on spots," Thackery said, and two overlapping circles of light pierced the gloom inside *Dove*'s hull. Only a single bridge station, dark and inert, and a few square metres of the flooring remained. Below it, somewhat more of B deck was intact, though the damage extended down through the systems corridor to the operations decks and the vicinity of the drive.

Exposed throughout were the hidden places of the ship, those known only to those who had built her: the conduits and cabling secreted into bulkheads, the plumbing and the gravity gridwork underlying the floors, the anonymous electronics packages nestled wherever space had allowed and function had demanded. Integument, axon, sinew, and skeleton were rent alike. It was a disturbing sight, far more disturbing than the simple news of *Dove*'s fate had been, for it drove home the reality that *Munin*'s crew were themselves living inside a fragile machine.

"There's no way she held any atmosphere after this happened," Thackery said, directing his spots toward the center of the ship. "The inner cylinder was breached along with the rest." He drifted in closer, and added, "I think I can get to the climbway through B deck."

The white figure disappeared from *Munin*'s view, and the attention of the spectators shifted to the relay from Thackery's camera. They watched as he gave the ragged metal at the edge of the damaged area a wide berth, then reached out for an exposed conduit and began to move himself inside from one improvised handhold to the next.

"*Dove*'s moving again!" Ryttn cried out suddenly.

The briefest glance at the display provided confirmation.

"Thack, get out," Koi radioed frantically.

"Too late," came the answer. "I'm too far in. Better come along."

"Thack!"

"Sorry."

"Navcon!" Koi barked. "Keep us alongside."

Ashen, Ryttn looked back at her. "We can't run with her.

I don't know how she does it, but she's got a fifty-seven degree
gradient."

"Then do the best you can, goddamnit. Maximum slope.
She let us catch her once," Koi said, unaware of how tightly
she was clenching the armrests of her seat. "Oh, Thack—"

Picking his way along one of the radial corridors to the
climbway, Thackery looked down through the twisted metal to
the far end, and his breath caught in his throat. Twenty metres
downship, in the long enclosed tunnel between Operations and
Survey, one of the drive access panels had been either removed
or torn away. A pale light from the opening played over the
ladder rungs and the opposite wall.

"Are you still monitoring me, Amy?" he called.

"Voice and video. Thack—we can't stay with you. We're
already a hundred klicks behind."

"What's the range on a suit transmitter?"

"About a thousand klicks. The signal is already weaker."

"I'm going downship, while we're still in touch," he said,
and reached for a rung.

"I love you, Thack," she said with despair.

"I love you, too," he said, and started down.

As he descended the last few rungs to where he could look
through the access panel, Thackery's heart was in his throat.
It was a struggle to force himself to look through the panel.
When he finally did so, he saw that the core was enveloped in
a soft blue glow that danced and clung like jellied fire. Even
where three of the coils were missing, the light conformed to
the shape of what should have been there, forming an unbroken
band around the rim of the drive core.

"Do you see it?" he demanded of his audience. "Do you
see it?"

"Yes, Thack," came Koi's voice. "We see it. It looks a little
like St. Elmo's fire."

"I'm going to go inside."

The expected protest did not come, and Thackery clambered
awkwardly through an opening which had been intended for a
maintenance tech in coveralls rather than an E-suited visitor.
Once inside, he could see that the blue glow enveloped the
entire drive core, forming a complete circle. He also saw that

the glow was not static but dynamic—he perceived it racing across the surface of the coils just as currents had once raced inside them.

"Is Gwen there? Can this be what's making her move?"

"Here, Commander. Yes, it would have to be," the exec said. "But don't ask me what it is. I don't do metaphysics."

"Could it be something residual—spontaneous?"

"No, sir. No drive damaged like that should run at all, much less more efficiently than it did before the accident. If your D'shanna are doing that, then they're magicians. Commander—I don't want to presume, but if I were you I'd get out of the core. If that field is the source of the energy that's driving *Dove,* I wouldn't want to predict what'd happen if you came in contact with it."

"I think I'll take that suggestion," Thackery said. "There's no one here, anyway."

But as Thackery turned to go, a tongue of jellied blue fire grew out toward him from the gap between coil 17 and coil 21 like an amoebic pseudopod. Deep in its substance appeared ghostly schlieren, like embedded threads of energy.

"Get the hell out of there," Koi shouted in his ear, half order and half plea.

But Thackery was paralyzed by childish wonder. There were colors in the pseudopod too, scarlet and canary and rust, whorls of inner light made pale by the blue glow in which they were embedded.

Like Jupiter—

"No!" Koi screamed as Thackery reached out a gloved hand toward the projection. The instant they touched, the light raced up his arm, enveloping him in its substance, spreading across his torso and down his legs, crawling across his faceplate. Koi screamed again as the display screen on *Munin* showed nothing but blue, but the sound died in Thackery's ears as the blue light and the ship around him both disappeared.

He was surrounded by currents of color, each different from the next in hue, in density, in brightness, in scent, in sound, in taste, all senses confused, all sensations mixing immiscibly in great swirls and whorls, both distant and near, both surrounding him and enveloping his—

His—

His body did not exist. He regarded the place he seemed to

occupy and found nothing. He opened his mouth but heard no sound. He brought his hand to his face, but his eyes saw nothing, his hand found nothing to touch.

= You are locked into the patterns of your material existence. Release them. Reach out to me and I will show you. Reach out to me and I will help you.

The knowledge that he was not alone sent Thackery twisting and jerking in a frantic effort to find his enemy. But there was nothing to push against, nothing to push with, and his most energetic contortions created not the least disturbance in the ebb and flow of the currents around him.

= You have been here before—you have been here before—do not be afraid—you have been here before. I have bound you to the spindle.

There was no climactic event, no clear moment of transition, but presently calm and reverie washed over Thackery, and his struggles ceased. He saw that there was order in the currents, and great energy. And he became aware of his companion as a complex resonance hovering nearby.

-You are D'shanna.

Thackery saw the thought enter the flux as a pattern, weakly formed but of clear meaning. Strangely, it had been stripped of the emotional overlay which he had thought integral to the concept. It was a label, not an accusation.

The answer came in the same wise, childishly simple and achingly complete. = I know and answer to that name, though it is not a part of me.

-What do you call yourself?

= We know each other in other ways.

-Others . . . -The incomplete thought was barely an outline, and vanished almost the moment released. Thackery reached out past his companion and saw a hundred resonances, a thousand, ten thousand, in the infinite expanse of his new universe.

-I have never been here before.

= You have. Once before I brought you across. Once before I bound you to the spindle. The memory of it has driven you to seek it again. But it was nowhere in your matter-matrix to find. Only here.

-Why me? Why did you choose me?

= You must stop. You must stop. = The patterns were bright and insistent. =I cannot do it. You must stop them.

In the pattern of the thought Thackery saw its meaning: the

survey ships turning back, retreating from the frontier. -You
destroyed four civilizations.

= I did not know that would happen. I saw only their yearning and that their yearning would carry them to danger. I meant
only to fill their need. I meant only to protect you.

-That's not true.

= A false thought will not form long enough to be perceived.
A false pattern is destroyed by its own dissonance. You know
this already. You thought us the destroyers, but you know now
that it is not so, because you could not make it part of our
namepattern.

Thackery could not argue; the very substance of the spindle
enforced the truth of the being's response. -Then what danger?
Why did you bring me here?

= I do not understand what moves you. I have been watching
you across ten million fibers of the spindle. When I look on
the matter-matrix of your existence, I see the shadows of what
it was and what it will be. The full Greatcycle is contained in
the thing itself, its origin and destiny. But you are different.
The origin is there to see, but I cannot see the destiny.

-Are you . . .- The word "God" had never come easily to
Thackery's lips, but in the ideogrammatic communication of
the D'shanna it could barely be formed at all.

= You wish me to be more than I am.

-You are not the force to which so many of my kind have
looked.

= I am and am not. I am only what you see, not the answerer
of orisons nor the bestower of eternal life—except that those
pleas helped stir me to take note of you.

Not God—Thackery felt emptied, deprived of the only label
he had which seemed appropriate for the being before him.

-Gabriel,-Thackery said on a sudden impulse. -I will call
you Gabriel.

= When I first looked out and discovered you, the idea that
matter could be animate and self-directed was beyond formation. It took much time to find the pattern and confirm that it
was a true-thought. Even then, as I watched you and came to
know you, I believed that the consciousness of those like you
was imprisoned in the matter-matrix. I tried at first to free you.
But when I first brought your kind across, they could not keep
themselves whole. Their energies lost coherence.

-They died?

= Some died. Some I returned to the matter-matrix, but even there they could not restore their coherence.

-Will I die? Will I go mad?

= No.

-Why not?

= Because you have come ready. You have prepared yourself in the searching. I knew one would come looking, and not die.

-Then I am not the only one?

= You are the one who came.

-But there were others.

= In a thousand ways, a thousand others were touched. Some were touched too deeply, and they lost their coherence. Some were touched too lightly, and were not changed. In the craze these last sense the nearness of the spindle and remember.

-Amelia—McShane—

Each name was a tiny resonance in the greater dynamic. = Yes.

-We're not in control—we never were. You've been watching us, guiding us, manipulating us—what are you?

= I am as you perceive me. Nothing is hidden.

-But what are you? What is this place?

= This is the other face of reality. The birth and death of your matter-matrix are linked here, in the fibers of the spindle. We ride the fibers of the spindle and draw our energies from the cataclysms at both ends.

-If you can do that, then what use are we to you?

Thackery sensed puzzlement. = I have tried to protect you.

-From what?

= Look outward and find it. The spindle holds the reflections of the entire Greatcycle.

-Is this what you did to the Sennifi? When I look will I know what Z'lin Ton Drull knew?

= You will know more.

-What the Drull knew destroyed him and his kind.

= If you are not ready, then I will wait for another to come. If there is time.

-Time before what?

= Look and you will have the answer.

-I am afraid.

= You do not yet know why you must be afraid. Look.

It was like learning to read all over again. Just as there was far more contained in writing than the simple black marks on white paper suggested, so too there was far more to seeing than the eddies and currents he had perceived so far. He opened himself up and the Universe poured into him, finite in extent and infinite in detail, bursting with energy and activity. He saw the Universe for the first time as alive and interconnected, not hostile and empty.

-I can see the ships!

The sudden thought was jubilant, a glittery grid of harmonic energy.

= Yes. Your vessels draw their energy from here, disturbing the spindle at the interface.

Thackery perceived each ship as a snag, an imperfection, where the fibers of the spindle were drawn outward across the boundary between Gabriel's universe and Thackery's. He saw each ship distinctly: the packets shuttling between Earth and the Advance Bases, the survey ships scattered beyond. How tiny is the part of it which we know, how tiny the steps we have taken. But he swelled with pride nonetheless as he found *Dove* and *Munin* playing fox and hound among the stars of Lynx.

-You always knew where we were.

= But you guided your own ships, set your own destinations—as did your Forefathers.

-Can I see them?

= You must.

-Where? How?

= Each fiber encircles space and partitions time. If you would look elsewhere, then you must move in-matrix toward centrality or out-matrix toward horizon. If you would look elsewhen, then you must move uptime toward origin or downtime toward terminus.

-I can go to any time or place?

= If you can find the proper place in the spindle and can look with sufficient skill. I will guide you.

-No,- Thackery said, retreating. -If I am to believe what you show me, there are things I must see alone first.

= I will wait for you here.

Moving required Thackery to employ a conception of direction. Unconsciously, Gabriel's ideograms had already tapped

Thackery's library of schema for the words most appropriate to describe the undescribable. Following that lead, Thackery completed the image of a great translucent cell caught in metaphase, the birth and death of the universe forming the poles of the mitotic spindle.

Time flowed along the fibers of the aster, past to future, centriole to centriole. Across the breadth of the aster stretched the expanse of space, its geometry reflecting the slowing expansion and inevitable contraction of the cosmos. And beyond the cell membrane lay the matter-matrix of Thackery's Universe.

The image was incomplete and imperfect, but it sufficed. He crossed space in great dancing leaps. His self-resonance propagated from one fiber to the next to the next. The leaps were made with more confidence than was justified. Deceived by his own heliocentric mentality, having forgotten that the shape of the Universe reflected not human coordinate systems but the dictates of the physics which spawned it, he quickly became lost, looking out on nameless suns with no conception of which of the Galaxy's billions they might be.

His very conception of Gabriel's universe buckled at the realization that, again the victim of ethnocentrism, he had failed to factor in the infinitude of galaxies. Burdened by that complexity, he lost his perception of order, and with it very nearly lost the coherence of the resonance which was his entire existence.

-Gabriel, help me. Guide me to Earth.

The call did not bring Gabriel, but other D'shanna came to cluster around him as though examining a curiosity. They sent thought-pictures to each other, but not to him.

<Another discordancy.

>The matrix is disturbed here.

<I will erase it,> one thought, and stirred up a swirl of ocher energy which crashed down on Thackery and further weakened him.

:It persists.

-Call Gabriel, Thackery pleaded.

>See, you have disturbed the disturbance into an imitation of life. A good joke, --namepattern--, I will remember to speak it when I return downtime.

With that, the D'shanna moved off. Thackery was too feeble to follow, his resonance half the amplitude and a far paler hue than it had been. He did not know how much time passed while he languished that way, carried toward terminus by the current of the fiber.

= Merritt Thackery.

The ideogram came out of the distance, bright and clear. Thackery seized it and molded what remained of his self to its contours.

= Merritt Thackery.
= Merritt Thackery.

Each repetition strengthened him, for the name was more than a label—it was the pattern of his consciousness, taken in totality. It came to him that the D'shanna were not immortal, that they required the mutual reinforcement which came from other-recognition to persist as coherencies. As he thought that, his own resonance acquired a new harmonic.

-Gabriel,- he called as the alien appeared in the distance. It was then that Thackery realized Gabriel's resonance was far more complex than those of the D'shanna who had found him a curiosity and nothing more.

= Have you found what you wanted?
-No. I was lost.
= Show me where you wish to see.
-Earth.

The glittery thoughtpattern was blue, brown, and white, as beautiful as the planet itself.

= I will take you there.

Together, Thackery and Gabriel flew across the aster, a hundred thousand light-years compressed into a thousand multifilamented fibers.

-Where are the people?- Thackery demanded as he looked down on a world of stone and ocean and cloud.

= You came a long way downtime in your wandering.
-This is the future?
= You can see only the impulse of the inanimate future. Extend yourself against the current and we will find the present.

Though the fiber itself was tranquil and turgid, unlike the leaps across the aster, there was resistance to their passage uptime. As they neared the present, the complex turbulence which had surrounded Thackery in the beginning began slowly to reappear.

-Is this why some D'shanna live downtime?

= Not some but most, living between the boundary of now and the terminus of the spindle. In the far downtime the spindle is undisturbed. It demands less of them and offers freedom to construct a self of such form and dimension that could never exist here.

-But you choose to be here.

= It is the only place where your world and mine can touch.

They soon reached a point where Thackery could look out on a populated world astir with activity, and did so without Thackery requiring further reinforcement from Gabriel.

-Let me go on alone, Thackery said, his confidence restored.

= I cannot make you see what is not there, nor stop you from seeing what is.

-I am not finished.

= Time passes both here and in the matter-matrix. = The thought was tinted gray by Gabriel's ill ease.

-I will not be long.

The old woman in the chair was dead, her face a cold blue and drawn tight in the rictus of rigor. Except for the light from the video screen, the room was dark, the environmental system having noted the lack of movement and followed its energy-conserving instincts. On the top of a nearby bureau, a photograph of a boy and the boy-as-man gathered dust.

-Andra...

But he could not complete even the namepattern, because he did not know its shape or details. He no longer saw her with the clarity the ideograms demanded, and she could no longer remind him of what he had forgotten or never known.

Mourning without tears, he drifted downtime until the body was discovered, then followed it through autopsy and cremation in the hope of learning where she rested. It was a shock to discover there was no marker, no memorial, because nothing but energy proceeded from the combustion chamber, energy to brighten hallway lamps and power the lifts that brought the next cargo of bodies to the processing center.

Anguished, he scrambled uptime until he found her alive. Watching her eat a meal, then fall asleep watching the NET in the chair where she would die, brought paltry comfort. And so he crawled still farther uptime, until he found her standing in a field of Queen Anne's lace, milkweed, and wild wheat, gazing up at the sky with an expression that was both wistful and peaceful. That was when he constructed the namepattern to which he would cling, and that was where he left her for the last time.

Withdrawing from all but the most superficial contact with the matter-matrix, Thackery drifted downtime, past the departure of *Tycho,* past the death of his mother, watching the comings and goings of the packets serving A-Cyg. Presently he drew in closer as the packet *Audubon* docked at Unity and disgorged its human cargo. Hovering over the proceedings, Thackery watched as a tall, raven-haired woman led a buoyant, gap-toothed eight-year-old girl by the hand down the walkway.

-Diana . . . Andra . . .

Suddenly it was not enough to watch. With a fury fueled by anguish, Thackery drove himself downward against the barrier, meaning not only to draw close but to cross, to leave the spindle and enter the scene presented so vividly before him. He drove himself down again and again, summoning not only his own energies, but momentarily marshaling the currents of the aster itself against the obstacle, reaching out with both love and guilt to take the girl and her mother in his arms.

But the only result of the effort was to weaken him. Failure slowly but patiently taught him that Diana and Andra were in a place that he could not reach, that he was seeing not reality, each microsecond frozen and preserved in an infinitude of Universes, but waves of causality—that what propagated across the barrier to the spindle was not a reflection of a substance still existing, but an echo of energies past. That which could be seen from Gabriel's spindle was true but not real. Only the present, from which Thackery had come, was both true and real. And realizing that, he had a sudden hunger to be finished and return there.

-Gabriel,- he called out in despair. -I am ready. Show me what you must.

=I am here,=Gabriel said, gliding out of the colorclasm toward him. =We must go farther back.

The planet he looked down on was Earth, but it was not Thackery's Earth. It was the Earth of the geologists and paleontologists, the Earth of first chapters and prehistories. A heavy cloak of ice and snow covered its surface well into what Thackery had learned to call the temperate latitudes.

On the face of the great glacier were the cities of the FC.

They were not cities as Thackery conceived them, with spires of steel and roads of stone. They were cities the way a sponge is an organism, thousands of small structures conjoined to form a greater whole, but each still capable of existing apart.

The cities of the open ice were carried along southward by its inexorable but fitful advance, reforming and reconnecting as fissures and ridges spoiled the neat tickweave pattern. The heart of each city was comprised of hundreds of domed storehouses, containing the harvests of the past held for the hunger of the future. Of the cells surrounding the core, some held the tools of their artisans, some the creations of their artists. The remainder of the shells were home to the city's inhabitants. From them came the people who manned the hunting sledges and snowboats, who kept the great articulated infrastructure of the city in repair, who bore children, laughed, and drank wine over the dead.

The cities of the mountains were anchored to the rock side walls of their valleys with cables of tantalum, each shell gliding in place on its runners and clinging to those around it as the glacier slid by underneath. By that means they held station with the honeycomb of mines from which one city extracted coal, another tantalite, and a third ortholite. Gasified, the coal provided the energy to warm the shells and run the myriad engines. The tantalite and ortholite together had built the cities, the former yielding the metals used where stress or heat was greatest, the latter the catalyst for the icesteel used everywhere else.

Seeing them, he could no longer think of them as the FC. The name was hollow and faceless, a linguistic convenience inadequate to their humanity. *What did you call yourselves?* he asked, but his seeing was too unskilled for him to have an answer. *The Weichsel was the last of the Pleistocene glaciations—the name belongs to your time, at least, if not to you. You are the Weichsel.*

The Weichsel had not fled south ahead of the ice but had adapted to it. The adaptation had taken two thousand years; the glaciation had now lasted ten thousand. In the face of it, they had retained their culture, their staunch meliorism, and their sense of community. But they had been forced to give up something in exchange: horizons. With the food resources limited, the cities could not grow. With material resources limited, their technology was frozen. It would be that way until the ice retreated.

The one horizon lay overhead, in the night sky. The Weichsel learned of hotter suns and warmer worlds, and yearned for freedom from the bondage of the ice. In time, there came a generation for whom yearning was not enough.

And it was they who built the iceships.

Amy—Derrel—I'm sorry. You were right.

But only partly so, Thackery learned as he watched. The iceships did not go out in clusters attached to a single mother ship. Each iceship was an entity to itself, attached only to a great interstellar bus which was little more than a great block of icesteel encasing the hardware of propulsion.

For what the Weichsel could make, they could also unmake. Using solar heat to begin the process and chemical catalysis to continue it, the icesteel reaction mass was reduced to hydrogen and oxygen. In perfect proportion, fuel and oxidizer flowed through tantalum tubing to an array of combustion chambers, where pressure switches and spark generators turned them into the explosive pulses which drove the iceships up out of orbit and toward the stars.

But that was not what struck Thackery dumb with awe. That was not what made a mockery of the exploits of the Service and the putative courage of its surveyors.

For the Weichsel had learned not only how to live on the ice, but had been forced to learn how to live through it. Despite their best efforts, over the centuries the pressure on the population of the cities had continued. A lesser culture might have clamped a firmer public hand on private matters of reproduction, or consigned the excess infants to the glacier. But in their mastery of chemical polymorphism, the Weichsel had found a way to make room for the new young.

In every city, there were dozens of shells which held nothing but bodies—the cold bodies, not of the dead, but of the waiting. The water of their cells, though supercooled, had not frozen. The blood in their veins, though sluggish, had not stopped flowing. Their hearts beat once a minute, their minds dreamed languid dreams. They were fathers, mothers, and just ordinary people, stepping aside in favor of the new generation, and then waiting for the sun to grow warm again.

And it was thus that the Weichsel made their journey. Each crew of twelve chose its own destination star according to its own criteria, then boarded an iceship and settled in for the coldsleep with the gray wolves they regarded not as pets but as companions. It was audacity that powered their ships, Thackery thought, the audacious confidence which allowed them to set off believing that somewhere, sometime, the warmth of another sun would awaken the engines of both the ship and their bodies. And the knowledge that, for many, their journey would end otherwise raised rather than lowered Thackery's profound esteem for them.

So it was with both shock and horror that Thackery watched the black star enter the solar system and rain death on the cities of the Forefathers.

The moon-sized ebony sphere with the indistinct surface was not a star, and yet he could not find another name by which to describe it. Nor could he name or even categorize the weapon, except by its effect. As though it were tuned to their resonant frequencies, the intruder's weapon splintered the Weichsel structures, then vaporized the splinters. A filthy gray steam rose in great clouds, and the ground shook as the Weichsel cities fell. One orbit sufficed to destroy that which had survived all challenge for millennia.

On the second orbit, those humans who had not drowned in the sudden floods or been perforated by exploding icesteel found themselves torn apart from inside by energies they could neither feel nor flee. The blood of an entire civilization ran together to tint the newborn rivers red. Nor were the Weichsel the only life affected. Everywhere the great beasts were falling, mastodon and cave lion, megatheroid and dire wolf, glyptodont and short-faced bear. And when the black star left and the clouds vanished, the places which the Weichsel had called home were bare and dead.

-Why?- After witnessing the carnage, even mustering the control to ask that simple, poignant question was an all-consuming effort for Thackery.

=For that answer, we must go elsewhere.

To Thackery's relief, they began to move uptime again. But the sight of the gallant Weichsel restored to life was hollow and bittersweet, for there was no erasing the memory of what lay in their future.

=That one, Merritt Thackery, Gabriel said, directing Thackery's attention to a departing iceship. =The answer lies with that one.

Crossing the spindle at an angle that carried them both downtime and across space, the D'shanna and the human followed the tiny Weichsel iceship through the void. As they left

Earth behind, the vividness of what Thackery had seen mercifully began to fade as his consciousness edited away the intolerable details. But he could not stop thinking about it or, when he grew stronger, talking about it. -Gabriel—did they all die?

= There was a great dying.

-But not the plants—the sea animals—the equatorial life—

= The sudden changes pressured many. Most survived.

-But none like me.

= No.

-Then how did there come to be people there again? Did one of the iceships return?

= No. Men returned to Earth because, at long last, I ceased only to watch.

-You?- The query was colored by both wonder and gratitude.

= When the colonies were strong enough to give back to their homeworld. It was a difficult thing for both them and us. Many died, and their deaths created a great disturbance in the spindle, a disturbance which began the migration of the D'shanna into the far uptime and which weakened me greatly. Those who did not die lost coherence and memory. When they weakened I brought more, until in time they bred and survived. They were your Forefathers, not those who lived in the cities of ice.

The tiny ship and its frozen cargo raced on, until it neared a place where five suns whirled in a graceful ballet: greater twins at the center, so close they nearly touched, and orbited by a lesser trio. The iceship's engines, facing the brightest of the suns, began to slow her, and its crew began to stir.

But before they could even have discerned whether the complex system before them harbored planets, a black star rose up from the neighborhood of the twins to meet it. The encounter was brief, silent, and telling. One moment the iceship was diving toward the system, the engines giving it an orange halo as they contributed their braking force. An eyeblink later it had been reduced to a spreading cloud of disassociated molecules which glittered prettily in the light of the five suns.

Thackery cried out in pain and turned away. Why the loss of a single ship cut him more deeply than the ravaging of all Earth he did not clearly understand even later, except perhaps because it was the second blow. But at that moment, he was consumed by an excruciating dolor.

-They were so close—

= This happened first, = Gabriel said. = This is what led to the greater dying.

-There was no reason, no need ...

= You have seen the reason.

-For trespassing?

= For invading. As they did once. As you stood ready to do again.

-Why? Where are they now? Where are the Sterilizers?

= Where they have always been.

-Where is that?

= Look. You know the place.

Compelled despite himself, Thackery dragged himself back uptime and watched again as the Weichsel ship neared its destruction. A double star orbited by a triple—

He drew back along the ship's line of approach and considered a larger volume of the matter-matrix. Close by was another bright binary, and far beyond a delicate whirlpool of stars. A spiral galaxy, viewed from above, the most spectacular vantage—*but there are galaxies in every direction. Have I seen this one before, or does the clarity of seeing deceive me with false familiarity—*

That's M101—

-Gabriel—I do know this place. Gabriel, you have to tell them.

= If you have seen, then I have told them.

-You have to stop them.

= How, Merritt Thackery? How can I quell this impulse in your kind, that rises up again and again? After all this time, I still do not understand you, what drives you. *You* must stop them. If I knew the way, it would be long done. I have done everything I am able to. I stopped the Sennifi. I stopped the Wenlock, too well as you saw. Yet even as I saw to it that there was no danger from the colonies, you came out again from Earth. There are too many of you, and I am much diminished now. You must stop them. I have stayed here amidst the disturbances which I created too long already. I cannot do it. To bring you here and teach you is my last service. Through the spindle, you have the ear of all your kind. You must stop them, Merritt Thackery. It is why I touched you. It is why you came here. You must stop them.

Gabriel's insistent repetitions battered at Thackery until he was forced to close himself off, to shut down the new senses he had only just learned how to use. There was too much power in the D'shanna's ideograms, the waves of energy too threatening to his coherence. He turned away and folded himself into a ball of cold light as tenuous and fragile as a soap bubble. But as he huddled there, keenly aware of his mortality, he sensed Gabriel's resonance enveloping him, cocooning him once more.

And when Thackery at last felt strong enough to unfold again and look around him, it was the inside of *Dove*'s drive core that he welcomed back with joyful tears.

chapter 17

The Horse by the Door

For a long time, Thackery did nothing but shake inside his E-suit and cling with an iron grip to the reassuring solidity of the drive core bus conduit. His body was numb and unfamiliar, yet his nerves jangled with intense sensory messages.

While he struggled to reassert control over his physical self, Thackery was also fighting wave after wave of unchecked primal emotion. Bound to the spindle, he had had no outlet for the intense feelings evoked by what he had seen and heard there. Without a physical existence through which to cry, shout, strike out, or flee, the normal homeostatic mechanisms were short-circuited.

Now those bottled emotions broke over him in concert, terror and awe, anger and grief. Later, Thackery would wonder if that were not the explanation for what happened to the unprepared who found themselves in Gabriel's universe. Strong emotions could be debilitating enough in the matter-matrix world. On the spindle, they were a short road to death or madness.

But for the present, Thackery simply clung to his handholds in a state of agitation for which he had no name. He kept seeing the black star and the Earth wearing a deathmask of gray steam, and the glittery remnant of the Weichsel iceship.

Presently the blue glow still dancing over the drive core reminded him of *Munin,* and he came to understand that the presence of the intrusive energies meant that Gabriel was still in control, slowing *Dove* and bringing her to a second rendezvous with her sister ship.

"Did you get it?" he paged eagerly. "Amy? Gwen? Derrell? Did you see? Did you hear?"

There was no answer, and Thackery's mercurial spirits fell precipitously. If *Munin* were not close enough to hear him and answer now, then *Dove* must have kept her distance throughout Thackery's time on the spindle. *Or did it matter? Would the suit cameras or transceiver have relayed anything of what I experienced?*

That line of thought led Thackery to wonder how long his communion with Gabriel had lasted. Subjectively, there had been no reliable indicator of time, and even recalling the sequence of events he could not say how much time they seemed to require. The suit chronometer showed something less than two hours had passed, which jibed with the healthy oxygen and water reserves reported by the environmental monitors. But he could not say how much of that time he had spent cowering after his return, or even be confident his body had stayed behind while his consciousness had crossed over.

Unable to cope with the uncertainty required to further pursue the question, Thackery shifted his attention to more concrete matters. His body was still conspiring to overload him with input—the variation in temperature between his torso and feet, the smell of his own fear-sweat, the hundred and one places the suit bound or chafed or pressed against his skin. It was as though every set of nerve endings which he had learned through years of living to ignore was suddenly clamoring for attention.

Trying to give his thoughts focus, Thackery repeated his call to *Munin*. There was no response. *If only some of this power were available for the ship's systems—then maybe they could hear me—*

The idea of asserting himself by taking action, even in pursuit of such an unlikely goal, appealed enough to Thackery to loosen his grip on the conduit and send him out into the climbway and down. Though each step, each individual volitional movement, seemed to require a distinct decision, his progress filled him with confidence all out of proportion to the achievement.

Three bodies were drifting free on E deck, all bearing stomach-turning witness to the sudden decompression *Dove* had undergone. Barely aware of what he was doing, Thackery brushed past the corpses and moved toward the contact lab. The lab was deserted, the equipment intact but inert.

There was one last possibility. The gig should be undamaged, and its communication systems were far more powerful than an E-suit's. If there were still power, he might reach *Munin*—

Returning to the climbway, Thackery continued his deliberate descent. From there he could see that the pressure hatch at the foot of the climbway was sealed.

It took nearly five minutes to manually retract the outer hatch and enter the dress-out compartment. There he found the suit racks full, and two more bodies, both wearing blissful expressions that suggested a quiet drug-aided death.

Thackery pressed on into the gig bay, where dozens of pieces of equipment loosened from their tiedowns by the collision floated in the open spaces. He made his way through them to the gig itself, which he found still held a pressure-normal atmosphere.

It had also retained the bodies of two men and three women. This time Thackery could not help but take note of their open-eyed stares and shrunken, gangrenous skin. Cocooned in the protective shell of the gig, the corpses had had days or even weeks to decompose before the systems failed and slowly falling temperatures halted the process. Thackery did not even trouble to try the gig radios; it was clear that the gig's final task had exhausted its power generators. Fighting a rising gorge, Thackery fled the gig and the bay.

As revolting as they were, the corpses were as a bright light to Thackery's mental fog. In their blank, decayed faces he saw Jael and Mike, lying dead on the boards of a Gnivian dray, hanging naked from the branches of a waxtree. The emotional jolt of that reminder awakened Thackery's somnolent faculties. *None of this matters,* he chided himself as he climbed upship. *Why are you avoiding what does?*

The blue light still filled the drive core, but Thackery climbed past it until he reached the open expanse of the edrec deck, where he used a short tether to secure himself. Only then did he begin to try to come to grips with the responsibility with which Gabriel had charged him.

He soon began to wonder whether his earlier dimness hadn't been a defense against thinking about what seemed an insolvable problem. Yes, the Kleine would allow Thackery to reach the other twenty-four survey ships. But that was meaningless, for he did not have anything approaching the authority to recall them. Only the Central Flight Office could do that, or the Chairman of the FC Committee above it, or the Director of the Service above it.

What all three had in common was that they were based at Unity, a fifty light-year craze away. Would *Munin*'s log records of the encounter with *Dove* be enough to persuade them to call a halt? Thackery decided it would have as much impact as throwing a marshmallow at an advancing tank. He did not even know yet if he would be able to convince Amy and Derrel, his closest friends and the nearest witnesses.

Hell—I barely can believe it myself, and I'm the one that has to do the convincing. If I wanted to, I could probably persuade myself that I'm suffering from a nasty shock to my nervous system and the disorientation that goes with it. I can't even prove to myself that that experience was real.

Those thoughts reflected despair, not real self-doubt. Just as he had admitted, Gabriel clearly did not understand the human mind. The D'shanna did not realize that human communication was not restricted to true thought, or that others Thackery tried to tell would require proof. Waiting for the welcome sound of *Munin*'s page, Thackery started numerous imaginary conversations, none of which he could make end satisfactorily.

(Supervisor, there's an alien species inhabiting the Mizar-Alcor system which poses a threat to all the human settlements.)

(Very interesting theory. Any evidence?)

(There's my testimony on the subjective out-of-body experience I had aboard a derelict survey ship, culminating a period of erratic behavior that began when I threatened to lock up one of my officers—)

(Next!)

On top of all the other problems, the unhappy fact was that Thackery could not even be sure that the Sterilizers were still in, or only in, the Mizar system. What if, just like humans had, they had gone through a period of expansion? What if they were now scattered all through the Ursa Major Cluster, or even farther afield? If so, then any ship could stumble on them—not just in Lynx, but in any neighboring octant. It's been twenty thousand years or more. Where might they have gone in that time?

(Chairman, you have to recall all the survey ships.)

(Why is that?)

(Because the Sterilizers could be anywhere.)

(Well, now, that seems a little extreme. I'll tell you what, we'll just send a ship on out where they were last to collect some more data—)

No, that would not do. The survey ships had to be recalled, or someday they would find—and arouse—the Sterilizers again. Thackery had witnessed their savagery, and knew that there could be no halfway measures, no investigations, no studies, no indecision. That meant that the person he had to deal with was the Director. That way Thackery would only have one performance to give, only one person to persuade. The Director was the highest authority in the Service; decisions bearing that office's stamp were final.

Now, if I only knew who the current Director was, Thackery thought, and laughed sardonically. The Director's authority reached out into the Service's operating theater impersonally, through channels—the same channels Thackery was determined to bypass. The last Director Thackery had taken note of by name was Anton LeGrande, and that only because it was LeGrande's name which appeared on Thackery's commission.

His ignorance on the subject was not a source of concern. Accessing a complete biography of the Director would be a matter of only a few seconds with *Munin*'s library. But Thackery's thoughts kept returning to an obstacle that did concern him: space itself.

Whoever the Director was, Thackery would have to make his case with him through the Kleine. That was a far from ideal situation; though the lag was only a matter of a few minutes, it was enough to kill off the rapport and feedback a real-time link provided. But there was no other way. Thackery could not even consider taking *Munin* back to Unity for a face-to-face encounter. The ships were already too far out for that. Every second *Munin* was traveling inbound, the other ships would be forging farther and farther into unexplored regions, at terrible risk. It had to be the Kleine. As Gabriel had warned, time was short.

Gabriel—Thackery had a momentary impulse to blame Gabriel for not arming him with some bit of knowledge so compelling that no one could fail to believe him. That was followed by an equally brief urge to blame himself for failing to ask the right questions—the location of the undiscovered colonies, or the exact year of the Sterilization, or some less dramatic but more readily verifiable fact which he could not have learned except through Gabriel.

But he quickly saw that both impulses were wrong-headed. In his own way, Gabriel was as limited in what he knew as was Thackery. Gabriel had all of time and space open to him— but he was not omniscient. As powerful as he had seemed, he knew only that which he had sought to learn and then made a part of his pattern. To know all there was to know about the Universe, Gabriel would have to *become* the Universe.

As for himself, Thackery found it hard to envision what he could say that would have the desired impact. *How can I ever make them believe me? I feel as helpless to stop us as Gabriel did. I can't take the Director where I've been, and I don't have the first bit of tangible evidence. How can I make anyone believe?*

And even as he thought the question, he suddenly saw a way—a way so simple, so certain of success that he wondered why he had not devised it sooner. *He has to do it. He owes me.* Suffused with hope, Thackery unhooked his tether and started back down the climbway once more.

The glow in the drive core had grown pale and weak, and fluctuated alarmingly as it coursed around its path. Thackery stood where he had stood the first time and called out, "Gabriel! I need to talk to you." When nothing happened, he moved to the gap in the damaged core and bravely placed his hand in the flux. For a moment, he stood straddling the two realities.
—Gabriel!
= I am here, Merritt Thackery.

Thackery was shocked at Gabriel's appearance. The sharp definition and strong amplitude of his inner resonances were almost completely gone. Thackery formed the most perfect namepattern he was capable of for the D'shanna and sent it in Gabriel's direction. When it was received and absorbed, Gabriel seemed to flicker, then reformed into a better likeness of Thackery's memory.
-I need your help, Gabriel.

= Your ship and companions are near. You will rejoin them soon.

-Not that. Something else, Gabriel.

Thackery made the name the center of every thought, and each time he did the D'shannan grew incrementally stronger.

= Show me.

-Gabriel—when I transfer back to *Munin*, I want you to take *Dove* to Earth through the spindle, the way you did the Weichsel for the reseeding.

= No, Merritt Thackery. I cannot.

-Why, Gabriel?

= Look at me, Merritt Thackery. Look at me. You ship has great mass. It would have been a difficult task for me then. I am too weak to even attempt it now.

-Gabriel—are you dying?

= I need the sharing of other D'shanna. As soon as you have rejoined your kind, I must go downtime.

Thackery thought furiously. The *Dove* was a unique and unmistakable artifact—to have it suddenly transported fifty light-years, to have it disappear from the screens of *Munin* and reappear moments later in the skies of Earth, would have given Thackery's message all the credibility that it required.

But the bodies downship were likewise unique and unmistakable, and could serve the same purpose. Eagerly he posed the question.

The answer came back tinted a ruddy red. = No, Merritt Thackery. You have lessened the task, but you have not strengthened me. When I have brought *Dove* to its rendezvous, I will have only enough coherence remaining to reach the D'shanna downtime. I have stayed too long and done too much already.

Both chastened and profoundly discouraged, Thackery withdrew from the flux. He hooked an arm around a brace and remained suspended there, shaking his head and muttering, "How, how, how, how? Oh, Gabriel, they won't listen to me. I've tried before to tell them things they didn't want to hear. And there's nothing that they're less eager to believe than what I have to tell them now."

But Gabriel had made clear that the most Thackery could expect now was to be reunited with *Munin*. Coordinating and channeling the energies required to stand in for the damaged drive had already taxed Gabriel to an alarming degree. *I sup-*

pose I should be grateful if he isn't forced to abandon what he's doing for me now.

Wait—that's the key. If Gabriel didn't have to exert himself with Dove—if he weren't transporting inert mass, but another intelligence from which he can draw sustenance—

A hateful thought brought Thackery up short. *You'll pay the cost that he doesn't,* he reminded himself sternly.

Or rather Amy will.

It isn't a choice. There's no other way to do the thing. There's no other way you'll be believed. She would understand—just one more Hobson's choice in a life of them.

The truth is that you won't be hurt by it, she will. You'll know why. She won't.

A tone sounded inside Thackery's helmet, but he ignored it. *It has to be done now. If I wait until I can explain it to her, Gabriel will be too weak, or will have gone downtime, out of reach. The window of opportunity is closing quickly—not just for me, but maybe for all of us. The truth is that I love her, and I don't want to leave her. But I also don't want to fail and know that there was more that I could have done, except that I was too selfish or too frightened to try. And I can't have it both ways—*

So decide! goddamn you, decide!

A grimness had gripped *Munin* since Thackery had entered the derelict three hours earlier, a grimness which set jaws in hard lines and put an edge on every utterance. The tension was greatest and the accompanying silence the most inviolate on the bridge, where Koi and the command crew continued to track their decelerating quarry. The two ships were moving toward an intercept less than thirty minutes away.

But that was not enough to relieve the crew's concern. Lying ahead of both ships on their current course was the system 211 Lynx with its red supergiant, six planets, and halo of minor bodies. If for some reason *Dove* again changed velocities, as it had already done four times since it was first detected, it would smash through the system like a self-destructing battering ram, completing the job started years earlier and light-years away at 61 Canum Venaticorum.

So when the comtech saw an encouraging change on his displays, he offered the news in a cautious tone. "We're back within range of the Commander's transmitters. I've got a weak locator signal and some telemetry." Everyone turned toward the comtech as he studied the incoming data. "And he's alive," he added at last.

The words swept away the tension like soap touching water. "Thank God," Koi said fervently.

"Heartbeat and respiration are elevated—," the comtech went on.

"Are you paging him?"

"Auto repeat, every fifteen seconds. It's on general relay, so you'll all hear him when I do."

Silence returned to the bridge, but it was a new kind: hopeful, anticipatory. The comtech turned up the gain until they could hear Thackery breathing and the grunts of exertion deep in his throat as he moved.

"Why doesn't he answer?" Koi demanded plaintively. "Why doesn't he say something?"

The comtech raised his hands in a show of helplessness, and as he did Thackery spoke at last.

"GABRIEL!" he cried.

Koi stabbed for her com controls. "Thack! Are you all right?"

But there was no answer.

Thackery's plan was a thought of greater complexity than he had yet given form to. But at its heart was a strong and simple image, rich in shades of blue and pristine white and smelling of forest.

Gabriel answered: = You are bound by time just as I am. There is no undoing what has happened.

A torrent of ideograms, insistently colorful, poured out of Thackery. -Not the past. The present. Not to prevent. To prevail.

For a long moment, Gabriel did not respond. = Yes. I understand. Will you stop them?

-I will, Gabriel. I swear I will.

= Then come to me.

Ryttn hated being the one to have to say it. She hated the look that she knew she would see on the others' faces, especially Koi's. She hated having to follow the Commander's strange outburst with unwelcome news. But it had to be said, nonetheless. "I mark a change in *Dove*'s delta vee," she said with effort. "She's no longer decelerating—holding at four percent, zero slope. I read normal displacement mass only— no AVLO field. No power generation."

Emotionlessly, Koi nodded acknowledgment. "Come on, Thack," she urged. "Come back on and tell us what's happening."

"I don't think he's going to answer," the comtech said slowly, sitting back from his station. "I've lost the Commander's biotelemetry."

"That could be anything—"

The comtech shook his head, his expression pained. "I'm still receiving telemetry from the suit." He swallowed hard. "The environmental monitor suit just reported a sudden drop in internal pressure."

Refusing to credit the comtech's pessimism, Koi prolonged the pursuit. *Munin* paced *Dove* until, five hours later, deflected by the gravity of the largest planet, the derelict slipped into the gravity well of the massive blood-red star and dove inward toward its seething surface.

"Commander—with that much velocity, there'll be a major flare, and probably some X-ray activity when she hits," Joel Nunn said gently. "We shouldn't hang around."

It was the use of the title as much as anything that forced the truth on Koi. "All right."

"Where to, sir?"

Koi was slow to answer. "I don't know. Poll the crew and see if there's any strong sentiment against going back to A-Cyg." Then she bowed her head and covered her face with her hands. "Oh, Merry," she whispered plaintively. "Good-bye."

chapter 18

Monody and Monition

Sunlight from a familiar yellow star warmed his naked body. Hot white sand scorched his feet, and the roar of the surf and the pungent salt smell curled his mouth into a grin. He was home, and he reveled in the thought for a long moment. Then he remembered why, and the grin faded.

The minor thunderclap that accompanied Thackery's appearance on the Cape May Point beach had been swallowed up by the white noise of the modest breakers churning the water just offshore. Moreover, the beach was crowded enough that relatively few noted that, in the infinitesimal crack between one moment and the next, the population of the beach increased by one. Nor did Thackery's nudity create any stir, for a healthy minority of the vacationers shared his condition—though he was by far the palest of the lot.

Only a few lying close enough to be dusted with the blast of sand which came as Thackery's materializing body threw back the blanket of air, and a few more who happened to be looking in the right direction at that instant, noticed anything out of the ordinary. Yet even those who saw did not quite believe, and turned to those around them in a fruitless quest for confirmation. Very quickly, they concluded that they had seen nothing at all.

But witnesses were not critical to Thackery's purpose, and he made for the stairs leading to the street as oblivious to those around him as they were to him. His mind was filled with thoughts of *credit—netlink—transportation*. He did not see the beach police angling across the sand to intercept him.

"No beach pass today, mister?" said one, catching him by the arm.

"Beach pass?" Thackery suddenly became aware that everyone was wearing a plastic wristband, most of them green, a minority red. "No. I'm afraid not. But I'm leaving—"

The second officer had withdrawn a wallet-sized case from a pocket and flipped it open, unveiling a keyless comlink complete with tiny screen. "It's pretty clear you're not carrying your cards, either," he said. "Your Citizen Registry Number, please."

"I'm afraid I've forgotten it. I can give you my Service commission number—"

The first officer squinted at Thackery. "You a starvet?"

"Yes, I—"

"It figures," said the other. "Four times out of five when you find somebody walking in circles, it's a starvet. How long you been back?"

About five minutes, Thackery thought. "Not long."

"I think you'd better come with us."

Thackery nodded agreeably. "That might be the simplest way, after all."

Thackery would have preferred to make the call himself, but the district supervisor of the Atlantica Peace Force had other ideas. Instead, Thackery provided the supervisor with the necessary numbers and names, and received in return a plain brown detainee's wrap.

Several minutes later, the supervisor returned to the holding room. "They're going to send somebody. You can wait in the lobby."

"Thank you."

"And, Commander Thackery—next time you decide to take one of these little excursions, make sure you've taken the trouble to learn the local laws, all right?"

"I will," Thackery promised.

Nearly two hours later, a two-seat air skiff bearing the Service's emblem set down on the Peace Force's flight pad. From the excitement the sleek little vehicle engendered among the staff, including the clerk who came to fetch him from the waiting room, Thackery knew that he was getting special treatment.

Inside, the skiff was quiet and comfortable, and seemed capable of largely flying itself. The only thing the young awk did after keying in a destination was to make a brief report.

"Ellit Donabaw reporting. I've picked up Commander Thackery and we're en route to the Wesley Space Center. Estimate arrival in one hour." Switching off, he settled back in his seat and cast a glance sideways at Thackery. "This is a pretty silly place to be caught, don't you think?"

"Excuse me?"

"They were talking about you around the office before they sent me out. I heard you were on contract to *Munin.*"

"That's right."

"*Commander* of the *Munin.*"

"That's right."

"They're going to hit you hard, then—AWOL, dereliction of command—you'll be looking at a fitness review the minute we reach Unity."

"Don't be dim."

"I'm not kidding. You should have been smarter."

"Can you access Flight Office files with that?"

"Yes—"

"Why don't you find out where *Munin* is?"

Donabaw narrowed his gaze questioningly, then turned to the comlink. "Way the hell out in Lynx," he said presently. "So?"

"So how am I supposed to have accomplished this dereliction?"

"On her last call here—"

"*Munin* is a survey ship, not a goddamn packet. She doesn't come to Earth."

That stumped the runner. "I don't understand."

"You're not supposed to. I suggest you get on your little box there and alert the Director that I'm on my way to see him. Time enough's slipped by already. I don't want to have to wait while he digs the sleep out of his eyes."

"You mean *the* Director? Of the Service?"

"Of course."

"Then you're dreaming. The Director doesn't drop everything to see any old person who asks for an appointment."

"I'm not 'any old person,'" Thackery said. "I'm Commander of a survey ship. There are only twenty-five of us. The Director will see me."

"Uh—sir, I don't even know if she's on station at the moment."

"Then you'd better find out, hadn't you? Because if the Director's not at Unity, we're sure as hell not going there." He crossed his arms over his chest, snuggled back into the comfortable seat, and directed his attention outside, at the surface of the ocean flashing by beneath the skiff.

"I can't say I ever thought to see you again," said Alizana Neale, placing her folded hands in her lap. Apparently she had been on station for some time, for the gap in their ages had widened. She had let her hair go to gray, and there were soft but definite lines in her face, but her eyes were as steely as ever. "And I'm a little confused about why I am. When did *Munin* put in?"

"She hasn't."

"That was my understanding. So how are you here?"

Thackery smiled. "There are two parts to the answer. The easy part goes: by way of the Cape May Shore Patrol, the Atlantica Peace Force, Wesley Space Center, and the shuttle *Ticonderoga*. The hard part I'd like to leave until I've had a chance to tell you *why* I'm here."

"That's no surprise. You've always preferred drama to straight answers. Well, go ahead, then," she said, settling back.

Thackery took a moment to collect his thoughts. "When you allowed me to have *Munin*, you hinted that you had become frustrated with the colony problem—as I did, and as everyone before us had," he began. "But it wasn't our fault that we couldn't make the puzzle come together. We knew that some of the pieces were missing. But we had no way of knowing that it was the most important ones.

"I have those pieces now. I know what happened."

In simple sentences which had sweeping power, Thackery proceeded to tell the story of the beginning—but not its end—of the First Colonization. He spoke of cities on the ice, of tiny ships and their crews, of a will for life so strong and a meliorism so great that those who possessed them dared to vault to the stars.

"In all, they sent out eighty-two ships before their time ended. Just seventeen of those ships founded colonies—the rest perished. Even so, they did more with less than I ever dreamed they could."

"You are something of a master of that yourself," Neale said dryly, "considering what you are able to do without proof."

"If you mean physical evidence, you can start with the 241 artifact on 7 Herculis. I'm sure we'll find more like it quickly, now that we know what we're looking for. Very possibly there are discoveries to be made among the archeological reports that have already been filed. And there are four more colonies. I'll provide the Flight Office with the information they'll need."

"How is it that you've come to be so blessed with knowledge? —Let me say in advance that I regard your answer with some dread."

Thackery smiled faintly. "I made contact with a D'shanna."

"Ah. Like your friend the Drull, who tried to tell you that the Universe is closed?"

"As it happens, it is."

Neale sighed. "I would have thought that in all this time, you could have taken the trouble to check your claims against the facts. The Universe is open, expanding. There's not enough mass to stop it."

"No. The Universe is closed. The Greatcycle will have an ending—just as the Sennifi told us. The missing mass-energy is in the spindle, in the energy-matrix inhabited by the D'shanna.

"How does the AVLO drive make phantom matter? The energy required for the feat flows to us from the spindle. What magic ties the Kleine transmitters together? The shortcut which allows us to call across the light-years leads through the spindle. It has to be considered the other half of reality. The spindle exists. I know. I was there."

"Invited, I presume."

"Yes. Not by the D'shanna collectively. By a singular individual I call Gabriel. He is—or was—an extraordinary representative of his kind. Alone among them, he took note of us, and realized what we were. Gabriel has watched us, worried over us, and been our friend.

"And we badly needed a friend. I haven't yet said why the Forefathers ended their period of colonization. It came because we're not alone in the Galaxy. One of the Weichsel iceships stumbled into the space another species regarded as its own— the Mizar-Alcor multiple system, in Ursa Major. The Weichsel vessel was destroyed. Then these—I name them for what they did—these Sterilizers followed its trajectory back to Earth, and coldly and efficiently eradicated all human life here. Nor were we the only victims. We've known for a long time of mass extinctions of megafauna at the end of the Pleistocene Epoch. Now we know why."

Thackery labored to make Neale see the images which were still so clear to him, to make her feel the horror. "Strange, isn't it? For twenty thousand years we've been pointing out the Big Dipper to our children without realizing what happened there. Those stars signify above all our greatest humiliation, and the beginning of the blackest chapter in our history."

There was a catch in Thackery's voice as he spoke those last words, and he paused. When he continued, it was in a softer voice. "When the Sterilizers struck at us, Gabriel was consumed by a moral dilemma. He could not stop the attack— just because I've named him for an angel does not mean he has the powers imputed to one. But he did have the capacity to intervene. He thought on it a long time, and in time decided that there was a wrongness in what had happened to us.

"Mind you, that was as much a revelation to him as was our existence. From what I saw of them and gleaned from Gabriel, the D'shanna do not have a particularly elevated moral sense even as regards each other. But Gabriel rose above that denominator. It was Gabriel who reseeded Earth, giving us back our home world."

"But the colonies were never touched?"

"The Sterilizers destroyed us as casually and reflexively as you might swat a fly. It did not occur to them to see if the fly had left any eggs."

"And now the eggs are hatching."

"Yes. As the colonies grew and flourished, Gabriel tried to protect us from ourselves. It was he who stopped the Sennifi and the Wenlock and the other advanced colonies from regaining space travel. But he wasn't here when he could have stopped us."

"And now he can't, is that what you're saying?"

"His final gift was the knowledge of what will happen if we don't cancel Phase III, if the ships aren't recalled." He leaned forward earnestly. "Alizana, we have fifteen hundred stars and five hundred thousand cubic light-years of space. That's enough for us, isn't it? Worlds enough? We've been in such a hurry these last five hundred years, always pushing on to the next star. It's time to go back to some of those worlds. It's time for us to rest."

Neale shook her head slowly. "I will give you credit, Thackery. The story has grown in the telling. I am impressed. Or perhaps 'entertained' might be a better word." She spread her hands palm-up in a gesture of resignation. "But how can I believe you? How can you expect me to?"

Thackery nodded. "I understand that you have to object. I'm grateful to you for hearing me out before you did. We're back now where we started. You asked how I came to be here. Because I knew that I would need proof, I had Gabriel bring me here, through the spindle. I'm sitting here with you now, but less than eight hours ago I was aboard *Munin*."

Neale regarded him with an expression that was both affectionate and sad. "Is it that you can't realize how insane that statement is?" she asked gently. "Or is it that you think that I'm insane enough to believe it?"

Thackery smiled knowingly. "If all I had to go on was my word, I don't think I'd believe me either. But you don't need to take my word for it. You have a netlink there. Use it. Call *Munin*. Ask them where I am, when they last saw me. Ask them what happened to their ship's Commander," Thackery said, standing as if to leave.

"Don't you want to stay for the finale?"

A wistful look came into Thackery's eyes. "No. You'll need some time, as I did. And I left some people I cared about back there, under circumstances not of my choosing. I can't go back the way I came, and I can't rejoin them. So I think I would rather not hear their voices again. If possible, I would ask that you not tell them that I'm here on Earth. It would just be the cause of unnecessary pain."

Neale nodded. "Where are you going, then?"

"On the way in from the shuttle I saw a restaurant that claims to serve 'traditional' meals—which I presume means food recognizable to people of our vintage," Thackery said with a weak effort at a grin.

"The Archives."

"You know it, then. I'm running short about three meals, so I'm going to go back down there and test their authenticity. When you're ready to see me again, you can find me there."

• • •

The restaurateurs were not immodest—their *bill du fare*
featured everything from Italian garlic bread running in melted
butter to a pot roast containing potatoes which had been grown
in soil, not aquaculture tanks. Thackery ordered impulsively
and eclectically, as though he had to make up for all his dep-
rivations in one sitting.

But when the food came, it passed through Thackery's mouth
tastelessly, as though it was just another shipboard platter in
which no real pleasure could be taken. The fault was not in
the food, but in Thackery. His mind was full of thoughts of
Amy. He wondered if what he had said to Neale was really
true. Was there no way that they could be reunited? If he were
to board a ship and head for Lynx, and she were to turn *Munin*
for home—yes, it was possible. They could be together again.

But even without having heard from Neale, Thackery knew
that that option was not open to him. He would be needed
here. There were things he knew that would have to be recorded, decisions to which he would have to contribute. He
could not drop this on them and then scamper away. The Service
was poised for change, and he would be expected to take part
in the transformation. He did not belong to himself—in truth,
had not since Jupiter. It was a fact he had both fought and fled,
and now, finally, accepted.

"Commander Thackery?"

Blinking, Thackery looked up into the face of a young awk.
"Yes?"

"The Director would like you to meet her in Gallery B of
the Service Museum."

"The Museum?"

"Yes, sir. In Kellimore Place."

Thackery wiped his mouth and pushed himself away from
the table. "I'm afraid you'll have to show me," he said with
an apologetic smile. "The last time I was here, there was no
Kellimore Place."

The museum was putatively closed, but that was no obstacle
for the Director of the Service. Neale was waiting in the entry
rotunda, in the star-dome of which hung models depicting the
long-ago encounter between *Jiadur* and *Pride of Earth*. The
awk delivered Thackery there, then silently excused himself.

"Walk with me this way, will you?" Neale asked, and they

started down the leftmost of the three broad corridors leading out of the rotunda. "I could not reach *Munin*—"

Thackery's face whitened with sudden panic, but Neale placed a comforting hand on his arm. "She's in the craze, legging from 211 Lynx to A-Cyg. But there was an exit dispatch—in which you figured prominently. There was sight-and-sound of you boarding the wreck of *Dove*—all time-stamped, of course. And video of what's left of *Dove* falling into a star, as well."

Calmed by the news, Thackery nodded his approval. "I asked Gabriel to leave her on a course that would make that happen. I didn't want them to keep chasing it, or risk someone's life trying to board her. I wanted them to think I was dead."

"You succeeded," Neale said succinctly. "Do you know why I asked you to meet me here?"

A small smile creased Thackery's cheeks. "You have a display of antiques you want me to be part of?"

"There's something I want you to see."

They walked until they reached a spot where several life-sized photographs had been melded to the wall in such a way as to make it seem that the people represented were actually standing there, engaged in conversation with each other.

"Do you know who she was?" Neale asked, stopping in front of the figures and gesturing at the proud, haughty face of an aged Oriental woman.

"No."

"Her name was Tai Chen. Five hundred years ago, she was one of the three most powerful people on Earth. She was instrumental in Devaraja Rashuri's struggle to build and launch *Pride of Earth*. But unlike Rashuri, she believed the aliens were a threat—that *Pride* should be not an envoy ship but a warship. She was overruled—no, better to say outmaneuvered. It was the residue of that xenophobia that saw to the arming of the Pathfinders."

"Is this why you asked me here? For a history lesson?" Thackery asked, bristling. "Or are you comparing me with her?"

"No," Neale said, shaking her head. "I asked you here to tell you that I believe you. The survey ships will be recalled. The orders should be going out even now."

Thackery sighed, and allowed his shoulders to slump. "It had to come, in time. The farther out we went, the more ships we would need. We couldn't have continued the way we were forever, Sterilizers or not."

"Nor can we stop cold out of fear. Merritt, you understand the situation of the moment perfectly. But have you looked past the moment, and thought about the impact news of the Sterilizers will have?"

"It will have to be carefully handled—possibly restricted—"

"And say what about our sudden loss of enthusiasm? No, Merritt. It's not possible for us to simply call the ships home and hide. We'll end up destroyed by the fear that they would find us again." Neale shook her head. "No—if we're going to keep what we have, we're going to have to go looking for them." She looked up at the picture of Tai Chen. Her eyes were wet, and her next words were directed to the lifeless image, not to Thackery. "It seems we must build your warships, after all."

For a long moment, Thackery said nothing. "I won't enjoy seeing that."

"It won't happen quickly. Nevertheless, I share your sentiment," Neale said. "I've postponed retirement a half-dozen times already. Now the problem that has been keeping me here has been solved, and I do not find much appeal in the one that will replace it. I've seen enough time and enough change. So I have already decided I will be resigning in short order."

Thackery's eyes flicked back to the portrait of Tai Chen. "I'm going to need to stay a while, at least."

Neale nodded. "Then you will need one of these," she said, and extended her closed right hand toward him. When she uncurled her fingers, she revealed a black ellipse lying in her palm. "I presume that if yours had come through the spindle with you, you would be wearing it?"

Thackery stared at her, then slowly reached for the emblem.

"No," Neale said, "Let me." She stepped toward him and pinned the emblem on the left breast of Thackery's collarless wrap. "A lot has happened since the first time I did that," she said, backing away. "I told you then that you didn't deserve to wear it. Today no one deserves to wear it more. You did a hell of a job, Merritt. They'll remember your name for a long time."

"I never wanted that," he said hoarsely, fingering the black ellipse.

"I know," she said. "But for a long time I thought you did— because I did." She smiled wanly. "I can still remember how excited we all were when *Jiadur* came. It was like the whole world had changed. We just couldn't stop talking about it. I wanted to know everything, stayed up through the night to watch the net when the first exploration team boarded. I wanted to be the one who was first—the one they were talking about.

"It wasn't until I was back here the first year after joining the Committee that I realized how little the citizenry cared, how little notice they took of what we were doing. That was when solving the colony problem began to matter most."

"Is that why you let me have *Munin?*"

She nodded. "I wanted to see them shaken out of their complacency. I wanted to make them raise their eyes from their own little comfortable nests and come to grips with the new history. It didn't matter to me who accomplished it.

"And now you have. The changes *Jiadur* brought are nothing compared to what your news will. The discovery of the colonies is nothing compared to the discoveries you've made. We now know that we are just one of three great intelligences in the galaxy, three intelligences which stand isolated from each other by their very essence. You've brought us knowledge of both a friend to whom we have a debt we can hardly begin to discharge, and an enemy against whom we have a grudge we can hardly begin to assuage. No one man will ever change the world more."

"The World Council I knew frowned on hero-making."

"It still does—except when there is no choice, as now. The Service will start it, and the nets will do the rest. I'm afraid you are to become one of those historic figures you learned about in school, the ones who always understood what was at stake, seized the moment, and never had any regrets."

"That's not the way it was," he said softly, remembering.

She smiled wistfully, sharing his pain, and took his arm as they started back down the corridor. "It never is, Merry. It never is."

ABOUT THE AUTHOR

Michael P. Kube-McDowell was raised in Camden, New Jersey. He attended Michigan State University as a National Merit Scholar, holds a master's degree in science education, and was honored for teaching excellence by the 1985 White House Commission on Presidential Scholars. Mr. Kube-McDowell's stories have appeared in such magazines as *Analog*, *Asimov's*, *Amazing*, *Twilight Zone*, and *Fantasy and Science Fiction*, as well as in various anthologies published in the U.S. and in Europe. Three of his stories have been adopted as episodes of the television series "Tales From the Darkside." His highly praised debut novel, *Emprise*, was published by Berkley in 1985.